THE SAPPHIRE HEIRESS

The Silver Order
Book 1

by Ella Leon

ARE YOU SIGNED UP FOR DRAGONBLADE'S BLOG?

You'll get the latest news and information on exclusive giveaways, exclusive excerpts, coming releases, sales, free books, cover reveals and more.

Check out our complete list of authors, too!

No spam, no junk. That's a promise!

Sign Up Here

www.dragonbladepublishing.com

(

Dearest Reader;

Thank you for your support of a small press. At Dragonblade Publishing, we strive to bring you the highest quality Historical Romance from some of the best authors in the business. Without your support, there is no 'us', so we sincerely hope you adore these stories and find some new favorite authors along the way.

Happy Reading!

CEO, Dragonblade Publishing

PROLOGUE

May 1809, somewhere on the Atlantic

ETHAN LOCKE STEADIED himself, ready to run. The distant high-pitched screech of a whistle signaled departure. He had only a few minutes to make it back to his ship so he and his crew could set sail.

But he couldn't go. Not just yet.

Mixed in with the mahogany furnishings, gold glittered. Behind red, velvet curtains swaying with the ship, a small, golden chest fell in and out of view. It had been hidden for a reason. Without a doubt whatever was inside would be valuable, indeed.

Of course he couldn't leave now. Greed beckoned him. Disregarding his need for haste, he pulled back the curtain and lifted its unsecured lid.

Disappointment flooded him. Without a lock on the chest, whatever was inside might not have been valuable, after all. But as soon as his eyes met the contents, his breath caught. Two items were suspended in black velvet. The first he noticed was a small, blue bottle attached to a silver chain. That didn't seem worth much. But the other item, also on a silver chain, was a sapphire stone, blue like the deepest ocean. As if in a kind of reverent protection, it was wrapped in swirling, silver filigree. Deep within the sapphire, a dazzling fire blazed.

The door screeched open behind Locke, startling him back to reality. Time since opening the chest seemed to have stood still. How long he had been staring, he didn't know.

"Cap'n. We be castin' off soon." The crewman, newly cloaked in fine leather, heaved with exertion while his captain stood there as calm as the day's sea, as if he had all the time in the world.

"Aye." Locke willed himself to drop the sapphire into his coat pocket before that same strange calm swept over him again. For good measure, he plucked the bottle up too and followed after the crewman.

Abovedeck, white sails stretched taut against a perfect, blue sky. About a dozen men lined the ship's railing, their hands secured with rope. Pistol in hand, another one of Locke's crew held ready.

To his relief, the deck was free of bodies. Blood too. His heart thudded against his chest at the thrill of yet another clean victory.

"You there!" A voice interrupted his thoughts.

Locke stomped toward its source, the wood of the deck creaking beneath his buckled boots. In a black, woolen coat lined with gold buttons, the man was no doubt the ship's captain. The grim-faced gentleman couldn't have been more than twenty-five, far too young for the part, but, at that very age now himself, so was Locke.

"That's no mere gem." Eying Locke's bulky coat pocket, the man seemed to warn him. Something told him this was no mere merchant ship, either.

Locke lifted his shoulders. It made no difference. Gold was gold and a rock was a rock. Locke placed a protective hand over his pocket, feeling the sapphire warm beneath his touch.

Whatever it was, it was one spoil he didn't plan to give up, even if it meant keeping Alastair in the dark. Locke swiped a blade free from his waist and flicked it into the deck. Inches from the captain's boot, it vibrated from impact.

"Try not to cut yourself."

At last, he gave the signal for his pistol-bearing crewman to retreat. Then, placing a hand on the ship's railing for support, he lifted his body into the air and landed back aboard the pirate ship endearingly named *Hell's Teeth*.

CHAPTER ONE

The Storm

33 years later
April 1842, Bristol, England

LIGHTNING CRASHED ON the moor, this time nearby. When her horse reared skyward, Mae Blackthorne strained to stay upright.

"Stand firm!" she shouted. Her dapple-gray gelding jerked back before righting himself. *"Easy."*

With the threat of rain imminent, their only cover was the Northern Woods ahead, but not even her horse, Thomas, dared to enter. Gaining on a web of lifeless trees, he snorted and pulled back.

"Quiet…" Mae rubbed his black mane. "It's no more than a bunch of trees."

The words worked to reassure Mae, too. It took only another glance to freeze the blood in her veins. The trees were so dense that the ground had darkened to black, and inside, all was still and silent. Not a single insect, bird, or other small creature moved in the brush. There was only the whispering of leaves.

She risked a look behind her. The last of the evening's light was gone. Dark, angry clouds rolled over the horizon. In the far distance, rain fell in thick, hazy streaks and bursts of lightning tore through a slate-colored sky. *Blast.* She'd thought she had more time.

Mae considered her options. There seemed little else to do but risk an awful cold. Her breaths grew shorter. She was far not only from the Rosewood estate, but from town, too. She had one option. Cutting through the woods had always been an obvious shortcut, though she'd never dared take it. Just the thought made her tremble. She cursed herself. What did she have to fear of the dark forest? No matter how difficult the terrain, Mae was sure she could cross it.

To hell with the servants' ghost stories. Yanking the reins, she twisted Thomas toward the trees. Snorting again, he continued to resist. Only after the second pulse of thunder did he ease forward.

Past the threshold of trees, the darkness deepened. Cold moisture coated Mae's skin. Amidst the rocks and fallen branches, Thomas struggled to maintain his footing.

Mae mouthed a silent prayer. She had assumed she was alone, probably for miles, and therefore helpless when a white light flickered out in the distance.

"Who trespasses here?" A voice broke through the still air.

Mae's throat tightened before she could respond.

The white haze grew brighter in the mist, approaching rapidly until it stung her eyes.

"Whoever you are, you encroach upon private property," a man said, his voice unrecognizable. Not a local, nor vagabond, given his accent and well-formed words.

"I—I didn't know anyone owned this land." Mae squinted.

The man lowered his light. He eyed her the same way everyone did when they noticed her deep-olive complexion. With practice, she had become skilled at ignoring it.

"I was only trying to escape the storm."

"I imagine you were. And your companions?" Locke swung out the lantern to pan the forest.

"I have none, sir. I was just out for an evening ride."

"I see," he said, though he continued to eye her suspiciously.

"Your destination?"

Mae straightened, the personal inquiry giving her pause. "Home. No more than an hour's ride—"

"*An hour*'s ride!" he exclaimed. "The storm will be upon us at any moment. You must allow me to escort you to my home. It's not far." He lifted his lantern, once again shining the light in her eyes. "What, may I ask, is the name of my guest?"

She swallowed. The last thing she wanted was to establish an acquaintance the man might soon regret. In this case, it was entirely unnecessary. "Sir, please, I wouldn't like to intrude... The distance will be no trouble at all." Mae jerked the reins to pass him, but his horse moved too, blocking her path.

Damn stubborn man.

"If you care to divulge your name, I can judge that for myself. I know every prominent family in the county *and* the distances of their estates."

Silhouetted in the weak light of the lantern, she struggled to make out his face. Whether friendly or harsh, she could not tell.

"You are the lady of the estate, are you not?"

He clearly could not make her out in this darkness, either.

"No, sir. I didn't mean to imply..." Mae blushed. "I have no estate. I'm no more than a governess."

"Ah."

"Sir, if you please..."

Lightning crashed again.

The man's head tilted toward the sky. "The storm's gaining on us. Come. I live just beyond those trees."

To Mae's shock, he pointed west. The forest went on for miles in that direction. The distance to another home in that direction would be greater than that to her own destination. *Unless...* Mae's breath caught in her chest. He couldn't possibly live *within* the Northern Woods. She lifted a cynical brow. Impossible. She would have heard.

Before she could question him, he disappeared. Curious now, Mae clucked her tongue, ordering Thomas forward. Between the trees, she could make out a subtle path, allowing for a safe gallop. Perhaps the home would be new.

Thunder roared again. As heavy sheets of rain crashed down, she quickened her speed. Shearing through the forest, she gained on the man. Skilled as she was, she sped ahead in a spray of mud.

But keeping her fast pace was no easy task. Her horse writhed with each long stride. Battered by the rain, her hands stiffened. Every muscle ached with fatigue.

The fog had thickened too, transforming the trees and rocks into dense, black shadows. Seeing a boulder, Mae yanked the reins just in time to leap over a fallen tree.

When she landed, the shadow of a building appeared seemingly out of the mist. She breathed in deeply with surprise. Not once had she heard of this man. All along, he had been her neighbor.

She pulled Thomas to a skidding stop. In the clearing stood a stone manor, stately yet modest in size. A burst of lightning illuminated the ivy that crawled its walls.

Mae swept round. A set of hooves squished in the mud, effectively catching her off-guard. The stranger was by her side.

"'Tis by good chance I found you." He laughed, lifting his face toward the sky as if to relish the rain.

"And the name of my rescuer?"

"Forgive me. Ethan Locke."

For a few moments, Mae forgot the rain. She held his steady gaze, his eyes no more than two glinting lights in the gloom. How on earth had she never heard of this man? The mystery surrounding him made her instantly suspicious.

"Shall we proceed inside, Mr. Locke?"

"Yes, of course." He snapped to attention and trotted past her.

Mae followed him through a gap in the iron fencing. Holding out his lantern, he revealed a half-moon portico. An iron knocker glinted in the glow.

She hadn't even time to drop the reins when the man dismounted and extended a hand. Despite his ice-cold skin, the gesture warmed her.

She couldn't remember the last time someone had helped her off her horse, let alone offered her a hand. But like a lady once more, she thanked him, picked up her skirts, and rushed into the cover of the doorway.

Mr. Locke squeezed in beside her, his gaze tickling her cheek. She tried to glimpse his features, but she could still only make out the glinting intensity of his eyes. They were trying to take in her too.

"I'll take care of the horses and meet you inside." He unlocked the door with a click. "Take this."

The lantern, pounds heavier than she expected, nearly slipped from her grip.

So quick, she near missed it, he flashed a smile. "Careful."

He went and took the horses' reins. Soon, all sight of him and even the clatter of hooves faded.

Mae gathered her courage and went inside. A wild wind slammed the door shut behind her, silencing the pounding rain.

In the new silence, her breath quickened, each gasp taking in the aroma of dust and wet stone. Besides the first few steps of a stairway, darkness shrouded her surroundings. Mae gripped the lantern tighter. Mr. Locke would return any moment. She certainly could not leave. Her fear was cold, but the rain even colder. Her black dress, heavy with moisture, stuck to her skin. When she took off her hat, her braids were sopping wet too. Rather than drip, water streamed down onto the stone floor. She didn't dare step onto the rug that extended before her.

In fact, she wasn't sure what to do. She had anticipated a butler or a housekeeper, but in the darkness, she rightly guessed no one would arrive.

Shivering, she tried to reason away her fear. What other horrors could compare to being alone in that forest? In this rain, any shelter would do.

At length, Mr. Locke's figure emerged from a hallway. He

relieved her of the heavy lantern. "I've lit a fire in the sitting room and have a kettle on the stove."

Mae followed him through the dark hall. The parlor, also edged in shadow, was less welcoming. Dust floated thick in the air. Every furnishing was draped in white sheets.

"I see I've caught you at an inopportune time." She stepped closer to the blaze. Amidst the windows that still rattled from wind and rain, she welcomed the waves of scorching heat.

Mr. Locke set the lantern on the mantel, then assuming the role of footman, helped her remove her riding coat and threw it over a sheet-covered chair. "You were expecting some place warm and welcoming, I imagine."

"I didn't mean…" Her chin dipped down, her stomach swirling. "I should be thanking you."

"I suppose you should." He wrapped a folded blanket over her shoulders. "Rather nice feeling like the hero for a change."

Mae opened her mouth, prepared to counter what she thought would be modesty, but given his strange reply, knew not what to say.

She stepped closer until the glow of the fire raced across his face, finally illuminating his features. His dark hair was slicked back, drawing her eyes to the scar above his left brow. Was it from fencing? Perhaps first blood drawn in a duel? He couldn't have been much older than herself—in his late twenties, maybe early thirties.

With a stern jaw too, he seemed just the type of man accustomed to meeting other gentlemen at dawn. The rogue sort of men her father had warned her about. They cared nothing for honor and lived only for adventure.

She could not make sense of his incongruous accent, nor the odd tie of the cravat he promptly tore off. He looked rather like something of the past, his rather austere countenance reminding her of some military officer.

Mae cleared her throat. After that long pause, she desperately needed to revive the conversation. "How long have you been away?"

It seemed a safe enough question.

"Years." He glanced about the room approvingly. "But everything's just as I left it."

"The forest provides good cover, I'm sure."

"Indeed. Most are too fearful to step foot into my woods, let alone explore."

Mae stared into the flames.

"But you're not," he said. "Tell me, do you often go on rides this late? Alone?"

She wanted to ask him the same. Riding horseback to a home he hadn't been to in years seemed rather odd. Would not a carriage have been more appropriate? Did he not have belongings?

Mae looked at him again as if somewhere along the glistening skin of his face and throat, the answers might appear. She chewed her lip, her curiosity getting the better of her.

"What about venturing through dark and mysterious forests?"

Mae shrugged. *What business is it of his?*

"Don't pretend." He fixed his gaze on her, leaning ever closer to take her in. "I know what the country folk say about my land...*about me.*"

"You criminalize yourself. I haven't heard a word about you and I've lived here my whole life."

"Your 'whole life'? I might have guessed you hail from elsewhere. Or perhaps one of your parents." He reached out a finger, nearly hooking a wet strand of her dark hair before snapping his hand back and clearly thinking better of it.

"My mother."

"From an island is my guess. Someplace tropical."

"The Philippines, to be exact."

"I thought so."

"But I know nothing of the place."

"No?"

"Like I said…" Mae resisted an urge to sigh dramatically. "I've lived here all my life. Just like most of the other villagers."

"No, no, no." He shook his head, his eyes bright and glossy. "You're not like any of the villagers at all."

Mae huffed, not caring how indignant it came out anymore. He might have been kind enough to offer her shelter, but he was still being rude. The truth was, no matter how hard she tried, she would never be like everyone else. People here would only ever see her as different. This man was no exception.

She opened her mouth, set on telling him how different, he, himself, seemed, like someone from another world altogether with a strange way of talking and an even stranger way of dress. Then something red caught her eye. She gasped. Along his left knuckles, a streak of blood glistened.

"You're bleeding, sir." She reached out.

Mr. Locke snapped his hand back. "A stray branch must have caught me."

"You should tend to it at once."

"Nonsense."

"Don't you fear infection?"

He stared at her, considering. "Wait here."

With that, he strode off into the hall. *How terse and typical,* Mae grumbled inwardly. But she immediately chided herself for the thought. She should be grateful for his hospitality.

"Some tea should warm you." He reappeared, tray in hand.

He set the service down on a low table and handed her a cup. His knuckles were now wrapped with cloth. *Poor man.* A wound on such a spot would take weeks to heal.

"Thank you." She took up the cup in both hands. A sip warmed her on the spot.

"I must say your riding skills astounded me earlier," he said after some time, sounding genuine, as far as she could tell. "That horse is rather impressive too…for a governess."

"It isn't mine, not really," Mae corrected him. "He needed some exercise is all."

"Ah."

Just when she thought he could shock her no more, he pulled his sopping-wet shirt free from the waistband of his pants. Then, in one swift movement, he was topless. Mae could not help scrutinizing him.

The man was tattooed! The black lines of a fearsome, teeth-baring tiger stretched up his ribs. Across his chest were two words in loops of cursive: *Hell's Teeth*. What kind of man would mark such a curse across his body? It wasn't proper, to say the least.

Decency demanded she look away, but she could not. Rather, her eyes inched upward. Around his neck hung a small, bluish-green bottle from a silver chain. She wondered what it contained. It was a strange sort of jewelry for a man.

In stunned silence, Mae pressed her lips together. The man must have lived a perilous life, just as she had imagined. He was likely not a gentleman, after all. That fact did not frighten her, though—only stirred her curiosity.

"Where are you from—Mr. Locke, is it?"

"Everywhere." Twisting away to poke the fire, he revealed another tattooed design along the curves of his back. Although this time, it was not words or an object, just an unfamiliar pattern of swirls, maybe even a vine. She might even call it *art*.

"Why do you ask?" He turned back at her. "Do I seem foreign to you?"

"Your accent, perhaps. I can't quite place it. But seeing that we've just met, it's only natural to wonder."

"Perhaps, one day, I shall tell you all." He laughed, though she wasn't sure why. "At which household did you say you are employed, miss?"

Mae paled at the question. It seemed to give way to all sorts of possibilities, and Mrs. Rosewood had been clear. Liaisons of any kind would not be tolerated. Mae had to stop this now.

She cleared her throat and moved toward the window. If she had to risk a cold or her position, it would be the former. She had already let this go far longer than she ought to have.

"The rain has slowed," she lied. "Perhaps I should move on."

"Don't be ridiculous…" He stepped forward as if to bar her exit. "You'll catch your death… Surely—"

"Please." Her tone was firm. "I must insist."

Mr. Locke's jaw tensed, but after a moment, he conceded. "As you wish."

He relinquished the blanket from her shoulders and held open her still-wet riding coat and floppy hat. Heavy with rain, they both weighed her down.

"My employer would not be pleased if I returned past midnight."

"Yes, well, meet me out front." He put his coat on over his bare chest. "I'll bring you your horse." He sounded slightly affronted. Though Mae could not fathom why. He should understand someone in her position could not take such risks. She'd had no right accepting his offer of shelter in the first place. She had merely been desperate to stay dry. She couldn't help wondering what kind of house was out here in the woods too—and what kind of man lived there.

Outside, the rain still poured and strong winds surged from every direction. In the complete darkness and this time without a lantern, Mr. Locke brought Thomas forward. Her foot nearly slipped off the soaked straps, but Mr. Locke held her firm.

"Perhaps, one day, we shall meet again."

"I think we'll have to leave that to fate." Mae lifted her chin. She was glad to have met him. But he had to know meeting again was out of the question.

Betraying the slightest of frowns, he finally seemed to realize this. He slapped the rear of her horse. "Ride swiftly, Miss…?"

She stared ahead, glad she had kept her surname. If nothing else, it would save her ears from itching when he asked about her. Better yet, it would rob her neighbors of the gossip they took far too much pleasure in.

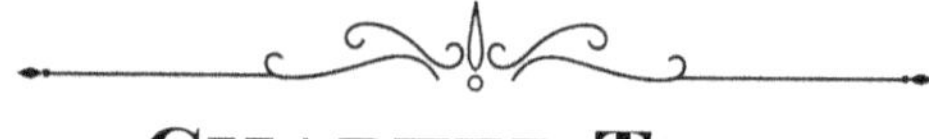

CHAPTER TWO

The Guest

ETHAN LOCKE TOOK in the crisp, cool morning air. Salt-less and thick with rotting leaves, it was nothing like the smell of sea he had grown to admire. The sky at dawn was different too. Instead of the brilliant blues and deep purples, the color of yolk stretched across the sky striped with a stir of dull oranges and sharp reds. There was no sound of sails snapping against the wind or the roar of waves, either—just the chirping of birds.

He let out a woeful sigh. *My business of piracy and constant travel is over,* he reminded himself. *Land will have to do.*

And among these land-dwellers, he would have to fit in. Last night, he had come off as a gentleman splendidly enough. Certainly, that woman would not have accepted shelter otherwise—no matter how ill the weather. She seemed a good judge. Like most English ladies, she had airs that hinted at her past within the upper classes.

He wondered what had happened to bring her down in the world of servitude. In her fine, quick eyes, she certainly held an interesting tale or two. He could tell that much. Any woman brave enough to traverse his woods on horseback was quite unusual. Then again, so was her background. At the same time, there was something familiar about her. The mystery of it had needled him all night.

At the end of the drive, he reached what was once an iron gate. Since he had gone, a web of dead, leafless vines had ensnared it shut. Without an ax, there was no hope of getting it open. At the moment, though, it suited his needs. Down the dirt road, carriage wheels ached with speed. He took a knife from his waist and cut away the brittle vines, creating a makeshift window.

The carriage, opulent with black, lacquered doors, rolled to a halt. A man dressed in a green waistcoat and top hat descended with several delicate steps. He brushed himself off, straightened his jacket, and, removing his hat, revealed a gray mountain of hair.

"Frances Ellsworth, are you?" Somehow, Locke imagined the man who had written these last few weeks to be younger. But he knew him only by his fine and delicate signature. More importantly, Locke wanted to know how the bastard knew about the Blackthorne fortune and his interest in it.

"Things aren't as they once were, are they?" Ellsworth lifted an emerald-embossed cane and stabbed the vines with a crunch.

"That was clear enough in your letters." A fact that made Locke ache for the prosperous days of old. "How long has Alastair been cold in his grave?"

"'Bout six years."

Locke was surprised at the pain that took hold. Rival or not, Alastair had once been family. *Adopted* family, but family nonetheless.

"I hoped to find you sooner, but it proved no easy task."

Locke clenched his jaw as he usually did to control his anger. He did not like the idea of being used for the man's own design, but if it meant recovering the stone so that he could finally return it, hell, anything was worth that.

Running from country to country smuggling just enough to stay alive had seemed like a decent alternative at first. After a few years, it had worn thin. He simply could not go on living like that. It was the stuff of cowards. But until he got those men off his back about the stone, he'd always be running.

"And your plan will work?"

"I've not a doubt." Confidence glittered in Ellsworth's translucent, blue eyes. "Together, we shall find the Blackthorne family vault in no time."

"By the end of the year, I should hope."

"Possible." Ellsworth jutted out his lower lip. "Tired of the tempest seas, are you?"

"Ready to retire is all." Nearly halfway into the nineteenth century, times had changed. It was the end for men like him. Like Bristol, the seas had changed too. A bit of quiet would do him good, though—better than good. To own it, he *was* rather tired. "You're certain the estate's current owner will be amenable?"

"Oh, yes."

In his mind, Locke noted the plan—as laid out in Ellsworth's letters—had seemed cunning enough; supposedly, Ellsworth had some precious clue. The only things that worried him were how he had gotten that clue and the abruptness of their acquaintance. Locke did not have a good feeling about him and he always trusted his instincts. He would simply have to be careful. Recovering a dangerous and powerful gem from a dead thief would not be easy. He had come prepared for that.

"Fear not." Ellsworth lifted his chin and smiled friendly-like. "You can trust me. You were Alastair's enemy, were you not? That is enough to make us instant friends… Or partners, at the very least."

Locke *huffed*. "What else do you think you know of me?"

"I did hear a fanciful tale or two, but I'm sure it's no more than conjecture."

"Rumors are hardly ever true." *Yet the ones circling the county about me probably are*, he thought. The sapphire had changed him in ways he could only hide for so long. It was a wonder the villagers hadn't yet called for his neck in fear of witchery or some other nonsense. Though they'd always seemed to sense something unnatural about him, it hadn't been enough cause for true concern.

And if there was one thing he remembered of the people of Bristol, it was that they enjoyed all tales supernatural. Better yet, they feared them.

"Don't worry." Ellsworth smiled. "I don't pay much heed to wild tales."

"Are we to split the profits, then?"

"Why, of course. But before we get into such details, first allow me to properly introduce myself. I am Francis Ellsworth." He stepped back and gave a deep bow. "And you are Ethan Locke."

Locke almost corrected him. Captain *Ethan Locke*, he wanted to shout in his usual commanding tone that struck fear into many a man's heart. But considering the ill-repute of pirates these days, he reconsidered. Instead, he gave a half-hearted nod.

"Now that we are acquainted, how about a cup of tea for a weary traveler?"

Locke paused. His old self would never have allowed this. The man could very well stab him in the back. Rather than unnerve him, he smirked at the thought.

"One moment." Locke turned round and headed for his ax.

He had bigger fears than death. Imprisonment, he knew firsthand, was a far worse fate. He might not have been trapped behind a cage, but given his fifty-eight years of the same sunrises and sunsets, that was what life had become. And although he was aging again, as the years went on, he found himself increasingly eager for escape.

MAE STIRRED IN her bed. The light in the room, though still dim, intensified as Grace pulled back the curtains.

"How you feeling, miss?"

Of all the servants, Grace had been kindest and most loyal

through all this. Despite Mae's change in station, Grace still considered her the true lady of the house. To her, Mae wasn't different. She was the same as she had always been.

"Grace, you don't have to—"

"I'm in no mood to argue, miss. Richie says you took quite a lashing in last night's storm."

Mae moaned into her pillow. The night before seemed more like a strange and distant dream. A near nightmare.

And yet she didn't quite regret it.

"Your dear brother would not have approved of such late rides and well you know it." Grace refilled the corner basin, a few grays poking out from beneath her white cap. At her age, she ought to have retired. Instead, Grace had stayed, taking care of her like family.

Mae nibbled her bottom lip. She had only stayed out so late because she had not wanted to return. She had wanted the feel of the wind and the smell of the moors to continue on forever. But Grace was right—if Mae's brother had been alive, he'd have scolded her too.

She didn't care. Riding far beyond where she ought to had helped her feel like her old self again: the person who would cast aside anything for a thrill, who found pleasure in all things dangerous. She refused to be defined by any other term.

"I don't think your dress will ever dry out." Grace looked pointedly at the dripping-wet mass hanging over Mae's desk chair.

Mae groaned as she threw the covers aside. "What time is it?"

"Eight A.M., miss. And I daresay, today is not a good day to be sick." Grace kneeled next to the ash-filled fireplace. "Just as I thought." She clucked her tongue. Tossing in more coal, she returned to the topic at hand. "The house is in a throes over Mr. Rosewood's most important guest this evening. A great dinner being ordered no sooner than this morning."

"Mr. Rosewood wastes no time."

"And I've been told—" Grace's face scrunched, as though

repulsed by the words to follow. "I've been told to send you to the kitchens after your lessons. I tried to tell 'em, I did. I told 'em you haven't chopped, stirred nothin' in your whole—"

"It's fine, Grace." Not yet mustering the strength to rise, Mae dragged her fingers through her thick, dark-brown hair. It was just one of many sacrifices, she was sure. Last night included.

"Is someone ill?" Mae asked.

"That be another matter entirely. It seems our Katie has been relieved of her duties."

"For what?"

"Displeased Mrs. Rosewood with some impropriety. I hear she means to find work in London."

"Oh, dear." Mae had considered the same thing once. But she had heard too many woeful tales. For the rich, London held the promise of endless social engagements, whilst for the poor, the place was often hard and cruel. There, one could easily starve. She had heard about the seamstresses who, widowed and without relatives, had had to resort to less savory forms of income. She could only hope that fate did not become the poor young woman. Perhaps she would find work and be happy. Lord knew happiness could not be found here amongst strict and unforgiving employers like the Rosewoods.

Mae stepped onto the cold, hard floor. Out the window, it did not look much like day. Gray clouds still lingered over the tips of the trees. As her eyes wandered toward the endless horizon, the sudden image of Mr. Locke's piercing gaze made her wince.

She wished she hadn't been so timid. So much seemed possible now. A promise for a visit? Someday…more? But she had no wish for that sort of trouble. She would never see the likes of him again. It was better that way.

The fireplace restocked and the ashes cleared, Grace rubbed her hands over her apron. "Well, good day, m'dear."

"Thank you," Mae said as Grace shut the door behind her.

Selecting a dress for the day had never been a joy. But looking back, she should have relished every one of those colorful gowns with their smooth, silky material. The task of dressing depressed her now. In her wardrobe, she had only one spare. This one in gray.

She tried to picture how she looked the night before. Plain and utterly foreign. Like this estate had been the last place she'd belonged, though where else she might belong, she didn't know.

Before the basin, Mae dipped the folded corner of a cloth into the water—thankfully lukewarm—and smoothed it over her eyes. Despite her hopes, it did not erase her thoughts of Mr. Locke or the weariness that was beginning to well within her. It was nothing new—just the widening of a hole that had long existed. Only now, it gaped, impossible to ignore.

No one would have blamed her for telling him the name of the estate. Only she dreaded the discovery of her past. She cringed again at the implication. The last thing she wanted was to get the gossips started. It was too good a story. Last she'd heard, they had called her life "a riches to rags story."

It wasn't the least bit true. She might no longer have money or social standing, but her life wasn't nearly as horrid as one might think. At least working as a governess in her former home meant she could still enjoy its vaulted ceilings and the ancient, stone carvings grand enough to rival churches. Albeit a small consolation, she tried to let it comfort her.

Had the estate still been hers, she imagined herself nodding to Mr. Locke's requests for her to stay, thinking it nothing. She wouldn't care about rumors that might result if anyone saw her. As an heiress, she would have been free to do as pleased. As a governess, however, she had no choice but to obey Mrs. Rosewood's orders of pious propriety. It was either that or face the street. She squeezed her fists, hating that she had been so obedient.

She took a deep breath. This was no way to start her day. She patted her face with a dry corner of a cloth and set her jaw.

Then, like all the days before, she dressed, braided her long hair, and twisted it into a tight coil. Everything was the same, save for her roiling stomach.

As she descended the stairs, she realized she had forgotten Grace's warning and nearly collided with a servant. Weaving around her, a trail of three more followed, their expressions long and their arms heavy with linens and china. At the far end of the gallery, Grace worked a mop across the floor.

The estate had not seen this sort of chaos in years. Not since she'd been a child. Back then, the sight had meant an exciting ball, soiree, or dinner party. Now, she felt only the anxiety of the servants.

The schoolroom, at least, was completely serene. Not once rearranged, the room was the same as it had always been and yet so different. Exposed to the latticed windows, her favorite lavender chaise had long faded, its matching rug tattered and frayed at the edges. That morning, Mae felt equally worn, her smile more strained than usual. She could not continue like this.

Agreeably on time, Mae's two pupils were already seated at the table, but while Miss Lenore was reading, Miss Clarissa Rosewood seemed distant, her eyes far away.

"Daydreaming, are we?" Today's lesson would be harder than she thought.

"Haven't you heard? We are to have a guest for dinner this evening!" Miss Rosewood clapped her hands together.

"Oh," Mae replied stonily. "Fancy that."

"Well, whom do you think it is?" Miss Rosewood asked.

"I haven't the slightest. Whoever he is, you're sure to meet him soon."

"So it's a man. You think a *man* is coming for dinner?"

"Of course," Miss Lenore piped in, straightening up in her seat so she sat a little taller. "To ask father for my hand."

"*Sister,*" Miss Rosewood drawled. "You're not yet seventeen."

Though perhaps it wasn't far from the truth—just for the wrong sister.

Mrs. Rosewood clearly regarded her youngest, Miss Lenore, with her delicate features and thick, auburn hair, as the true prize.

Miss Rosewood, meanwhile, could not have been more different. Instead of pale, unblemished skin, she had dark freckles and red hair. But because she was the eldest, Clarissa needed to marry first. Mr. and Mrs. Rosewoods would be sure to pass her along quickly to the first half-decent man that came along.

Miss Lenore had something like real beauty and when it came to pushing an already wealthy but title-less family higher in society that—in addition to their wealth—was their best hope for leverage. There would be no settling on a husband with her.

The thought made Mae's heart ache. Even Miss Rosewood seemed to know she was second best.

"Do you think I'll like him?" Miss Rosewood asked.

"Of course," Mae replied. Truthfully, it didn't matter. As with any young woman of means, if her father thought he was good enough, what else was there?

"So you think—"

"Whatever your father intends, he has your best interests at heart. Now, please—"

"Had you no offers?" Miss Rosewood asked, too innocent to know the sting of the question.

"One," Mae said matter-of-fact. It was something she preferred not to think about. For two years, she had pushed it out of her mind entirely. The experience had been too painful.

"And you declined?"

Even Miss Lenore frowned.

Mae smoothed down her skirts, struggling to maintain her composure. Her pupils wouldn't give in until they knew. "Well…a merchant expressed a feeling or two for me, but that was years ago…"

"Is that so?" Mrs. Rosewood appeared at the doorway. Mae snapped to her feet. What was she doing here? And for how long had she been standing there?

"Was he not well-to-do?" the mistress of the house asked. Her features were as sharp and severe as her manners. With high cheekbones, she might have been pretty once—if she'd had a little more fat on her face and lips that weren't so razor-thin.

Perhaps knowing what her mother was thinking, Miss Rosewood's expression soured in her mother's direction, but the look went unnoticed.

"He was," Mae whispered, feeling rather like an old maid.

"And still you rejected the offer?" Mrs. Rosewood balked.

"I later broke off the engagement."

"Feelings for another man got in the way, no doubt."

Mae opened her mouth to argue but quickly remembered her place.

"It's a story we hear a thousand times, is it not?" Mrs. Rosewood began the lecture in a boorish tone. "The outcome is never as happy as the storybooks. Miss Blackthorne herself is proof. Once an offer is turned down, one can never be sure if there will be another—no matter how large the dowry. For someone with Miss Blackthorne's breeding, it's almost a certainty."

The last line about Mae's breeding, no doubt in reference to her mother's background, bit into her.

"Fact is, he was a terrible man." Mae could not help herself. "Life with him would have been miserable." *More so than this one,* she finished in her head.

The family business had rested on the marriage, but every fiber in her body had screamed against it. All the jewels in England could not have tempted her to accept him.

She didn't care what the local constables believed, her brother's death had not been a suicide. Beneath his veneer of fine manners, Ellsworth was a murderer. William's murderer.

"You have provided an excellent first lesson." Mrs. Rosewood smiled crisply. "But I'm afraid that will have to do for today."

She motioned Miss Rosewood to come forward. When Miss Lenore sat up, the lady of the house shook her head. "Not you, dear. Just your sister."

"Why only me?" Miss Rosewood asked but went forward nonetheless.

"We'll be going out in search of a new gown."

"For tonight?" Miss Rosewood nearly shrieked. "For dinner with father's guest?"

Mrs. Rosewood gave a quick nod, then eyed Mae. "Don't forget the kitchens, Miss Blackthorne."

Mae bowed her head, impatient for the clicking of heels to dissipate. Choking back a sob, Miss Lenore clearly had been affected by the visit too.

"Now, now." Mae knelt down before her. She felt her own pain surface, but having had much practice, forced it back without notice. "It'll be your turn soon."

"Yes, but how long might that be?"

"Soon enough." Mae picked a book from the stack and opened it. "Until then, you best mind your studies."

AT THE END of the lesson, Mae headed to the kitchens, as instructed.

Since that morning, the house had become only slightly less chaotic. Servants put the finishing touches to flower arrangements and ran rags feverishly over anything made of wood.

Meanwhile, Miss Rosewood's questions still plagued Mae. No matter how little she had left to lose, no matter how hard she tried to rise above, the tiniest reminder of Ellsworth still crushed her.

Members of the same trade, Mae's and Ellsworth's families had been at odds for generations, a rivalry that often amused her. While tense, it had sometimes proven beneficial, driving her father toward better and more innovative ship design.

Not once had she imagined what it might be like on the losing side, the bitterness that might arise when faced with failure. The kind of bitterness Ellsworth embodied for his entire family— all dead now.

The rivalry had destroyed them both. Mae hated that Miss

Rosewood had brought back those memories. Even if it had been well-intentioned on the pupil's part. Here, forgetting was difficult enough.

Mae hurried down the empty hall, glad for once that she would not be alone, that she had an hour's more work to free her mind of these things.

Upon entering the kitchen, the smell of fish and stewing vegetables overwhelmed her. Shelves teeming with pots, pans, and preserves lined every inch of available wall space. Above the hearth, a large pot bubbled to the brim.

Mrs. Jacobs, a well-rounded woman well into her later years, was stirring, her face slick with perspiration. On the large table centered in the room, Mrs. Dorris—a woman of equal age to the cook but meager frame—chopped carrots. She had a small space cleared out amongst a clutter of other ingredients.

Since the women had mostly been confined to the kitchen, Mae had only spoken to them once or twice. And yet, both women and even their mothers had spent their lives working there. They seemed content. As if the idea of a different life had never even occurred to them. Mae supposed that there would be little point. Here in the kitchen, they were even more confined than Mae. It was only she who had a taste, a dream of something better.

"Yes?" Mrs. Jacobs's stirring hand stilled as she looked up. The old woman wore her usual white cap.

"I was told you needed my assistance?" As the words had left her mouth, an idea struck. They, if anyone, might know about the modest manor in the woods. Her only challenge was how to bring it into conversation.

"I thought the work be beneath you, you being educated and all…" Mrs. Jacobs grabbed a handful of chopped carrots from Mrs. Dorris's pile and threw them into a second pot. "But I suppose we do need the help and things have changed, haven't they?" She turned her gaze to a pile of potatoes in the corner. "Those need peelin'."

Mae waited for further instructions, but, receiving none, reluctantly walked to the corner. Pulling up her sleeves, she shifted through her surroundings. Beneath a dirtied rag she found a knife.

Again, she hesitated. Her ignorance of such an easy, domestic task took her aback. Still, she was even more reluctant to speak up. So with a potato in one hand and a knife in the other, she tried to imitate what she had seen only a few times before. Careful not to cut herself, she slid the knife down a potato then again but with more force. Although she shaved off more than she would have liked, she thought she'd managed well enough.

"I'd wager the man coming to dinner is likely a suitor," Mrs. Dorris said after several minutes of silence.

"Says who?" Mrs. Jacobs sprinkled a collection of herbs atop the carrots.

"Why else would they be having a guest for dinner? Mr. Rosewood will likely secure an offer before the day is out."

"It may be their only chance."

"Mrs. Rosewood does seem to repel."

The two old ladies laughed together.

"Likely to be an ogre of a man," Mrs. Jacobs whispered, though Mae heard every word.

"And old, to be sure!"

They laughed again and this time, even Mae joined in. It was then that she realized her opportunity.

"I encountered something strange in the Northern Woods yesterday," she began. Both women turned sharply, as if noticing her existence for the first time.

"You rode through the Northern Woods?" Mrs. Jacobs asked in harsh disbelief.

"Only to escape the storm. I met with a home there."

Mrs. Dorris gasped. "'Tis abandoned."

"Not anymore." Mae moved her knife down a new potato. "A Mr. Ethan Locke lives there. He had just arrived."

The two women looked at each other, their eyes as wide as

their open mouths.

"I'll be…" Mrs. Jacobs mumbled, evidently deep in thought. "Came in with the storm this time, did he?"

Mae did not catch her meaning. "You know of him?"

"We both do," Mrs. Jacobs answered. "Your father knew him well enough."

"When?"

"When he was young, of course. They were like brothers, they were. But that was years ago. Before you was born."

"Like brothers?" Mae's heart jumped. She hadn't heard a whisper of him her whole life. How was it that this cook—someone to whom she had not spoken more than a few words—knew more about her father's past than she did? Following his death, she had searched her father's office for clues, a journal—anything that might reveal more about the family—and had come up with nothing. Now there was this. Though little and seemingly insignificant, that detail had brought her father's hazy memory more to light. And for a moment, she felt less like the last surviving Blackthorne whose past was better off forgotten.

She wondered more about the man. How had he come to know her father—so much older than he? What had ended their connection?

Before Mae could think to ask these questions aloud, Grace's head popped in the doorway.

"Mr. Rosewood's guest has arrived," she said. "He has asked for some tea before dinner."

"I'll bring it out to him." Mrs. Jacobs whipped out a towel and grabbed the kettle hanging in the hearth.

"But that's not your job. And you smell of onions," Grace protested.

"Mr. Rosewood won't notice. Get me the china."

Mrs. Dorris nodded, feverishly arranging the tray while Mrs. Jacobs collected herself, straightening her cap and pushing back loose strands of gray hair. Then tray in hand, she walked out of the kitchen with more poise than Mae thought possible.

It was a severe slip in conduct and decorum, they all knew this, but the servants had learned enough about the Rosewoods to know they wouldn't notice. The Rosewoods' wealth was so new, the finer details regarding hosting and the servants were lost to them.

Mae had already finished peeling, but she could not bring herself to leave. Rather, she took in the grand display before her. The gravy Mrs. Dorris carefully spooned into white porcelain. The large and impressive roast mutton on its silver platter, the glossy oysters, the fish consommé still brewing, and the bright-pink salmon. She had never really thought about the work needed to create the meals she'd once taken for granted. Nor the intense heat of the kitchen and the abhorrent smell of fish. Burning pencil shavings did little to cover the stench.

She felt silly standing idle while Mrs. Dorris arranged adornments of foliage. But at last, Mrs. Jacobs returned, her face flush and her voice ripe with excitement.

"You didn't get in trouble, did ya?" Mrs. Dorris asked.

Mrs. Jacobs waved a hand and rushed over, short of breath. "It's just as I suspected! Just as I suspected…"

"What?" Mrs. Dorris demanded.

"It's none other than Mr. Locke himself. And he hasn't aged a day, I tell you. Not a single day!"

"Impossible." Mrs. Dorris stilled in her work.

"Mr. Locke is Mr. Rosewood's guest?" Mae asked.

The two ignored her.

"He should be—" Mrs. Dorris attempted to count on her fingers. "Not much older than me. Nearly sixty."

"*Sixty?* Perhaps you've mistaken father for son?" Mae interjected.

Mrs. Jacobs collected the potatoes from Mae's corner and began chopping. "No, no, dear. There's no chance of that. I suspected the same thing when Mr. Locke visited your father oh, 'bout seven years ago. He was supposed to be fifty just like your father, but he wasn't. I couldn't be sure, but now that all those years have passed…"

"He has sold his soul to the devil." Mrs. Dorris gripped a knife in consternation. Mae stifled a laugh. It was the odd sort of story all the servants there loved to gossip about.

"In sheep's clothing, he is," Mrs. Jacobs said. "For he's certainly no ogre."

Certainly not, Mae thought. And likely from a place entirely unknown to her. Someplace that had to be far grander.

So why was he, of all places, here?

"Where do you think he has returned from?" Mae asked.

"Who knows where." Mrs. Jacobs shook her head.

No doubt somewhere distant, Mae thought, envying him at once. Maybe Spain, among the matadors. She tried to imagine Italy, the West Indies, China—the places she knew only from books and the globe collecting dust in the schoolroom. It would likely take her a thousand years to guess.

"He can't be all bad," Mae found herself murmuring. She had always thought her father brave for traveling in his younger years, for venturing beyond England and all that was safe. Her mother too. Before they'd settled down in England after they'd married, she'd traveled alongside him. What she would do to travel to the places they all had been, whatever places those may have been. She didn't care.

"Don't believe us?" Mrs. Jacobs knifed off a few of the potato skins Mae had missed.

"It is quite the claim."

"No claim. 'Tis the truth." She bristled. "And if you're wise, you'll stay away."

Mae flushed again, not sure why the cook had given such a warning. What would *she* want with him? She certainly wasn't so disillusioned to think that last night had been anything more than a kindness.

Beside her, the chopping continued. Mrs. Dorris tilted her head up. "We got it from here."

Mae brushed off her hands and went into the hall. The tale

those women spoke of could not be true. They were impossible, not to mention ridiculous.

Mr. Locke didn't seem far in age from herself. He hadn't the look of a man nearing his sixties, like Mrs. Dorris.

Perhaps these were the rumors he had expected her to hear. He had practically admitted his notorious reputation himself. Well-bred accent or not, a man with those tattoos was no doubt involved with some scandal or another. Whatever his connection to her father, she had a feeling it hadn't been good.

There were tales that circulated around her family too: particularly those of how they'd risen to grandeur. One called her grandmother a mistress to a king, another said the house itself sat on a goldmine, kept secret to avoid taxes.

A sudden rap of footfalls stilled her thoughts. She prepared herself for Mrs. Rosewood, who would likely have a new set of demands. Ones she'd be forced to obey, no matter how late the hour. But when she looked up, another figure closed in.

Mae stepped back. She recognized his deep-blue, almost-black riding coat at once. Swallowing her shock, she regained her composure. Mrs. Jacobs was right about one thing. Given the proximity of his home, there was a good chance Mr. Locke's father and maybe even his grandfather had been acquainted with her family. Now it was more important than ever to keep her name—or better yet, her existence—secret from him.

Mae picked up her pace, hoping to pass him unseen.

"Is it really…" His voice stopped her.

"Mr. Locke." Mae lifted her gaze off the floorboards and caught his bright eyes. All at once, the other words she meant to speak caught in her throat. He looked so different than he had the night before. His hair, bronze when dry, was no longer wild but coiffed back.

Thank God they were alone. What would Mrs. Rosewood surmise of the charming gaze he was giving her? What would the servants?

"Fate smiles upon me." He gave the slightest twitch of a bow.

"You are in good health, I hope?"

Recalling Mrs. Dorris's words of the devil, she studied him. Aside from his utterly charming appearance, he didn't seem a man of evil or darkness. Then again, who could be sure?

"Yes, thank you." Mae curtsied and waited for him to continue on.

"I feared you might have caught cold after last night's ride." He stood his ground. "I should have been more persuasive in my efforts to make you stay."

Was he truly this concerned? It was polite of him to inquire after her health, of course, but the question surprised her all the same. Most people above her station didn't bother with pleasantries.

She stumbled for something to say. Somehow, the words were lost to her. Nervousness was building in her chest, twisting her insides into a tight coil ready to explode. Alone or not, they still ran the risk of being caught. Mrs. Rosewood's assumptions would have no bounds. She was known to accuse a maid or two of theft when something had been misplaced. Who knew where else Mrs. Rosewood's imagination might lead her—or for that matter, Mae's own.

"I am quite well," she finally managed, though meekly. When she stepped forward, Mr. Locke blocked her escape.

"Do you mean to trap me, sir?" Mae's voice was even with propriety, but her eyes fluttered with anger. She wouldn't stand for these games.

"You seem flushed. Not from fever, I hope." His brow wrinkled and drew together.

"No, and if you don't mind…" Beneath his teasing eyes, Mae was sure she flushed even deeper. "I don't think Mr. Rosewood would be pleased to discover your absence."

"Gracious host as he is, he left me to admire the drawing room and soon I came to admire the hallway too…and now"—he smiled with practiced charm—"you."

She hardened her gaze. He was doing this on purpose, trying

to embarrass her. He probably thought that the slightest flattery would make her weak in the knees. No doubt he enjoyed toying with the servants too.

As if to confirm her suspicions, he smirked before turning his eyes to a portrait that hung on the wall beside her. The grim expression of an old, white-haired man stared back. "A Rosewood ancestor?"

"No, an ancestor of the last family that lived here."

Although the words tickled her tongue, she couldn't bring herself to ask if he had known the family. It was far too risky. The question could give her away and for some reason, she also feared the answer. She had a feeling whatever this man had to do with her family, it couldn't be good.

"That's right. Mr. Rosewood came into his money rather late in life, didn't he? Grew up a farm boy. Hardly the type of upbringing—"

Mae cut him off. She would not be caught listening to such insults. "How long have you known Mr. Rosewood?" But her question wasn't entirely innocent, either. She was eager to discover the purpose of his visit. Did he really intend for Miss Rosewood's hand? It didn't seem likely.

What did a man, inked on all over his chest, want with marriage? He didn't belong in fine drawing rooms. He belonged elsewhere. She didn't know where.

"Since this morning."

"And you are not acquainted with Mrs. Rosewood, either?"

"We are neighbors." Mr. Locke's face hardened.

"How nice of you to visit," Mae replied with even civility. "And so soon. Do you plan to visit the Nettle family too?"

"My, you ask a great many questions." He pulled at his white sleeve cuffs, drawing her eyes to his hands. "What are you, a damn detective?"

Mae barely registered his words. Along either set of knuckles wasn't the gash she recalled from the previous day. There wasn't even a scar.

When her eyes lifted, the gaze she met was no longer teasing, but stiff and serious.

"I daresay there are some things you may not wish to know," he said.

Like what? The black arts that had healed his wound so quick? What else might give him the ageless life the cooks had claimed him to have? Perhaps they hadn't been telling lies, after all. This man was beyond all logic.

"You must be fascinated by me," he continued, catching her unfocused stare. "Out of boredom, I suspect."

"You flatter yourself." People thought governesses were all the same: timid, lonely, and obscure. If only she could show him who she really was. The person she so desperately wanted to be.

"In that case..." Mr. Locke stepped aside, allowing her to pass. With a sweep of the hand and a twinkle of the eye, he dared her.

Taking her chance, she picked up her skirts and left him behind. She refused to let his comments faze her. Even if he was right, even if she wished they had done so much more than talk that stormy night, even if she had thought of little else...

She slowed her steps. A new, unfamiliar atmosphere seemed to surround her. And it wasn't just through the eyes of her role as governess, either. Her home, once constant, had changed somehow, as though teeming with secrets she couldn't quite see. Mr. Locke was one of them. If Mrs. Dorris had been truthful and her father had known Mr. Locke, then he had likely ventured here before. But when? As a child? How close could he and her family have been? What else might she discover?

It had long troubled and shamed her that she knew so little. Despite the long, distinguished line of ancestors behind her, their rise to prominence had been a complete mystery. Like every family of significance, they had to have started somewhere. A grand story, no doubt. Why had her father not shared it? He had told her so many far-fetched, wondrous tales she'd taken then as truth. Naturally, she'd questioned their veracity as an adult.

Though she wanted to believe again. She wanted to feel that same wild sense of longing to be among the waves, to be brave, to find riches beyond imagining. A child's hope just as far-fetched as her father's stories. She opened her bedroom door and shut it behind her, feeling it rattle through the latch.

CHAPTER THREE

The Pocket Watch

MAE SPRUNG UP in her bed, not sure what had woken her. Darkness closed the space around her. Cold air breathed at her neck. Her fire had gone out hours ago. She clenched her blankets tighter, but it was too cold to wait for the morning sun to warm her.

She twisted out of bed and plunged into the darkness for the fireplace. The floorboards creaked as they always did, but something else sounded too: a dull thudding.

She was inclined to think it nothing—particularly with the house thawing in the warmth of spring. But Mae knew every groan and ache the house made and—though faint and obscure—that noise was not one of them.

She gasped, her exhale visible in the freezing night air. She could stand the cold no longer. Tomorrow, she would demand more coal from Mrs. Rosewood. What remained in the fireplace was no more than sparkling embers.

She yanked her robe free from the bedpost. The cold cloth clung to her, sending shivers along her body.

She recoiled. The thuds came three in a row. Had Richie's dog made its way into the kitchen again? Groaning inwardly, she moved out into the hallway to begin her investigation.

She refused to think anything of danger. Not when they had Moore—Mr. Moore, as she now needed to call him—butler and habitual sleepwalker. Twice, she had caught him walking the halls like a God-damn ghost.

Loud in the silence, her feet thumped along the floorboards. She had no more candles left to guide her. Luckily, she didn't need one. She knew the halls well enough to walk them in absolute darkness.

After a few moments, her eyes adjusted to the night. She expected to hear Mr. Moore or the dog at any moment, but as she walked along the staircase, all seemed calm. She sighed, waiting for another sound. If it was Mr. Moore, she needed to remember not to wake him this time. Months ago, he had gone on a rampage at her disruption, waking the entire house.

She heard it again. Something tumbled from below. Muffled too, it was undoubtedly nefarious. Whatever was happening, the culprit was trying to keep their actions hidden.

More cautious this time, Mae descended the staircase and caught the glow of a lamp. Down the hall, she realized its source: her father's old office.

It was one room the Rosewoods had kept unchanged. Since her employer had decided to take another office closer to his personal library, no one had stepped in the room in years.

She stilled. A series of whispered curses caught her off-guard. The terse words were not Mr. Moore's. She wished she had stayed in the safety of her room. In the dark of night she would only encounter trouble.

The sound of ruffling papers sent her backward. Steps resounded throughout the room. Fear urged her to run, but no matter how terrifying the sounds, she could not get help until she knew their source. She had to be sure it wasn't some disgruntled servant who likely deserved to take a few things.

Easing herself along the wall, she peered one eye over the threshold.

In the dim light, stood the man from the woods. Her mouth

dropped in horror, still frozen when they locked eyes. In the next moment, he pulled her into the room against the wall. Though indecency was the least of her worries, she was suddenly aware of her scant robe and nightgown. Pinned down with a hand over her mouth, her mind raced with devious possibilities and violent ends. The previous cold that had stiffened her body lifted away, replaced by the warm rush of panic.

"Quiet, you," he commanded with ragged breath. But in his tone, she sensed he was scared too.

"Release me." Mae panted beneath his warm palm. Though futile, she struggled against him.

"I'll not hurt you," he said, as though it were obvious. His hand fell away, his face crumpled in shame.

"What were you searching for?" she asked, straightening her meager gown.

He looked about the room, as if contemplating how much to tell her.

"I could report this," she added.

He snapped back to meet her gaze. "You mustn't."

"Then tell me why you are here."

He pulled away, pacing. Then, reaching into his breast pocket, he came close again.

"What if"—Mr. Locke reached his hand down to her waist—"your master found you here with my timepiece?" He plopped a heavy thing into the pocket of her robe. Mae waited for him to pull away, but he held fast. She did not wince, though. She would not give a man the pleasure.

"How then will you explain your presence here?" She lifted her chin in defiance. "*Uninvited?*"

He set his jaw and took back his timepiece. "Why couldn't I have awakened a foolish maid?"

Mae looked him up and down, still vexed by his needless contact. No one had ever touched her like that. Had not even come close. "Wot'll it be, then?"

She didn't like this sudden air he'd taken on. He sounded too much like a criminal, though he looked anything but.

"Come on now." He dropped the timepiece back into his pocket. He moved behind the desk, collecting papers and putting them back in place. "Everyone has a price."

"Money, you mean?"

"Indeed. Name your price."

Mae studied his hands as they shifted the papers, once again noticing his knuckles, completely healed.

She should turn back and get away. But she didn't. She remained as still as the wall behind her, considering. The temptation to take advantage was unbearable. If nothing else, she needed to risk the one question that had gnawed at her since she'd offered her assistance in the kitchen. She had to.

"What do you know of the Blackthornes?"

Mr. Locke stilled in his work. "Who?"

"The Blackthornes. Were they not your neighbors once?"

"This interests you? Why?" He narrowed his eyes.

She swallowed. "They lived here. They're in the walls, in the still-hanging portraits. There are stories…"

"I won't stand for the slanders of gossips."

"You knew the family, then?"

"No." He looked to the ground briefly.

He was lying, Mae was certain of it, but what could she do? What else could she say?

"Here. Why not keep this, after all?" He tossed her the watch. "You wouldn't tell anyone *now*, would you?"

Mae looked at the shiny object, suddenly abuzz with shame. *Idiot.* She should refuse. But what then? What might he do? What else was a man who rummaged through offices willing to do for silence? She did not dare think of it. The worst of it was, he needn't give up his watch.

"I was only curious."

Her threat earlier had been an empty one. She would much rather not get involved with any of this. Whatever it was.

He dropped the papers. "I know."

When he stepped close, Mae stared at the mangled skin above his left brow. Perhaps from a similar incident, it seemed to speak of dangers yet to come. She straightened, summoning her voice to scream.

"Not a word." He clenched his teeth. Then, as if suddenly summoned, he stalked out of the room.

There are serious consequences for walking about past midnight, Mae thought with her chest heaving. This encounter had been one of them. Events could have gone far worse. For a long while, back in the relative safety of her own room, she could think of nothing else. When she settled back in bed, the cold seemed a trifle. Now she had the emptiness to think of.

CHAPTER FOUR

The Uncertain Betrothal

"YOUR MOTHER?" MR. Rosewood sealed the last document of the marriage settlement and extended it over his desk.

"Dead too, I'm afraid." Taking the precious papers, Locke sank back into the leather chair.

"A man with no family. No wonder you are so eager for a wife."

"Yes, companionship is truly something to be cherished." Locke suppressed the urge to make his leave at once. All he had to do was sit through a few more odious drinks with the man. That was it.

After exhausting negotiations on the settlement, Locke could hardly stand his presence. He had underestimated the family's social ambitions. Money wouldn't do. Rather, it was his large plot of land and this notion that by combining their estates, Mr. Rosewood would have the largest in the county that finally sealed the deal. It had taken two days and all his land, but finally, Mr. Rosewood had agreed to let Locke help handle the mismanaged estate—just the role that would allow Locke to search the place without question.

"I think you should like my darling Clarissa." Mr. Rosewood gave Locke a wolfish grin that disturbed him.

Like most country men, Mr. Rosewood's peppered hair was an uncombed, frizzy rat's nest atop his head. The type of suit he donned reminded Locke of his earlier days in England. No doubt it had gone out of style by now.

In hopes of ending the conversation, Locke gave a nod and rose to leave.

"She is quite accomplished, I'll have you know."

"Yes." Locke sat back down, his eyes flashing to the mantel clock. Why Mr. Rosewood still felt the need to convince him of all this, he had no idea. "I experienced them all last night."

The singing, the piano playing—it had all been quite exhausting. He had no interest in the woman—who seemed far more like a girl, in his opinion—or any woman, for that matter. All he wanted was access to the estate. But if everything went according to plan, he'd disappear long before they had to marry. He wasn't sure where he'd go, but he'd have plenty of time to think on it. Wedding arrangements often took months and he planned to drag them out as long as necessary.

"Her governess had a world-class education herself. She's skilled in almost every subject most useful to the ladies these days, so I'm sure you will find Clarissa readier than ever to run the household. Miss Blackthorne has even—"

Locke sprung forward in his seat, his eyes widening with interest. "Miss Blackthorne?" He gripped the armrest tighter.

"Yes. Her governess. You know the lady?"

So that was why she had been asking questions. He was an imbecile for not realizing it sooner. He thought he'd recognized her face. She was Alastair's daughter. He should have known. It all made sense, why Mae's mother was from where she was from.

Alastair had clearly met his wife overseas and brought her home sometime after their partnership had ended. He had even read their names, Tala and Mae, in the papers he had dug up before meeting Ellsworth. He just thought Blackthorne's daughter would have been married off by now. Given the family business's downfall, he hadn't expected she would reside so close, within such easy grasp. He almost could not believe it. Though it made perfect sense.

Locke focused back on Mr. Rosewood. "I knew her father."

"Ah. The man is dead, you know. Died six winters ago of pneumonia."

Locke nodded, tapping the edge of the envelope on the arm-rest in thought. The night prior had played over in his mind a thousand times. It all made sense now. He had been impressed by her quickness. Of course she wasn't just some governess. In the face of his threats, few had dared express the same fortitude. And her brazen questions! The truth had been obvious from the first.

"Luckily, he died before he could see the girl sink his business into ruin," Mr. Rosewood went on. "We did her some charity taking her in when we brought the house two years ago."

"You know how she lost the fortune?"

"Tragic story, that. From what I've heard, it all started after her brother, William, had gone missing at sea. He returned sometime within the span of four years, but not soon enough, I'm afraid. Miss Blackthorne trusted the wrong manager. Their shipbuilding business—a longstanding one, have you—fell to the wayside some months later. T'was around that time the brother killed himself."

Locke had read just that. "What tragedy."

"Alas, her story is not unique here. Among shipwrights, at least."

"You mean the bankruptcies?

"Indeed. Several more will likely follow…"

"That's too bad."

"Yes, well, regardless, Bristol will always be a port and a port will always need its warehouses."

"You're not worried, then?"

Mr. Rosewood laughed. "It's what attracted me here in the first place." He waved his arms up. "Plenty of empty estates ripe for the taking."

"Cheap too, I imagine."

"They have their history and austerity…"

Locke drowned out the rest of the man's words with his thoughts.

Despite Locke's doubts, Ellsworth was right: Alastair's heirs hadn't found the fortune. What was more important, the revelation meant his revenge might still be possible. Since the day Alastair had left him for dead, he had thought of little else. He should be imaging a knife at his daughter's throat. Instead, he felt a pang of pity.

Chances were, she didn't know a lick about the crimes her father had committed. Her questions—asked so unflinchingly— had proven this.

She was an innocent. Untouched by the vulgarities of the world. Lord knew he had seen too many. It made her the worst kind of enemy. But an enemy nonetheless.

Now she'd have to get involved. The lady would prove most useful in the ways of finding the family fortune hidden some-where in the manor. And yet, part of him hesitated. He wanted that way of life behind him. He wasn't prepared to face this kind of enemy again. After his failures the last time, he did not think he could bear the consequences.

☾

THANKS TO THE household's first guest in months, rumors of Miss Rosewood's betrothal spread like wildfire. The following day, Mae could hardly go an hour without hearing the man's name. Talk of balls, engagement parties, and receptions were already stirring. A new stream of gossip had erupted about Mr. Locke's background as well.

To some servants, the mysterious man was a successful inves-tor ready to settle down after making thousands speculating on diamond mines. To others, he was the son of a wealthy merchant residing in Australia.

They reminded Mae of the tales the servants told about her own family. The stories of long-lost hordes of Roman coins and gold from shipwrecks. They were really just dreams of how they themselves might attain it.

Compared to her family's origins, Locke was far more mysterious. Not even Miss Rosewood knew the whole truth of his affairs. And yet, the rumors surrounding Mr. Locke only seemed to heighten the lovesick young woman's admiration of the man. To Mae's ears, it all sounded like fanciful fiction.

There had been not a single explanation as to why he thought it fruitful to marry the young lady. Surely, he wasn't stupid enough to risk disgracing the innocent lady—nor would Mrs. Rosewood have allowed such an opportunity.

They were simply ill-suited. Why didn't Mrs. Rosewood see that? Their marriage would be a disaster from the start.

Mae had caught him rifling through her father's things, for heaven's sake! What he had been looking for, she still had no idea. The truth seemed out of reach. Even the cooks—despite being known for adding fuel to the gossips—had kept quiet about him. Though she couldn't quite call it bliss, Mae had to live in ignorance.

When Mae retreated to her room for dinner, time seemed to stretch forever. She ought to have been doing something else. Anything else. But as the sun sank reluctantly beneath the horizon, no book could quell her mind. The previous night played over and over: the peculiar way his eyes had burned, the intense heaving of his chest...

In the end, she couldn't help herself. She was determined to find answers about Mr. Locke, no matter how much he poisoned her mind with dreams far beyond her present reality.

In hopes of learning the latest rumors, she even offered to help with the kitchen duties.

"That is not what you were hired for." Mrs. Rosewood's hand stilled over the letter she'd been writing. Judging from the swirls of the letters, it had been some sort of formal invitation.

"You are to focus on Clarissa's dancing instead."

"Dancing? What happened to her dance master? Mr.…." Mae struggled to remember his name.

"He's occupied with other families. Regardless. We need to save what we can." Mrs. Rosewood turned to Mae with a stern eye. "Once Locke officially proposes, a betrothal ball will soon be upon us."

"No visit to London, then?" Mae felt the blood drain from her face. Were the rumors really true? The notion sickened her. "Miss Rosewood was so much looking forward to her first Season."

Dropping her pen back into the inkwell, Mrs. Rosewood stood up. Her pale-yellow skirts billowed behind her. "Those engagements are not only costly, but unnecessary. We are lucky to have found Clarissa a match so quickly. One that will add greatly to our estate and reputation, no less. The gentleman is perfect… Well, for *Clarissa*, that is."

Mae could not believe her words. Perhaps she'd be able to convince Mrs. Rosewood of a more advantageous match. Not out of jealousy, of course, but for Miss Rosewood's own protection. Mr. Locke was, after all, as good as a burglar. "Are you sure they are well-suited? Perhaps—"

"Of course I am sure they are well-suited!" Mrs. Rosewood's mouth fell open in stark horror.

"I didn't mean to suggest…" Mae sputtered. "I-I just…"

"Tame that tongue of yours!"

Mae bit her lip, stifling the unruly anger that would only serve to get her sacked. She looked down at the black ripples of her skirt.

Mrs. Rosewood let out a breath. "If it's London you crave, you'll soon have it when Lenore is out. For her, we'll accept nothing lower than an earl."

"Yes, of course."

"You see, I have a plan. As I said, Clarissa's fate is already settled." Mrs. Rosewood released a terse breath and focused on the flames dancing in the fireplace. "Now, go. Do as you are bid."

Mae nodded as obedient as ever. "Yes, ma'am." But inside, she was cringing.

Of all the men she had imagined the Rosewoods throwing at their eldest daughter, a man like Mr. Locke was certainly not one of them. She had expected them to force her to marry a much older bachelor or widower. Locke, though, was so young, cultured, and charming... She swallowed, then taking a deep breath, confined the jealousy that threatened to possess her.

For now, she'd have no choice but to obey her employer.

As the days passed by, they began preparations for Miss Rosewood's betrothal ball. Every other so-called "useless" subject they'd spent years improving upon dissolved away. Dancing and etiquette became their sole focus, subjects Mae hated most of all. Standing over Miss Rosewood's curious eyes, Mae paced back and forth in the dining room. She debated whether she really needed to refresh her on this one topic.

Miss Rosewood fumbled with a fork. In front of her was every imaginable bowl, plate and piece of silverware she could expect to encounter.

"What is it?" Miss Rosewood entreated.

"I'm not certain, if I..." Mae clasped her hands tightly. "But you do want to make it a success, don't you? And since it's often expected..."

"Miss Blackthorne." Miss Rosewood frowned. "Just tell me. *Please.*"

"It's just that I know you can be rather talkative at times." Mae cringed, preparing herself for Miss Rosewood's reaction. "On the night of the ball, however, that might not be wise."

"Do you fear I'll forget my steps? But, Miss Blackthorne"— Miss Rosewood blinked rapidly—"you've seen how well I dance the quadrille."

"That matters little. Talking, I'm afraid, as a reminder, should always be kept to a minimum."

Miss Rosewood's eyebrow furrowed. "Am I to be utterly silent?"

"For the most part...yes," Mae replied, struggling to keep her smile. "And do refrain from whispers."

"But why? If I'm disturbing no one—"

"Because it is unladylike." Looking away, Mae caught a glance of herself in the polished mahogany of the dining table. Who had she become? Were these not the rules she herself had rebelled against at Miss Rosewood's age? She remembered how her father had chastised her for riding astride, but she had never obeyed that old-fashioned ideal. Riding that way was needlessly difficult, uncomfortable, and even dangerous. She didn't care how unladylike it might have been.

Miss Rosewood, meanwhile, gave no rebuke. She simply nodded in understanding.

The young girl, barely eighteen, was eager to have a husband. From the looks of it, she was willing to do almost anything to accomplish the task.

Perhaps Mae should've been just as willing. Didn't they want the same? To escape from this country estate and Mrs. Rosewood, her harsh and emotionless mother?

In that train of thought, Mr. Locke came rushing into her mind. After catching him in her father's office, his absence was to be expected, but she also couldn't deny how it filled her with disappointment. She couldn't forget the feel of his hands on her or the breath of his words against her ear.

"Miss Blackthorne?"

"Yes?" Mae snapped back to reality.

"What if he doesn't like me?"

"What? Why wouldn't he like you?"

"At dinner, he barely looked at me. Even when I sang."

"Sometimes it's like that at first. First, he needs a chance to get to know you." The words gnawed at her as she said them. They just didn't sound right.

"And if he still doesn't like me?"

"You'll be stuck with him either way." Just as Mae was stuck here—a harsh reality to which they both needed to resign themselves.

CHAPTER FIVE

Revenge

"Why did you not tell me of her existence in the first place?" Locke's clenched jaw barely allowed the words to escape. He threw his gaze across the modest sitting room to where Ellsworth sat a good five yards away.

His mere presence made Locke uneasy. Ellsworth might have called himself a guest in Locke's home for the moment, but that did not make them friends. Locke would sooner slit Ellsworth's throat. Their newly struck deal certainly did not make them partners, either. Not with his pathetic excuse for strategy and rather lacking arithmetic skills. The man hadn't even surmised that Locke should have been just as old and gray as he.

"Don't tell me you fancy she will help us!" Ellsworth laughed in a storm of exaggerated outrage.

"If we are persuasive enough, why not?" Damn it, he wanted his freedom. He needed to recover the stone and soon. It was only a matter of time before his enemies returned. "Don't be a fool. She would go to Mr. Rosewood at once. She'd like nothing better than to see me hang."

Locke's patience with the man had grown so thin these last few days, he would hardly mind the same. At the moment, though, Ellsworth and his precious clue were necessary.

"I don't care what your reasoning. Only a Blackthorne is meant to find the vault. She is the last one!"

Only an idiot would let such a detail fall between the cracks. Not including the land they owned, Blackthorne Manor was extensive. Without Miss Blackthorne's assistance, the search could otherwise take months, maybe even years.

The sooner they found it, the less time he had to spend in the company of that Rosewood girl. Ellsworth frowned. "She's shiftier and more conniving than one might think."

"How curious." Locke crossed his arms. "That was hardly my impression." Nor how he would describe her. A word more like *frustrating* seemed more fitting. Not to mention *distracting*. Far too often, she occupied his thoughts. The things she had said seemed to linger. He was still waiting to see a wisp of Alastair in her, but there was no likeness yet. Which made her more intriguing.

"Pretty, don't you think?"

Locke shrugged.

"I suppose she might be to some. But don't be deceived." Ellsworth leaned back and sipped his tea. "You mustn't forget who raised her. Blackthorne was a shipbuilder, but a dirty, shifty one at that. I say"—Ellsworth's lips flattened into a quivering line—"their downfall could not have come to a more deserving family."

Locke resisted an urge to roll his eyes. He hated when Ellsworth turned the conversation away from their goal, but at the same time, he took an interest in Miss Blackthorne's past.

"Your families were competitors, then."

"Bitter rivals," he replied. "My father built up the business. We were one of few that could keep pace. In my hands, I had not a doubt of our continued success. Like my father, I have an ambitious nature and a talent for innovative ship design. Nothing dared stand in my way..."

"Yet the business failed?"

"Just about. The Blackthornes undercut our prices at every

turn. We couldn't compete." He rose from his seat in a tremor of anxious movement. "We lost thousands. A fair price. That's all I wanted, but the prodigal son was ruthless."

"'The prodigal son'?"

"Miss Blackthorne's late brother. William Blackthorne." He stilled before the stone fireplace tinged with decades-old soot. "I had to dismiss dozens of my men and still, we were in debt. I even…" He cleared his throat. "My father gave me every opportunity." He turned to Locke. "He'd later wish he'd saved his efforts. At least that's what he told me the night before."

"'The night before'?"

"He killed himself."

Locke almost smiled. *Fascinating what shame can do to a man,* he thought. *Or rather, those who are less.*

"Miss Blackthorne's brother." A dangerous glint took hold in Ellsworth's eyes. "How fitting for him to have died of suicide too."

"Quite."

Locke bit back his growing frustration. He wasn't at all pleased with the bitterness that would undoubtedly plague their plans.

"Now I intend to set my business to rights. With my cut, I could reinvest in a new venture. I could create the empire I was always meant to, give people the jobs my father had intended for them. Perhaps then she might finally see her mistake."

"What are you talking about?"

"For rejecting me! Miss Blackthorne had her chance. We didn't have to be like everyone else. If we had wed, our business-es combined would have been saved. I had the land and supplies for it…but what did she do? She chose to become penniless. She chose the life of a *governess.*"

Locke's stomach twisted, the notion of Miss Blackthorne marrying the man making bile rise in his throat.

He fought to keep his face from screwing up with disgust. "I suppose I'd feel insulted too."

Mae's life would have been easier in a lot of ways if she had accepted. And yet she'd refused. That had taken some backbone and plenty of courage.

"She wasn't fit for the type of life I could offer, anyway. Couldn't dance or dress worth a damn, spent far too much time on that horse of hers…"

"Outrageous for a woman."

"Almost wasn't worth her father's assets."

"Maybe you should be relieved, then."

"Not in the least. If a penniless immigrant would not have me, who else would? Society turned on me. 'There must be something wrong with me,' they said. 'Madness in the family,' that sort of nonsense."

Locke sniffed, shoving down an urge to laugh. The only one who was mad was Ellsworth.

"Now you want her to suffer, eh?"

Despite himself, pity blossomed in his heart again for Miss Blackthorne and when it took hold, the anger he had felt for years toward her father seemed to cool. But like an ember, it remained, ready to burn bright again.

"Indeed." Ellsworth brought Locke back to his pathetic tale. "In the name of the men I put out of work, for the very families that starved at my hand. Quite frankly, she may never suffer enough."

Locke was tempted to call him *a bitter fool*, to tell him all the revenge in the world could not have made him a better man in the eyes of his father, but he held his tongue. Wasn't revenge exactly what he, himself, once wanted? Seeing Ellsworth's sudden rage, the sickening, maddening kind of rage that had simmered and festered for years, Locke felt disgusted with himself.

"No shame in trying this out, I suppose. Nothing ventured…" Ellsworth re-lit his pipe and breathed in the calming effects of tobacco. "I'm just not certain it is worth the risk. How do you expect to make her agreeable?"

"Through deception, of course." Locke chose his words carefully. "We promise her a third of the fortune and—"

"And the moment it's within our grasp, we break her neck, eh?" Ellsworth's eyes gleamed.

Locke went rigid, tasting bile again. He'd had enough of bloodshed, distrust, and betrayal. He needed no more fuel for his nightmares. The look she'd given him in the office that night when she caught him had pained him enough. Just thinking of it, his throat went dry, rendering him barely able to speak. He knew that look too well. It brought back memories, dreadful ones his mind would never let him forget.

"I-I…" He swallowed. "Yes."

Although he wanted to scream out against the notion, Ellsworth would take it as a sign of weakness. Maybe it was.

Locke was already starting to have his doubts about all this. But he still needed to get to the vault. He clenched his teeth.

"'Tis an excellent plan." Ellsworth stood up and slapped him on the back. "I suppose you'd like to be the one to finish her?"

Locke swept round and met his eye.

"No need to feel guilty," Ellsworth said. "The Blackthornes took a whole fortune and then some from you—just like they stole business from me."

Locke cringed at the similarity Ellsworth had drawn between them. The idea that they were anything alike dug at his pride.

"I don't think revenge would be too much out of order."

"The fact does not escape me."

Locke looked at the floor, in need of masking his true feelings on the matter, particularly his intention to stay well-armed. If Ellsworth tried the smallest thing to hurt the governess heiress, Locke swore to himself he'd stop it.

"Would you rather I dispatch of her? Perhaps I could throw her into the ocean. Make her walk the plank, as it were. You'd like that, wouldn't you?" He smiled with cruel mirth. "Perhaps I might even have a moment with her first. I would hate to see her die unspoiled…"

Locke's gaze fixed on him. He had no control over what

followed next. Ruled only by his fury, he thrust a hand onto Ellsworth's chest and slammed him into the wall. "Say not another word," he growled in the voice from his earlier days, his crueler days.

"Fine, fine." Ellsworth let out a slew of choked laughter. "She's yours." But when Locke held still, all hilarity left him.

"You need me."

"Hardly." Locke shoved him backward. He was so disgusted with the man, he took three strides backward. He needed every bit of distance between them. "With a Blackthorne in my sights, do you really think I need your measly clue?"

"Your task will be easier with my clue. Faster."

"How is that?"

With some satisfaction, Locke noted a bead of sweat glistening down the other man's temple. Ellsworth smeared it away, his expression lifting back to its usual zeal.

"I'm a new man since all that's happened," he said. "I'm quite well-known in London. The bad parts of town, mostly. I've started a few…let's say, *illegitimate ventures* there. They've kept me afloat these last few years."

"How wonderful." He rolled his eyes.

"I employ a great many men, Locke. Dozens, in fact. All of whom I think you shall find very useful. Londoners are quite different from country bumpkins. I daresay"—he pointed at Locke's neck with his cane—"they notice things like men who wear necklaces."

Locke touched the small, glass bottle hidden beneath his thin, cotton shirt. "It's a lucky charm, is all."

"We could be partners well into the future, you know."

Locke grumbled. *Not in a hundred years*, he thought. And time these days was precious. He was aging again. He had been for the last seven years. Right where he had left off. He at least had the blue elixir.

He touched the smooth surface of the bottle. There was a reason the two items had been paired together. The sapphire he surmised could only stop the aging process but it couldn't heal one from injuries.

"I'll be retiring," Locke said. "A portion of the woman's fortune is more than enough for me."

"Is it now?"

"Believe me." Locke opened a window to release the gathering smoke. "The Blackthorne fortune is generations in the making and with what I have added to it, you will be able to live like a bloody king."

More importantly, once Locke retrieved the stone from the vault, he'd be able to shake off his last and final enemy. A man he only knew by the name Pierce. He wouldn't have to run anymore.

"I'll have my men attain Miss Blackthorne tomorrow." Ellsworth pulled him out of his reverie.

"No!" Locke near shouted. Was it not enough that they were taking her inheritance—what might be her only ticket out of her pitiful life as governess? The woman deserved better than that. No, he would not risk hurting her in the process—especially in the grips of the scum Ellsworth employed. "Would it not be easier if I brought her to you instead?"

"Whatever you say." Ellsworth blew out a puff of smoke and grinned like the crackbrain he was.

"Wait." Locke stilled Ellsworth's retreating steps. "Before we take it all for our own, I want your word on something."

"Anything."

"You'll shed no blood of Miss Blackthorne's. Not a drop. Not even a bruise until the vault is discovered. Only then is she fair game."

This would give him time, he reasoned with himself. During their search, he'd think of a way to keep her out of harm's way.

"Want her to yourself, do you? Unspoiled?" His eyebrows rose suggestively.

"And unscathed."

"I give you my word." Ellsworth bowed his head, his eyes

sardonic.

"Good." Locke nodded. But as hard as he tried to accept their plan, he knew he had handed Miss Blackthorne a blow from which she would never recover. And each day led closer to her ruin.

CHAPTER SIX

The Hunt

THROUGHOUT THE DAY, Mae found herself staring longer than usual—for whole minutes at a time until something caught her attention and forced her to look up.

Mr. Locke's presence had become all-consuming. Her questions never seemed to still.

What had he been searching for in her father's office and what parts of Mrs. Dorris's tale were true? There had to have been something. Was it not her father who'd told her that all tales, no matter how wild or abstract, always had some basis in truth? He, who—like the servants—had warned her never to venture into the Northern Woods?

She was restless. Her only hope for calm was her afternoon rides, which Mrs. Rosewood had hesitantly allowed. Out there in the fresh air, she felt like her old self again. Even the harsh, cool winds of early spring soothed her.

Beyond the misty hills, the faintest glimmer of sea enticed her forward. Beyond that was a world she could scarcely imagine, a place that seemed exclusive to Mr. Locke.

She envied him the privilege, of all that he had seen. The icy mountains of Sweden, perhaps? The deserts of Africa? Likely not a single dull moment.

She pulled back on the reins, the vastness of the green, gray moors no more. In her aimless ride, she had somehow led herself to the edge of the Northern Woods. She kneed Thomas an inch closer toward the tall, pillar-like trees, a strange sensation coming over her. Rather than the repulsion she'd felt all those times before, she felt drawn to its danger.

Mae searched the horizon like she might search a face for answers. Before her with the trees casting strange shadows and the eerie silence all around, the woods seemed more haunted than ever.

If not for the betrothal ensnaring him in reality, she might not believe Mr. Locke existed at all. That night of the storm, he'd seemed more like a ghost. The kind that appeared only at dark when one was alone.

Possibility had seemed so ripe then and she had failed to seize it. More likely, she never would. She was not one to take such bold actions anymore. That night, breaking decorum should have seemed easier with him, a man who was less so a gentleman.

In a coming breeze, the collective rustling of leaves resonated low and vast. Strange shadows flickered. When the crows began to caw, she needed no further warning. She twisted Thomas round and raced back to the manor with vigor.

Miss Rosewood awaited her at the stables. Perfectly poised in a new pink, muslin gown, she brushed the mane of her pristine, white mare.

"Miss Blackthorne!" She ran forward.

Mae brought Thomas to a walk and dismounted.

"Oh," Mae gasped when Miss Rosewood took her in with a tight embrace.

"You will not believe what has happened." Miss Rosewood pulled back. "Mr. Locke has proposed. I am officially engaged!"

Mae's breath seemed to escape all at once, suffocating her for a moment. She should not have been so disappointed. She should feel nothing but the utmost joy for her pupil. Miss Rosewood expected it.

Her mind worked for something to say. She had to say something wise, something optimistic, but the words seemed impossible to conjure. She resented the very thought of marriage. A feeling so strong, it frightened her. When had she become so bitter? When, exactly, had her life become so hopeless that even love seemed dismal?

That day you became a governess, a voice answered. Men married for money and status, not love. A truth that dragged her down with the weight of a thousand stones.

Miss Rosewood, unfortunately, was not oblivious to Mae's less-than-thrilled moods. Her gazes directed at her governess had often dripped with pity. "Father will throw the grandest ball." In Miss Rosewood's round, green eyes, the same pity caught Mae again. "Promise me you'll attend."

Mae shook her head. She could not endure all the familiar faces. She absolutely refused.

"But why?"

"Must I explain?" Mae turned to the horizon. Though it had been a beautiful violet that day, she saw nothing.

"Do you really want to be a governess forever? When Lenore's married off, what will you do?"

"Seek another post, of course."

"But surely, you don't want that."

"Then my only escape is what? Marriage?"

Mae didn't fear solitude. Rather, she feared a life of poverty of shameful begging and charity.

"I meant you could meet someone. You could fall in love."

Something in Mae responded to that remark, but she could not forget how sheltered Miss Rosewood was. Miss Rosewood had never experienced the harsh realities of life, nor did she understand the sacrifices of marriage.

Now wasn't a good time to speak ill of love, though. Seeking marriage was the point of every young girl's existence, particularly those of consequence.

"Promise me you'll attend," Miss Rosewood asked more

sternly.

Mae stared on, silent.

"Please? Just so I could introduce you to my cousins. They have heard so much about you in my letters. They don't mind that you're—"

Mae snapped away. Worse than cruelty sometimes was kindness. She didn't want it. "Forgive me."

The concern in Miss Rosewood's eyes didn't last longer than a moment. How could it when she was only a step away from freedom?

"If you but knew how it feels..." With another wide, unable-to-contain smile, the naive pupil grasped Mae's hands. "I love him."

Mae studied her face so full of triumph. Miss Rosewood didn't even know what love was. And neither did she, for that matter.

"You must meet him!" Miss Rosewood linked their arms and dragged Mae toward the manor.

"I mustn't." Mae wanted to pull back, but she found her feet stepping forward, eager to see Mr. Locke, if but for one more moment.

Entering the tearoom, however, Mae immediately regretted it. Mrs. Rosewood sat tall at the end of the settee in her best gown, the sea of grass-green taffeta far too much for the occasion.

Porcelain clinked atop the table.

"Clarissa." Mrs. Rosewood stood up and tugged her from Mae's arm. "Your father and Mr. Locke will be back at any moment." She wrinkled her nose. "Have you been in the stables again?"

"I must introduce Miss Blackthorne, Mother."

Mrs. Rosewood seemed about to object when Mr. Rosewood entered through double glass doors. Behind him, an even more distressing man followed.

"Mr. Locke," Mae said, uneasy.

By then, it was much too late to disappear. He would finally know her family name. Why had she been so foolish, so curious for another glance? So lost was she in that desire, the consequences had not even occurred to her.

She wrung her hands and looked down at the carpet. She was tired of the embarrassing stories that passed around the neighborhood like a bad cough. The fact that he would soon know them too made her want to dissolve away. Like all the times she passed the servants and they stilled in their chatter, she felt herself trembling. *Be stronger; don't care; just survive*, she told herself. But that wasn't living, was it?

Mrs. Rosewood shot her a hard look, probably planning punishment later, as Mae had spoken out of turn. "Yes, this is Mr. Ethan Locke. Mr. Locke, this is Miss Mae Blackthorne, my daughters' governess."

At the mention of her name, Mae waited for a bewildered expression, but Mr. Locke betrayed none. He swept back and gave a bow. Today, he wore a waistcoat of black and gold buttons, his scandalous tattoos hidden from view.

"How do you do?" he said with all the manner of a gentleman. Except for the slightest hint of self-scorn, he played the part well.

As if there was any hope of improving her appearance, Mae tucked back her wild strands of hair and gave a quick curtsey in return. Her skirts, she realized as she lifted them, were covered with splashes of mud and she was certain some covered her face. She could feel the splotches crack as she forced a smile.

Mr. Locke, polite as ever, smiled back, but unlike their last meeting, his eyes were lifeless.

What had she been thinking, agreeing to meet him now? Even if it hadn't been Mr. Locke before her, she was mortified. She could barely summon the words to speak.

"She is quite the horsewoman, as you can see." Miss Rosewood strode over and touched his arm.

He flinched ever so slightly but covered it with a cough. "Yes, I can see that."

"If I had known—"

"Clarissa, what were you saying earlier about a possible fox-hunt this week?" Mrs. Rosewood returned to the tea service and began to pour.

"Oh, yes. I daresay I shall impress you with my equestrian skills, Mr. Locke. Miss Blackthorne's advice in addition to my lesson has improved my skills vastly. She's won many local races and she too has been trained by the best."

"I would be happy to witness her skills—in addition to your own—firsthand come Thursday." His gaze connected with Mae's and held firm.

"Oh." Mrs. Rosewood cleared her throat. The invitation was clearly not her intent in changing topic. "If that would please you, sir."

Mae trembled at the idea. She must refuse. But instead, she was nodding. "I shall look forward to it."

Mrs. Rosewood's eyes widened, a sneer overtaking across her face. She quickly fixed it and turned to Mr. Locke.

"How do you take your tea?" she asked him.

Rather than await her own offer, which would surely never come, Mae curtsied again. She was desperate to take her leave.

"Excuse me. It was wonderful meeting you." With a quick glance in Mr. Locke's direction, she rushed out of the room.

In the windowless hall, a heavy darkness came over her. She could hear shrieks of laughter echo down the hall. Why couldn't Mae find that same confidence?

She had had it once. Not more than a year prior, she could command an entire room, practice well the art of conversation. But stripped of her jewels, gowns, and fortune, her confidence had dwindled to nothing.

With a sigh, she stilled her fervent steps and steadied herself against the banister. She was still cringing from the look Mrs. Rosewood had directed at Mae after his invitation. She had been expected to decline.

What had caused her to accept? Perhaps Mr. Locke had

drawn something out of her. Something that had been building since his arrival. Something dangerous.

☾

MAE PULLED ON her cracked and faded riding boots, her stomach twisting in a tight ball of excitement. For the entire morning before the hunt, she couldn't help but give in to her daydreams. In her thoughts, she had grasped him and so much more that night in the office. Now she might have another chance. Miss Rosewood and the rest of the family would be miles away. She saw only herself and Mr. Locke surrounded by bare, leafless trees with just enough cover to… She bit her lip, stifling the thought. How could she think like this? It was so wrong. As a governess, she must be stalwart and chaste at all times. She would display her skills, perhaps offer a tip or two, and that would be it. She would not endeavor to enjoy the excursion, either. That way, she could not be disappointed.

Not even when she arrived at the stables and found herself alone. Her stomach dropped. Had they left already? She would not be surprised if they had. But why hadn't she heard any of the dogs or the guns?

Still unsure, she headed toward Richie, a rather scrawny young man, who was sweeping one of the stalls. A harsh wind brushed past her, bringing with it the sharp scent of manure. Despite the cloudless sky, it was not a good day for a ride, anyway.

She started. A figure appeared out of nowhere, blocking her path.

"Good morning to you." Mr. Locke walked along the stalls, stopping at a beautiful chestnut gelding that was quite intimidating in size.

"I'll require my mount," he said to Richie, who rushed to oblige.

"Have you heard from the others?"

"I'm afraid none of them are coming."

"Is everything all right?"

"It was upon my request." The smallest trace of a smile on his lips. "I said I was feeling a bit under the weather and they elected to go to town instead."

Mae was silent. She did not know what to think, what to do. For a moment, she simply stood there.

"Where is your horse?"

Mae looked to the stall across from her. Following her gaze, he went inside. Mae watched, stunned, as he proceeded to pick up her saddle and throw it over Thomas.

"I don't understand." She entered the stall in a daze. "What are you doing?"

"Saddling your horse. Today, you shall have a riding companion."

"I don't want one." Mae ripped off her gloves. "It will seem odd and people talk, you know, and—"

"They always do."

"I have a lot more to lose than my reputation, Mr. Locke. Mrs. Rosewood might—"

"I insist." He tightened the saddle straps.

"I'm afraid I must decline."

For some rebellious reason, he would not accept the imprudence of all this. The sharpened edge to her voice only seemed to rile him. He veered toward her with such a look of determination, she stepped back.

"I care little for these rules."

"Well, I do. I must set a good example for Miss Rosewood." Of course he was too much of a brute to realize that unlike some people who went rummaging through offices, she had a moral code.

"Even after all you have endured?"

Mae clenched her gloves. Of course he'd brought up her past. He was bound to.

Her only defense was to feign ignorance. "I don't catch your meaning."

"Why should you abide by society's dictates?" he asked. "Society's shunned you. After losing your fortune, they have left you to live what really isn't a life at all."

Mae wished he would cease all this. She had expected him to find out the scandalous tale from any number of people but never did she think he would speak about it with her, much less come to her defense. Once she'd thought it better to have all the gossip that way, behind her back. Now she wasn't so sure. It felt freeing to have it out in the open, like she was more than just some caricature rather than a person.

He was right, of course. All of her friends—the ones who had gone with her to dinner parties and balls and who had made frequent calls for tea—had abandoned her at the mere rumor her business had been in trouble.

"It doesn't fit you, a life obeying orders." He curled his lip. "You don't belong here like this. Rather, I think you're fit for someplace else."

"And where is that?" she demanded. Even if she had the courage to leave, she certainly hadn't the means.

"Do you really not know anything about where your mother's from?"

Mae stared ahead.

"I think you'd like it. I know I did."

"You've been there?" She blinked. Of course he had. She wanted to ask so many questions. Mr. Locke nodded. "What I remember most are the sunsets. How they make the ocean look like a pearl. And at night, there are so many firebugs, the island practically glows."

"What were you there for?"

"Work." He quirked a brow. "I'm well-traveled. So was your father."

"I'm aware." Mae let out an exasperated breath. Whom would he mention next? William and his travels? All it had ever brought to him had been pain. She felt that ice water again, beginning in her heart and spreading outward across her chest.

"Maybe you don't belong here, in such constraints."

"Why do you say these things to me?" Despite herself, her voice croaked.

Mid-motion, he stilled. "I didn't mean it as a slight." He snapped the final buckle in place. "What I mean to say is that I, myself, care not for rules. Especially those that get in my way."

Mae stepped back as if the words themselves had reached out and groped her.

"Please," Mae ground out. "Leave at once."

He laughed. "Still playing governess, I see."

Mae's cheeks flamed with offense. She had been quite wrong in coming here. She had not been thinking clearly. She had been consumed by his presence and now his words. *"You don't belong here like this. Rather, I think you're fit for someplace else."*

It was a longing she'd carried every day, whether she admitted it or not. Her father, mother, and brother had all traveled from place to place, so why not she? Traveling was in her blood. But Mr. Locke had been the only one to confirm it, the only one to see the part of her eager for something better, no matter how difficult or scary that path may be. No matter how endless. His bold honesty made her long for something different, something new, burn brighter. A hopeless flame that had nothing on which to burn.

"I thought you wanted answers about me and my associations with your family. That night in your father's office, you were pretty eager."

Mae hesitated, her heart ticking with both excitement and fear. She wasn't sure she liked the word "eager," but she nodded nonetheless. "I do."

"Very well, then." Mr. Locke tipped his head toward her horse.

She did not like games like these. The stables, though empty, seemed suddenly full of onlookers. At any moment, the Rosewoods or some loose-lipped servant might appear. From there, rumor would carry like fire in the wind. Richie alone was enough cause for concern.

If they were to continue to speak in this manner, it could not be done here.

She hoped whatever he had to say, he would relay at once before the Rosewoods returned. She didn't know what consequences awaited governesses who went on morning rides with engaged men—and a man betrothed to her own pupil, no less. It wasn't respectable. Nor dull or uptight. She hated the rules. She wanted to forget them all. Pretend decent society didn't exist. Beside him, it seemed easier to do.

Mae shot Mr. Locke a hard glare, then, mounting Thomas, raced out into the fields. Did he really think she was fit for someplace else? The words should have provoked bitter shame for all she had once been and for all she was fated to become. Instead, she felt mad with excitement, as if maybe she was something more than a penniless governess with only fond memories of the past to keep her warm.

She couldn't forget her position in life, the horse that didn't truly belong to her anymore, nor the cotton dress that had replaced her silk ones. She struggled not to slump out of her tall posture. One look at her and it was evident why Mr. Locke was marrying Miss Rosewood. Her pupil was proof that respected family names and money did not always go hand in hand, but if there was one that could stand on its own, it was money.

Mr. Locke closed in, a loud crunching of grass indicating his proximity. She tried so hard to be brave, but her stomach still wrenched with worry. What would happen if the Rosewoods returned early? What possible explanation would she have, would *he* have?

"You had some business with my father." Mae severed the silence. "Alastair Blackthorne. He died, you know, in the winter of '35."

Locke remained silent.

"If he owes you some debt. It can't be repaid."

"There is no debt." This was a surprise. "What other reason have you to speak with me alone like this?"

"Seeing that you are the true lady of the estate, I thought I might indulge you with its fate." He cleared his throat. "My marriage to Miss Rosewood means I will be the estate's new master… at least while the Rosewoods are in town."

"Mr. Rosewood will give you full rein?"

"It's the least he could do for taking the whole of my land. So you can rest assured the estate will be in better hands."

"What does that matter?" Mae snapped her gaze away.

"Because. If you care not for the estate, then why are you here? The question has plagued me for days now. After your descent to governess, do the memories not overwhelm you?"

"At times, but—"

"You'd rather stay?"

"How could I leave? I thought…" She fought to keep her words steady. "Childish though it may be, I feel safe here."

"Why, you're holding on to something you should have resigned years ago. Change is—"

"Inevitable? I know. No matter if I stay here or not, I'll pass on. The estate, all the generations before me, the legacy they hoped would last forever will cease to exist, everything to be forgotten."

Mae looked out into the distance, where a line of trees met the pale-blue morning sky. A bright green was already beginning to make its way across the branches and the dead silence of winter was no more. Weaving in and out of the sky, birds chirped one by one, each adding different notes, pitches, and rhythms to the first.

She wondered why Mr. Locke cared to tell her this at all. How easily it seemed to wash away her previous notions of him.

"Have you fallen for the beauty of the home too?" she asked. "Is that why you wish to marry Miss Rosewood?"

He gave a little laugh. "Material things have little sway over me, Miss Blackthorne."

"I know you do not love her."

He smiled, his eyes twinkling with mischief. "How do you know that?"

"You've met her all but once and you two have barely even talked," she said with outrage. "Not to mention the utter lack of compatibility."

"Oh?"

"Because of the life you lead," Mae explained.

"And what life is that?"

"One that must be far from dull, to put it kindly."

"Bristol is my home too. Why not settle here after my travels? Ever consider that?"

Mae lifted her shoulders. He had successfully put her in her place. But she had yet to run out of questions. She half-opened her mouth to ask another—particularly about his travels—when he interrupted.

"But alas, you are right. I do not love her."

"Then—Then…" Anger lit inside her like a torch. "Why must you do it? If you have no want of fortune…"

"I have my reasons."

Mae opened and shut her mouth. She wanted to convince him to do otherwise, but what hope had she of that?

"Do you think me incapable of making her happy?" He pulled back in evident outrage.

"Of course I do. You do not love her. If I could keep her from you, I would."

"You must have a very ill opinion of me…and care for her a great deal, too, I suppose." He raked a hand through his hair, his face full of thought.

"She may not be beautiful enough to tempt a duke, but she has enough wit and generosity of heart to make any man willing to see that happy enough."

"You think I cannot grow to love her?"

Was he teasing her now? Mae gripped the reins so tightly, she feared the leather might melt in her hands. "I happen to think a man like you incapable of loving anything."

The rogue jerked in his saddle. "'A man like me'?"

"Yes." Mae kept her chin high and her words strong. "You haven't the manners fit for a saloon. Like Mr. and Mrs. Rosewood, you have not a hint of decency. You know nothing of honor, dignity, or kindness, let alone love. Like I said, you are incapable of it." As soon as the words had left her lips, she regretted them. Nonetheless, she followed it up with a weak mumble. "I am sure of it."

What about the shelter he offered me that night in the storm? she immediately thought. *Then again, what about the night I caught him in my father's office?*

Mr. Locke shifted his horse closer so that he brushed against her. Then, taking her gaze, he held it. "Unwilling, perhaps. But incapable, no." His eyes held a feverish, lewd gleam, sending her imagination flying.

She shook herself free of the thoughts at once. She couldn't forget where he'd be mere months from now: in Miss Rosewood's arms.

Frankly, Mae had given up on any notion of love long ago. His warm, brown eyes were nothing to be fawned over. Not even his smiles.

"We're near your woods." Mae slowed her pace. The wall of trees loomed higher, their limbs stretching toward the bright, cloudless sky. "You can leave me."

"It is a warm day." Mr. Locke's hard gaze fixed ahead. "Some shade would do you good. For a moment at least."

Mae knew she should refuse. The forest offered far too much privacy. She had to say *no*. But on this path of defiance, there seemed no hope of slowing. Without a word, she galloped ahead.

Just as she entered the darkness, Mr. Locke, who trailed behind, called out. The shout dissipated, unintelligible, within the confinement of trees.

CHAPTER SEVEN

Family Legends

LOCKE RACED AFTER Miss Blackthorne, kicking his horse, Gambit, faster toward the wood. His eyes searched for any sign of Ellsworth. The man was already here. Somewhere, he stood hidden, waiting.

Locke forced Gambit to slow. There was no turning back on this now. The knowledge of what he was about to do already had his heart thrumming with regret. He was not a ruthless shark, as he'd once believed. Knowledge of what was to come tugged at him. *No.* He set his jaw. The deal had already been struck.

He had to get that sapphire back, no matter what the cost.

Despite a voice that begged him to stop her, warn her, he shoved it down.

His mind focused on the need to act first, feel second—if at all. But for too long, smuggling and the solitude that had come with it had been his life. He had never grown numb to it. Recently, the sting of loneliness felt sharper, especially alongside her.

When all this was over, when the sapphire was recovered and returned to Pierce, its rightful owner, he knew the life he would return to. A life in which he hadn't a single friend, only enemies.

Locke ordered Gambit to gain speed.

The trees grew denser, his eyes taking a moment to adjust to the darkness. "Miss Blackthorne?"

A *thud* broke out, sending a shower of dead leaves fluttering in its wake. About fifty yards away, two men had pulled Miss Blackthorne from her horse. Like hungry beasts ready to devour their prey, they lunged at her.

Dread stabbed Locke in the gut. He had brought her to Ellsworth himself, but now he wanted to pull her away. She was an innocent. If he did nothing, he feared this moment would haunt him always, forever on his conscience. What peace might he have then?

Yanking the reins, he brought Gambit to a rearing halt.

A man twice the governess's size seized her in his arms. He flashed a toothless smile and nuzzled his dirt-lined face into her neck, undoubtedly whispering unspeakables. Miss Blackthorne jerked away, her expression filling Locke with swift and utter anguish.

If the man wanted to see another day, he would release her. But at Locke's approach, the man—likely from the booming slums of London—did not so much as pause. He ran a knife back and forth across her dress, catching and pulling the fabric.

His companion, a skinny lad of no more than sixteen, whipped out his own blade and pressed it over her cheek. Miss Blackthorne's eyes, shiny with desperation, flashed to Locke.

He couldn't deny her call for help for a moment longer. He had to stop this now. And since the type of men Ellsworth had hired were not likely to give into his demands, he had to go with a more violent alternative.

Within a matter of seconds, Locke dropped from his horse and drove his fist into the first face he could find, then into the next.

Miss Blackthorne grabbed on to him.

"Your horse…" She clearly expected for him to pull her away from the madness. She clung so close, he could feel every shiver, hear every grasp. But when he failed to act, confusion and worry washed over her features.

"What the devil?" The younger lad came back to his senses and staggered up.

"Mr. Locke!" Miss Blackthorne shook his arm as if to wake him, but he didn't budge.

"This bloke ain't here to help ye, fool!" The other accomplice wiped his face, throwing a spray of blood to the ground. "You oughta fear 'im more than us."

Among lowly men like these, Locke was not surprised these men revered his pirate past. Whether or not that served to instill some respect had yet to be seen.

Miss Blackthorne loosened her grip and stepped back. She stared at him, not blinking There was no doubting his part in this. She had had a low opinion of him from the start and now always would.

"Giving you trouble, is she?"

At the sound of Ellsworth's voice, Miss Blackthorne froze in place.

"Rather, your men are," Locke said. "You agreed there would be no blood. These men have knives."

"We couldn't risk her getting away. These Blackthornes, they're full of tricks."

"Two men against one woman and you thought knives necessary?"

"She kicked and elbowed me, I'll 'ave you know." The younger lad gripped his side.

"In any case, she seems fine to me. Just as beautiful as ever." Ellsworth craned his neck to get a better view. He even went so far as to brush the back of his hand along her face. Locke expected her to shiver, or at least back away, but she clenched her teeth, her previous fear replaced by some fierce disgust.

Ellsworth, however, didn't seem to notice. He turned back to his men, pain and embarrassment still reddening their faces.

"There's no need for knives, is there?" Ellsworth asked the governess.

"Just get to the whole of it," she barked. "How, exactly, do you expect me to help your struggling business this time? With my limited funds, I can't even imagine."

"Help? You think I'm asking for help?" He widened his stance and crossed his arms.

"How often did you seek out my brother? How often did you *grovel* for his mercy?"

"Your brother was so drunk half the time, it proved less useful than talking to a wall." Ellsworth sneered with a ferocity equal to her own. The same way men looked at one another before going in for the kill.

And Miss Blackthorne did not even flinch. Her face remained hard and unyielding.

"Why don't you tell her our plan, Locke? Why don't you tell her how we plan to take back what has always been ours?"

Locke hesitated, unable to find the words. He saw only her angry, unblinking stare.

"Go ahead," Ellsworth pressed. "You're a ruthless pirate, aren't you? Strike fear into her heart! Have your revenge!"

Locke winced. So the truth was out. The once-elusive Ethan Locke was elusive no more. He could fade his tan and hide his tattoos, but he could not escape his past. No matter how much he wanted to shake free of it.

Miss Blackthorne went quite pale. Her mouth contorted, but no words came. If she had not sensed true danger before, she seemed to sense it all around her now.

And to imagine, he had secrets far worse than this one. A secret that had left him constant and unchanged for twenty-six years. A secret she would never be able to comprehend.

The danger of such a secret, he could feel now.

"On the other hand, I think I shall take the privilege..." Ellsworth cleared his throat. "You see, Miss Blackthorne, that former estate of yours contains a fortune that belongs to myself and my associate here. And we'll go to any means to get it."

"He nearly owns the estate now." Miss Blackthorne turned to

Locke, her voice shaky. "Take it. What do you want with *me*?"

"I'm afraid it's not that easy." Ellsworth approached with power in each step.

Despite the lurch in the pit of his stomach, Locke decided it best not to act. They had some time before the task was accomplished. Even if every fiber of his being screamed to separate the villain and the lady, he had to restrain himself.

Ellsworth reached into his waistcoat and handed the parchment to Miss Blackthorne.

"What's this?" She opened the letter with its already sliced seal. "This is my father's writing." The governess shot Locke a look. "Written weeks before his death."

Ellsworth motioned her to read on. The effect of the letter was instant. Her eyes glazed over as they flew across the sheet.

Locke could only imagine what the words meant to her. He had seen the alternative will betrothing a particular key to her brother himself. As soon as Ellsworth had revealed it that morning, Locke had read it a dozen times, eager to decode the secrets that would lead to the vault, but in the letter, he could find no clues. His only hope was that Miss Blackthorne could.

Her face grew more somber. Then a realization seemed to dawn on her. She turned to Ellsworth.

"You did kill him," she uttered in a low voice that was quickly gaining volume. "All these years, I've suspected it. I drove myself mad with the knowledge of it—without any proof, any real indication but my imaginings. But you did it for this, didn't you?" The parchment shook violently in her hand. "For this!"

Locke choked back some surprise. Ellsworth had confessed his hatred of the family, but not this. Though Locke yearned to ask more, he kept quiet, anxiously observing.

"I did what I had to. Just as your brother did when he undercut our prices." Ellsworth drove his cane into the ground. "I see no difference."

"So this was why you were searching my father's office." Miss Blackthorne directed her anger at Locke now. Only then did he notice the tears glistening on her cheeks. "You were looking for this key. Do you mean to kill me to get it?"

Robbed of his ability to speak, Locke shook his head.

She did not believe him. Her eyes fell back to the letter, as if seeing her father's ghost risen from the grave. "What am I supposed to make of this?"

"You really are daft." Ellsworth laughed. "Can't you see? The legends are true. Hidden somewhere within the manor lies gold, rubies, diamonds—a treasure trove!"

"That child's tale?" Mae crossed her arms.

"What tale?"

At Locke's approach, Miss Blackthorne gave a look worse than the one she had given Ellsworth, as if he had slapped her across the face.

Though the same dread returned three-fold, Locke straightened, immediately disposing of his feelings of remorse. Why the devil must he care so much? Yes, she was tempting, but that would not put the sapphire back in his hands or Pierce off his heels. Nor did it negate the crimes of her father.

Like Ellsworth, he had let his anger simmer for years. His only comfort being the revenge he hoped to enact someday. And now was his chance. He could inflict his vengeance and utter ruin to a Blackthorne. But why her? Anyone but her…

"Excuse him," Ellsworth said. "He pays little heed to our folklore."

The stories, however, did not surprise him. He could imagine that any family that went back as far as hers must have been ripe with legends.

"The local townspeople were always wrongly questioning my family's wealth," Miss Blackthorne explained with an exasperated sigh. "Rather than attribute it to hard work, they preferred to make tales. My ancestor stole jewels from a king or the one about the ancient burial site stuffed with gold. All of it hidden away in some vault. It's ridiculous. If there were a fortune hiding somewhere, I would know."

"Yes, you do know," Ellsworth said. "I imagine you know many of the home's secrets: the hidden compartments, tunnels, doorways—much of which are still kept secret from the Rosewoods, the servants, everyone…"

Mae rolled her eyes. "Of course there are tunnels. The manor is the oldest in the county. Built during far more dangerous times when there was need to escape persecution, sieges, invasions… My mother even used them to store wine."

"And a secret fortune?" Ellsworth's face pinched.

"If my father left a fortune, William would have told me."

"It exists." Ellsworth persisted. "That very letter is proof!"

"It proves nothing. There's no knowing what the key leads to—"

"Doesn't matter." Locke bit back his growing frustration. "Only a Blackthorne can unravel your family's clues. And unfortunately, you're the only one left."

Terror flashed anew over the woman's features. She was shivering again. "Then you will never find it. My father left everything to William and he is dead." She turned to Ellsworth. "You killed him, or don't you remember?"

Locke fought to keep his face unchanged. Ellsworth was truly the lowest of villains, the type of scum he didn't mind killing himself.

Guilt swallowed him up again. Whole this time.

Miss Blackthorne had altered entirely. That pained look, the new hardness in her voice—it affected him. He wanted to erase it, to reach out and bring back that bold, blithe spirit that had taken strange control of him since their acquaintance. It was still there, just far away.

Miss Blackthorne yelped, forcing Locke to attention.

Ellsworth had beckoned his men forward, one of them taking her arm.

"*Wait,*" Locke commanded. "What about our offer?"

Miss Blackthorne pulled herself free. "What offer?"

"For your assistance and your silence, we're offering a third."

"A third? As in a third of the fortune?" She sniffed. "Do you think to play me for a fool?"

"We could take the alternative and force you. I find this simpler."

"Take the deal." Ellsworth's voice strained with desperation. "You'll get nothing better than this."

"I'm giving you the chance to escape," Locke reasoned. "You hate this life. Admit it."

Despite the doubt that flickered in the governess's eyes, Locke was certain of her acquiescence. Even if she went to the constable, she had to know no one would believe such a wild tale—especially from a lowly governess like herself. Not to mention the fact that he, the so-called criminal, was soon to marry an heiress of the estate.

If she wanted her old life back, any freedom at all, she had to agree. It was this or nothing.

The seconds pressed on. She glanced between the two of them, then looked off into the distance. There was no other way, Locke wanted to reiterate. No other possible escape from her false life here. But judging by the intense wrinkle between her brows, she was proving stubborn. He could not expect concord yet.

He put a finger to his chin and began to pace. "These so-called 'tales' you spoke of, did they happen to concern a vault?"

"If I don't answer..." Miss Blackthorne swallowed. "What will you do?"

"Oh, come. It's an easy enough question. We're only talking rumor."

"Well, of course there were rumors. Suspected locations, even."

"And the most likely of those locations?"

"This is ridiculous. This treasure trove doesn't exist!"

So that was her concern. Locke cursed. He had no choice now. He had to go with the alternative.

"Still have my timepiece?" He moved close, looming over

her.

Miss Blackthorne stammered for words.

"You must be good with your hands to have snatched it so surreptitiously. And from my own front pocket, no less."

"Don't forget Locke is in the family's favor now," Ellsworth added.

"But—But, what if it turns out that the fortune does not even—"

"Then you'd like a life to go back to, wouldn't you?" Locke struggled to summon the devious smile the statement called for. With what little she had, save for her post, cornering her had been too easy.

"With or without your station, you'll help us. Now tell me about these suspected locations. A guess. That's all I want." Everything rested on her. She had to know something.

"The western wing, I suppose," Miss Blackthorne finally answered, deflated. "A large cellar near the west courtyard has been abandoned for years. But you can't possibly think—"

"It will do. You'll meet us there at midnight."

"Just one moment!" Ellsworth erupted. "Don't tell me you're going to release her. She'll run!"

Damn it, Locke almost said aloud. He had hardly finished. He let out a calming breath and turned to Miss Blackthorne. "So much as pack your things and it'll only cement your crime. Second window from the left, correct?"

"You're despicable." Mae spit, her voice shaking with emotion.

Locke could not argue that. To retrieve the sapphire, he had little choice.

"Now, now," Ellsworth taunted. "Try to be a little pleased. You'll still have your third, remember?"

Locke itched to use his fists and shut him up. If he made his hatred for her any more obvious, she'd never believe they were going to split the profits. Despite their threats, they needed to act like allies now and establish a kind of trust with Miss Blackthorne.

Otherwise, she would lead them astray, send them looking for clues that didn't exist just to stretch time. Locke was tired of waiting. How could Ellsworth not see that?

"Come." Locke motioned her toward Gambit. "Best get you back to the estate before the Rosewoods return."

Spooked, her horse had likely returned to the stables by now. Looking around, Miss Blackthorne seemed to realize this too.

"Fine," she agreed in a hard, cold voice.

Locke felt some relief at this small concession, but as he gripped her hand to help her atop his horse, pity crept over him. He reminded himself he hadn't a choice. If he wanted his freedom, he had to recover the stone. Pierce would soon have his throat if he did not retrieve it. He doubted the sapphire or the blue elixir could save him from that.

☾

WITH EACH GALLOP of the horse, a bolt of fear coursed through Mae. She was surprised she didn't fall off altogether.

Mr. Locke—no, *Locke*, she corrected herself. A man like him didn't deserve her respect anymore. She didn't think he ever had.

At the mere mention of his notorious profession, she was finally beginning to see him for who he really was. His tattoos; the dark, unfashionable way he dressed; the angry scar above his left brow; not to mention the wild look in his eye... She was in the hands of a bloody pirate. The cutthroat, evil sort of men she had only read about in novels. She should have guessed.

As if he hadn't just brought her close to death, he held her tightly in front of him, almost protectively, so she wouldn't slip. She hated that she could feel the warmth of his back behind her and the in-and-out of his breath.

A sob crept up her throat, straining for release. But rather than give him any more satisfaction, she swallowed her pain. What could tears do to ease her distress now? With no relatives, she was at the mercy of these men.

"You need not fear me." Locke slowed the horse to a walk.

Mae started. How could she not? Even if he had pulled her away from those vulgar men earlier, he had also led her straight to them. Ellsworth was ruthless. He would not let anyone stand in the way of what he wanted. Helping them would simply delay her demise. No, her only hope was to give the devils up to the law. A plan that could easily backfire, thanks to that damn watch.

"You will not be harmed during our search," Locke said. "I promise you."

"That's laughable."

If he expected her to feel comforted, she felt nothing of the sort, only suspicion. Everything he had ever said and done had been carefully planned. She had no doubt of that. Even his flirtations had been a lie. Her face flamed. She had been so easily fooled.

"I give you my word," he added, honor and pride ripe in his voice.

"Your word?" Mae laughed. "What good is the word of a pirate? That is who you are, isn't it? Admit it."

"Fine. I'm not ashamed. I was a captain once and a well-respected one, at that."

Mae shook her head, incredulous. He spoke of piracy as though it were nothing. He wasn't a law clerk, banker, or clergyman, for heaven's sake. He was a murderous pirate. The word alone was enough to rattle her.

"What kind of pirate promises safety?" Mae asked. "Why, you must have found God."

She felt his body tense. "I may not be a saint, Miss Black-thorne, but I'm no liar."

"And things of material consequence do not sway you, ei-ther?" Remembering those self-righteous words of his, Mae felt her fury rise. The statement was so far from the truth.

"I'll have you know that *a third* of what lies in your family vault belongs to me. I'm simply retrieving it."

"Really. You cannot expect me to believe you." Least of all this little deal of his.

"I do have *some* honor," he said. "Enough to keep you safe."

"Your kind has no honor."

"Perhaps it's my one weakness. Even heroes have flaws, you know."

"Please."

He was wasting his breath. She would pay no heed to his words. She had to keep on her guard.

Mae searched the horizon. They were still headed east through the moors. In less than a mile, they would be back within the safety of the estate. Feeling some comfort in that fact, she reconsidered how she might tell Mr. Rosewood and the constable Locke and Ellsworth's plan. He might believe her. No, of course they would. She could picture it now, the shocked faces of the servants, the squeals of fear from Miss Rosewood and Miss Lenore.

"How long do you expect it to take?" She tried to glean more damning evidence.

"To find my fortune? Not long. If it does—"

"The manor will be as good as home."

Mae remembered his convenient, sham of an engagement to Miss Rosewood. "How clever. What then?" Her heart sank for Miss Rosewood's sake. "Did you plan to disappear?"

"That's likely to happen, yes. The fortune does belong to me."

"All of it?"

"Most."

"Again, I am to believe the word of a pirate."

"Excuse me?"

"I captain my own ship. Captain. Chief Commander. Either is a fine enough title for me."

Mae scoffed. "Whatever you call yourself, you are nothing but a scoundrel with rivers and rivers of blood on your hands."

"'Rivers'?" Locke glanced back at her. "Nah. Most are quick

to surrender and death was often avoided."

"And if they choose to fight?"

"Then we forced our way to their captain and took him for ransom."

Fear pricked its way into Mae's heart. This man was merciless. Who knew how many men had suffered at his hands?

"It's only a matter of time before you hang." Justice would be her mission now. She had to find a way.

Locke merely laughed, defiant even at the prospect of death.

"They could never harm me," he said with surprising confidence. Perhaps it was true. Withstanding the cooks' supernatural tales, the man seemed nothing short of dangerous.

He flicked the reins, sending the horse into a faster gallop. The villain was close enough that she could feel his pulse and breathe in his pinewood scent… There was no avoiding it.

By the time they had returned to the estate, it was already late afternoon. The early spring air had taken on an icy chill. Locke dismounted first, then just like that night of the storm, he offered Mae his hand. The contact seared her fingers like hot coals. This time, she didn't thank him. She clenched her arms tightly across her chest as he mounted the horse again.

"Till midnight," he said meaningfully. Then, with one last tunneling stare, Locke reared up his horse and ventured back into the moors.

CHAPTER EIGHT

Midnight

MAE STILLED IN her pacing to glance at the small clock atop her nightstand. At ten-thirty, her candle was nearly spent.

Though Locke was likely watching every accessible door, she had the tunnels. Her father had told her and her brother about them for good reason. She might very well make it. She could run to the next town, sell what little items she had. She could not sell the watch, of course, since it might only be a matter of time before the police…

She turned to her bed and snapped back open her half-filled carpet bag. She couldn't do it. After spending her whole life within the comfort of the estate, she feared the harshness of the outside world.

And when it came time, she had failed to tell Mr. Rosewood too. The fool would never believe the tale, let alone notify the constable. Locke, the devil he was, had known this all along.

She really only had two choices: run away or give into the bastards' blackmail. Either on the street or by Ellsworth's hand, death seemed inevitable.

She shut the bag again. Perhaps she would rather starve. She hoped that hadn't been the fate of the scullery maid, but the truth was, new employment would be impossible without the proper references, not only in Bristol, but elsewhere too. It might even be assumed she'd stolen the items she'd be selling—or perhaps done worse.

Would it be so terrible to agree? a voice whispered again. She had been miserable these last few years. She could not blame that solely on the wretched Mrs. Rosewood, either. She hated this new post and that would never change, no matter where she escaped. Every one of her pupils would be the same. They'd never value their education like they ought. Even fascinating subjects like astronomy. They'd bemoan anything that hadn't to do with catching a husband and she'd spend the rest of her life fighting for their attention.

She could become a companion, she supposed. But what freedom would she have then? This fortune—if it did indeed exist—was her one and only chance for true independence.

She was no fool, though. She did not believe Locke's promise of protection for a moment. They only wanted her to agree to their plan. Though his days of piracy were over, he still craved his gold. And this was his only way to get it. Sure, they planned to keep her alive long enough to open the supposed vault. Afterward? They would not risk a witness to their crimes, much less losing a third of the fortune. Pirates were not known for their generosity. No, they were known for destruction, theft, rape, and murder. Ellsworth's sudden zest for generosity had been even less convincing.

Helping them for now would at least give her time to think and plan, however. And she might even discover clues about her family along the way. But more than secrets and possibly gold, she wanted Ellsworth to suffer for what he had done, to personally swipe that wicked smile from his face.

After all her family's misfortunes, it'd be better than doing nothing, as she had been. It was high time she righted those wrongs. She could not simply run as they raided her family home. Any Blackthorne—having discovered the fortune's possible existence—would at least try to take it back.

Ellsworth and Locke were just desperate enough that maybe it was real. The letter, too, had been in her father's own hand. Even if she did not know how or when her family had earned that money, that didn't mean it didn't exist.

But if it did, it was hers.

She blew out her candle, preserving its final hours for the night ahead. She laid out her warmest cloak and sat down atop her bed.

She could outsmart them. She was sure of it. She had been raised a Blackthorne. All she needed to do was think.

NEARING MIDNIGHT, MAE waded through the darkness of the corridor, the light of her candle surrounding her in a halo. It proved useful on the stairs, but as far as finding the right passage, she relied solely on her memory.

In the silence, she struggled to control her loud, rapid breaths. The night seemed to hum with possibility, the still air full of mischief. Though no one seemed about, she did not quite feel alone.

Her hand shook as she braced the wall for balance. She was in the old gallery now. The one her ancestors had built almost a century before her grandfather had added the new wing. Mae knew it best by the air that had grown wet and stuffy and the stone floor that felt gritty beneath her feet. Here, the contrast between past and present felt more distinct. Her mother's memory stark and painful.

The room had been her mother's favorite. She'd walked through here every day until her death. Mae had been just nineteen. Doctors hadn't known the exact cause. All they could say was that it had had something to do with inflammation.

On her death bed, Tala had finally begun to miss home, growing homesick alongside her other illness. Perhaps to soothe herself, she'd told stories set in her faraway homeland. She'd describe days so hot and humid, one could squeeze water from the air. Origin stories of the moon and stars had cajoled Mae to sleep. Unlike the wedding ring and so many other items Mae had been forced to sell, no one could ever take those stories away.

Maybe her mother was here with her now. Covered in dust, the room certainly looked haunted.

Years ago, its white marble and etched plaster walls had glittered with cleanliness. Today, its present condition was an insult to her mother's memory. The gallery would never return to its previous state. The manor's oldest wing had been neglected too long for that.

But tonight, its abandonment would serve her purposes well. She could go about the search for the vault without a sound reaching the Rosewoods. Searching in the emptiness of night—that had probably been Locke's thinking too.

Mae swept the candle across the room. Stripped of furniture and paintings, the room lay barren, yet there were still marks of the past. Sconces held half-spent candles and the outlines of paintings stretched long, like scars.

Mae froze. A clicking of claws came nearer. Likely a tiny, harmless mouse. Still, she didn't dare linger. She sprinted toward the double doors and swung them open, setting off a low whine.

Mae stepped back, a near-scream escaping her lips.

A man stood in the opening, the moonlight gleaming off his black waistcoat.

"Locke." Mae sank with relief. The weak glow of candlelight had sharpened the angles of his face, making him look grim yet enticing all the same.

"Did you think me a ghost?" He laughed, its low, masculine thunder strangely comforting.

Mae shook her head. She believed in far too many ghost stories for her own good. "How did you know to wait for me here?"

"This is the closest door to the courtyard."

Mae eyed him. "You're rather intelligent for a pirate, aren't you?"

"Intelligent enough." Locke licked his fingers and smothered the wick of her candle. In an instant, the darkness closed in. Only a feather of his outline remained.

"Light carries for some distance," Locke explained. "You wouldn't want to risk us being seen…"

"'Course not." Mae agreed, still skittish when Locke reached in for her candle. He dumped the melted wax and pocketed it.

"Lead the way."

Picking up her skirts, Mae took off across the courtyard. In the dark of night, the dead emptiness made her skin crawl. Only the ever-persistent ivy had managed to survive. Its still-dormant tendrils streamed down the stone walls, giving the manor a sinister, if not altogether *haunted* atmosphere.

"You won't regret this." Locke swooped beside her. "You've made the right choice."

"I made the *only* choice."

Mae shivered in the cool, night air. He had been watching in case she decided to try and run, hadn't he? He had *threatened* her.

"Still brave of you, especially in the face of Ellsworth. Foolish men are dangerous men, I always say. They're not easy to predict."

"That applies to both of you, then."

He laughed. "Perhaps Ellsworth is the one who should be afraid."

"Don't mock me."

"I'm serious. You didn't crumble—you stood your ground earlier. Less could be said of most men, given the circumstances."

The words gave her pause. What could he mean by telling her this?

"You wanted to strangle him right there in the woods had you the opportunity. I could see it in your eyes."

"He deserves nothing less." Her brother had been strong on her mind, then. No matter how long she had tried to ignore it, the intense anger that gripped her years ago had never faded.

The local vicar had often told her to forgive Ellsworth. Sometimes she even thought she had. Then something would remind her, she would find a favorite book or trinket of William's and that deluge of anger would return.

"Around Ellsworth, my temper makes me feel capable of all sorts of things. More likely, it will get me killed."

"You have your doubts that we'll succeed, I take it?" A piece of pottery cracked beneath his step.

"I do."

Mae paused at the cellar doors. Heavily rusted chains and a padlock barred their entrance.

"Allow me." Locke pushed her aside. A loud crack resonated, followed by a clamor of chains.

Mae stared stunned at the remains now piled on the ground, barely noticing when Locke returned her candle. In an even gentler, smoother motion, he struck a match and connected flame to wick.

"Ellsworth should arrive at any moment." Wearing his most inviting smile, he opened the door and waited for her to proceed.

Mae nodded false gratitude and stepped around the broken rust. Her previous strength seemed to vanish within the deeper darkness ahead, her knees weakening with each step of the descent.

She worked hard to regain herself. It had been so easy to foresee success from the warmth of her bedroom, but here in the darkness, she doubted her survival, even more so her ability to hand Ellsworth's death. She had never before faced danger like this. She was not strong or brave and she certainly was not prepared. Rather, she had mostly been prepared for a life of parties, frivolity, and dependence. None of which had done her any good.

Even her anger was not strong enough to sustain her. If only she had been trained in more practical matters, taught how to fence or throw daggers like her brother. Against these men, her weak, skill-less limbs were useless.

Her rushed and panicked mind had remembered something, though. In her father's library, she had read the ancient works of Greek scholars. She had learned something of the art of war and strategy. That the blade itself—had she to obtain one—incited violence. She could use it as well as they. It was a simple act of driving metal through flesh, wasn't it? She could do it. She just hoped her determination would be enough.

Stepping farther inside, she made a feeble study of her surroundings. The low-ceiling cellar her family had once used to store vegetables and fruits was as deserted and decrepit as the courtyard before. Illuminated by candlelight, empty barrels and broken crates lay scattered beneath inch-thick cobwebs. Like the moors after a heavy rain, cold moisture hung in the air.

"This is where rumors say your fortune lies?" Locke asked.

Mae's heart still roared in her chest. "I was never one to believe in legends."

"Servants were likely to frequent here." Locke stepped onward, eventually disappearing into the darkness. "But if there was any indication of a vault, word would have spread quickly."

Mae said nothing. She no longer had the strength to deny the legends. For years, they had seemed so outlandish and implausible, but now she feared she was falling victim to hope.

Lantern in hand, Locke stepped back into the light. "Do you mind?"

Mae placed her candle inside and watched as he slipped it onto a nearby hook. She imagined him doing the same below the deck of a ship. Only those surroundings, even aboard a pirate ship, had to have been more hospitable than this.

At the sound of the door, the image faded like a cloud of smoke. She hadn't even time to calm herself.

"Didn't run off, I see." Ellsworth sauntered in, the two men from earlier gathering behind him.

When they eyed her crudely, she stared back with daggers. She wouldn't let Ellsworth or his men think she was afraid of them, not for a moment.

Ellsworth reached into his waistcoat. A timepiece and chain swooped out of place. She recognized it at once.

"Look familiar?" He dangled the glistening disk in front of her face. Mae blinked. It was her father's, given to him by her grandfather and so on. Before the auction, she had wanted so badly to keep it. In the end, when the items had not brought in what had been expected, she'd had no choice. She had not known Ellsworth had been the one to claim it. The thought filled her with so much disgust, she snatched at it. When he pulled it back, she cursed herself. Of course he would do that. She hated herself for giving in, for submitting to his games. Not to mention this whole charade.

"Every day, it serves as a reminder…" Ellsworth studied the watch in reverie. "That no one, not even a Blackthorne, can best me."

Looking into his pale, emotionless eyes, Mae saw her brother once more, a mangled sight of blood and flesh.

"You're wasting time." Locke moved between them. Even Ellsworth's men were smart enough to step back.

"You are nothing." Mae stepped to the side, letting loose the words she had held in too long. "Even now that they're dead, you're still nothing."

"With your lot in life, you should look upon me with envy."

Mae despised that priggish grin of his. He had wanted it all, most rapaciously her family's social connection, merchants or not. Ellsworth would kill if it meant he could accomplish the same.

To him, reputation and appearance meant everything, though his own were far from intact. Since their broken engagement, his good name had never recovered. Now he was on a quest to restore it. She couldn't bear the terrible acts he might commit for that purpose. It brought on the urge to turn back and run. But, clenching her fists, she forced herself to still, to face this adversary like her father and brother might have.

"How wonderful it is to be in the Blackthorne Manor once more," the villain said. Mae's unsteady eyes followed Ellsworth as he weaved around a crate. "Fills me with memories. I can almost smell your brother's cologne. Whiskey, was it? He always wore too much."

"Get on with it." Mae's temper simmered.

"If you insist." He patted down his waistcoat and took out the same letter from earlier. "Something's missing. A clue."

Mae grabbed it. Swallowing the urge to shed more tears, she shrank back and read once more.

William,

As all the Blackthornes before us, I bequeath you a most profitable key. One that shall be known only to the flames. Find the key swiftly, for you are not alone in your search.
Beware of Ethan Locke. He is your enemy.

A. Blackthorne

Mae looked up at Locke, wishing now that she could heed the warnings. What's more, she knew nothing of what her father had meant for William to do.

She didn't understand it. Why go through the trouble of keeping the so-called "key" to their inheritance known only to William and said flames? Surely, that meant she should burn this paper. Still, why such secrecy? Could it really have been necessary? Could a bank not have sufficed?

"Think," Ellsworth demanded. "We haven't all night."

Not knowing why, Mae turned to Locke, but in the darkness, his expression was impossible to gauge.

"Surely, your father told you something." Ellsworth paced. "Maybe as a child?"

Mae worked to remember what seemed a thousand years past. Between managing the business and estate, her father had spent little time with her. Though she could recall every rare moment, he had said nothing about a fortune. When she had been a girl, it had seemed to be all around them.

"Did he pass anything down to you? Anything at all. Perhaps a locket?"

"A key…" Locke drawled.

Mae shook her head.

"Think harder." Frustration rippled across Ellsworth's face. The men behind him kept shifting, moving from leg to leg, restless too.

"Maybe…" she started. Her father's note repeated in her mind. *Known only to the flames.* It wasn't quite right, was it? After reading the note, William would have known about the fortune too. Why had her father written that? It couldn't mean…

Letter in hand, Mae moved to the single lantern that hung low enough to reach. She opened the glass door and brought the letter close.

Ellsworth grabbed her wrist, but Mae was resolute. "I must." She took the lantern with her other hand and freed it from the hook.

Ellsworth squeezed tighter but did nothing as she shifted the paper closer to the flame. Then, all at once, brown letters leached out across the paper. Mae held it closer. More words came to life, their letters darkening to match the other writing. It was as if they had been there all along. She put the lantern back on the hook, near laughter.

That was why her father had been so intent on playing that invisible word game with William. It was a delicate balance of getting the parchment close enough to warm it without setting it aflame. William had shown her once. She, of course, had not been allowed to put her fingers anywhere close to invisible ink, let alone a flame. *Unless I did so in secret, that is.* After some practice as a child, she had mastered the trick.

That wasn't the only thing her father had insisted on teaching her. There were also the tunnels, hidden throughout the house like veins that were each marked with the Blackthorne sign of escape: two horses rearing toward each other in a perfect mirror image. He'd wanted her to know how to navigate them just as well as the halls. She'd thought it had been just so she didn't get lost if she happened to stumble upon them. Rather, it had been so she could escape men like Ellsworth and Locke. They both gave a whole new meaning to the term "fortune hunter."

"Well?" Ellsworth pressed.

"It's the heat. My father left us another message."

Behind her, Locke's breath caught. She balanced the letter in her hands, her heart shuddering in her chest.

On the parchment she read:

Ars Gratia Artis

Genuine excitement sparked inside her.

Latin. The phrase spoken so often by her father seemed to whisper in her ear.

"What does it mean?"

Mae nearly jumped at words. For a moment, she had forgotten Ellsworth. Best of all, her shaking hands.

"'Art for the sake of art,'" she answered.

"And just how will that tell us where the damn key is?" Ellsworth grumbled.

Mae closed her eyes, letting the words transport her back to childhood. Her father had been near fluent in Latin, it being the official language of the Romans. Unlike her tutor, he had respected the ancient society more for their war generals than philosophers. With unmatched fervor, he had told Mae tales of conquests that had known no bounds, not by way of land nor morals. It had always fascinated her that men could want power so badly they would kill not a few, but *hundreds of thousands* of men for it. At times, it had even seemed part of the fun.

"Well?" Ellsworth barked. *He, for one, is like the Romans*, Mae thought, *thinking of death as little more than a means to an end.*

She searched her memories again. This time, it was clear.

"My father's garden…The key my father mentioned in the letter has to be there. I know exactly—"

"What about the vault?" Locke asked, his eyes aglow.

"There can't be a vault in the gardens," Mae said. "It has to be here. This letter is only meant to direct me to a key." And perhaps another clue, but Mae didn't want them to know that. If she found the clue first, there was a chance she could keep it secret.

"Which wing?" Locke focused on her intently.

Everyone stood to attention. Ellsworth's men prodded at each other, already celebrating.

"Here, near the west wing."

"Go with her," Ellsworth ordered. "Keep to the shadows."

But Locke, who was clearly unaccustomed to taking orders, did not move an inch.

"That, I'm afraid, must wait till morning." Locke took the letter from Mae. "Miss Blackthorne is finished for the night."

Ellsworth's face scrunched up. "We've just arrived…"

"It is night. We can't very well search the garden in the dark."

"And if she lied? Don't be an idiot. Let her go and she'll find the key for herself."

"Go."

"Not so quick." With the swiftness of a vulture, Ellsworth snatched up Mae's arm. His men closed in too, ready to pounce. "First we'll show her what we do to betrayers…"

Mae stifled a squeal, expecting a blow at any moment. She had little faith in Locke's protection, but desperate, she turned to him still.

His face had shifted, his displeasure needing no words. Almost instinctively, Ellsworth shoved her away. Her hands thudded to the floor. Yet the dirt, dust, and cobwebs were far more preferable than his touch.

"Mercy? For *her*?" Ellsworth recovered his dignity with a storm of laughter. "Not many women aboard those pirate ships, are there?"

As the London scum joined in the laughter, Mae stayed low, inching backward along the cold dirt.

With practiced swiftness, Locke unbuttoned and pushed aside his waistcoat. The hilt of a blade shone in the darkness.

Mae was certain of violence now. At any moment, he would take that knife and send it sailing through the air. Instead, he folded up her father's letter and tucked it into his pocket, the faintest smile touching his lips.

Quite visibly, the men relaxed. One of the London men even let out a low chuckle. Had she the air left for it, Mae would have cursed at him for his little game. She could not deny that part of her had wanted him to kill them all.

She cringed at the thought. Even in her head, it sounded harsh. She should have been ashamed. How had she, a simple governess, come to desire such violence? She should have been praying for the constable to arrive. She wished they would because even if Locke did take these lives, who would protect her from him, this bloodthirsty pirate? Alone, she was ripe for the picking. Vulnerable to his needs and desires, as the London men had suggested. She was caught up in this patched-up partnership now. At the mercy of whoever earned the upper hand.

Gathering herself, she inched to her feet so as not to gain notice. All the while, an even deeper terror cut through her. Ellsworth would be a much worse fate than Locke. She hadn't the bravery for that. She knew all too well what he was capable of. She had seen it firsthand and had heard from servants too. His bouts of violence came without warning. Even now, there was no knowing how he might react to Locke's defiance. But if he did lash out, it would be without hindrance, without restraint.

"You cannot be serious." Ellsworth eyes flickered. He couldn't have been afraid, could he? "She's a pretty lass. But to accomplish anything, we must take on unsavory tasks, instill fear…"

"Mmm. Machiavelli." Locke darted forward, his still-open waistcoat flailing. "A wise man."

Inches from Ellsworth, he tightened a hand around his right shoulder, the fine silk of Ellsworth's coat crinkling beneath Locke's grip.

Though the other men tensed, they stayed in place. It was

astonishing, really. In a matter of hours, whether from the reputation behind his name or the blows he had delivered in the woods, Locke had instilled a fear deep enough to keep the scum in place.

"You want the key for yourself. Is that it?" Ellsworth asked. "You're trying to leave me out of whatever you discover."

Locke did not argue and his grip did not falter.

"You shall have to kill me first," Ellsworth said. "I shall stop for nothing else."

"Ambition is not always a virtue." Locke finally relaxed his hold and patted him hard on the back. "One day, it shall be the death of you. Just as it was your father's."

When Ellsworth went rigid, Mae could hardly suppress a feeling of triumph. She was no stranger to Ellsworth's undying respect for his father. He idolized the man more than Christ himself. Any other man saying these words about his father would have suffered.

Locke, she was sure, would not.

"Go," Locke said a hair more softly to Mae. "Meet me in the courtyard again at first light. I'll be alone."

Without further delay, Mae headed to the stairs, the last words lifting her.

"As for you two…" he continued loud enough to hear. "Tonight, you will search the cellar. I'm sure the vault is here."

Mae raced up the rest of the steps, trying not to think of what awaited her. After tonight's confrontation, Locke's partnership with Ellsworth was shaky at best.

One thing, however, was certain: within the bricks of her family's manor, she was no longer safe.

CHAPTER NINE

The Key

GRASS AND WEEDS crunched as Locke cut across the quiet lawn. Birds chirped overhead and the scent of dew hung heavily in the early-morning air.

Recently, mornings in the country had become far more tolerable. Hell, *life* had become far more tolerable. Something he suspected had everything to do with Miss Blackthorne. In this world he knew so well, she was something entirely different. Not at all what he'd expected to encounter here. Her strength was unlike any he had ever seen in her father.

He liked to think she was not Alastair Blackthorne's daughter. But he couldn't deceive himself, no matter how difficult the truth.

He still found it hard to believe that Alastair—the man who had been both a brother and enemy to him—was six years dead. His body eaten away to the bones now. Nathaniel's too.

The thoughts wore heavily on him, depressing him anew. He needn't another reminder of his unnaturally enduring youth. Not now. Not when *she* was so close by.

Leaning against a tree, Miss Blackthorne hadn't yet noticed his approach. She didn't seem much aware of her surroundings at all. She looked to be thinking to herself—about what, he feared to know. Standing there, she had that pained look again. Her eyebrows were drawn together and wrinkled—something he knew had everything to do with *him*. The vivacity that had once surfaced in her smile was gone. A vivacity he'd likely destroy entirely when all this was over. And that was the best of outcomes.

Locke squeezed his eyes shut. A comparable piece of his past clawed at him again. Watching her alone and unawares seemed to evoke the memory even stronger.

The smell of sea was back and just as he had done for Miss Blackthorne, he was making a promise. One he would fail to keep. He shook himself from the image, from the stark splash of blood. He had to keep control.

And that meant freeing both himself and Miss Blackthorne from Ellsworth. The plan would indeed protect the sapphire. *It's about nothing other than that*, he told himself. His cares were focused on the sapphire alone. He had priorities, after all. He hardly thought of revenge anymore—and never like Ellsworth did. Finding the key needed to come first. And if there was another clue to be discovered with it, Ellsworth was right: Locke wanted to be sure the other man wasn't there to find it.

He cleared his throat, prompting Miss Blackthorne to look up. The keen eyes he had meant to avoid caught him now, pulling him down into their depths. The moment put him on edge. Like a sudden storm, the feeling struck without warning. And now that he was caught in it, he feared he was already lost.

"I feel I should thank you," she said.

"For what?"

"For insisting on meeting me alone."

"Yes, well…" He stumbled, surprised that her trust had been so easily gained.

"Did you find the vault?"

He shook his head. "We'll search again…"

In the growing silence, Miss Blackthorne leaned back against the tree, careless of how the bark might catch her dress. "May I ask," she began with caution, "*why* you insisted on meeting me alone?"

The question brought his eyes back to hers. The fearful gaze he remembered from the previous day was gone, replaced instead with a calm resolve. He blinked hard. He hadn't done it for her sake, if that was what she was asking. "The man irritates me. Nothing more."

"If you really wanted to get rid of Ellsworth, you could…you know…" She held a hand to her throat, her eyes cast down, too afraid to say the actual words.

He almost smiled at the idea, save for the contempt that laced each word. It was one form of disrespect he could never stand. "Kill him, you mean?"

"You're a pirate, aren't you? It would be easy for you. As much as I despise the man…" Her hands quivered. She couldn't even bring herself to finish the words.

"Say I do kill him." Locke crossed his arms. "How would you look upon me then?"

"With gratitude." She looked up, locking eyes with him, almost hopeful.

"No, you would be disgusted. You would look upon me with fear."

"*Now* you venture to be noble? When all this time—"

"Just how should I act?" Locke demanded. "Like a vagrant? A common thief? Piracy may not be the most noble profession, but for more than a century, it was noble enough for your family."

Miss Blackthorne stared at him, evidently still working to make sense of the words. He was surprised he had said them at all. He hadn't meant to reveal that fact. Not yet.

"What I mean is that your father was no better man than I," he clarified. Perhaps if she knew the truth, she would look upon him with less scorn. "He was a man of fortune." He spoke louder, hoping to evoke her this time. "A pirate just as I."

Miss Blackthorne's sneer of incredulity shifted to anger with one fierce blink of her lashes. Even then he could tell she was beginning to entertain the possibility. She'd likely had an inkling of it all along.

"We're not all toothless savages—" he began. "Some of us even have great houses, even great names."

Mae just stared off, ignoring him.

"Why do you think your house has all those tunnels you mentioned? They were pirates with a great many enemies and an even greater deal of loot."

"But you kill the innocent. You kill for greed."

"So did your father when it was necessary. He had everything a pirate needs: a flag that struck fear into the hearts of men and a bloody fast ship."

"No, I don't believe you."

"On my honor, you come from a line of pirates. Every ancestor as far back as five generations has taken to the sea in search of wealth."

Miss Blackthorne looked away, her eyes searching. Had she really never heard the rumors? Had her family managed to keep her that sheltered? "Your father's father was a pirate too just as he was a shipbuilder."

"My grandfather?"

"Nathaniel Blackthorne." Just saying the name brought him back. "We traveled the high seas together, sailed waves the size of mountains."

"What are you saying?" Miss Blackthorne laughed.

"The truth. Nathaniel, Alastair, and I captured more precious cargo than you could ever dream of. Of course, Alastair later betrayed me and stole my share of the profits. Typical pirate, eh?"

"Wait," she held up a hand. "You're saying that you and my *grandfather* worked side by side? He stopped sailing in his thirties. And you're, what? *How* old, exactly?"

"Thirty-two." Locke cleared his throat. What choice had he but to reply? There was no disguising his youth. She shook her head. "You're lying. You would have been very young at the time." Locke cursed the slip. Sooner or later, she might very well discover that truth. Just not now. She would think him the devil.

Her opinion of him was low enough.

"My family, we were merchants."

"Until they fell upon hard times. Had you the opportunity, would you not have seized it too?" How could she be so naive about the ways of the world, particularly how the higher classes attained their wealth in the first place? They took it.

"Don't you see? It became a shroud," he continued. "Your father's business was nothing more than a lie to keep hidden their true line of work. That way, they could still parade around society with their ill-gotten wealth. What?"

Mae looked away and bit her lip. He could tell she didn't believe him. "Pirates don't spend all their lives at sea. They have to retire sometime."

"It can't be."

"Your family brought me into it. I must say, I helped increase their profits a great deal."

At that, Miss Blackthorne's face soured with pain.

"Why do you think your father spent so much time at sea? Haven't you ever thought of it?"

"I-I thought it was just part of the business."

"What did you think he was doing all those weeks? Why do you think your brother—"

"Stop it!" Miss Blackthorne screamed suddenly and loudly. She twisted away and sank onto a large stone at the base of the tree. "They're dead. They cannot defend themselves. I won't hear you blacken their names."

"I speak only the truth."

"I told you it's impossible."

Locke released a stream of frustrated curses under his breath. He regretted disclosing her family's long-established venture into piracy, more so that he had been old enough to partner with her father. Now she only thought him madder than she already did.

Arms crossed, she sat there, obstinate.

"So you're one of those," he said.

"One of what?"

"One of those people who has to see something to believe it."

"I'm certainly not fool enough to believe everything I hear. Especially your far-fetched claims…"

"Enough of this." He let out a long breath. Something about her regarding him as a liar bothered him. *But I don't have that time to dabble with that now*, he lashed at himself. "This key, where—"

"Here." Miss Blackthorne lifted her arms to encompass their surroundings.

Amidst the languid flowerbed and brittle branches that had once been bushes, the only living thing stood in the center. A tree so ancient and wide, it provided shade to almost every corner of the courtyard.

"Here? At this tree?" Locke studied its gnarled, twisted bark. He had seen it before, but where, he could not be sure. The species, whatever it was, was not native to England. He picked at a leaf, taking a small seedpod in his hand.

"What kind of tree is this?"

"The poisonous kind. Particularly those seeds you're holding." Her lip quirked almost to a smile.

Locke dropped them. "How do you know?"

"My father told me. He said that this tree is really a work of art. And yet, it also serves a purpose: shading us from the heat, poisoning our enemies. But more often, art has no purpose. It's just art for the sake of art. *Ars Gratia Artis.*" She shrugged. "It's a simple enough clue."

Yet only one she could decipher.

"Hardly the words of a pirate," she added.

"Not *your* notion of a pirate, at least."

Locke walked around the tree. Was there some convenient nook? "Where is it hidden?"

"I have a suspicion…" Miss Blackthorne rose, her arm bracing what appeared to be a petrified root. She moved back. Without her there to distract him, the beauty of the object was impossible to ignore. Made of some brown and green marble, it blended in with the bulbous, moss-covered roots of the tree. A bench.

Locke pressed a hand to the roots, feeling the intricate engraving.

"Somewhere in here, I should think." She bent down and peeked through the structure's dozens of cavities. Even Locke got down in the dirt. He squeezed in right up against her. Once again, he had no choice. But this time, she didn't shrink away like she had all the times before. Despite himself, he wasn't immune to the contact, either. It flooded him with craving. Now he could barely concentrate. He could only stare at the dirt.

They had barely searched for five minutes, when Miss Blackthorne suddenly grasped his wrist. He swallowed. Was she—

"Did you hear that?" she whispered up against his ear. In response, his whole body went warm.

Then a voice came some distance off.

"What on earth are you two doing?"

Locke almost choked on his next breath. The clock had not yet chimed six and the day was already proving a disaster.

Locke quickly stood. Miss Blackthorne followed suit, brushing the dirt off her arms, her face a brilliant red.

From the edge of the courtyard, Miss Rosewood came closer, a shaky smile on her lips. The young woman was still jittery around him, but for all the wrong reasons. Guilt swung at his heart. Though ridiculous and plain, she seemed sweet enough, if not the personification of naiveté. With her wild sway of moods and often ridiculous manners, she was still very much a child. Locked away in the country, who wouldn't be?

"I was taking a walk and lost one of my earrings…" Miss Blackthorne glanced hurriedly at the lifeless leaves that littered the ground. "Mr. Locke here was kind enough to aid in my search. He was just passing through to see you."

Though seemingly momentarily distracted by the promise of a visit, Miss Rosewood caught sight of Miss Blackthorne's ears. "I didn't know you owned earrings. Did you lose both?"

"She did." Locke cut in, not surprised Miss Blackthorne wasn't much for lying. "Faulty clasps, didn't you say?"

"Yes, I should get them fixed, shouldn't I?"

Miss Rosewood narrowed her eyes, all too similar to her mother, but before she could speak, her governess gave her a pointed look. "What about you? What are you doing about so early?"

Locke smiled, thinking her rather clever for turning the question back on Miss Rosewood. Maybe she was a fine liar, after all.

"I saw you two from the window. You seemed to be arguing."

"Spying is unbecoming," said Miss Blackthorne. "And you shouldn't walk about the western wing. It's dangerous."

"I was only trying to relieve my restlessness. With the ball tonight, I could hardly sleep."

Locke groaned inwardly. How could he have forgotten their betrothal ball? He hadn't the time for their sham of an engagement. He had a fortune he was damn close to finding. But he could not turn his back on Miss Rosewood now. He needed to keep up appearances.

"You couldn't sleep, you say?" Locke drew Miss Rosewood's attention. "Nor I."

"Is that why you decided to call on me so early?" She sucked in a deep breath and held it for a moment.

"Why else? To take tea with you is one of my greatest pleasures." At this, he caught Miss Blackthorne's subtle eye roll. He grinned. "Perhaps you might request a tea service while I resume my search?"

"Why, of course."

"Oh, no, don't do that," Miss Blackthorne said. "You must accompany Miss Rosewood, Mr. Locke. I won't detain you a second longer. You have my thanks."

Damn lady. That was the last thing he wanted to do. They were so close earlier and in more ways than one. Now that was what he wanted to resume.

"Are you certain? I..." He struggled to find the right excuse. He clearly wasn't as quick as Miss Blackthorne had been.

"Please, Mr. Locke, with your betrothal ball tonight, you are far too busy. You two should enjoy each other's company whilst you can."

"We shall have our whole lives to get acquainted," Locke countered, not meaning the lie but knowing the governess was well aware of the pretense. What was she about?

"And yet, it still doesn't seem quite long enough, does it?" Miss Rosewood sighed.

Locke near grunted aloud. Alas, he had no choice but to surrender. He hardly had the time to step forward when Miss Rosewood hooked an arm through his. Forcing a smile, he led her away from the dingy, aged bricks to the more modern parts of the manor. What was Miss Blackthorne planning, forcing him to leave like that? Sooner or later, she would find that key. And betrothal ball or not, he would claim it from her.

His heart pounded faster, the thought of seeing her alone again thrilling him far more than it should.

"You should be glad I found you." Miss Rosewood patted his elbow. "Miss Blackthorne can be quite depressing at times. But of course, she *is* a governess."

"I was doing her a kindness." Locke snapped back, knowing that Miss Rosewood had slung the insult out of jealousy.

"Yes." She patted his arm. "It was very kind of you to help." When Locke said nothing in response, she frowned. "How drab it is today."

Locke followed her gaze. The sky had indeed been overcast. From the looks of it and the feel of the gusty wind, rain was likely. Though he hadn't noticed.

Oddly, it wasn't the vault that distracted him, either. Even now he was too busy thinking about Miss Blackthorne to care.

☾

ON HER KNEES, Mae saw it: a tip of silver gleaming in the soil, inside the tiny cavern of stone.

Most inconvenient. She had no choice but to get in the dirt on her stomach. There were spiders to fear too. As she reached in, cobwebs coated her hands. Cold as ice, the key was heavier and thicker than she imagined. She tugged with all her might. It wouldn't budge.

Her fingers dug deeper, her nails filling with dirt until at last, she yanked it free. She held it out in the light. Intricate bands of gold and silver peeked through clumps of dirt. Something so delicately designed could not have been forged by pirates.

Mae pocketed it and kicked her way through a tangle of shrubbery.

She had heard plenty of stories about her family, plenty of slander meant only to please the gossips. They were all meant to explain how her family attained their wealth that, to them, seemed far beyond that of a simple shipbuilder. But not once, not even from the squawking servants, had she heard a tale as wild as Locke's.

To think, her father a pirate! The idea was laughable.

If only William had been there to hear such a tale. He would have laughed with her. It was a lie, she was sure of that. The nerve. Locke simply wanted to blacken her father's name.

But as hard as she tried, she could not ignore how it explained her father's long absences and the recent wealth her family had acquired before William had left for sea.

Not to mention the need to keep their fortune hidden in such a way. And what about that dreadful spring when the business had lost three ships to hurricanes? They hadn't gone bankrupt. Not in the least. They had actually been richer than ever.

Consequently, they'd taken on a new rise in status. Her mother had become revered, not just in the county, but across London's highest circles, for her frequent parties and new carriages.

So long as Tala had had money, what did they care about her background?

What Mae wondered more was if Tala had known. Her parents had been too close for her not to.

Her mother had to know. Tala—a name that meant "bright star" in her language, she'd told Mae once—had been too smart.

Then there were the bedtime stories she'd told her. The ones that featured great battles on the sea. Perhaps Mae had always known her family's true profession, after all—just as a tale.

But she didn't want to think like that. She didn't want to believe it, even if every clue led her to the same truth, even if Locke's eyes had been nothing but sincere.

Mae stilled her steps before the back door. On the other side, she could hear the staff milling about. She let out her breath, wishing she had sought a different entrance.

When she passed through the hall, there was no avoiding the melee. At every turn, servants swept past with candles, garland, and whole armfuls of roses. The adornments were like nothing from her past. In her mother's time, the flowers, shipped in from the most distant parts of the world, would have been orchids. The finest delicacies would come still alive in water bowls.

No theme or motif had been out of reach. One season, she'd even gone so far as to cover the ballroom in dozens of mosaic mirrors and colored glass—just to emulate how the Amber Palace of India gleamed at night.

The vulgar extravagance had offended no one—at least none of those invited. Still, the planning and expense required made Mae shudder these days. But as a child, she'd seen none of that— only a room that had seemed to change with the seasons.

The Rosewoods, who must have hired a dozen additional staff for the occasion, were doing their best to compete— particularly for those who still remembered.

"We're to have a crush on our hands," one of the servants said. And it was true. No one in the county, no matter how socially superior, would dare turn down an invitation to Blackthorne Manor.

There were too many memories here.

As Mae climbed the stairs, she could see the guests between the banisters again. An apparition of her mother was there too, greeting everyone with smiles and nods. Mae closed her eyes and returned to the ballroom. Great swells of skirts soared across the dance floor in smooth, gentle waves, breaking apart, then pulling together again.

But those were the golden years, long past, Mae thought. *And these are the dark ages.*

Reaching her room, she plopped down on her bed. From her bodice, she pulled out the key. The metal was so tarnished, it didn't shine, not even in the window light. Scratching at it, Mae barely caught a shimmer.

How strange that this one key could change her life forever. That if she managed to find the vault first, she might not only elude Locke and Ellsworth, but poverty itself.

She could not let Locke's words distract her now. She had to toss emotion aside and trust no one. His promise of protection had to be little more than a manipulation, just another tactic to keep her agreeable. She had to think. Where else might the vault be, if not the cellar? Where else might she find another clue?

A knock shook her door, shattering her thoughts. She tucked the key into her bodice and sat up. "Yes?"

"It is your employer. Let me in."

Mae unlatched the lock and stepped back. Before "Come in" could so much as leave her mouth, Mrs. Rosewood stormed forward her eyes surveying her room, undoubtedly for tidiness.

"It has come to my attention that there will be an uneven number of guests tonight," Mrs. Rosewood began immediately, needing no preamble to speak with her inferiors. "Therefore, it is incumbent upon me to offer you an invitation."

Mae stilled, the horror of such a request stealing her breath. "Mrs. Rosewood...I cannot."

She might as well get on her knees and beg. It would be a far more bearable indignity than enduring all the people who had once dared to call her friend.

Already, she could hear the whispers. It was enough to send her stomach roiling with anxiety. Surely, this fact had not been lost upon her employer. Mrs. Rosewood knew as well as anyone that she would face these people no longer as an equal, but an inferior. For those considered high society, it was reason enough to attend.

Mae grit her teeth. More likely, it was the reason behind Mrs. Rosewood's invitation. Perhaps her employer had been planning it all along.

"You know as well as I the importance of this ball," Mrs. Rosewood said.

Yes, Mae had been acquainted with enough social climbing lackwits to know that tonight would set the stage for Miss Lenore's debut in a couple of years. If the Rosewoods were to attract the highest-ranking members of society for her hand, they had to uphold every decorum and, more importantly, fulfill every expectation.

"I will not risk violating proper etiquette," Mrs. Rosewood continued. "And I will take no refusal."

Mae's heart sank. Begging would prove useless to a mother with her sights on a title. To Mrs. Rosewood, Mae was just another rung on the social ladder. To fail now would be as good as death.

"I have nothing to wear."

"Your usual gown will do. Goodness, I don't wish you to attract attention." She released a wave of ugly laughter.

Mae bit her lip, tasting blood. "Of course not."

"And do be on your best behavior. In exchange, I will have Mr. Rosewood introduce you to a few of the gentlemen. Who knows. Perhaps a woman of your background might chance upon a desperate bachelor. Wouldn't that be lucky?"

Lucky? Mae wanted to snarl. That was the last thing she considered herself. Still, accepting the introduction meant she might not have to be alone. She would need the distraction, so perhaps a companion would help stifle the humiliation.

"Please do," Mae said weakly.

Mrs. Rosewood nodded and stalked out of the room, leaving Mae with a heavy sense of dread.

Damn Ellsworth and Locke, she should leave now. Run off to London like the scullery maid and, and…starve. Mae paced back to her bed, drumming her fingers. More than ever, she needed to escape this life of taking orders. She didn't care what the cost. If it meant she would die in those efforts, so be it.

CHAPTER TEN

The Gown

A GENTLE TAPPING sounded at the door. Mae cursed. She was hardly in the mood to see anyone and stupidly, she had left the door unlocked.

"Miss Blackthorne?" Grace stepped inside.

Mae lifted her head from her pillow.

"Good heavens, dear. It's the middle of the day. Are you all right?"

Mae held back a yawn, not wanting Grace to know she had been up morning and night. "Just suffering from a bit of a headache is all."

"See here." Grace threw open the curtains, letting in a rush of light. "'Tis no use moping."

Mae winced, squeezing her eyes tightly against the sudden sunlight.

"So you heard?"

"I thought maybe I could be of some assistance." Grace clasped her hands together.

"How is that?"

"By making you beautiful, of course. Turning you back into your former self."

"Don't be ridiculous. Of her, there is nothing left."

"Bosh." Grace cupped Mae's face in her hands. "Tonight's guests may not envy your wealth, but they will envy your beauty." Her hard tone meant she could not be bargained with. Whatever Grace had in mind, Mae had no choice but to follow along. Perhaps it would not be such a bad thing. In some ways, Mae had missed being pampered.

"This is kind of you." Mae smiled, suddenly racked by emotion. "But I would be impeding upon your duties. I'd—"

"Not in the least. Mrs. Rosewood hired far more help than needed. No doubt she wishes to impress tonight. Half the county is expected to attend, you know."

"How am I to endure it?" Mae closed her eyes, hoping that when she opened them, all the chaos of the last few days might disappear. She barely had the time to catch her breath when the next troublesome event was upon her.

"By looking your best and accepting my help, of course."

"Fine." Mae outstretched her hand in offering. "You may do your worst."

Grace didn't hesitate. Taking Mae's hand, she yanked her out of bed and into a run. "Not a moment to be spared. The others will soon arrive with your bath."

"Wherever are you taking me?" Mae's sluggish limbs barely kept up pace.

"To get your gown! It will fit. I am certain of it."

Mae dragged her heels. "How could you possibly—"

"No questions." Grace tugged again, her face lit up with excitement. "It's a surprise. You'll be right pleased, I know it."

At last, Mae gave in, allowing Grace to haul her up the stairs to the third floor—a portion of the home used exclusively by the servants.

Grace collected a candle from a wall sconce and started toward the attic.

"Wait." Mae gave pause again. "Anything you find there is going to be ages old. I greatly appreciate the effort, but—"

"But nothing," Grace said. "Do as I say."

Dust swirled as Mae stepped across the creaky floorboards. Except for a few trunks and some outdated furniture, the small triangle of a room was dark and almost empty.

Where the ceiling met the floor, Grace cast the candlelight upon a dust cover. Ripping away the sheet, she revealed a strikingly white box. With a flattened red bow to boot, it stood out in stark contrast to the dust-covered surroundings.

"Right as I left you." Grace lifted its lid and pulled out a sheen of silver moonlight.

Equal to the shade of twilight, the silk was beyond decadent and French, to be sure. Gold ruffles of lace edged the deep-scoop neckline and short-cuffed sleeves. She didn't even care that the high-waist bodice was slightly old-fashioned. It allowed the silk to drape just so and it would doubtless suit her figure.

"How did you get this?" She remembered her mother sitting in the dress before her vanity, another grand ball ahead of her. After all these years, it was as beautiful as ever. "I never thought I'd see it again." Like so many of her family's possessions, the dress was supposed to have been sold at auction.

"I snuck this off to the attic before you could sell it." Grace held the dress over Mae's figure, her old, crinkled eyes filling with tears. "I know material things shouldn't matter, but I just couldn't let you give up all of your mother's possessions. She would want you to have at least one item. And if you were to find a husband, I knew you'd need a gown."

Mae hovered a hand over the material almost too delicate to touch. It seemed to embody her mother's spirit, her sense of adventure—memories that were part of a life so different to her now that they were beginning to feel like they belonged to someone else.

The sea, travel, and romance, it had called out to her, her mother once said, like a song always playing in the back of her head. So at twenty-three, she had taken to the sea with Alastair, not thinking of danger. Nor had she thought how her skin, features, and even religion might be welcomed in a place like

England. But she'd married Alastair and settled here with a baby in her arms all the same.

At first, she had simply done as the Romans did. The missionaries had already taught her some English and with the help of private tutors, she had even mastered a proper aristocratic accent. Like any wealthy English woman, she'd dressed in the finest, smartest clothes and loved playing host.

But she would never truly be considered one of them. Rather, it had been curiosity that had eventually brought her into the neighborhood's highest circles. She'd held a "sweet, exotic allure," she'd overheard a crass gentleman whisper one of the rare times Mae had been allowed to formally greet guests before bedtime.

Regardless of how crass the word seemed to Mae, it was a role her mother had decided to embrace. That was when she'd begun to theme her parties after every corner of the world. Soon enough, everyone had talked of them and no one had dared miss them. At a time when Mae was so focused on the bad, the gown had brought up all the good parts of her past. And something else too.

Her lips fell, a coldness coming over her. She had long wondered what business her father had had in the Philippine Islands. Neither her mother nor her father had told her. Locke's claim offered one explanation, though.

She clenched her fists, hating that he knew her so much more than she knew herself, more so that he'd been right.

She didn't belong here. Though everyone thought it, he was the first to make her think that maybe she was better off. That maybe she could actually escape this place. Something in his eyes had awakened that long-dead desire. Made her want to do it, tonight.

"What is it?" Grace asked.

"Nothing," Mae said, her words raspy with emotion. "I—I just don't know how to thank you."

"No need." Grace folded the gown back up into the box and

took Mae in for an unexpected embrace. "Just promise you'll do everything you can to catch someone's attention tonight. Your mother would have wanted it so. She'd want you to leave this place."

⌐

LOCKE TRAMPLED DOWN the hall, violins strumming caution in his ears. A few more steps and the ballroom opened up before him.

He swallowed a breath, the crush of gowns and evening coats taking him aback. He hadn't expected a crowd this large, not by half.

Amidst the romantic glow of candelabras, he entered the same Blackthorne ballroom of decades past. But there was something different about this gathering, something much more sinister behind the quiet whispers and concealed laughter. This crowd hadn't come for his recent engagement. Rather, this crowd had everything to do with the years-old scandal surrounding Miss Blackthorne.

No one cared for him. He was halfway through the room and not a soul had noticed. Their shifty eyes were all searching for the heiress-turned-governess.

His goal remembered, he set his sights on a slim figure in black. Every muscle went tight with anticipation. Since Mrs. Rosewood had confirmed Miss Blackthorne's attendance that evening, he had worked up an excuse to abandon his duties as host. Greeting guests had become a surprisingly tiring charade.

He wanted to see if she'd discovered the key, of course, but something else had his feet moving faster through the room.

Catching up to the familiar figure in black, he set his shoulders back, prepared to steal her away. To hell with what these people might think.

He had just reached out when the woman turned around. Locke stepped back. A face that wasn't Miss Blackthorne's regarded him, blinking rapidly in confusion.

"Excuse me." He swept past her.

Where is she?

He paced the ballroom, the whispers of those around him ringing loudly in his ears. *Miss Blackthorne, Mr. William Blackthorne, shameful, pitiful.* There was no avoiding it. At length, he could take it no longer. He escaped to a secluded spot near the window.

He could not shake this constant feeling that she was in danger. His heart began to pound. A panic that wouldn't cease until he found her. He needed to do so at once. It was all he could do to keep from screaming out her name.

Through the glare of the window, a flicker of movement caught his eye. His heart stilled. There was only one person who might seek the refuge of a patio on such a chill night.

Nodding to the occasional guest who now began to recognize him, Locke made his way through double doors. Behind him, the chandeliers and candelabras of the ballroom lit up the night.

He found her figure beside the marble balustrade, its once-pure-white glimmer stained with green. Though her back was to him, a tightness in his gut left no doubt. Her silvery dress swooped low, exposing gold, gleaming shoulders. Her dark hair had been braided more intricately than usual with ribbon weaved throughout. He struggled to get out a single word, much less make his approach.

As he feared, his first step gave him away. She swept around and moved more visibly into the light.

He stared. The woman who stood before him was no governess, no woman who had lost everything. Before him, stood the true Mae Blackthorne. The woman who lived deep within her, who held the kind of emboldened spirit he had only ever met at sea. A spirit he might very well kill if he kept a man like Ellsworth at his side.

He swallowed, wishing he had some champagne to relieve his suddenly dry throat and something, *anything*, to occupy his heavy, foolish hands.

"You should be with Miss Rosewood," she said. Setting his pulse to quicken, she picked up her skirts and came close. "Dinner will soon begin."

"Hang dinner." He wanted nothing more than for the entire event and all who came with it to disappear. He nearly said as much when she stepped back, casting her face in shadow.

"What is it?"

Miss Blackthorne eyed the guests beyond the window glass. "We should not be seen together."

"Come now. You're already ruined. We've been alone. I've touched your waist. A few decades ago, that would have been enough."

Amidst Locke's short-lived laughter, Miss Blackthorne's stoic face didn't shift. He almost apologized. He was being insensitive again when for once he wanted to be something other than a brute.

"Not me, *you*. Soon they'll be whispering about you too."

"And you think I give a farthing?"

"If you are to secure Miss Rosewood's hand and this estate, perhaps you should." She clutched her hands and eyed the room nervously. How many years might have passed since she had last seen these people in the ballroom? How many of them might she have asked for help as they'd turned on her one by one?

"Hang them," she cursed bitterly. "Hang them all."

He reached out but thought better of it. He couldn't risk scaring her away. She was more valuable than he had imagined. Her first guess about the vault being in the cellar had been right. After searching for some time the night before, Ellsworth and his goons had found it.

Earlier that day, he had been the one to discover it. He'd merely kicked aside a stack of crates and swiped away two layers of dust. The simple yet sturdy trap door had hardly been hidden at all. Beneath it, there could be no mistaking the heavily padded vault. He imagined that barrels of wine had once covered it. The location still seemed strange to him, though. It was too obvious. Any servant who happened upon it would tell others at once. It was likely how the legends had begun.

"When I was inside…" Miss Blackthorne's gaze hardened toward the windows. "This man—a man I thought had been a friend of my father's—was speaking the most terrible slander against my brother. I had expected all talk to center around me. At first it had, but…"

Locke almost demanded whom. Which of these bastards had he greeted and smiled at? He would demand an apology, rip it from the man's throat with his bare hands.

Right now, however, he wanted to remain at her side. Ellsworth had censured Miss Blackthorne for her lack of dancing, fashion, and even domestic skills, none of which mattered to him. She had something like true bravery in this quiet countryside. Most would be broken down by these tragedies or changed into something wretched. Miss Blackthorne hadn't been. Not at all.

He knew only a few men half so strong as she. One of them her own grandfather.

Forgetting his trepidations, Locke stepped closer, mere seconds from crushing her into him. He wanted so badly to complete the movement, to press into her, when the sharp arch of her brow gave him pause.

In her eyes, he could read her words perfectly. *Scoundrel. Killer. Pirate.* Names he wished had never belonged to him.

Locke stepped back and forced his desires into retreat, feeling them sizzle down inside him until he felt raw.

"I know what you want," she whispered.

"You do?" The words chilled him from raging fire to sudden ice.

"Yes. And you'll be relieved to know that I did indeed find the key."

"Oh, yes." Locke jolted. He had almost forgotten. "Hand it here."

Miss Blackthorne tilted her chin away.

"You don't trust me?" Locke balked. "We have an understanding, remember?"

"*Trust* you?"

"I've kept you from harm, haven't I?"

"You want me on your side is all."

"Of course, I do. As partners."

"No, not the same," she said in sudden passion. "You want my help. Your kindness is all a manipulation."

"So I should be cruel to you? Is that what you think you deserve? I say, you must have a very low opinion of yourself."

"If you are kind to me, it is only for the basest of reasons."

"I see…" He broke off, momentarily shaken by that truth. "It's myself you have a low opinion of."

He thought to try to dissuade her, but as long as he was little more than a scoundrel to her, what was the use? She would never trust him. Christ, she barely trusted their deal. The idea distressed him, reminding him in one harsh blow of the life he needed to change.

He forced a smile. "I suppose now is not the time to ask for the honor of a dance."

"No." Mae eyed him. Did he really mean that? Did he even know how? She couldn't even picture it. Or was it just another one of his flirtatious manipulations?

She held his gaze. "Have no misgivings. I won't let the key out of my grasp. Not for a moment."

"Whatever you like," Locke said. "Meet us back near the cellar after the first dance."

"'*Us*'?"

"You can't expect me to keep Ellsworth away for good. He's even managed to secure an invitation to tonight's ball."

"He has?" Miss Blackthorne visibly shivered.

"You'll have no trouble getting away?"

"No, but surely, you will."

Locke grinned. "I have a feeling I shall take badly to the mussels this evening."

Miss Blackthorne didn't return the smile. She just stood there staring. "Are you certain we must meet so soon?"

"The ball provides a perfect distraction and we may very well leave with our shares tonight."

"I don't understand." Her mouth hung open.

"Don't you? The vault, Miss Blackthorne. I've found it."

MAE STARED AT the gold-rimmed dinner plate, its red-rose design peeking out beneath a scattering of peas. She smiled to herself. She hadn't seen these plates in ages. Mr. Rosewood must have attained them at the auction, along with the furniture, before finally deciding to buy the whole damn house.

She trembled, remembering the relief that had fallen over her. Now she wished she had refused. How differently her life might have been.

Damnable regret. She hated the feeling. No one, no matter how wealthy and well-connected, was immune to that bitter poison. She had felt its strong effects most as a heiress. There was the boy to whom she hadn't spoken, the horse on which she hadn't cast a high enough bid.

How trivial and foolish she had once been. She had endured too much since to let such a thing as pointless as regret consume her.

If nothing else, the decision to stay had brought her the truth. And it had brought her adventure, even if it had also brought her Locke. She had so many reasons to be angry with him for what he'd pulled her into.

But at the same time, the last few weeks since she met him had been utterly enthralling. A feeling she had known so briefly, it almost felt new. With this search for the vault, he had set her stagnant life in motion. Though minuscule, she still had a chance at getting all she wanted. Her old life. Revenge. Love? But that was only a girlhood dream. As an adult, it was a notion she had given up a long way back.

Roused by the thought, Mae looked up. At the same time, a dozen or so guests hurried away their gazes. Mae sighed inwardly, fighting to keep her chin high.

The guest next to her, a Mr. Cummings if she remembered correctly, had been the only one not staring. He seemed nice enough, just not quite to her taste. He'd been quiet and reserved the whole evening, seemingly not yet mustering the bravery to join the surrounding conversation, either.

"Mr. Cummings." Mae turned to him with a smile. "How is it, exactly, that you've come to live in India?"

Mr. Cummings glowed with eagerness. Mr. Rosewood had introduced his cousin as a visiting businessman, but his mission was clear enough. Like so many Englishmen who resided in foreign lands, Mr. Cummings had returned for the sole purpose of finding a wife.

"My family's long been involved with the country's silk trade," he answered her.

"How interesting." She forced cheerfulness in her tone. "Your forefathers must have worked very hard to establish themselves in that part of the world."

"Of course we owe much of our success to the East India Company. A pity their own success was so short-lived. Are you much aware of them?"

"I am." In the heyday of piracy, she imagined her grandfather commandeering their ships, perhaps taking their vast shipments of silver. As much as she wanted to dismiss the notion, she found herself holding on to the hope that the pirate treasure did indeed exist. Not only for her own livelihood, but because she couldn't stand the idea of William dying for less.

Unable to stop herself, she cast her gaze several seats down from her toward Locke. Still handsome in his black-and-silver-buttoned evening coat, he too, had been staring. Before he snapped away, his face reddened.

She was surprised at his jealousy. His feelings for her were supposed to be a manipulation just to get her to do what he wanted. Maybe she was wrong. Maybe Locke had been genuine. She couldn't help but smirk at the thought.

Nearby, Miss Rosewood hardly seemed to notice him. She was in the midst of laughter and, down another seat, so was Ellsworth.

At the mere sight of him, Mae jerked with sudden rage, her fork nearly slipping from her grip. She clenched the utensil tighter, so tight, it cut into her hands.

That man should not have been allowed to come anywhere near someone so innocent. Although Mae wanted to demand he leave at once, she was powerless. These guests, who also chatted with him, seemed to suspect nothing. He hid his venom well beneath a veil of good manners and fine clothing.

She turned back to Mr. Cummings. He was, after all, a gentleman many women would've found attractive. Why shouldn't she?

"I hear India has the most wonderful weather. Much nicer than our often rainy, overcast skies, yes?"

Despite her lacking interest in the man, Mae couldn't help but imagine what it might be like to live in such a country.

Mr. Cummings gave a slow nod, his gaze calculating. "Does travel interest you?"

"Quite." Mae rested her chin over her hand, struggling not to look bored. She should've been fluttering her eyelashes and smiling widely. *After all, what is stopping me from running off with this very man?* Mae thought wildly. Likable or not, the man could afford to take care of her.

Maybe she didn't need her fortune. Maybe she could live off a generous husband instead. Only the idea revolted her. It was the sort of life that would only end in imprisonment. That was all a loveless marriage could ever be.

It didn't seem to offer the same excitement it had her mother. It was about social connection, money, those who gained and those who lost. She wanted none of that. She only wanted love, but that sort of marriage didn't seem to exist anymore. She wasn't the sort of fool that thought it did.

"*Miss...*" The voice of a servant rang in her ears, his tone exasperated, no doubt from repetition. "More wine?"

Bewildered, Mae shook her head vehemently.

Mr. Cummings gulped down the rest of his glass. "I prefer something a bit stronger myself."

Not sure how to respond, Mae smiled. Charmingly, she hoped. But in fact, she was cringing. Ever since her brother's problem, the notion of drinking—especially strong liquors—had never sat well with her. More often than not, men abused liquor and the consequences were often less than favorable...

"You seem to have a great deal on your mind."

"Forgive me." Mae's cheeks burned. "I'm afraid I'm not much for witty conversation."

Mr. Cummings eyed her unabashedly. "You're a far better dancer, no doubt. Perhaps as the evening progresses, I may have the pleasure."

The haughty undertone of his statement had Mae buzzing with discontent. And yet, she could not politely refuse. Before she could stop herself, she was nodding her consent.

Dinner after that seemed to stretch on forever until Mr. Rosewood stood up from his seat and announced the start of the evening's amusements.

As Mae began to rise, she sensed Locke's presence behind her.

"May I escort you to the ballroom?" he asked stiffly, shooting Mr. Cummings a glare.

She tensed. He'd broken decorum again. He was supposed to be among the first in line toward the ballroom and she, the last.

Mae searched the shifting bodies for Miss Rosewood, her biggest fear becoming reality. With one hand holding Miss Rosewood's and another shielding his modest laughter, Ellsworth walked to the head of the line. Even Mrs. Rosewood looked pleased.

How had Ellsworth done it? What lies might he have told this time? That his home at the edge of town was three times the size of Blackthorne Manor? That this was a mere hovel in comparison?

"Miss Blackthorne?" Locke repeated.

Mae sent an apologetic smile in Mr. Cummings's direction. "I shall see you for our dance later."

"I am sure the wait will be well worth it." Mr. Cummings bowed his head and waited there, his eyes expectant. She sighed inwardly. He was no doubt waiting for her to offer her hand. If only to be rid of him, she offered it. Rather than simply grasp it, which would have been more bearable, he pulled it in for a kiss.

The smile that followed sent a shiver of ice down Mae's spine. Grateful for his presence now, Mae took Locke's arm and mingled inside the crowd.

"You accepted a dance?" His whisper burned hot in her ear.

"That is none of your concern."

"We haven't the time for such frivolity. We should leave at once."

"You're mad," Mae whispered. "I have to at least make an appearance." Otherwise, Mrs. Rosewood would have her neck. And more than that, she needed to plan. Everything was happening so fast, so soon.

"The key is safe?" Locke opened a door nearest to them and forced her inside.

"Of course."

"You have it on your person?" He backed her deeper into the empty butler's pantry.

"Perhaps…" She wanted to shove him for the way he looked down into her bodice, perhaps thinking it was there.

"We should leave for the cellar now."

"You—we can't. Not before you complete a dance with your betrothed."

"She is not my betrothed," Locke said, hard and cold. "At least not truly."

"You signed a contract, did you not? Only the Rosewoods can release you—"

"Not if they can't find me."

So that was his plan: to run off someplace.

"You'll cause a scandal. You'll ruin Miss Rosewood…and Miss Lenore too. I can't let you do it."

"What society believes makes no difference to me."

"How could you do that?" Mae's voice wavered. "Ruin some young lady like that. Never mind her feelings for you and the heartbreak she'll have to go through once you run off."

"I have to do what I have to do. At this point, what would be worse? Starting a little scandal that will undoubtedly blow over in a matter of months or marrying a woman who doesn't interest me when all I can think of is someone else entirely?"

It took a moment for her to understand what he was saying. Did he mean her? *Of course he did*, she chastised herself. *Who else could he mean? Mrs. Rosewood?* And yet, she just stood there, too stunned to speak.

Before Mae could find the words, Locke jolted away, dragging a shaky hand through his hair. "This evening has been the most torturous—"

"And it's almost at an end."

He regarded her, his expression softening, then, in his usual abrupt manner, fled into the hall. It didn't bother her this time. Rather, Mae brightened. If what he'd said was true, if all along he'd actually been genuine, at the very least she'd be safe. Locke wouldn't let Ellsworth hurt her, no matter what she did.

MAE'S LAST STEP of the quadrille could not have come sooner. With anticipation roiling inside her, she curtsied.

"A glass of punch?" Mr. Cummings offered, probably noting her shortness of breath.

Mae shook her head, her gaze searching for Locke. "I'd much rather have a bit of fresh air."

"I could join you."

Good heavens, the man was persistent. But the moment she caught his hopeful stare, her anger subsided. She pitied what would prove to be a difficult pursuit for a wife. After all, the women willing to sail halfway across the world must have been few and far between. The least she could do was be honest with the man.

"My regrets, Mr. Cummings, but I'm afraid I must wish you good evening."

Mr. Cummings's hopeful smile dropped to a frown. "Is something the matter? Something I've—"

"I'm afraid that's all I can say on the matter."

As Mae raced away, a gathering of young women swelled around her. Their delicate, white dresses made her stand out with such bold starkness, she didn't dare linger.

Impatient for the cool, crisp air of the patio, she weaved her way through the faceless figures, her face pulsing and her hands still shaking with fear. Then all at once, the crowd parted. At first, she was relieved, but to her dismay, a small yet obvious circle had formed. Previous glances became stares, the warmth of before intensifying. Something in the air had shifted. Whatever it was, she felt herself choking on it.

"There she is…" Miss Rosewood shrieked down the clearing. Mrs. Gertrude Wilson followed. *Wonderful.* Mae took a ragged breath. Years ago, Mae had known the woman well, but even as an heiress, they had never really been friends. Straddling the line of very rich and moderately rich, Mrs. Wilson had an easy propensity toward jealousy.

Before Mae could escape her, the woman closed in.

"Miss Blackthorne." Mrs. Wilson swept up Mae's hands. In her smile, it was like no time had passed at all. But her eyes held something different, something horribly false. "You are well, I hope. The Rosewoods do throw a good party, don't they?

Everyone says it's the best they've ever attended." Her eyes went round, inching from Mae's face down to her feet. "My, you look lovely this evening."

"Mrs. Wilson. If you don't mind. I have matters to attend to."

"Surely, your duties can wait for an old friend. Your dress doesn't disappear at midnight, does it?"

Miss Rosewood turned to Mae, her gaze darting back and forth between them. The young woman was not prepared for this sort of cruelty. In the face of it, Mae needed to show strength, not weakness, good humor not ill will. In the schoolroom, she would have told her pupils to act the better person. So Mae kept her smile.

"That Mr. Locke is quite the Prince Charming," Mrs. Wilson went on. "I daresay you yourself seemed quite taken by him."

All around Mae, the room seemed to still. "I-I don't know what you mean." Who else had seen her on the patio earlier? It had been foolish to speak with him given the windows. Now she was caught. For a long, languishing moment, she felt herself grow hotter.

"Tell me, Miss Blackthorne…" Mrs. Wilson's whisper chilled away the heat. "How was a young lady like Miss Rosewood here able to catch such a handsome husband?"

When Miss Rosewood looked to her feet, Mae could stand the insults no longer.

"She has tact," Mae said. "A trait you don't have the fortune to possess."

Mrs. Wilson covered her mouth, her eyes wide and staring. She clearly hadn't been expecting an insult so loud and without guise. Mae did not care. She could take the veiled venom no longer. She steeled her face determined to retain her composure.

"*Heavens,*" Mrs. Wilson said, as if Mae had as good as spit on her. "What in the world has gotten into you these days?"

"I'll thank you to step back." Mae straightened, looking upon Mrs. Wilson with such defiance that her old companion's confidence finally began to waver. Her jaw slackened—most unladylike, but still, she did not budge.

"I only wanted to see how you were faring."

Mae decided there was no need to wait or ask a second time. Even if it would only make matters worse, it could not be helped. Mae refused to stay another moment. So she strode forward, bumping Mrs. Wilson square in the shoulder. Mae had even put some force into it. Frankly, she did not know what had come over her. Or perhaps she did. All the whispers of that evening, the quiet betrayals she had endured these last few years, her anger over William's unexpected death, Ellsworth with his harsh words… It all seemed to coalesce into one flaming ball of *go to hell.*

In a most un-Christian way, Mrs. Wilson cursed too. The words—shrill and clear—set off its own eruption of gasps and whispers.

As the crowd parted further in her wake, Mae smiled to herself. That little victory felt good. The air tasted calm again. And making her way toward the west wing, she felt ready for the trials ahead.

CHAPTER ELEVEN

The Vault

BENEATH THE SHADOWS of the courtyard, Mae's unease continued to build. As hard as she tried, she had failed to come up with a plan. Not just the *perfect* plan or a *good* plan, but *any* plan at all.

Once she handed over the key, there was no knowing what might happen. Ellsworth had already proven himself capable of murder in the name of greed. And Locke, even if he did indeed plan to share the profits, could not hold up against three men.

Out of options, there was little for her to do but take her chances and pray. She crossed her arms tighter across her chest. In this frigid air, she did not know how much longer she could wait. For the hundredth time, she searched the courtyard, waiting for Locke to show. Strange shadows crisscrossed along the dark, green-less expanse. Empty.

What was keeping him? Miss Rosewood? She imagined the young woman had him in her arms somewhere. Miss Rosewood considered herself so in love, maybe she had grown bolder, and Locke, unable to cause a scene, had acquiesced, humoring her with a few light kisses… She shook her head to banish the dark thoughts. She couldn't continue to wait here much longer.

She jolted. A flutter of movement caught her attention. The source was likely a bird, but beneath the cloak of night, the courtyard was too ominous to indulge that possibility.

At times, it was like her family had never lived there at all. *But they did*, she reminded herself. For over two centuries, her bloodline had laid claim to this land, this home, this courtyard.

Mae took the key from the bodice of the simple dress she had changed into and studied it. The weaving of the handle was so worn and tarnished, time—not just its exposure to weather—was to blame. Several generations of her family had handled this key. The knowledge of this seemed to tremble through her.

She squeezed it tighter, feeling years of grime give way beneath her fingers. She looked at the key again. This time with the same wonder and awe she reserved for her family's oldest possessions.

Her eyes widened. Beneath her fingers, she began to feel an engraving. Along the stem of the key where the grime had been was another design. Words.

CROW'S NEST

Only a few of the letters had been rubbed away, but she knew the name at once. Mae gasped, loud and unrestrained. *Crow's Nest* was the name her father had once called their now-abandoned summer cottage on the coast.

She shuddered, the key shaking violently in her hand. It was as if everything her father had ever spoken or shown her as a child had had some hidden meaning. No one save for William and herself would realize that the vault in the cellar was a red herring Thanks to the wagging tongues of servants, it had distracted from her fortune's true location. Perhaps in cases like this, her family had prepared.

Mae looked back up, a realization sweeping through her all at once. It was at the same moment that her body began to hum with fear. Someone was watching.

Eyes searching, she could see little more than shapes in the darkness. With the passing of an icy draft, the courtyard shifted from ominous to deadly.

"Miss Blackthorne."

A touch on the back of her neck sent shivers knifing through her body. She swept round and saw Locke, his eyes glistening like crystals. She shrugged out of his grip. He needn't use force to imprison her—he did as much with his gaze.

"You have the key?"

Hesitantly, she nodded.

"Then we mustn't delay."

Not bothering to take it from her, he led the way across the lawn. Mae tried to take solace in his presence. If she ever needed protection, it was now. Of all the people in the world, this pirate was her only ally. He had kept her uninjured thus far and he still needed her, didn't he?

Whatever partiality he held for her—no matter how base— she prayed it would be enough to keep her alive.

As she stepped into the darkness of the cellar, cigar smoke clouded her vision and stung her eyes.

Within the gray haze, Ellsworth and his two men sat huddled around a small table. The three of them had likely found it buried beneath the dust. Compared to how she had left it the other day, the place appeared tidy. Most of the debris and clutter had been cleared away.

"You have the key," Locke prompted.

Mae nodded and slid the key over the table toward Ellsworth.

"Perfect." He dragged the pipe from his lips and signaled one of his men. "Show her."

The man, sporting new bruises along the side of his head, kept a wide berth as he walked to the end of the room. From the dirt floor, he pulled up a large hatch. Until then, Mae had never known of its existence.

"Go on." Ellsworth motioned her.

At the opening, one of Ellsworth's men had already descended. He was much younger than he should have been for such a task. His face, though drawn, still had some baby fat, and, showing no fear, he exuded the kind of bravado that only came with young age.

Even in the dim light, she could make out the black iron of a vault door. Well-crafted, it had an etched frame of gold. What a wasted expense for a mere decoy.

"So the rumors are true." Mae didn't quite succeed in keeping her voice from shaking.

Ellsworth held the key out to her. "I'll give you the honor."

Mae swallowed, fear holding her back. She chided herself. No man would think twice about this. Closing her eyes, she summoned the memory of all of Ellsworth's furtive glances, the unease that inched up her neck every time she'd met him at a gathering. She remembered her brother next, their races across the moor followed quickly by the sight of his broken body. Anger swelled, uncontrolled. She had to act. It would be a matter of duty, of justice.

"Best you do it," she said.

Of course he would believe her refusal to open the vault herself. To him, she was a flighty, emotional woman like any other. But for a long while, Ellsworth said nothing. He took another puff of his pipe, inhaled deeply, and shrugged.

Mae waited for no other confirmation. She hurried away to the corner where Locke stood. Whether it was from her rapid breaths or sudden proximity, he seemed to sense something amiss. He turned to her, his expression questioning. Then, with eyes wide, he seemed to realize. And yet he didn't speak. For some reason, he kept silent.

Ellsworth, meanwhile, had closed in on the trap door. Rather than descend, he tossed the key toward the man inside. Mae shot a worried glance at Locke. As wicked as the London thugs were, Ellsworth deserved death above them all. What could they do? They hadn't the time to act when a loud, jerking sound resonated through the floor beneath them.

Ellsworth, the fool he was, smiled at her, his eyes brimming with delight. Though sure enough, her previous notions had been correct. The lock had triggered a trap sure to be lethal. After a pause of silence, a strange rumbling grew louder, vibrating the room with intensity. Next came hissing.

Ellsworth's confusion changed to panic. Even at that distance, Mae could see the smoke streaming to the surface, its chemical aroma stinging her nostrils.

"Shut it!" Locke roared.

When Ellsworth didn't move fast enough, Locke pushed him aside. He kicked down the door himself.

Mae wondered about the man still inside. But against the door, there was no sign of struggle.

It was too late for her too. With Locke distracted, Ellsworth was able to close in. The next moment, he had her by the arm. Her resistance did little to thwart him. With red-hot fury fueling his strength, he flung her to the ground.

Locke, who had finally turned around, was coming for her. But he wasn't alone. Ellsworth's other London man was already on him.

Locke twisted around and, leaning back, managed a punch right into the man's face. Blood streaked down his cheek. Before Locke could get in another blow, the bastard sprung at him again. He grasped on to Locke with both hands this time, locking her ally in a struggle that was enough to hold him back. For a moment, his eyes flashed to her as they jerked from side to side, even as they fell to the ground. Locke grunted and shifted toward her if only by an inch.

He wasn't going to make it. He wasn't going to be able to make true on his promise. Still holding her gaze, he seemed equally certain of the violence that was to come. But after that moment, all she would remember was the rage dancing in Ellsworth's eyes.

HEAD THROBBING, MAE shook with a fear deeper than she had ever known. Her eyes opened to blackness and a horrible silence came from all around. A nothingness that seemed equivalent to the depths of hell. Was she dead? If not, it seemed only a matter of time. Death seemed to breathe at her neck.

Where was Ellsworth? Locke?

She shifted an arm to get up but quickly slammed back to the hard, dirt floor. Pain blossomed—an intense burn that stretched across her head, cheeks, and arms.

Several moments passed before the wave of torment rolled away, leaving numbness in its wake. Her surroundings were clearer now and so was her memory. She was still in the cellar amidst dirt and dust.

She lifted a shaky hand to the areas that pulsed with the deepest pain: her cheek and a swollen gash on her arm. Still spilling with fresh blood, the wound was severe, if not lethal. Each breath hurt and her throat ached with thirst. But she deserved it all, didn't she? This was where her plan had gotten her.

Why hadn't she stopped it? Rather, why had she tried to kill Ellsworth in the first place? Had not *somebody*—be it her father or mother—taught her that such a vengeful, hateful act could only end badly? Or was it common sense? The act made her a murderer now, as good as damned in the eyes of the Church. Just like Ellsworth, just like Locke.

Whatever punishment God had handed her now, she deserved.

Like a nightmare, she remembered flashes of pain. Most of all, Locke's efforts against Ellsworth's men. The fight in him had shocked her. He hadn't been thinking anything of gold, then. He had been focused on her.

With a gasp, she tensed, forcing herself to keep still. Even the slightest movement meant needles and daggers of pain.

"Miss Blackthorne?"

At the aching, groaning sound, fear gripped her again. Footfalls resounded, gaining on her.

"Who's there?"

A flash of light—strangely blue—erupted. Though little more

than a shadow, Locke entered her field of vision. She recognized his frame at once, his presence bringing a relief so deep and total, she had to force her hands to keep from reaching out.

But unlike the strong pirate she expected, he looked a mess. Hunched over, he limped as he came forward. Dirt, blood, and cobwebs covered his arms. Her own state was far worse, no doubt. The pain had already returned. The numbness was gone as her shoulder pulsed, blood gushing out, wet and hot.

Locke crouched down before her. Judging by the tenseness of his brow, her wounds were severe. She would likely die, the horrible truth making her want to scream out, to weep.

"Rest easy now." He wafted a hand over her injuries. "You'll be fine."

Mae hadn't the will left to argue. She wished he would leave her, as he had probably done to countless others. And yet he remained, holding eye contact when, without warning, he placed something cool to her lips. Despite herself, she swallowed the liquid that followed.

It took a while for her to realize what was happening. At first, it felt like warm honey spreading through her body. Then finding the sudden strength to pull back, she saw it. In his hand, a small, blue bottle shone as brightly as a thousand candles. Her mouth rounded to speak when she realized something else.

The pain had all but gone, the wounds disappearing from her limbs. Only their horrible memory remained.

Like a body thawed from ice, she snapped to attention and reached out for the odd bottle. In her grip, the chain around Locke's neck pulled taut. Suddenly and seemingly without provocation, it lit up again. She stared, waiting for an explanation, but Locke didn't speak. He barely even moved.

She was equally still when he took her wrist and put the small bottle to his own lips. The bruises along his brow faded until they disappeared altogether.

She remembered all those days ago when she had met him in her father's office. She wasn't mad. She hadn't been seeing things when she'd thought that gash upon his left hand had disappeared.

"How is it possible?" she asked, breathless. Who was he, really? With this kind of item, he had to be much more than a snarling, bloodthirsty pirate.

Locke took the bottle from her hands and stuck in a stopper like it was no more than a syrup. "I'm afraid there's little time for that." He put a calming hand to her face. "Are you faint? That would be perfectly normal…"

The question was so ridiculous, Mae almost laughed. He'd spoken as though she hadn't been gushing blood a second ago. But laughter in that dark, dank cellar was too much to muster.

"You can stand?" Locke offered a hand.

Mae nodded, getting to her feet with little effort. Although a bit hungry, she felt perfectly fine. Not even tired.

"Where is Ellsworth?" Her muscles tensed again.

"I was sufficiently outnumbered." His voice was hard and regretful. "Alas, he managed to escape me. He bolted the door and in time, he'll be back with more men. Though there is no knowing when."

He paced around, searching the broken crates piled along the edges of the room. "Perhaps I can find something to break it down."

"And leave your precious treasure?"

He turned, a smile playing on his lips. "The treasure isn't here. It's not anywhere near here."

"How do you know?" She crossed her arms and took him in. He was smarter than he had initially seemed.

"Your family was far too clever to make it that easy."

"But you still don't know where it's hidden. It could be any-where in the world, for all you know."

She touched her lips, not sure if she wanted to let on all that she knew.

"That's why I need you. Help me find it and you'll have your inheritance. You'll have your old life just as it once was—financially, at least."

So that was why he had healed her. He was trying to make it seem as though she would get Ellsworth's half. Once again, he wanted her to trust him. Which she didn't, of course. But what other option was there? Stay here and wait for Ellsworth to return? Wait for him to beat her an inch from her life again?

"I could find it without you."

He pulled something out of his pocket. For a foolish moment, Mae feared it might be a knife. Instead, he presented the key. "Without this?"

"How did you get that?" Mae fought her urge to snatch it from him. She would lose. Of that, she was certain.

"It wasn't pleasant. And not just because of the fumes." He tucked it away. "Now tell me, what's Crow's Nest?"

Mae crossed her arms. He'd found the clue, yes, but at least he didn't know what it meant.

"Come now." He flashed his most charming smile.

"As if I'd make it that easy. I'm a Blackthorne, remember?"

He grunted, lifting up one of the crates that littered the ground. "At least help me find something to break down that door. A wrench, a crowbar—anything."

"If I told you the location"—Mae blocked his path—"you'd simply abandon me."

"How else are we to—"

"I can show you the way."

"To Crow's Nest?" He stood up straighter, his eyes wide.

Mae nodded.

"At least tell me the distance I can expect—"

"A few days' ride is all you'll get from me."

"Then it's here." He brightened. "Somewhere in England."

"Perhaps."

"And the profits…we split them equally?"

Mae nodded. "I want your word—for whatever it's worth."

"You have it." Locke held out his hand.

Mae took it, feeling somewhat reassured when he smiled. As reassured as she could be dealing with a pirate.

"Now this door…"

"That won't be necessary."

"No?"

"I know another way."

She went to the wall and worked her finger along the stone until something snapped at the pressure. Almost instantly, it gave way, revealing an iron staircase spiraling into darkness. The escape tunnel was still there, just as William had shown her. So was the Blackthorne sign of escape.

"I knew I saved your life for good reason." Locke moved ahead.

Mae bristled. She had hoped that he might have saved her for more. Whatever existed between them, she didn't know what to call it, but didn't he feel it too?

"The manor has a series of connecting tunnels," Mae said, changing the subject. "There's hardly a room in the west wing without one."

"Fitting for a house of pirates."

The echo of his descending steps seemed to emphasize the emptiness below. She forced herself to follow nonetheless, pushing back any lingering feelings of unease.

"Locke?" In the darkness, she struggled to make him out. Then, like a flame, light flickered across his chest. It was the blue bottle again. "There."

The thing baffled her. Mrs. Jacobs's tales seemed less far-fetched now. Perhaps this strange bottle was how he had managed to stay young and immortal like the cook had said…

"Don't fuss now."

"You've made a pact with Lucifer," Mae blurted out before she could stop herself. "You must have."

Within the glow of the bottle, his jaw clenched. She could practically *see* the harsh words waiting to burst from his lips.

Then all at once, the light shuttered to black.

Before Mae could suck in her next breath, Locke came close. She considered moving away, but the effort wasn't worth it. Not when his body radiated delicious heat in that freezing underground tunnel. She stared at the smooth skin of his shoulder where his torn shirt had left it bare.

"If you must know, I *found* this healing serum and for all I know, it may indeed belong to Satan."

"You mean to scare me."

"Perhaps you should be scared."

A long beat of silence commenced. The air was suddenly so hot and thick around her, it seemed as if nothing could break it. Every fiber of her being begged to pull him closer, but as hard as she tried to smother it away, her longing pressed on. Something about the darkness, the remoteness of the tunnel, made her lust grow even stronger. And with each breath, her hindrances were flitting away.

But she could not give in to these desires. She couldn't let him know such a weakness existed in her.

"Just trust me, will you?" He plucked a piece of cobweb from her hair and broke away into the darkness. "After saving your life, haven't I warranted as much?"

Still pinned to the wall, Mae felt her head spin.

She had no reason to trust this brute. He simply needed her to help him find the vault, and what about the fact that he had led her to those brutes in the first place? That fact could not be forgotten. He wanted her fortune equally as much as Ellsworth. Possibly more. He was a pirate, wasn't he? Though now it seemed he was something much more.

"You said you found that serum?" Mae gripped her mud-drenched skirts and followed after him.

"Yes." Without warning, he whirled again. Mae flinched.

"Must I keep repeating myself?" He groaned. "We're partners now. What reason have I to hurt you?"

"You're a killer. I should expect no less."

"So are you, darling. Or have you already forgotten?"

Mae stilled at the image of the slamming hatch and the man still inside. She saw his drawn yet youthful face again. Whatever his name, he had died too young, far too young.

"It's not always avoidable, is it?"

"I didn't mean for it to happen. I was only guessing it might be a trap." Mae clasped her neck, as if feeling that harsh, chemical sting again. "Ellsworth was supposed to be the man caught inside."

"So you knew there was a risk to whoever went down there. To be honest, I didn't think you capable."

Mae shot him her hardest glare. She did not find it amusing at all. She felt sick. With the exchange of a key and the slam of that hatch, she had become no better than he. What did one do now? Beg for forgiveness? Give oneself up to a life of debauchery?

"Don't worry. It improves with time."

"What does?"

"The guilt. Not that you should feel sorry for the bastard. He would not have hesitated to do the same to you had the order come. Given the circumstances, you did well. If it frees us of Ellsworth, I'm glad of it."

"Please don't try to justify it."

"The man was scum. No different than Ellsworth."

Mae tensed, unable to erase the memory or the feeling sinking deeper in her stomach. If only she had time to think. But holding that key, she had felt only anger and a desperate need for revenge. She hadn't thought of the consequences. She'd simply wanted to be free of that horrible, blood-soaked memory. She wanted her brother back.

"Think of it as an act of courage. You did what you had to." Locke shrugged as if her act had been nothing more than the swatting of a spider. "You did what needed to be done."

"A sort of means to an end?" Mae thought of the Romans again. How their ambition had turned into the bloodlust and ruthless cruelty that had eventually been their downfall. She refused to be the same. "I won't become a monster," she said, more to herself than anything.

"Impossible. Though it does help to take up a few charitable subscriptions."

"Is that what soothes you?" She mocked, not believing him.

"I find it best in easing one's conscience, yes. Give it a try when you have the means. Might I suggest St. Aubin's Orphanage in London?"

"And here I thought you grew up in a gutter."

"No, actually. I happened to be luckier than that."

"Then what's your connection to them? Or is the place just a guise for something else?"

Was he teasing her? He could not be half so considerate. She almost didn't believe it, but in his shameless eyes, she sensed that maybe he had actually donated to the group. And likely more than once.

"All I know is that some men would not be half so rough had they some decent care early in life. Sometimes I wonder who I might be without...well, *my father...*"

Stunned, Mae stilled her steps. Locke's act of charity seemed more unlikely than her own act of violence.

Disgusted with herself again, Mae could not help but remember all the morals her mother had tried to instill. *The Ten Commandments. To treat others as one would want to be treated.* She had tried to obey those simple rules, but that was before her brother had been taken by the sea, before she had been betrayed.

Circumstances could change anyone. Even Locke.

Clearly, something had to have happened in his life to provoke this empathy. To even *think* of the poor while he was out stealing from others—how was it possible?

She wanted to study him in this new light, see if his expression might betray it all as a lie, but he raced ahead, distracted by a new series of bricks and a change in the air. She, too, felt the slightest wisp of a breeze. They were getting closer.

A few more steps and Locke stopped altogether. He held up the bottle and light spread over the wall. It's a dead end," he said without a hint of fear.

"Let me." Mae reached out, searching for the hatch. She

wondered how long it had been since it had last been used. Years? Decades? She and William had never gone this far. There were too many things that could go wrong: a cave-in, a flash flood…

Faster now, her hands ran up and down the bricks until finally, she paused. Then, mustering her strength, she pulled hard. A clicking noise echoed so loud, dirt vibrated down from the ceiling above. One final shove from Locke's shoulder and the door gave way.

Together, governess and pirate stepped into night and atop a mass of dead vegetation. They were in another one of the manor's courtyards, the scent of grass strong in the air. Like ghosts, white, marble statues stood scattered among the weeds.

Locke picked up his pace and looked about. "Come quickly," he whispered, as though he had seen something. Mae did not bother to ask what. She simply ran. Along the grass, thick droplets of dew tickled her ankles.

Besides her own rapid breaths, the night was silent. Music from the ball had completely died away.

The manor, however, was still aglow. In the tall windows of the ballroom, a lone figure stood unmoving, seemingly in thought. Mae had a feeling that person was in anguish. She had an even stronger feeling it was Miss Rosewood.

She should tell Locke to get down, to hide, to do something that would make their long shadows more obscure.

But it would only delay the truth. Whether or not Miss Rosewood had seen, there would be no avoiding Mae's and Locke's absences the following morning. Mae wished she had written a note and offered some explanation.

It was too late now. Up ahead, Locke had reached a large cluster of shrubs. His horse was tethered there, sniffing in his eagerness for release.

Locke lifted her up and mounted the horse behind her.

"Our destination?" he asked as chirping birds signaled the approaching dawn.

"West…to the coast."

As he twisted Gambit around, Mae glanced back at the estate shadowed against the golden haze of dawn. The figure was gone now.

CHAPTER TWELVE
Night at the Theater

UPON REACHING TOWN, Mae did not want to stop.

Against the cool, morning air, Locke kept her warm, his arms encircling her while his hands gripped the reins. She should have been used to the close contact by now. But she wasn't. Every now and then, she still shivered.

These last few hours had offered more close contact with another person than she had experienced in all of the last decade. She no longer doubted. The contact between them, closer than necessary, said so much more than Locke dared to.

She wished they could ride on like this for days. She rather liked the quiet determination of their journey. Every mile they distanced themselves from Blackthorne Manor, she felt more at ease. After all that had happened, even the bricks seemed a lie. It was a place unknown to her now, with new memories of pain and danger—of things she wished she hadn't done. The ominous darkness of the cellar, that hissing noise—it all seemed to follow her. From that, no distance seemed great enough.

Locke, however, demanded rest. Town offered them a place to get food. If they were lucky, safety too. At least for a time. With Ellsworth quite possibly on their heels, Locke said they would blend in best on foot. And they could not very well run like this forever, could they?

After stabling Gambit, they made their way toward the heart of town. The smell of freshly caught fish steeped the air. At the pair's passing, shopkeepers sprang to life, shouting and motioning toward their goods.

Locke, the only one with any money on him, picked up as much food as they could carry. Although he made no issue of it, Mae was reminded yet again just how much she'd left behind: everything save her dress and boots.

It had been months since Mae had been to market. As the morning carried on, new stalls of fruit and flowers opened all along the streets. Around her, the crowds doubled. People burst forth down the alleyway, spitting, shoving, shouting.

She enjoyed scenes of customers bartering for a cheaper price, the cliques of women deep in gossip, the casual *how-do-you-dos* between acquaintances. Furthermore, all the different styles of dress: some dirtied and ragged like theirs and others of the finest and latest styles.

"A rose for your wife," a man called out to Locke.

Locke stumbled for words, clearly caught off guard.

"No need." Mae clutched his arm and pulled him ahead. "I have a whole garden of those." Maybe one day, she would.

"Thank you." He tilted his head toward her.

"Just trying to blend in." Mae raised her chin. In the crowd, it was easy enough.

Only once did she worry when she saw children running unchaperoned. While pitiable, they also seemed suspect.

She feared the worst when Locke had caught the hand of a rough-looking boy. A silver coin glistened between stubby, dirt-lined fingers. Mae pieced it together. The boy was a pickpocket. Sadly corrupted at so young an age.

"Oh, please let him go." She could only guess what Locke might do. The small lad could be no more than twelve. But while she expected curses and maybe even a hard knock, Locke held still.

"Please, sir." The boy twisted and tugged.

"You're clumsy." Locke released his hold. "And not a quarter as fast as you should be." Reaching into his pocket, Locke tossed him another coin. The boy grinned, then, without a single word of gratitude or apology, ran off into the crowd.

Mae stared at Locke, aghast. Though she had feared Locke being too harsh, she still thought the boy had deserved some sort of punishment. Certainly not a reward. "I hope you don't think that an act of charity. You're only encouraging his criminal behavior."

"He steals to survive. There's no crime in that. The only criminals are those who steal out of greed…like myself."

Mae laughed, at last endeavoring to relax.

At least a decade had passed since she had traveled this far away from home.

Only a few of the same buildings she had visited with her mother still remained. For those sights and memories alone, Mae relished the visit.

She froze as a horse-drawn omnibus whizzed past.

"Careful." Locke yanked her back.

She flushed. "The streets get busier every year."

"Towns change without warning, don't they?" Locke took in the vastness of the buildings, their height reaching four, even five stories. "It's remarkable, really. How nothing stands still."

"Not so," Mae countered. "In the country, the moors, prairies, forests… None of that ever changes. But if you wait long enough, even their beauty in your eyes begins to fade."

How often during the lull of afternoons had she stayed indoors, gazing at a book without reading a single word? She had had enough companions to occupy her then. But eventually, she'd found them dull too. Time spent with them had always led to the same gossip, the same compliments.

A certain restlessness had begun growing in her then—urging her toward something more exciting. A feeling she'd thought had died with her brother. Though now she wondered if it had ever died at all. It was in her blood, hidden but eager to re-emerge. All the Blackthornes before her had known and experienced it…at sea, as pirates.

A woman screeched nearby, an argument ensuing with a wagon driver. Mae waited for the shouting to recede into the distance. "How do you remember it?" she asked the pirate. "The town, that is."

Had he actually been alive to see it in its early days? She hated that she had even entertained the possibility. But given that strange, blue serum, it had to have been true. Furthermore, who would invent such a tale? Secret betrothals, affairs, even women being with child had been invented, but nothing like what Mrs. Dorris and Mrs. Jacobs had suspected of Locke.

"Less busy." His eyes narrowed at the chaos. "I notice the same in other places. Forests are downed, farms and villages taking their place. Villages become towns, towns become cities. Any forests in their path gone in a matter of years. In fact, that could very well be the fate of the Northern Woods. You would miss the place then, wouldn't you?"

Mae nodded. "That's the trouble when things are taken away. You finally realize their worth." She thought of the forest, its crisp, mossy smell, the quiet whisper of leaves, the vibrant color of grass after the rain…

Along the street they walked, there was not a single tree to speak of, let alone a patch of grass. She still appreciated the town for its ability to change, though, for the shops and buildings both old and new. "I think I've had my fill of forests and moors," she said.

"For good?"

"Perhaps." She couldn't deny how much she enjoyed this new taste of freedom. "So long as my surroundings are thrilling enough, why not?"

"How, may I ask, do you find our adventure?" Locke quirked a brow. "Thrilling enough for your taste?"

"More like *dangerous*."

By now, Ellsworth could have discovered their escape. For all they knew, he could have been searching for them.

"There are far worse enemies in this world than Ellsworth, Miss Blackthorne… and far worse ways to die."

A glimmer of something she didn't recognize took over his eyes. Whatever it was, something clearly painful to him had crossed his mind. To witness it felt intrusive, as if she were unearthing a private, uncharted piece of his life. So, quickly, she looked away.

A church served as a perfect distraction. Sunlight sparkled off the tall, white dome, rising far above than any other building.

"Nice to see that some things have remained," Locke said.

Clearing their view, a flock of birds dispersed and something within Mae sparked. The way Locke talked about this town, how it had and hadn't changed over the years, made it all too clear. Locke was much older than he appeared. She was growing certain of it.

"What is it?" he asked, his strikingly familiar face confirming her suspicions. "You've suddenly gone quite still."

How had he managed it? How had his serum been able to heal her so quickly? There was nothing within her logic to explain any of it. Since the moment they'd met, he had been nothing short of perplexing.

He had saved her in the cellar, but first he had put her life in danger. And for what? Gold? Vast amounts, yes. Though perhaps he had been after something different, something far grander, since the beginning. Something she could scarcely imagine. She would like to think he hadn't been lying. That material things did not sway him like he had once said. That he wasn't some bitter pirate desperate for glory that could no longer be had at sea. He could not think gold was worth her life. The very idea had likely been borne out of some idle hope that he cared for her, that his charm wasn't founded on lust.

"Miss Blackthorne?"

"We best find a place to sleep."

Locke looked around and nodded in agreement. "Indeed."

LOCKE SPLASHED THROUGH the puddles of the alleyway, not surprised when Miss Blackthorne lagged behind.

"You're not taking me to an inn, are you?"

Locke grumbled a curse. Their trip through town seemed all he could endure. His body ached everywhere and he was in desperate need for a good night's sleep. Food was definitely in order too.

"No time to argue." Locke waved her forward. "Quickly now."

Miss Blackthorne sighed and lifted her skirts an inch higher. Evidently all too aware of the stagnant puddles, she took slow and careful steps. Even now when she was undoubtedly exhausted from their journey, her skirts already ragged and dirty, she was as collected as ever.

She didn't need the ostentatiousness of silks or furs. Even without, she stood far above the likes of him.

Still in her fine dress, she held whispers of her true self. Perhaps it was their escape from the manor or their near encounter with death, but that bold, wayward air of hers seemed clearer and more apparent than before. For once, it wasn't so fleeting, hidden or aloof.

"Over here." Locke shot down the alleyway. If he was going to get through the night, he needed to keep her at a distance.

"You'll get us in trouble," she whispered harshly. The longer she took in the ominous grayness of the surrounding buildings, the more questioning her eyes became.

Locke thrust his elbow into the glass of a door. "We'll be fine." He reached through and unhinged the lock.

Miss Blackthorne inspected the alleyway. She picked one of many crumpled show-bills and dropped it.

"A theater?" She gasped. "You can't be serious."

"I won't risk discovery at an inn."

He could not shake this constant feeling that Ellsworth, in a rare moment of intelligence, had lingered behind and had seen them leave the estate. He was likely following their trail. Their route had been too direct. Too easily, it could be followed.

More than his life was at risk now. He didn't like that Miss Blackthorne's life seemed to balance in his hands. The least he could do was play the gentleman. Even if he hated the theater for its cheap laughs and overacting, the grandeur and stateliness before them made good manners seem possible. At an inn, he couldn't be sure.

She bit her lip. "They could be rehearsing..."

"The place is closed for the season. Said so on the marquee." Locke offered his hand.

After a tense moment, she grabbed it, much to his satisfaction. He wasn't completely sure if she trusted him, but his efforts to keep her safe had at least not gone unnoticed.

The glowing necklace guided them through the dark, windowless lobby. The fog of light just enough to make out a glistening staircase. In its pristine, nearly dust-free condition, the place had likely closed only weeks ago.

Still, Miss Blackthorne kept close, searching the floor, probably for rats.

"It's not so bad." He gave her a reassuring smile, his eyes lingering then snapping away.

He relaxed his tensing muscles. The baser parts of him knew all too well that inn or not, they would be alone. But, hang it, he could not think of Miss Blackthorne like this.

For decades, he had been waiting for his chance to reclaim the sapphire. He could not let some woman, some short-lived attraction, get in the way. She was useful for now, but she would not be so always. Finding the sapphire might not call for saving her life like it had in the cellar. More likely, she would only stall him. He should leave her behind and take all the treasure. A pirate would think nothing of it. A true pirate wouldn't care.

Though somehow, that had ceased to matter. He was leaving that life behind, wasn't he? The one ahead of him seemed much brighter with her in it.

As they climbed the stairway, her father's betrayal was forgotten. The sense of revenge that had fueled him in the beginning had been squashed to nothing.

He had once despised Alastair's ruthless, unforgiving nature—traits he'd expected Miss Blackthorne to share. Yet she was different somehow. She had always been. He was sure of this now. In her, there was modesty, uncertainty, and a kind of yearning. Something he wanted deeply to indulge.

"There's nowhere to sleep," Miss Blackthorne said.

Locke mounted the last step and led the way into one of the private balconies. Sooner than he had expected, night had descended. Moonlight spilled in from a nearby window, casting the room in a silvery hue.

"Right here." Locke slapped a plush, velvet seat.

Miss Blackthorne shuffled past him and leaned over the railing. Weak sunlight streaked through the skylight, illuminating a long stretch of aisle and row upon row of seats. "I've never been to a theater this empty."

"Nor I." From a bag, Locke pulled out the supplies they had purchased. Kneeling on the carpet, he worked quickly to arrange the blanket, taper candles, and much-needed bread, cheese, and wine.

But as perfect as he thought the spread looked, Miss Blackthorne did not seem to notice any of it. Leaning against the wall, she stared straight ahead, her pale cheeks flickering in the candlelight.

"You must be hungry." Locke uncorked and handed her a bottle of wine. But she didn't drink. Instead, her face crumpled.

"What happened in the cellar, what I did… I'll never be able to forget it, will I?"

She was speaking of that man's death. Something that would

likely trouble her for months, if not years. Her eyes watered and she bit her lip. He should have been the one to bear it, the one who had killed that man instead.

"You'll forget soon enough," Locke lied. His first kill had been just as horrifying. He couldn't have been more than eighteen and it hadn't taken much effort. It had almost been an accident. But he'd known the sharks had been in the waters that day. They'd been following his crew's ship since they'd entered the Pacific. When the man had come at him with a knife, Locke had simply shoved a shoulder into him and he'd fallen overboard right into the circle of sharks. The blossoming of blood had been almost instant.

"I suppose there's no going back now, is there? If we don't find the vault—"

"We'll find it. I've never let anything half so valuable escape my grasp and I don't intend to now."

"What about Ellsworth? After all this, he might still seek me out." She tipped the bottle into her mouth and drank.

With an arm resting on his knee, Locke bit heartily into a chunk of bread and thought it over.

"There are plenty of places to go. Rome. Egypt. India…" He pointed his half-eaten bread at her. "You've never been to any of them, have you?"

"And you have?" She passed him the bottle.

"I've seen 'em all." And thus, he had paid a price. Aside from Miss Blackthorne and the wretched Ellsworth, he hadn't a single acquaintance left.

She came closer and, spreading out her skirts, sat down on the blanket beside him. At last.

"One can't travel forever, you know. With your share, you'll have to settle down sometime."

"Perhaps." He paused to consider it. "Say, what does a respectable man with a fortune do?"

"I suppose he would marry." She took up a slice of cheese and placed it on the bread. "Attend the opera, throw dinner parties."

"Dinner parties? As in the one that I attended the second time we met?"

"Similar, yes."

"I'd rather hang myself."

She laughed in a breathy, cheerful way. It lifted him.

"You have a bit of that wanderer's spirit yourself," he said after a pause.

"When I was younger." She blushed, as though it were a silly notion. "I remember asking my father over and over to take me to sea. Of course, given that I was no more than a girl, he refused."

"He was trying to protect you."

"If only he had wanted the same for William…"

"But it wasn't the sea that claimed him."

"Ellsworth…" Locke remembered, his face falling.

Miss Blackthorne rubbed her arm. "It was right when we'd lost everything. Everyone thought he'd gone mad and maybe he had. The sea and whatever tragedy he'd faced out there had done that to him." She squeezed her fists. "But I refused to let that scare me off from ever leaving home—had I the chance."

"Good." Locke gave a single nod. When traveling, or going to any place unfamiliar, really, the first thing one must overcome is fear. Otherwise, it will swallow you up."

"How did you overcome it?"

"I try not to focus on the dangers. And I never look back."

"That's no easy thing," Mae said. "I'm starting to miss Blackthorne Manor already."

"The place doesn't suit you."

"Oh? And what place does?"

"That, you'll have to discover for yourself."

"Tell me." A glimmer of bold curiosity brightened her eyes. "Tell me about the places you've been."

Glad to have distracted her from her moroseness earlier, Locke worked to come up with the single, most romantic place. "The Tuscan countryside. The wind there isn't sharp. It's warm and soft. And saturated with the scent of leather." He breathed in deep, almost fancying a hint of it.

"And the people. What are they like?"

"I don't know. I—uh, didn't stay long. The smugglers I banded with, well, they didn't last."

"The law caught on to them?"

"Not quite. More of a coup, and things…turned violent. Didn't even get my cut. This, after my days at sea. I hadn't much money then…"

"So what did you do? How did you survive?"

Locke looked down at the wine bottle. He'd been an idiot to bring up Tuscany. He wished he hadn't.

"I went as far as I could afford. I suppose it will disgust you that I stole from families when I needed to, even the elderly."

"Why not search for work somewhere else? Become a sailor, perhaps." Mae fumbled with another slice of cheese.

"I've heard enough dark tales to know that's no easy life, either."

"So what *did* you do?" Miss Blackthorne seemed afraid to ask.

He was just as afraid to answer. He wanted the story to encourage her wanderer spirit, not scare her away. "I did what I had to until I could afford a ticket someplace promising. I haven't lived an easy life." *I should stop now*, he thought. All he had seen and experienced—it wasn't fit for her ears.

"Perhaps if you had tried to make an honest living—"

Locke clenched his teeth. She insisted on marking him dishonest. But what of his privateering days during the American War of 1812? What would she have called him then? A soldier? A good man willing to die for his country, though his acts had been no different?

"You don't know the truths of this world as I do," he said, calmer now. "It's one where honest men starve and dishonest men feast, and sometimes violence is the only choice we've got."

"Good speech. Though I doubt it'll keep you from hanging."

"Still mean to turn me in, Miss Blackthorne?"

"Mae, if you please."

"Friends now, are we?"

"Hardly. The name is just—just too reminiscent of things past…"

"That's behind you now," Locke reminded her. "Don't look back."

"For that, I am grateful to you. Grateful enough to call us friends."

Mae, he repeated in his mind, was easier on the ears. Blackthorne held too many dark memories for him too. Mae, he liked much better.

"Do you think I'll ever return?" Mae asked.

"For your sake, I hope not."

Mae crossed her arms. "Being a governess wasn't all bad, I'll have you know… I still had use of the library. I've even read of that Tuscan leather you spoke of."

"Much to learn from reading, but you'd do better to experience it firsthand. How can books possibly capture the smell of the Indian market? The colors of the sunset over the Mediterranean? The majesty of the ancient pyramids? We all see the world differently, Mae. The point is that you have to see it for yourself."

In her expression, a bit of that hope-filled wanderer spirit emerged. Renewed and strengthened, he'd like to think. Though only for a moment. Soon after, her face dropped, returning to reality. "We can't all be fearless pirates."

"'Fearless'? I'd sooner be dead. I have fear—just not enough to imprison me."

"What of men like Ellsworth?"

Locke clucked his tongue. "The world is full of betrayers—no matter where you run." *Except here*, he thought. Mae could trust him with her life. For however long it lasted, for this moment at least, they were bound to the same cause: they both sought freedom and soon, they would have it.

"You know…" He offered her another slice of bread. "You need never fear starvation with me. Tuscany was a long time ago and I—"

"How long, exactly?"

"Years. I was younger then, more foolish."

"Hadn't you any family? Parents, siblings…"

"To rescue me, you mean? To try to convince me of a better life?"

"Forgive me, I—"

"No." He rubbed the back of his neck. He just wasn't like her, with a respectable name. Even if that name hid a past as unconventional as his own.

"What about the father you spoke of?"

He was surprised she remembered. The mention of him had been an afterthought. A little fact he hadn't meant to reveal. Hell, that never happened. He was never this forthcoming.

"There was him," he admitted. But there were also his original, biological parents.

Mae waited, expectant. There was no evading her questions now. But why not tell her? What harm could it do?

"If you must know, both my parents died long ago, when I was a lad." His voice dropped to a whisper. He didn't know why. It wasn't as if someone else stood near.

"It's difficult, isn't it?"

"Yes. We're similar in that. We're both very much alone."

Mae lifted a shoulder. Her dissent, though subtle, seemed outright. He happened to think that they were very similar, and in more ways than one. How did she not see their likeness? With her, these traits were oftentimes hidden, but they were there nonetheless.

"To an extent, we're similar in that way, yes."

"'To an extent'?"

"Well…" Mae swept breadcrumbs from her skirt. "Unlike you, I don't always wish to be alone."

"What makes you think I wish to be alone?"

"Your desire for smuggling and travel, of course."

"Suppose I don't travel so much anymore… There *are* downsides. Piracy, for one, is full of enemies."

"As I would expect."

"But I despised that bit. Through and through. I've come to realize that gold is not worth that price."

Mae let out a beat of laughter. "All this time, is it not what you've been after?" When Mae looked at him with an arched brow, he near snarled.

"It's not as though I am incapable of feeling…" he whispered. She didn't understand, but how could he explain things without revealing his aims for the sapphire? He didn't want to involve her in that mess. Instead, he fought for other words, eager for her to know at least a portion of the truth. He wasn't the same cold-blooded killer as Alastair. He was certain of that now.

Mae laughed. "The only thing you should care for are gold doubloons."

Lord, he didn't know what had possessed him. Perhaps it was his frustrations—but drawing a breath, he took her hand and brought her dainty fingers to his lips.

"You're wrong," he said, holding her hand tightly, using all his strength to keep still.

Mae's eyes, meanwhile, grew wider. She ripped her hand out from his grasp, her eyes skidding over her surroundings, as if noticing for the first time that they were alone. When she backed away, all anticipation drained out of him, replaced by the icy chill of her gaze.

"You don't still see me as a threat…" He shifted closer.

"*Don't.*" Mae's tone turned as hard and cold as iron, freezing him in his tracks. "I've agreed to help you find my fortune— nothing more."

"As I'm well aware." Equally insulted, he rose to his feet.

He cursed himself. What the devil was he thinking? Certainly, this was not the place to get what he wanted. Yet he could still see it in her eyes. The look that had yet to fade. Why didn't she simply give into it already? He growled inwardly, like the savage she thought he was.

What did he have to do? Call her beautiful, write her hourly poems, pay her a thousand more compliments before she might agree to a kiss or more? He hated how much he longed for it. He might have agreed to do anything for it. How she could quite easily make him a fool.

"I've done nothing wrong." Here, he was in a room alone with her—an accomplishment he might never have deemed possible with such a woman—and he couldn't even manage to kiss her hand, much less the other things he'd dared to imagine. He hadn't even the hope of a "good night."

"It doesn't matter. There are certain rules men and women are supposed to abide by. We should not be alone like this." She pushed her hands out.

"I did nothing out of line." He raked a hand through his hair. "We've been alone plenty before and I've never... You're not even a lady any longer."

Her mouth went slack in a silent gasp.

He was certain she was being unreasonable, but when he saw the flicker of fear in her eyes he understood. She wasn't truly free. The straight-laced rules she'd been forced to follow had never left her. "Why are you so fixed upon these dictates?" He demanded to know.

"I-I..." she stammered as she pressed back against the wall, letting her eyes drift to the floor. If only he could see what she wanted him to do next and how he might give that to her...But she was impossible to read. Her eyes were mysterious now more than ever.

"I don't know!" she suddenly screamed. She pounded her fist backward against the wall and spun around, covering her face with her hands.

"It is fear holding you back?" Locke said. "I fought enough battles to know fear when I see it. No matter what kind...even fear of who you are. You're not just your father's daughter."

"I know that."

"Yet you've denied the rest of you for so long."

"Because it's only brought me pain."

"It could bring you peace. If you embraced it, your wanderer spirit, and perhaps…"

She scoffed. "Do what? Travel?"

"Why not? Deep down, that's what you were meant to do. I'm certain of that."

When she turned around, he stepped closer. For a second, Mae seemed certain of it too.

"You have no wish to travel in your heart?"

"I always have." Mae shrugged. "Though I've never spoken of it."

"Ah…" He brushed her chin with his thumb. "I thought so."

The sensation, the warmth of her skin radiating into his, surprised him. It had been some time since he had been this close to another woman. Years, even. But he was sure it had never felt like this, never so right.

She swallowed.

"You'll do it, then? Travel with me? When all this is over, of course."

She nodded, making his pulse throb with excitement. Somehow, she seemed to be agreeing to so much more.

The romantic side of him wanted to be gentle. Have her yield to him without trepidation. But the pirate side of him wanted to take the back of her neck and pull her against him, no matter what the consequence.

Taking in a deep gust of air, he let the pirate side of him win. To his amazement, she didn't resist.

CHAPTER THIRTEEN

A New Enemy

THE KISS HAD not been like what she had expected. Locke did not hold back.

In the midst of it, she struggled to find her balance. But in Locke's ever-tightening grip, it wasn't long before she allowed herself to give in. How easy it was for her to forget all that troubled her: all of who she was and who she had been. Impossibly easy.

A moan caught in her throat. His lips dug into her neck. A moment longer and she'd be letting him ruin her right there in that theater.

Mae twisted away, her virtue saved by the distant thunder of steps. Voices resounded from below, gaining volume. Panic hit her fast. Despite all their efforts to be careful, Ellsworth had found them. Who knows how many men he might have with him now?

"Not a word." Locke grasped her arm.

Footfalls echoed through the building. In the complete silence, they seemed to belong to a horde of beasts rather than mere men.

Straightening out her skirts, Mae tried to relax, but her heart still raced and her skin still tingled from his touch. She couldn't make sense of what she had done, or what she had continued to do. And trying to reason with herself seemed useless. Her heart paid no mind to logic. Recently, they seemed two entirely different things, sworn enemies at best.

"Locke?" A deep, throaty voice called out.

She didn't recognize it. A part of her relaxed, it wasn't Ellsworth after all. Who was it then? It couldn't have been the local police. Whoever this was knew Locke's name. She was breathless, not sure if she should run, not sure if she *could*. But as the footfalls gained the stairs, they could only wait.

A group of five men surged forward, darkening the hall with black cloaks and long shadows. These men were not the police. They didn't don the typical hats and slick silver buttons. Whoever these men were, they were dressed to blend in and attack from the shadows. Their grim and menacing faces marked them as killers.

"Ah, there he is." The figure of a man stepped into the weak moonlight. Sporting a short, peppered beard, Mae guessed he was in his fifties, though his eyes seemed far older. In them, he held a gleam of authority. "I'm in need of a few words."

"Then say them, damn you," Locke snapped.

"That's no greeting for a friend." The stranger cut across the floor, his face a map of sharp angles and deep wrinkles. "And to think, I thought you returned to England just for me."

"I'm no fool. You'll get what you want. Your message was clear enough."

"And yet it seems you two are running."

Mae stepped back, hoping to shrink out of view. Just like Ellsworth, this man was clearly an enemy. How many enemies did a man like Locke have? Despite her hopes, the man turned to her. Though she was in shadow, he seemed to see her clearly.

Locke stepped forward, shielding her from view. "I need time is all. Give me till the end of the week. Until then, you can leave us the devil alone."

Mae looked back and forth between them, her breath quickening. Neither side seemed interested in yielding. They were outnumbered too and she was unarmed. She needed a blade. How much time would that give her? A few seconds?

The stranger scoffed. "Am I supposed to believe you? After all these years of silence? We've offered you guineas upon guineas for what is rightfully ours."

Gold for more gold? Mae almost questioned aloud. It didn't make sense.

"Instead of giving us what we want, you run," the man said.

"Well, I'm tired of running!"

Mae trembled at the emotion in Locke's voice. She thought he loved this life of his. That he had no one to answer to, that he was free to go and do as he pleased.

In actuality, he was trapped. They both were. Whatever these men were after, they seemed the worst kind of enemy. How minuscule her own sufferings now seemed.

Locke backed closer to Mae just as the men seemed about to beckon. Turning back to his enemy, his words were stone again. "Leave us, Pierce, or you'll never get what you want."

Mae could feel the twitch of anger welling in Locke's limbs. Its release, even a breath of it, would undoubtedly mean death. But against these men, what hope had they?

"Two days' time," Mae suddenly said. "We'll arrive at the vault no later. What you want is there, isn't it? Whatever you want, you can have it. I don't care."

"Useful, this one." The man Locke had called "Pierce" smiled and turned his sights on her. "And where, pray tell, is this vault hidden?"

"West along the coast," she answered before Locke could stop her. She didn't know what had come over her, but she felt sure this was necessary—more than necessary.

Pierce's thin lips quirked. "Until the morrow, then." He pulled something out of his pocket. It glinted, a flash of silver. A sort of pin, Mae guessed as Pierced dug it into Locke's collar. "Or we shall cross swords again."

"Then I shall sharpen my blades."

"Better yet." Pierce's charming smile fell.

In another sweep of their cloaks, the men padded down the stairs.

"I wish you hadn't done that," Locke grumbled.

"Who was that? I demand to know." She grabbed at the pin on Locke's collar and ran a finger over the rose engraving. It was some sort of insignia. She couldn't even begin to imagine what it meant.

"The Silver Order."

"The what?"

"*The Silver Order.*" Locke ripped himself away, heading back onto the balcony. From the floor, he grabbed the wine bottle and took a large gulp. "Snakemen, the lot of 'em."

"But who are they?"

"I know little beyond the name. They're known to a select few of London high society. And among those sort, there are few consistencies."

"W-What do they want with you?" She deserved answers and he knew it.

"They're not after your fortune. *I* was never after your fortune."

Overcome by this revelation, Mae stumbled backward.

"Then what *do* you want?" she whispered. "Tell me now."

"Your father stole something else from me." Locke avoided her gaze. "Something infinitely more precious than gold."

"What, then?" Mae almost yelled. She hated having to drag each and every answer out of him. After all his lies, she would wait for the truth no longer.

"A necklace like this." From beneath his shirt, he lifted free the silver chain that held the "healing serum," as he called it. "Except this other necklace holds a gem. A very unique and powerful gem. A sapphire, to be specific."

"Then you lied to me. You didn't *find* these things. You *stole* them."

"Of course I stole them." He huffed.

"And you look young when in truth you're old. Very old. You should be closer to my father's age. But you're not."

His jaw tightened.

"How?" she pressed. Something told her that sapphire had everything to do with all her pressing questions, all of the cooks' claims, all her doubts….

When he didn't answer, she pressed again. "You owe me an explanation. Many, I should think. My grandfather—" She could not believe she was about to say the words. "You knew him too. How?"

"He wasn't there that day. I wish he had been."

When he quieted again, Mae tried to be patient. How far back might these memories date go?

"I was legitimate then. A privateer on paper, but with no true loyalties. Not when I saw their ship. Everything about it called to me. The gold-painted railings; the pristine, white sails; the deep-red rose insignia. No ship had ever looked so tempting. So my crew and I did what we did best, we overcame their defenses and in exchange, I took its most precious cargo: this serum and a sapphire…"

Mae held her breath, more than ready for the answers she had waited for.

"For years, I wore the sapphire as a good luck charm. I thought of it as nothing more. But the men we pillaged…they weren't mere merchants, Mae. They're something far more. They wield great power and not merely the political variety.

"You see, that necklace, it doesn't just hold a precious gem. It has mystical properties of some sort. I don't know how, but it sustained my youth. For as long as I had worn it, I remained young. That is, until your father took it from me. That was seven years ago."

"And you think it's in my family vault?"

He nodded. "It has to be. They'll soon kill me if I don't return it. Hell, I think I'd rather that than be on the run again."

"You were never after the fortune?"

"No."

Mae backed away, struggling to catch her breath. She was relieved his aims hadn't centered around greed, but a sort of panic surged through her still, making her feel faint. Locke's discoveries seemed so impossible—alluring, even. It had filled her life with the sort of intrigue she thought limited to plays and books. But all that had taken on a dark and sinister turn.

With Locke, death seemed a certainty. Even if he returned the sapphire those men demanded, there was no knowing what they might do. If *he* was powerless against them, what was she to do? In the face of those men, she was little more than a lamb.

Self-preservation demanded that she escape this now. She couldn't be a party to his troubles and she couldn't continue down this path of romantic abandon. Sure, he was thrilling and at times good-natured, but she couldn't forget his scandalous occupation, nor his bloody past.

"Pierce and those men. They're dangerous…"

"Capable of *anything* for the sake of secrecy. I learned that much."

"But they've no interest in my fortune?"

"No."

Mae let out a breath. There might still be hope for her, then. She had to be sensible. She'd claim her fortune and that would be that. They'd go their separate ways. There'd be no more of this lusty, kissing nonsense. Whatever feelings she felt for the man, she must vanquish.

With money on the horizon, she had so many options. She knew what her family would have wanted her to do: regain her propriety and build new her reputation. They'd have wanted her to move to London, where she could find a nice fellow with a good name and head on his shoulders.

But after Locke's offer to travel, she knew that wasn't what *she* wanted. With money, she'd be able to travel all the same. But it wasn't just the travel that she saw in her future. Locke had been part of it too. Something that seemed so possible a moment ago had vanished before her eyes.

"Mae…"

She looked up, noticing Locke's sudden proximity. She must've gone still.

"What is it?" he asked.

"I'm sorry."

"What for?"

"For earlier." She stepped backward. "I had no intention of leading you on."

Locke swallowed, his soft expression hardening in less than an instant. "Why must you do this? Why must you *lie?*" He pulled her close. "You want me. I know you do."

"Well, I shouldn't." Mae yanked free, his presumption filling her with disgust. "The woman I was never would've considered you. It is only now that I am desperate and lonesome that my standards are thus lowered."

"I see." He clenched his teeth. "No need to explain any further. You're a lady and I'm a vagrant. Clear as glass."

She could sense the storm brewing beneath his features. Struck now with guilt, she wanted to take it all back. He had proved to be so much more than a vagrant. She was still alive, wasn't she?

"Perhaps if things were different…" she began. "If you had lived an honest life…"

"I suppose you think I'd be respectable, then. For what honor does a pirate have?"

"None, I'm afraid."

He looked up at the ceiling and shook his head. "You might fancy yourself a lady, but your father was a pirate."

Mae narrowed her eyes at his words. She could have said something even nastier right back, but she didn't.

"I still loved him," she ground out. "To me, he wasn't a pirate."

He laughed. "Countless dead men would say you are mistaken…"

"And you're no different, but you stuck your neck out for me and vagrant or not, you deserve my thanks. I simply can't be party to this. I can't be around when they—"

"I know," Locke said as though everything were so obvious. "Of course not. I never should have asked."

Mae leaned her back against the wall, wanting to shrink down all the way to the floor. The words, though insulting and hurtful, were no less true. He had not forgotten his past. And neither could she.

"I suppose I'll have to collect my share quickly." There would be plenty of time for her to escape unseen, she hoped.

"Oh, indeed. The sooner, the better." There was anger in his voice now, an anger she realized she had wanted to hear.

"You'll be able to take your fair share too." She tried to sound optimistic despite the guilt that swelled in her stomach.

"No need." Locke turned his back to her, looking down at whatever lay in his hand. "You'll have your family fortune—all of it save for the stone. Tell me, how much honor is that worth?"

"You'll change your mind."

"I give you my word." He twisted round, looking gravely offended.

"But it's entirely unnecessary. It's yours. It belongs to you." More than that, he needed it to live off.

After all he'd done and all that he'd promised to do, it was the least she could do to show her gratitude. But if anything, her adamant refusal must have seemed mocking to him because without another glance, he left for the balcony.

Mae settled herself back into the window nook.

Somewhere within the following hour, she fell asleep. When she woke, she was wrapped in a blanket. The gesture should have warmed her. Instead, it only made her feel cold.

CHAPTER FOURTEEN

The Stream

THE HEAT THE following day had become an unbearable blanket of moisture. Without the slightest warning, spring had ended and summer had taken hold. Trees once brimming with buds had burst to life. And still, they offered little shade. It didn't matter much that Mae and Locke had left late in the afternoon. Despite the woods that surrounded them, the searing sun still managed to break through as strong as ever.

Once again, Mae had no choice but to ride with him. They rode the same way they had before with her in front and him pressed against her back. Even though his arms still held her, he didn't feel nearly as close. Maybe it was just the heat. Rather than pull away too, she should have savored this. Who knew when she'd feel this way again? Or *if* she ever would. Soon, he would be only a memory.

A realization that filled her with dread. She didn't *want* to cast him aside—she only needed to. Now she feared she wouldn't have the strength. The hurt on his face in the theater the night before had been so clear. She didn't think she could bear it again. She hated even having to remember it. In this new silence between them, she only had her thoughts.

But as the day wore on, she was too tired to think about

anything. Despite her well-trained riding habits, she nearly slumped off Gambit. Against the stabbing rays of the sun, she could barely keep her eyes open.

Locke, however, seemed no worse for the wear. Though the tip of his nose was raw and a beard was beginning to take hold, his posture was tall and confident, his eyes piercing and alert.

She envied this side of him so unperturbed by their journey. Constant change, nothing static—that was the life in which he was accustomed and the type of life Mae realized she wanted too. All this time, she had rather hoped for it. For however long their fates were tied together, equally uncertain, she would savor it.

At last, they closed in on the enticing trickle of water. Hidden amongst the trees, they had circled for nearly an hour in search of it. Strewn with rocks baking in the sun, the haven spread wide between the trees. The glasslike water glistened like a mirage.

"What do you think?" Locke pulled back the reins and brought Gambit to a walk. "Does it suit you?"

"Suit me? Whyever not? I'm no dandy."

Now that they had found it, she was prepared to walk through fire and broken glass to reach it. Before Locke managed to jump down, she had already disappeared into the ravine.

A breeze whipped past, but not even that could cool her. In this heat, she wanted the water to envelop her from her toes to the very tip of her head.

With no regard for her heavy skirts, she splashed into the water. She didn't care if it stained the dress or knotted her hair. Here in the wilderness, she did not feel the least bit need to be ladylike.

The relief of the water was instant. In its cool embrace, the heat of the sun no longer seemed as potent. She leaned back, gasping as the water inched up her neck. The weightlessness of her long, often-tedious hair felt so freeing. With a deep sigh, she brushed her fingers straight through.

From shore, she heard Locke's footfalls and sat up. When he pulled his shirt up from over his head and threw it away, the night of the storm returned to her. The dark, menacing lines of his tattoos were exposed again.

"Hell's Teeth," she yelled out at him. "What does it mean?" The marking had to signify something other than an obscenity.

"It's nothing."

Though terse, they were the first words he had spoken in hours. Ever since the theater he had been so closed off. During the ride, she had grown tired of the silence, of constantly looking behind her to catch a glimpse of Pierce and his men. If they followed, there wasn't the smallest trace of it.

"It can't be *nothing*."

"Fine." He looked out at the water rippling around the rocks. "It was the name of my ship."

"What became of it?"

"Don't know. Left her rather abruptly…"

"It was my father's ship too, wasn't it? You left because he betrayed you somehow…" Mae hated the idea. These were things she thought impossible of her father. To her, he had never been a pirate. To her, he had been a different person entirely.

"Is that how you ended up in Tuscany?"

Locke didn't answer. He continued to look out into the water as it tumbled unstoppable over the rocks and fallen trees. She didn't need him to reply to know the answer was yes.

"Looks deep, eh?" He had walked up a large boulder jutting out from shore. "This part is quite still."

Mae shrugged, leaning her head back into the water again. When a loud splash erupted, she snapped up. He was gone. Several feet away, he bobbed above the water and flung back his hair.

Mae struggled to find the right place for her eyes. She was desperate to fill the silence, to keep him from falling silent again. "We'd have been done for if not for this stream," she said. "It saved us."

"Don't forget it can drown us too." Locke swam closer.

"Of course you know that best of all." She couldn't help but tease. "I can hardly imagine all the poor souls you forced to—what do they say? Walk the plank, is it?"

"Nah. They didn't drown. More often, the sharks got 'em."

"How horrid."

"That's why I never committed the act."

"I don't believe that for a second."

"I swear it. That sort of walk-the-plank business is simply done to amuse. I only ever killed out of necessity."

"Gold is necessity enough, I suppose."

"Survival, more often. But if the men had any wisdom, they surrendered at the mere whisper of my name."

"Or else what?" At his ego, Mae could not suppress the incredulity rising in her voice.

"Death."

The word brought out a quiet intensity in his gaze.

"No code of honor for pirates, is there?"

"On the high seas, the rules are simple: divide spoils equally and never steal from your own. Beyond that, it's fight well or die well. That code is half the reason I'm alive… Well, amongst other reasons." He tapped the serum that hung from his neck.

She could only imagine how important it might be at sea. Her mind filled at once with blades clashing and blood spraying. Whole limbs severed from their sockets.

The gore brought her back to the cellar. The horrible beating she had endured. *The man she had killed.* She didn't even know his name. All she could remember was his young, fearless face and that hissing that had yet to cease. She'd heard it that morning when she'd opened her eyes. The worst was she knew his agony. She knew how it felt believing she might die.

"Does it sicken you?"

Mae jolted out of her thoughts with some relief. "Of course."

She wanted to hate those London men just as she hated Ellsworth, but part of her wondered if they deserved her pity. What if it wasn't greed that had driven them to kill? What if it had been desperation? Hadn't she heard that in London, if one couldn't find work, they had no choice but to resort to violence to keep from starving? No one should have to live that way.

Rather than dream of more, maybe she should have been grateful for the quiet, easy life that had once been hers. As dull as servitude was, so many had even less.

"With or without honor, my crew and I lived well. Far better than most."

In that particularly cultured tone, he was getting defensive again. She had not the slightest clue why. He shouldn't give a whit what she thought. Even if they had almost… Even if she still wanted to.

"Do you think I enjoyed it? All those inevitable deaths?" he asked quietly.

Mae was surprised at his increased asperity. The tenseness she had endured all throughout their ride had returned. She could stand it no longer. He had to know her regard for him had improved. He was not the devil Mrs. Dorris had claimed him to be. The more she thought of it, the more she realized how wrong she had been. Even if it changed nothing, he had to know this.

"Locke, I meant every word in the theater. I don't—"

"No need to spare my feelings. No need to tell me you think I'm anything other than scum."

Scum? Mae wanted to laugh at the accusation. "And what, may I ask, is your opinion of me? After what my father did to you, I can only imagine what you must think of *me*."

"Your father…" Locke trailed off, struggling against a tumult of emotion. Mae's heart sank. These past atrocities blackened everything she'd thought her family had stood for. Whatever had happened, those dark days had bruised him. In the reflection of the water, his jaw clenched.

"I don't think you're scum." Mae thought she should clarify. "I don't think that in the least."

"Then divulge me the location of the vault."

"What? Why?" She looked down at her fidgeting hands. "You wouldn't need me anymore. Just like you no longer needed

Ellsworth."

"I gave you my word. But still you think I'd—"

"Why not?" It didn't matter that he had saved her life with that bizarre serum. With his true mission in mind, gold or no gold, it did not make things any clearer. They were entangled in this. She didn't know how long. Soon, he'd be off again. She would be gone from his life.

"Is not everything to you temporary?" she asked. "Even your promises?"

She did not know what more to say. She wished he hadn't brought it up at all so that they could go about the day with their troubles left behind.

"Rather, I think it's *you* who would abandon *me* at first chance. If you'd prefer to fend on your own, then perhaps I should oblige…"

A splashing forced her to look up. Locke was stomping through the water. For a moment, it seemed he was coming toward her. Mae floundered back, but he continued past her, toward shore. He found his coat and, fidgeting through the pockets, pulled out the key and left it there, shining atop a flat stone.

"Take it." He pointed at it then off into the quivering trees. "And go."

Silence stretched on for a moment. He was bluffing. If she so much as grabbed it, he was certain to stop her. Mae bundled her sopping skirts in one hand and inched forward nonetheless.

"This partnership will never work," he said.

She felt his eyes as she took up the key. Her heart pounded. The air between them intense. Cautious, Mae looked up at him. Water still beaded down his face, his hair dripping at the ends. A sharp wind blew past. In her soaked clothing, she shivered.

She had every reason to walk away. She might be able to elude Ellsworth and those other men, but she could never leave Locke to suffer them. She wouldn't. Not even close.

The part of her that had always been suspicious had begun to yield.

She took the heavy warmth of his hand and felt the slightest of tremors. It seemed to slip into her skin, rattling down into her core. The need to reassure him overwhelming.

This wasn't about his word. It was about hers.

Turning over his hand, she slapped the key onto his palm.

Around the key, Locke closed his grip, but instead of seeming pleased like she'd expected, he gave a grunt and broke away.

LOCKE STILLED HIS brush over Gambit, the rustle of Mae's skirts unsettling him. He tried to prepare himself. All this time between supper and sleep, he had failed to find a worthy explanation for his rash behavior. The mere *possibility* of her departure had unnerved him. A terrible feeling he didn't care to dwell on.

He turned his mind instead to more practical thoughts: any deals he might be able to negotiate with Pierce and the Silver Order. First, he needed to uncover any weaknesses they had—anything he might be able to overcome. He didn't even know Pierce's full name. But they knew his and seemingly so much more. He hated that they were still out there, watching his every step. Perhaps listening to his every word.

"Night's closing in." Mae approached. "Suppose Ellsworth, too, is following…"

Locke had no doubt of that. He had sensed it as soon as they had left town and returned to the main road. The only question was when he might strike. It would likely be yet another sleepless night.

She retreated and Gambit snorted. Locke frowned at him. He could not face Mae. Not yet.

He still hadn't come to grips with what he had risked earlier. It had been one of his more reckless acts. He had been panicked with self-doubt. If she left, he could do nothing about it.

Thoughts of the sapphire had not even occurred to him. He could only think of what might happen to her. All the danger that might suddenly close in. In the end, all he wanted was to protect her. Didn't she see that?

And yet, stay or go, it didn't matter. He could not protect her from the Silver Order, no more than he could give back the time he had stolen. A fact that stabbed into him, robbing him of relief. Her disinclinations toward him had not been far from the mark. Since the day he'd stolen that cursed sapphire, he had been chained to Pierce. For years, he had been willing to do anything to break free. All that he had done and said had been aimed toward that end. He was ashamed of his lies, his selfishness, the fact that Mae would have to suffer the same fate as he.

Her steps closed in again.

Locke braced himself for anger, but no, everything in her tone signaled hurt. "I simply want to know *why*. I've seen this all before. Something is eating at you. I know it's none of my affair, but—"

"Leave it alone." Locke brushed more furiously. Gambit snorted again and shifted away.

"Did you truly expect I'd take that key? Did you truly think I'd leave?"

"It doesn't matter." *Was it not obvious enough?* he wanted to demand. He didn't deserve her trust.

"I've given you false hope," he finally said. "You are immersed in this now. It doesn't matter if I give over the stone—those men might still kill us both. Even if you manage to take your share and escape…even if you run now. If they mean to find you, they will… I can't stop them. There'd be no use trying. Pierce and his men, they're too powerful."

"But—But…how can you know that?"

"I just do. The secrets they hold…there's too much at stake."

And they were no one. Two nobodies no one would ever miss.

Mae clenched at her throat, fear gripping her, like it had in the theater. In an apparent daze, she moved toward the shore. Locke steadied her, helping her settle atop a large, flat stone.

"Here." Locke retrieved the canteen near their makeshift picnic area. She swallowed a gulp. After some collective breaths, she composed herself.

"Tell me all you know. I'll not wait a moment longer."

Locke cleared his throat, the words as difficult to get out as they were to face. "I know nothing. I can't even be sure they're mortal." And there was no predicting what they might do to ensure the stone's secrecy. He could not even endure thinking of it. The possibilities came near to driving him mad.

"This sapphire. The day I found it… I cannot erase it. I cannot change what will happen because of it." He was powerless. More than he had been against any enemy. He might not care. He might even find Pierce's plans—in the end—quite freeing. But not anymore. He had other priorities. New things that he had never wanted before, he wanted now.

"There's a chance that they might still show us mercy," Mae said. "What would they want of me? After we surrender the stone, what would they want of you?"

"Nothing, I hope." But he did not like leaving their fates to mere chance. Anything he had ever achieved, he had fought for and won.

"Then we'll have to hope." Mae sounded heartened. "And have faith. Trust, too."

"I'm not one to trust. Not any more than I can be trusted. I lie," he exemplified. "I've lied to you."

"Yes. I imagine you've lied to me about many things." Mae stared down at her jittery hands. She clasped them tightly to keep them still.

He was glad she didn't demand more explanation. She wasn't trying to leave, either. Though perhaps she should.

"I have killed more people than I can count." He was a monster, hardly even a human being. Didn't she see that? "There's only one I truly regret. Only one that I can never let myself forget." And soon there might be another. He clenched his teeth, hating himself once more.

After some silence, Mae touched his arm. "Tell me."

Locke stilled at this request. There was so much more to say. Details he had told no one. And Mae could sense it. Though he wasn't so sure she would understand, he didn't want her asking other questions, either.

What if she started asking about his other promises and lies? He didn't have the courage to tell her what Ellsworth expected him to do. It was more likely he never would.

"I took no pleasure in killing." He thought he should explain once more. "It was the strategy I liked. The game of it. The challenge of capturing a ship without a simple drop of blood split. Death, however—"

"—was necessary. I believe you. You don't have to—"

"I'm no farmer, Mae. I've done more than kill a chicken or two…though feed us, it did." He turned to her, a sudden flash of grief hit, but as quickly as it came, he steeled himself.

"We only ever battled the able-bodied. It was the high seas. A dangerous place as it was. So we rarely faced the weak and unabled. Least of all women."

His eyes focused back on her wavering reflection in the water, expecting some sort of outrage at that last damning word. He watched as she gathered her skirts and shifted closer. The steady humming of his heart was louder than the buzzing cicadas.

If she was wise, she would tell him to stop. A large part of him hoped she would. He had warned her about his past for a reason. There were dark things she would not want to know. Particularly this story. When it was over, any trust he had garnered would vanish. A man was only as good as his company. She would see that he was a criminal, nothing more.

"We infiltrated a whole fleet," he continued—toward his downfall. "With skill. Catching them off the coast of Veracruz, we blended in like one of their own. Then we waited for the proper moment. It was flawless, really. Perfect planning. Taking the first ship, we raised no alarms." He gripped a loose stone and tossed it skipping over the stream.

"But once we'd secured the survivors, I knew something was wrong. Just a sense, a sort of hunch. So I had my men search the ship. I remember hearing shouts.

"Her name was Mary. She was a captive, being held for god-knows-what depravities. I could see blisters along the skin of her wrists and all over, she was shaking. Of course I demanded her release. Gave her food, set her to rights. She wouldn't tell me much at first. But I wagered with her. After she had calmed a bit, I brought her on deck and turned her to the fleet, their great sails billowing in the calm. I told her if she could tell me the ship bearing the most cargo, the most wealth, I'd give her freedom and even some money to live off."

"But how could she know?"

"She'd sailed with them for months, she said. Was once a personal…" He hesitated, searching for a discreet word. "*Servant* to the captain. I simply asked her which ship he seemed to talk of most…and captured it."

Mae's eyes widened. They had indeed made off with a great deal of gold that day and yet it had never felt like a victory. What had happened had prevented that.

"We were miles away from the galleon…"

Locke trembled in the still, warm air. The sky had turned a blackish blue, the trees before them fuzzy around the edges. The stream had long ago faded into the darkness. Its presence marked only by a steady gurgling.

"What happened?"

"She died… and at the hands of my men… Lord knows how she suffered. I had to force myself to look. One glance. That's all it took." His voice hardened.

He would never know the full extent of his men's crimes. Didn't want to. "I left her in her own private quarters, locked the door. Told her she'd be safe."

"You can hardly blame yourself for their actions," Mae whispered, her hand hovering over his but not quite making contact. "You'd promised her freedom. You had a deal…"

"It proved not to hold much merit." He imagined again the flash of metal against the dead woman's throat. He knew that much had happened. If only he had done something at the first sign of abuse, come up with an agreement, an excuse to keep her to himself. "I would have been able to set her free at the first port."

"How could your men—"

"'You had no use of her,' they said, the three of them all in agreement. Your father was not among them."

Mae looked down.

"I was too angry to think. I punished them right then and there with my pistol. At times, I still think that was too merciful."

"They got what they deserved," Mae said grimly.

"Didn't change what had happened."

"Still. That wasn't your doing."

"But I had been one of them. For years." He went rigid as more pain pitched in his chest. New this time. Despite his best efforts, the past had repeated itself. With Ellsworth, he had been on the side of evil again.

Not a thousand virtuous acts could undo that mistake. He knew how Mae had perceived him. She thought he was purely after his own gains. But that wasn't true. At least not entirely. Keeping Ellsworth at bay had been a sort of comfort, a reminder they weren't truly the same. Perhaps he had always been soft beneath his steel exterior—which had been the mask he could no longer tell.

"If only I had abandoned smuggling after that Spanish fleet," he thought aloud. "Damn it, I wish I had." The sapphire would still have been in Pierce's possession. At least then Mae might have been safe. He would have lived his life already. If he'd lived long enough to see sixty, Mae wouldn't even have given him a second glance.

"But—why didn't you?"

"Greed." He sniffed. "Hardly clears my name, does it? At least not amongst decent society."

Mae shook her head. "Everyone, even those in high society, carries something dark and regrettable in their past. My family did for nearly two centuries."

Locke could not allow the statement to give him hope. He threw another stone, this one plunking straight down.

"You can't just take the sapphire, you know. You need money. If you do survive those men, how will you live?"

"Men like me don't live so long. It's not right."

He could never find the peaceful life he had craved for so long—not with all he'd done and what might still happen. If Mae's death was all the world had left for him…the best he could hope for was a peaceful end. That had been all he'd wanted since the start: to die not as a criminal or outlaw on the run, but as a free man.

The wound to his heart she'd given him in the theater would be his last, he decided. It certainly ranked painful enough. He'd wanted no more like it. He'd fulfill his promises to the Silver Order and be done with it. At least die with some honor. Perhaps even convince them to do the job.

He had always wanted impossible things. Death, for once, was easy. There wasn't much chance Pierce would let him live, anyway. Those men would be more than happy to do the honors. He was sure of that.

"Don't be ridiculous." It seemed to take Mae a moment to fully see the truth in his words. When she did, she grasped his arm, the color draining from her face. "You wouldn't…" Any other words seemed lost on her.

He swallowed a lump like acid, relieved that at least one person found no joy in it. So relieved, he wanted to pull her into him, just as he had in the theater…

At a sound, Mae turned away.

"We're quite safe here." He tried to reassure her. "In a forest littered with leaves, I'd hear anyone from afar." An attack that was more likely to happen at night than day.

She wasn't listening. "What if there's something you can do to stop Pierce? What if—"

"Then I'll do it. No matter what the price." Touching her arm, he brought her gaze back to him. "I won't go back on my word. I will return the stone and from the vault, I'll take nothing else. I swear to you."

MAE ROSE EARLY beneath another searing sun. Locke was already gone from his adjacent yet distant spot next to her. All the blankets had been gathered in a pile between them. That warm night, a barrier had been their only purpose.

Shielding the sun from her eyes, she looked out. The water glistened brightly in the morning sun. A flock of ducks down the shore didn't seem to notice them, even when Mae had slipped into the stream.

Locke too had been drawn to the water. Out in the stillness, he floated with arms stretched over his head. At the sight of him, any fear she had felt the night before seemed to dissipate. No matter how invincible Pierce and his men were, Mae didn't care. She was confident Locke could overcome them. She didn't know why, only that they had gotten this far. So how could they fail now? Perhaps it was naïve, but she believed in him, in all his pirate strength and strategy. Even if he didn't believe in himself, *someone* had to.

She glided out farther from shore, her toes sinking deeper into the warm, muddy sand. A cool breeze cut through the thick curtain of heat. The trees swayed restlessly behind her, reflected in the glasslike water.

The stillness reminded her of a nightmare she had had. The man in the cellar had been there; so had the blows she could only recall in bits and pieces.

"What might we have for breakfast?" she called out to Locke. She hoped that if she could ignore the memories long enough, she might forget them too. This morning, it seemed slightly easier to do.

"Should be some bread left."

"Not again," Mae grumbled. They had eaten nothing but bread and cheese for two days now. Luckily, she hadn't much of an appetite. More than eating, she wanted to enjoy the calm she knew couldn't last.

Used to the water now, Mae tilted her head back, trying not to notice how it made her neck tighten with pain. She jolted when Locke's shadow crossed over her.

"Try floating on your back."

Mae snapped up. "How do you mean?"

"Float in the water face-up," he said. "I find it much more comfortable."

"I've never heard of such a thing."

"Straighten out your legs and lean back." He demonstrated.

"What? No."

They exchanged unyielding glances. Though some distance had remained, the tenseness from the day before had gone entirely.

"Oh, come now." He righted himself. "Trust me. It's most comfortable."

The word *trust* hovered between them. Locke had almost flinched at the word. *Of course I trust you*, she wanted to say. Despite all that had happened, how he had used her and made it possible for Ellsworth to near-kill her, she had stayed. If any good had come from Pierce and his men, they had at least opened her eyes to the things he really wanted, transforming him in every way.

And she was determined to prove to him that he was a new man. Maybe then, he could be persuaded into taking some of the fortune. They had to survive those men. Just had to. He deserved to live a free and peaceful life. They both did.

"Fine." She lifted her chin in challenge. "I'm not afraid."

His crossed arms suggested he would not concede until she obeyed, anyway. So against the calm expanse, she lowered her shoulders backward and straightened out her legs. A breath of reluctance caught in her chest.

"Just relax." He stretched his arms out beneath her. Mae breathed out, still feeling some nervousness burn in the pit of her stomach.

She felt as if he were a magician ready to make her levitate in front of a crowd of onlookers. When he pulled his hands away, she struggled not to flinch. With her head half-submerged in water, she held perfectly still. For a moment, she didn't breathe.

To her astonishment, nothing happened. She was like a feather, floating weightless in the water's easy embrace. She took in the bright-blue sky and the tips of trees arching and shuddering against the wind.

It was all so beautiful. She had seen the same sky and trees, yes. But from that perspective, the sight was different somehow.

Locke's sudden grip brought her back to reality. She stared as if to see him for the first time. From that angle, he had not the look of a villain. Covered in moisture, he was iridescent in the sunlight—not entirely the pirate he was supposed to be, nor the rigid gentleman society had planted in her mind.

Suddenly, the prospect of never seeing him again made her ache. How could she even consider it? The thought evoked a feeling that seemed to freeze her up so she couldn't breathe, couldn't think. Locke and his way of life had intrigued her from the first. Since then, they had grown close, she felt, closer than she had allowed anyone to get to her in years. And yet, he was more lost to her than the stream that slipped between her fingers and continued toward the sea.

Did he sense it too?

Gathering her balance along his shoulders, she studied him. For a moment, they were frozen in time, the stream passing carelessly between them, until, quite suddenly, he found her lips.

It was familiar, like something they had done for centuries. The feel of him as natural and soothing as the water around her. She was blissfully weightless again, a leaf caught in the current. His grip all that held her in place.

But this wasn't like the theater. The truth of him had been such a revelation then, the road before them so open.

Rather, this kiss was subdued, a goodbye of sorts. Anything more would have been a lie. And that would have been too cruel.

Pulling away, they met each other's eyes in silence. A most heart-wrenching silence that left her despondent and continuing forward on their journey only because they must. She would have much rather stayed there at that stream. If not for the men following, she might have lived there with him forever.

CHAPTER FIFTEEN
The Cave

MAE KNEW THEY were close when the cawing of seagulls and the salty smell of sea intensified. She was glad she hadn't bothered to braid her hair that morning. It felt so freeing letting the wind take it in every direction.

There was a certain freshness in the air, too, as if with summer, the earth had become new and young again.

When the ever-expanding ripples of blue came into view, she could practically *taste* her freedom. They'd had to travel all afternoon to get there, but it had been worth it. They were finally here.

Flanked by tall grasses and a scarcity of trees, they followed a dirt road. Everything was just as she remembered. All except for one thing.

Inland from the coastal cliff, the building that had once been Crow's Nest, her family's old summer cottage, was boarded shut. Cast in the shadow of a drifting cloud, it appeared isolated and abandoned. The roof had caved in and its shutters hung crooked. Several large cracks ran up the plaster from the foundation. At one of the corners gapped a jagged hole. She winced at the thought of the vermin living inside.

In the garden, not a single vibrant flower had managed to

survive. The jasmine and fuchsias lost forever. Instead of a shock of colors, leaves and dead foliage piled high, overtaking the front gate and the stone path that led to a now-gray door.

All of it a reminder that her childhood and its happy memories were no more. The life that had once been hers some strange, half-remembered dream.

She closed her eyes, hoping the wild sounds of the waves and the hard thrust of the spring wind would bring her back to happier times. Instead, only painful memories surfaced.

They reached the edge of the cliff. The birds looked as they always did, sailing, drifting—

"Mae?" Locke jolted her. "The vault…"

"Of course." Mae turned her thoughts to the present. There was really only one place she could imagine it being hidden.

"That way." Still tucked in front of him, she pulled forward and pointed toward the steepest cliff overlooking the ocean. She hoped she was right. Otherwise, who knew how long they'd be searching? Then again, maybe a long search wouldn't be so bad. Miles ago, she had given in and decided to savor their closeness for however long it lasted. Getting comfortable in his arms was just too easy. "Toward the cliff?"

Mae turned over her shoulder and met his gaze. "I can show you better from there."

Gambit ambled forward, but the path did not prove easy. Jutting rocks forced them to take to their feet. With no trees nearby, Locke anchored a rope between two stones and left enough length to allow Gambit to graze.

"Careful," Locke reached out to grasp and ungrasp Mae's hand as they navigated the rocks. "You don't want to twist an ankle."

The closer they got, the harder the wind pushed, almost as if to force them back.

Locke stood tall to take in the dark, turbulent sea, the surrounding boulders and the pale grass. "There's nothing here."

"We have to climb down."

"Down there?" His eyes widened.

"Yes." Mae jabbed her boot into a break in the stone. "Don't tell me you're afraid."

William had managed to climb the cliff at age eleven, no less. Looking back now, perhaps it had been a bit of training so that one day, he'd be ready to find their inheritance she was sure lay somewhere below.

Locke wiped the sweat from his forehead. "I'm fearful for you is all."

Mae laughed, the sound of it washed away by the roaring waves. Killed countless men but nervous at a little climb? The thought amused her. There was nothing to be fearful of. With so many protruding stones and a gentle slope, Mae found the descent rather easy.

At the bottom, she wiped her hands and began to loosen and pull off her boots.

"What are you doing?" Locke jumped down from the cliff face.

She pointed to a small bay enclosed by a series of boulders. Then, undoing her buttons, she removed her bodice. "We have to swim. There's an underwater cave. You'll see."

When she moved her hand up her thigh to untie the ribbons of her stockings, Locke cleared his throat and turned around.

"Almost done," she reassured him. With her fortune and freedom in sight, now was no time for modesty. Finally, she pushed her skirts and petticoats past her hips.

Wearing nothing but her chemise, corset, and drawers, she bid him to turn around.

"Are you sure about this?" he cautioned. "It's chilly and it'll be pitch—"

Mae dove in, feeling the rush of icy water prick at her skin. She did her best to ignore the pain and swam with more force. In the sunless cave, the water became cooler and somehow thicker, darker, denser. But after a few more tense strides, she popped her head up above the surface. She shivered in the cold, the sight sending an even stronger chill down her body.

Just as Mae remembered, the cave ceiling shimmered with the blue illumination of tiny, worm-like creatures—their numbers well into the thousands. On the surface, the water shone sharp blue from a kind of glowing algae. The unearthly glow was so strong, it reached every corner of the cavern.

She could still imagine William sitting on the rocky shore, his eyes wide with wonder as he marveled at the biology of the strange yet magnificent worms. Somehow, being in that cave made her feel closer to him. As though in this cave seemingly made of magic, a part of him still lived on.

Disrupting the silence, Locke broke through the water. He opened his mouth not to speak, but in complete awe.

"Beautiful, is it not?"

"I've seen these creatures before. At night, they roll along the waves lighting up the darkness with color." He slicked his hair back from his eyes. "But I've never seen them in a cave."

Locke swam forward and lifted himself onto a wide ledge of the stone. Stripped down to nothing but his breeches, every hard line of his body gleamed in the blue glow. The bottle that hung at his chest, usually hidden beneath his clothes, stood out most of all, the brightest blue she'd ever seen.

"The place looks empty." He studied the stone walls. "There has to be a hidden door."

Mae climbed onto the ledge and began searching too. But in the small space, there was no sign of anything. Not even rocks that might have covered a clue.

"It has to be here." She searched along the ground, her bare feet scraping away at the sand. They went on like this for some time. Then, finally, Mae saw a glitter of blue in the sand.

"Here!" She motioned, excitement rushing through her veins. Locke was at her side in a moment, throwing back heaps of sand to reveal a reflective, metal latch. He tugged, but to no avail.

"I'll need to retrieve my tools."

"Where are they?" Mae asked.

"In Gambit's saddlebags—"

"Then I shall retrieve them."

"No, it's too dangerous. Ellsworth is still out there—"

"Exactly, and I can climb faster than you can." Mae turned around and began to twist back her hair.

"No," he said flatly. "You're under my protection and I say *no.*"

"I will only be a second."

"Mae, wait—" Locke yelled after her in protest, but before he could reach out and stop her, she'd taken the plunge once more. This time, the water felt colder. Even in the warm, afternoon sun, she continued to shiver in her sopping-wet underthings.

As Mae began her ascent up the cliff, her limbs ached too. While she had expected agility, her arms, her legs—her entire body—had gone stiff. Overpowered by exhaustion, her strength was finally fading.

She had expected it. They had spent too long riding without so much as a second's pause. She could sleep standing if she wanted to. But somehow, she pressed on. Perhaps it was pure optimism fueling her.

Half-undressed as she was, she didn't even feel the slightest bit cold. Dropping her heavy bodice and skirts had actually been quite freeing.

With Pierce and his men nowhere in sight, she couldn't help considering more of what the future held. Locke's words still rang in her head. *"The point is that you have to see it for yourself."* Maybe she would take his advice.

But in addition to excitement, she felt a sense of longing too. If she survived this, she would be alone again and of all the people she should miss, she thought only of Locke.

He had been right about so much. At the estate, she'd had nothing to hold on to. Any honor her family had held had been falsehoods. She couldn't continue to live within that lie and in that home. The pride she had once felt as a Blackthorne had all but disappeared. She could see no honor in the deaths her father had handed out for the sake of gold. In the end, William had died because of it. His downfall had started at the sea, where he'd plundered in the name of greed. Even if he hadn't died due to his own greed, he'd died due to another man's—Ellsworth's.

She still could not understand why her brother hadn't told her the truth about their family's profession in the first place. At the same time, maybe it was obvious. Hadn't he always treated her like a blissfully ignorant girl unknowing in the ways of men? Her only hope for success a marriage that might enhance the family connection? She hadn't even succeeded at that.

She could imagine what they might say about her going against the family and pairing with Locke. How it was just like her to defy them.

How it was just like her not to care.

She struggled her fingers into another stone, the climb far more difficult than the descent. She would not give up, though. She fought harder, at last pulling herself over the edge.

She fell onto the sandy stone, heart thumping, struggling to catch her breath. She dared not rest long. Between the grasses, she caught a flicker of Gambit's coat. Some yards out from the cliff's edge, he was well hidden. They both were. How clever of her family, indeed. The tall grasses that surrounded her kept away any onlookers. She wondered how long these plans went back, if they—

Breathless, she stopped in her tracks. A twig had snapped in close proximity. Just as she was hidden, so was the intruder. She was too tired to run, too far from Locke. How long might it be before he came looking? Before he realized something was amiss?

Someone called her name. The voice sounded familiar and so strangely harsh.

Then a hand seized her wrist, and out of the tall grasses, Miss Clarissa Rosewood stepped into view.

$$\smile$$

LOCKE CLEARED AWAY more of the sand. Barely able to see, he felt along the hard metal. The trap door wasn't the same as the one they had encountered in the cellar. It wouldn't reveal a vault below. This *was* the vault. And it had a keyhole. He need only…

Locke stopped himself. His partnership with Mae demanded he wait, but after all his years on the run, he could not. He had become overwrought with impatience.

He pulled the key out from his jacket and twisted it hard in the lock. Sealed with rust and grime, the hatch opened with a crack, a puff of stale air rising in its wake.

The fog cleared slowly, revealing an even more glittering blue. The light seemed to mesmerize, beckoning him down a rusty ladder and deep within the underground cavern.

The stored-up fortune that encompassed nearly two centuries of successful piracy held true to every expectation.

Twinkling in the glow of the blue creatures, piles upon piles of Spanish gold hadn't lost their luster. Overwhelmed by a scattering of silver coins, the floor—whether stone or sand— hadn't been visible.

He counted forty crates, most of them stacked to form leaning, precarious towers. Others lay on their sides, the stones spilling out as abundant and haphazard as dirt from a wheelbarrow.

Though none of it seemed arranged at first, he was sure a small valley down the center marked a pathway. As he walked along, various stones crunched beneath his feet. He recognized a gold-and-ivory pistol he had recovered during the War. Years later, he had given it to Alastair as a birthday present, only to find it here discarded. *The bastard.*

A short distance down, he passed a whole pile of granulated gold jewelry. He remembered Nathaniel, the man who had been as good as a father to him, carrying it by the armful, a burning ship at his back.

Locke was walking through time, it seemed, toward the very beginning of the Blackthornes' reign at sea. The cave had been set up that way. There was no doubt in his mind. On the cavern's walls, distinct, white lines marked the generations to which the spoils belonged. Toward the back, the piles were shorter, though bricks of gold, emeralds, and uncut diamonds were by far the largest.

Finding the sapphire would not take days, as he had feared. As with a long hall of carefully organized shelves, he need only search for Alastair's loot and focus his efforts there.

He stepped between the proper white lines and combed through whole crates of gems, overturning each one he crossed. Chests of every size littered the area as big as a sitting room—all of them disappointments. Then, buried beneath a glittering of coins, he saw the smallest yet. Although it was wooden like all the others, this one had a lock.

He didn't have time to dawdle. Without thinking, he slammed it against the stone wall. Amidst the explosion of wooden shards, he caught a tiny square of velvet. He picked off a few wood shards and unfolded it. At once, he recognized the sapphire's deep-blue hue and unique silver encasing. Amongst all the others, its brilliance had no rival.

Blue like the deepest ocean, the stone looked the same as it had the day he'd discovered it. And like that fateful day, his life had taken a dangerous turn. The thing was bad luck.

Damn it, was it beautiful, though.

Despite all the gems, pearls, and other treasures that cluttered the cavern, he wanted nothing more. Save for the sapphire, he was happy to leave it all behind.

MAE YELPED, HER exhaustion a part of the past as she embraced Miss Rosewood. But Mae felt no warmth in it, no grip pulling her in.

"How did you get here?" Mae looked around for her horse

and spotted none. She must have come with someone, then. But whom? She couldn't imagine Mr. or Mrs. Rosewood indulging their daughter on such a wild goose chase.

Miss Rosewood's face soured. "I should ask you the same."

Mae had no answer, no explanation. Stupefied, she stood silent.

"You're here with *him*, aren't you?"

"Miss Rosewood—"

"It's true." Her words seemed to condemn. "I didn't believe it at first. I said Ethan would never hurt me thus, but Mr. Ellsworth insisted. He said he saw you."

How could she have mistaken him for this slip of a young lady? *He* had been the figure in the window watching their departure.

"Ellsworth?" Mae grabbed Miss Rosewood's arm. "Where is he?"

"We tried to get you alone," Miss Rosewood said, unaffected. "When you reached this place we had no choice. We waited for you two to separate, but not once was Ethan out of your sight. Not once were you left vulnerable and alone, as I was."

"Miss Rosewood—"

A set of footsteps closed in behind her. Locke. She wished he had stayed away. The fact that, like herself, he was scantily dressed—and soaked—only seemed to cement their crimes. To any outsider, it would seem as though they were on holiday.

Miss Rosewood looked back and forth between them, her face paling. Though the silence seemed an eternity, it still wasn't long enough to explain.

"All this time," Miss Rosewood said, befuddled. "You were with a governess?"

Not *my* governess, Mae noted. Merely *a* governess.

"Miss Rosewood…" Mae struggled to take control.

"How?" she demanded. "How could you do this?"

"You should not have followed us."

"Because I'd see the truth in all your lies. Because I'd finally realize your treachery!"

"No, Miss Rosewood. Think of your reputation. Your parents must be terrified for you. Running off with some man…"

Save for the tears swimming beyond her lashes, Miss Rosewood gave no reaction. In Miss Rosewood's mind, Mae had betrayed her in every sense of the word. And there was little hope of undoing this. Despite all her hopes and plans, Mae wished she could give it all back. She didn't want to earn her fortune in sin.

"This isn't safe. Ellsworth isn't safe," Mae went on. "He's deceiving you."

"It is *you* who has been deceiving me. Mr. Ellsworth… He has been nothing but kind."

"You must believe me." She could not let Miss Rosewood fall into Ellsworth's trap, not as her brother had.

Before Mae could think to offer an apology, Miss Rosewood was off into the grasses.

Mae started after her, but Locke pulled her back. He seemed to sense that danger was near. Mae knew it with certainty. Ellsworth had followed them, as they both had feared. Like Miss Rosewood, he was hiding somewhere in the grasses. Their carriage and horses had to be somewhere out of sight too. Wherever he was, Ellsworth already knew they were there.

Wasting no time, Locke untied his horse and swung his leg over. Mae grabbed his outstretched hand.

Together once more, they seemed safe. Gambit had already begun to gallop away. They had even managed to make it inside of a clearing. Then came the sound of a gunshot. Startled, Gambit reared, his forelegs kicking circles in the air as they flew backward.

Only minutes ago, she had felt so determined, her climb up that cliff both arduous and worthwhile. Now her body flew airborne.

Landing took the breath from her lungs. White stars whirled across her vision. When they cleared, her worst fears materialized. Some distance away, Ellsworth came nearer.

She was a fool to think she could one day leave England. In truth, she might never escape.

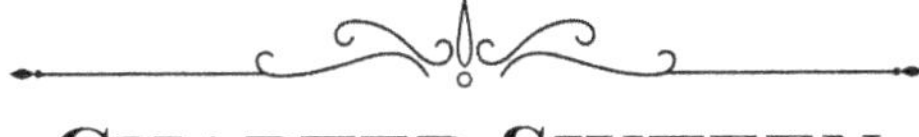

CHAPTER SIXTEEN

The Invitation

MAE INCHED AWAY as a river of blood cut through the grass. For a moment, she feared it was her own. But as Mae lifted her head, Locke's unmoving body came into view, the sharp edges of a rock protruding from his back.

A scream of dread seemed to empty her. She cast aside any thought of running. Thief or not, he was the only one to help her attain freedom from poverty, who believed she was meant for something better. The only one in the world she trusted. Finally, Locke would know it. Seeing her at his side, he would not have a doubt.

If only his eyes would open.

Where was the Silver Order?

Desperate for mercy, she looked skyward. Ellsworth came forward, his figure blocking her view. He hadn't broken his cruel, serpent-like gaze, and in the blinding light of the midday sun, a knife glistened menacingly.

"Miss Rosewood?" Mae made her out, standing arms crossed amongst the grasses. But behind her angry glare, she saw no pity. Her former pupil merely watched as Ellsworth dropped down from his horse and tore through Locke's pockets. A silver chain with a strange sort of blue stone pendant thudded to the ground.

The sapphire, Mae nearly screamed out. Ellsworth, thankfully, paid no heed to the seemingly useless trinket nor the strange bottle that hung at his neck, not when his focus was on finding the key. It took only a moment for him to find it in Locke's other pocket. He snatched away Mae's only future then took aim with his knife, daring her to object.

She remained unmoving. What did death matter? With Locke lying so helpless like that, she wanted the same fate.

"The vault's location." Ellsworth came upon her and grabbed the back of her neck.

Mae pressed her lips together, her skin stinging from his grip. "I'll lie," she spit out. "Just to see another one of your men suffocate."

"I do have a hostage, remember. She's ruined, yes, but that's still better than being dead *and* ruined."

When she remained silent, he shook her. "Tell me *now*."

Again she was silent.

Ellsworth turned the blade over, its gold hilt facing her. "Very well."

The hit reverberated in her ears before she felt it. The pain came slowly, settling deep within her skull. For a brief moment, she wanted to shatter. Then she felt an anger all her own.

"You deserved that," Ellsworth said. "So did your brother. That night when you thought I left? Well, I snuck back in. I made sure your brother got what he deserved too."

The strike pulsed with scorching heat. But Mae would not let that faze her. She secured herself along Locke's still body, gripping and shaking him. Even Gambit had been nudging his foot with his snout. If not Locke, *someone* had to make Ellsworth pay for what he had done.

Her hand graced across his belt. Feeling the cool metal of a blade, a sudden idea chilled her.

She had no choice. It was a simple trade, really. Seconds of violence for a lifetime of regret. She knew now she could never erase what she had done in the cellar. Nor could she reason it away.

The reasons didn't seem to matter. It didn't change what she had done, what she had taken away.

Her fingers wrapped around the hilt. The blade was unique with a smooth, onyx stone that winked at her in the sunlight. She swallowed. Whatever injuries she endured, if she lived, she could find Locke's healing serum. How could she have forgotten that? With it, she could cure Locke's injuries too. She had only to free them of Ellsworth.

She owed Locke this. He, she was certain, would have done the same for her. *Had* done the same for her.

The sun shone brightly over her, heating her skin. All the while, Ellsworth's knife, now righted, came closer. Beads of sweat swelled along Mae's forehead. The bugs, wind, the rustling leaves—everything fell away.

Knife fights never lasted long, according to some of her father's tales. Just another part of her past that added up to Locke's accusations. She could deny it no longer. Feeling a savage anger begin its steady release, she would finally live up to her family name and kill again.

Fearless now, Mae took a deep breath. Ready for Ellsworth to make one wrong move and end his life in a flash, she swiped the blade from Locke's waist. Though she expected to hear a *ping* of metal, a louder sound erased it.

Hooves trampled across the dry, dead grass. Branches snapped like gunshots.

Mae twisted around, frantic. A circle of men riding horseback closed in, her hair blowing wild from the rush.

Ellsworth looked around and began to step back, his eyes, uneasy. Whoever these horsemen were, they didn't belong to him.

Within the frenzy, Locke came to.

"Mae." Locke coughed, his eyes on the knife shaking in her hands. For a moment, she was still lost in the frenzy, frozen in shock.

"Mae," he repeated.

This time, she heard him. Still shaking, she dropped the knife.

Ellsworth and Miss Rosewood had disappeared. They'd already begun their retreat to wherever their carriage and horses lay hidden within the grasses.

"On their heels," a hooded man prompted.

Dressed in long, black cloaks, the horsemen were the same they had met in the theater. She recognized Pierce's tall posture and broad build instantly, though his presence was different now. She wasn't afraid. As silly as it was, she was grateful. She should have feared these men more than Ellsworth. Her and Locke's fates in their hands might very well be no different. They would die here in turmoil, not peace.

On the ground still, Mae had enough wits about her to pick up the silver chain Ellsworth had dropped and hand it to Locke. He gave her a weak smile and pulled her close, his right arm drawn across her chest. Only then did she remember how scantily she was dressed.

"He wanted something from you." Pierce galloped closer. It wasn't a question, but a statement, maybe even a prediction.

"What can I say? I am a man of intrigue." Locke beamed, the pain of his back seemingly no more.

"And a man of your word?"

Locke held up a silver chain and thrust it forward. A glinting sapphire encased in silver filigree swung back and forth from the movement.

Now that she had the chance to take it in, the jewel was unlike any she had ever beheld. It twinkled, not reflecting the dim light of the overcast sky, but from a sort of light source within. It was almost as if it were alive.

"Take it," Locke grunted. But Pierce didn't move an inch.

"Just like that? You don't wish to negotiate a price? It was, after all, fairly stolen."

"I owe you a debt." Locke looked off in the direction Ellsworth had taken. Pierce had saved their lives and they both knew it.

"So you owe me a favor." Pierce pulled back his hood, smiling.

"No. We are square."

"Keep the sapphire a moment longer." Pierce waved a hand of dismissal "We make our trade soon."

"I wish to be rid of you now."

"I'm afraid that's no longer possible." For a tense moment, they locked eyes.

What could they do? Surrounded by horses, they couldn't run.

Mae shrieked when someone yanked her upward and secured her arms. The hardness of a chest pressed against her back, falling and rising with each nasally breath.

"Don't." Locke took to his feet. His voice was fierce but breathless from the pain. "We go of our own accord."

He placed the necklace around his neck. Mae expected a transformation of sorts, for him to take on a new, immortal glow. But he remained unchanged. Just as he had for decades before her father had taken the necklace and locked it away in the vault. That time had added seven years to his once unaging life, putting him in his early thirties, when in truth he should have been much grayer. She could not forget how remarkable this all was.

"One conversation is all I ask."

"Fancy that. If I'd known—" Locke widened his stance and put his hands on his hips.

"Where are your clothes?" Pierce drawled.

"Down on the beach," Locke answered.

"Get them," Pierce ordered one of his men. Turning back to Locke, Pierce seemed to make sudden note of the blood still spilling onto the grass. "You need assistance with that?"

"Not at all." Locke lifted the serum from around his neck and raised it high, as if in toast. Instantly, it began to glow. With a nod, he took a tiny sip. "I still find your tools useful these days."

Pierce's men laughed, a low rumble that shook the ground.

Gambit, dragged along by one of Pierce's men, pulled up beside them.

"Don't worry," Locke said into Mae's ear, the breath of comfort hardly enough to ease her fears.

But following Pierce, there was no knowing what cold, dark place they might end up in now.

☾

LOCKED WATCHED THE red ember of a sun slide beneath the horizon. Atop Gambit, Mae and Locke had been traveling in and out of rain. At least the evening had turned warm.

As much as Locke wanted to hide his face beneath his collar, he had made a point of mapping their route. At first, he wasn't familiar with the unpaved, overgrown road they traveled. But during the course of the ride, it became fascinatingly clear. They were traveling on old Roman roads. He was sure of it. After coming inland for quite some time, they had landed on a route that ran north. The path was ancient and overgrown, yes, but probably the most direct. Very few knew about them and most known routes were incomplete. But flanked by ditches and slightly arched, the road was suited for all weather. He believed it had been paved once too. The occasional flat stone was hidden beneath a mossy overgrowth.

Wherever they were headed, it couldn't have been far if they were traveling horseback. Mae could easily find her way to London. From London, she could go anywhere. If he helped her escape that far, would she still insist they separate?

If only they could claim just ten percent of what was in that cave. They could have had a simple life, a nice manor on the coast not too far from town, but with enough land for riding. There would be no men to give them chase. Instead, there would be her face in the morning and his lips on hers at night. Everything about that kind of life enticed him. Nothing, not even the thrill of the raging sea, could hold a candle to it.

He would like to think it was possible. Something in her gaze when he'd come to had given him that hope. Still, there was no ignoring the well-armed guards, nor the power Pierce seemed to hold in his eyes alone.

Locke clenched his teeth. With the sapphire in Pierce's hands again, this business was supposed to be finished. He had no clue what else Pierce wanted, either. Not even an inkling.

He readjusted his grasp around Mae's waist, his cloak protecting her completely from the rain. She was safe for now, but for how long? He had to stay focused. He could not let himself get distracted. He would hold true to his promise. She would have her fortune and her freedom. He would do more than try. He would do everything in his power. It was all that mattered to him now. Sapphire be damned.

He lifted the cloak that shielded Mae's face. The blow Ellsworth had delivered had stopped bleeding. It was now just a swirl of black and blue. He covered her again. He hated seeing her like that and even considered supplying her with a drop of the serum. But it belonged to Pierce and who knew what he might ask in exchange.

She seemed at peace, anyway. She snored lightly, her body twitching every now and then. Was she dreaming? What kind of things did a woman like Mae dream?

In the past few days, his own had taken on a whole new theme. They were no longer sequences of blood sprays and fallen men. They were of a more pleasant variety. In each of them— often set in his woods or the endless expanse of the moors—she was just a glimmer of an image, a hazy apparition.

Dear God, what *was* she dreaming? They had likely turned to nightmares. Did she see Ellsworth now? That blade running into her shoulder that night in the cellar? The face of the man she had killed?

He wanted to wake her, only reality wasn't much better.

He'd give anything to change their stars and make new their

fates. But no matter what he did, danger loomed closer. Ahead, turrets made their first appearance above the treeline, their sharp roofs cutting into the sky like blades.

"We're here." Locke nudged Mae out of sleep.

She gasped. Buried within a valley of rolling hills stood a great, stone building seemingly preserved since ancient times. Pillared archways and high-pitched roofs were distinctly Gothic.

The cavalry picked up speed toward an iron gate. A man emerged, swinging the gates open.

As the group raced on, the building grew larger, its stone figurines and decorative, wrought-iron fencing more distinct.

Mae, with her chin slumped down to her chest, paid no attention. By the time he dismounted, she near-fell into his arms. She would not be carried, though.

"Please," she protested, her half-open eyes failing to sharpen to their usual vigor. "I can manage."

He watched with resigned amusement as she straightened and smoothed out her skirts. After a full day of riding, her efforts did little good. A fact, she irritably seemed to notice too. Locke laid a protective hand on her back, the touch jolting her forward.

From behind the gathering of horses, Pierce headed their way, his face serious and stern. "We'll need to relinquish your weapons first." He waved a guard over. "Search him. The lady too."

"She's unarmed." Locke pressed a hand against the guard's chest.

Eyes narrowed, the man—well-trained, he imagined—didn't move back an inch.

"Are we to take his word?" Uncertainty ghosted through the guard's voice. Locke could easily land a blow against the bastard's ribs. But against the two other well-armed guards, he could hardly hold his own.

"A quick patting," Pierce confirmed. Locke breathed in, anger burning his chest as the man signaled Mae to raise her arms. He forced himself to watch, ready to shout foul if the man so much as smiled at Mae.

"Nothing." The guard moved to Locke next, inching a hand up along his waist. He stopped at a knife—the very one Mae had grabbed.

The memory made him shudder. He should have gone after her the moment she'd left to get the tools. The vault had distracted him, overcoming his good sense. He had left her defenseless and she had been willing to fight. *To kill.* He didn't like the idea. The one man she'd killed had troubled her enough. It didn't matter if she had all the strength or reason in the world—he didn't want her to face that again. No matter what the circumstances, no one was immune to the nightmares. And he knew she had them. He knew every time her mind returned to the darkness of that wine cellar.

The sound of metal hitting stone forced Locke from his thoughts. The damnable guard had tossed his blade to the ground like a piece of scrap metal. He relinquished two smaller blades and a pistol next. With a careless hand, they, too, were tossed to the ground, quivering on impact.

"Is that all?" Pierce circled the pile.

"Afraid so."

"Then after you..." Pierce threw an arm out toward open doors.

Locke kept Mae close as they entered. Meant to impress, the expansive foyer had not a single piece of furniture, just long, intricate tapestries, marble pillars, and a staircase that could have led to heaven itself.

"Ben here will take Miss Blackthorne to her room." Pierce motioned for a footman with a thick, elaborate mustache.

Mae cast Pierce a suspicious glare.

"Please. You are my guests." He gestured them forward with a slight blow.

"By threat of force," Locke said. "So far as I'm concerned, we're enemies."

"Pity. In the ways of the old world, you can't accept a morsel of food, either. And you must be hungry…"

Locke swore under his breath.

"We'll have her put in one of our finest rooms."

"Then I go too," Locke said.

"If I must," Pierce said, sighing indignantly, "I shall take the two of you myself."

He led them up the green marble staircase. Taking note of the glistening railings, Locke wondered if, in all this opulence, they were actually solid gold. His heart pounded, reaching for anything he might do to escape all this.

He resisted the urge to take Mae by the waist. He could not meet her gaze, either. If he did, there needed to be reassurance there. At the moment, he could muster none, not even the faintest of smiles.

"Your finest room." He turned to Pierce, trying his damnedest not to look impressed with the surroundings.

"But of course."

Rounding a corner, they moved into a hallway wide enough to be a sitting room. Crystal chandeliers continued one after the other seemingly forever.

Distress crept over Locke with each step, an unease Mae seemed to feel too. Lest she touch anything, she kept her arms tucked against her sides tightly. The extreme size of the building did not bode well for an easy escape.

"After you." Pierce motioned Mae toward a doorway. Inside, an open armoire had been filled with dresses. An elegantly arranged tea service complete with iced finger cakes graced a low table. They had been expected.

Trying not to let that fact unnerve him, Locke turned his attention to the bed. There seemed enough pillows and furs to satisfy Mae's former lifestyle.

"Is it to your liking?"

"Quite." Mae clasped her hands, waiting for them to step out. It wasn't good manners that kept her from collapsing. Fear shimmered in her eyes. A look he knew all too well.

"Capital. Do ring the bell, then." Pierce slid out.

"I won't be far," Locke promised quickly, though it could very well have been a lie. What else might be said? There seemed no other possible words for what might await them. Still, Locke wanted to take her hand and make the promise again. He wouldn't fail her like he had at the coast. She had to know he—

"Go," Mae ordered, her eyes finally lowering. "You must."

Nodding, he quit the room, wishing later that he had said something more. She had to know it was not hopeless.

"She'll be safe?" He met Pierce in the hall.

"Without question," Pierce said quickly with a hard glare. He seemed to be playing host now.

"What of Ellsworth and the other woman? Have your men recovered them?"

"Worry not, my friend. The moment they arrive with my men, they will be taken into immediate confinement."

Considering Mae, Locke paused. He needed to put his next request in the best possible light. "I trust you won't treat the young lady too terribly. She is a great friend of Mae's. A pupil of hers."

"If the younger one's release would please the lady, I shall do so at once."

Locke bit his tongue, knowing full well Mae would want the same. Yet it was far from the safest option.

"I'm afraid that might not be wise." Locke lowered his voice. "Miss Rosewood is not yet to be trusted. She has become too close with Ellsworth these last few days. A man who certainly can't be trusted."

"I see…"

"But if she is to be confined, it should be in the utmost comfort."

"Yes, of course. I shall give the order at my first opportunity. Now, please. A tête-à-tête is all I ask."

"Nothing more."

Pierce strode down the hall, his steps quick and animated.

What for? He had made it clear the sapphire no longer interested him.

Pierce moved into the dining room. It was no less extravagant than he'd expected. The place was a castle fit for a fairy tale. All around Locke, a series of candelabras gave the room a flickering glow. Marble walls rose an impressive two stories and through latticed windows, the moon hovered low in the twilight.

"Please." Pierce motioned Locke to his seat while he was no doubt gaping. "You're warm enough, I trust?"

With the evening proving warm, two pillared fireplaces went unlit.

Locke nodded, his sights on the long, polished table set for two. Heaping platters of sliced fruit, chicken, and bread drew him nearer.

Like Mae, he suffered from exhaustion. To his luck, a servant, well-dressed in all silver, placed a steaming cup of coffee before him. Locke dropped into the chair and took it up in his hands. Steam wafted over his lips, its effects working instantly.

"I never meant for us to become enemies." Pierce took the seat opposite. "Why you decided to run, I have no idea."

Locke, with a mouthful of coffee, nearly choked with laughter.

"So far, we've benefitted mutually," Pierce went on.

"How do you gather that?"

"When you overcame my ship's defenses, you showed me my weaknesses. Your gains, I think, are obvious enough…Most would consider it a gift."

Locke pressed his lips together. Perhaps it was a gift, one that with time, had made him realize how meaningless his life had been. A gift that had given him Mae. A gift Pierce had likely hoped to keep for himself.

"Have you ever made use of it?" Locke asked. "I rather hoped but could never be sure that my seven years without it meant…"

"You were aging again?" Pierce said plainly. "Indeed. You are."

Locke breathed out. "And you yourself never used it? Before I..."

Pierce closed his eyes briefly and shook his head, as if such things were beneath him to speak of.

"It's not too late to change your mind." Locke cast an eye over Pierce. He had been rather young for his position when they'd first crossed paths. Now his face hung heavy with wrinkles. His hands shook as he gripped his napkin, not much differently than when he had reached for his gun that day at sea. But these were memories Locke didn't care to recall.

"Here." Locke pulled the serum and sapphire free from his neck. In a clatter of chains, he dropped them atop the table. He wished he could say that he had never wanted any of these things, but the healing serum had saved his life and the life of his crew on more than one occasion.

Now it seemed he owed a debt.

"Whatever this place is, I want nothing to do with it." With this royal treatment of sorts, Locke saw where this was going now. Though it would make little difference, Locke needed to say the words.

"We must interest you to some degree." Pierce picked up his fork and served Locke several slices of meat and bread. "I know you've been asking questions."

They were good. Better than any organization he had ever heard of.

"What have you discovered?" Piece asked. "Please, indulge me."

"Nothing," Locke answered, ashamed of the fact. Only that Pierce must have had some sort of power to track him down as he had. The sapphire was only the tip of a much deeper truth.

"Please." Pierce motioned to the food.

Locke took up a fork, growing more uneasy. He didn't like sitting there in the company of even one Silver Order member. Not when he knew Pierce's power. Not when the man was holding Mae against her will. He was growing impatient. "Tell me what you want," he demanded, almost *roared.*

Pierce, however, didn't even blink. "First…let me enlighten you. Our power, you should know, is not the result of some political connection, money, or even cunning manipulation. Rather, we owe our power to one single asset." He pointed to the chains atop the table. "Interesting how some items can prove profitable and others not. Neither a stone nor a serum, this one asset is an elixir, a drink, if you will, one that allows us to see things…things that have not yet come to be."

Just as Locke had predicted, the man was only getting stranger, especially since Locke and Mae had arrived here.

When Locke failed to show surprise, he continued. "Just hints, flashes—never much. But as you can imagine, for this advice of ours, people will give almost anything."

"Why tell me this?" One reason Locke knew was that he would never leave this place alive.

Locke debated whether or not he should try to find Mae and make a run for it. But when shadows drifted past in the hall, he reconsidered. He remembered they weren't alone.

"I confess you surprised me in retrieving the amulet. Any other man would simply go on running forever. But you didn't, did you?" His eyes gleamed.

"I'm done running. I'm done with that life of crime."

"Indeed. Who wouldn't want to settle down with a woman like Miss Blackthorne?"

Locke gave in and took a quick bite of chicken. He didn't care if this man was impressed with him. He had only one thing on his mind: escape. For that he'd need energy.

"The serum, elixir, this gem—how'd you get your hands on it all?" Aside from his own curiosity, Locke hoped to distract the strange man. Anything he could do to buy himself more time. He still had yet to come up with a plan.

"The same way a pirate comes upon a precious cargo. We're far from the first to have stolen it. My ancestors, like your own, were explorers."

Locke placed his fork back on the table and tugging the chain, slid the healing serum into his grasp. He had a hunch he was going to need it. He could go without the natural order of things a little while longer. He had more to protect than just himself.

"My father, for one, was constantly searching the world for these kinds of discoveries. That sapphire, we found amongst the ruins of a much older society in the Pacific. Lord knows how those devils attained it." He let out a boom of laughter.

"Thing must be worth a kingdom."

"The sapphire? I suppose." Pierce gave a lofty wave of the hand, as if it were all so provincial. "But one cannot go about selling such things…"

"That would mean parting with some of your power."

"Ah. Not just some stupid pirate, are you? Can you read?"

"Of course." Locke narrowed his eyes. "In fact, I'm well-read."

"I was just teasing." Pierce laughed. "I never thought you a stupid pirate. Not once."

"Then be blunt. Given your abilities, you should know more about myself than I do."

"Perhaps I do." Pierce drummed his fingers together. "Even before you utilized certain…*abilities*, you were quite famous, quite feared too…"

At this, Locke wanted to laugh. He wasn't proud of these things. In fact, he would trade it all just for a normal life, or rather, *any* life with Mae.

"That day at sea when you overcame my men, I was in a state of shock. I had prepared, I had a large crew, and still, the way you came at us… If my crew faced you again, they said they'd surrender at once."

"I did what any pirate worth his salt does best. Induced fear."

"A useful tactic and exactly what we need. If our ships are to be protected, we need someone like you."

Locke snorted. "What of my future?"

"Are you so eager to hear it?"

"Why not?" He didn't have to believe him, did he? For all he knew, it could have been some lie and manipulation. He'd decide for himself.

"Quite simply, you become one of us. Your seafaring abilities and travels have made you quite successful in protecting our assets. You're a wealthy man. In want of nothing."

Locke's stomach twisted with disgust. "And that's the future as you see it?"

"That's what will pass, yes. No matter what you do. These visions are set in stone, Mr. Locke. They cannot be undone."

"'Cannot be undone...'" Locke repeated in breathless amazement. "Then what the devil—"

"—is the use of knowing?" Pierce finished, as he probably had a thousand times before. "We can prepare."

"Sounds like a curse. Or at least a story that will soon end in tragedy."

"Knowing can be a burden. Fate is a powerful and sometimes cruel woman, but she did bring us together, didn't she?"

"This is madness."

"Is this not what you want? You miss the sea."

"But not the bloodshed."

"Oh, there won't be much of that. Not if you do your job right."

Still, it would add up, Locke thought. And it would not be few. For each expedition in god-knew-what kind of unexplored territory, there could be many deaths. The seas were dangerous; they both knew that. When he had met Pierce's men at sea, they had been well-armed for a reason. It was only strategy and good luck that Locke and his crew had even pulled through. The man was ruthless. Locke had seen it then and he was seeing it now. Pierce was even more ruthless than Ellsworth; the only difference was Pierce's wits, calm temperament, and his seemingly endless power and resources. Traits Locke didn't have the skills to defeat.

"What exactly would you have me do?" Locke asked. "Protect your finds of mermaids and unicorns—the stuff of fairy tales and myth?"

"Nothing quite so silly as that. You'll just have to take me at my word. In time, you'll find the opportunity rather fortuitous, I think…and exciting too—a life that could be yours for centuries if you wish it."

"And what becomes of Mae?" Locke wanted so badly to call Pierce's fortunetelling a lie, but something told him it wasn't. It made too much sense, especially if it meant giving Mae her freedom.

His heart started to pound just as it did before a fight. The type of power that surrounded him was starting to make him nervous. From the ancient bricks to the gold, hand-painted plates before him, there was simply too much majesty and authority here to ignore. The man lived like a king and Locke was beginning to think he *was* one.

"Strange pair you make. You and Miss Blackthorne. Her father did betray you." Pierce raised a brow.

"He tried to *kill* me." Locke straightened in his seat.

"She is very handsome, of course. Has a glow about her."

"That, she does."

"But you found other uses for her. Made plans. Good plans."

"I wouldn't call them good." Locke looked down at the sharp gleam of the table. Working alongside Ellsworth had been his biggest regret. The memory burned straight through his gut.

"She can't know everything in your past, can she?" Pierce smiled with cruelty.

"No." Locke kept a straight face. He wondered if it was extortion he hinted at. The question was undoubtedly a threat of sorts. "But she knows enough."

"And she's willing to look past it?"

Locke shrugged. He didn't know for certain anymore. If she ever did, he'd never know why.

"I find her very hard to read myself. Her own future is unwritten as of yet. Though I rather hoped she might make a place for herself here…*with you*. You'll travel but a few months a year—

that, I promise you."

"*No.*" He knew what Pierce was suggesting and he refused to submit her to this prison, to another life of taking orders. "I'll do your bidding, but you let her go."

Locke had promised her more than her inheritance. He had promised her freedom. Soon, she would have it.

"Locke—"

"Take care of Ellsworth too." He shoved the sapphire necklace toward Pierce and rose from his chair. "And let me get some rest before I tell her the news."

"Very well. I suppose we have talked enough for now." Pierce rang a small silver bell. "Take Mr. Locke to his quarters. Spare no luxury."

The footman led Locke into a whole new set of halls. The place was a maze, making it difficult to gauge his distance from Mae. But he could hardly face her now after all that he had heard. He could hardly come to grips with his so-called future himself.

He had once been a captain, fierce and fearsome. He hadn't taken orders. He'd traveled the world because he had once been free to do it, not so he could protect discoveries some nob would profit from.

And yet, that was his fate. Already written in the stone. Despite his hopes and efforts, he would never free himself from Pierce's web. He had no choice. No matter what happened, Mae would get her fortune and her freedom—even if it cost him his own.

CHAPTER SEVENTEEN
William

MAE GRIPPED A clump of smooth silk. The images of the nightmare were still fresh in her mind. She let out a calming breath, trying to ground herself back to the present. She saw the same cellar that had stolen away much of her sleep these last few days. But never before like this.

Illuminated by the weak flicker of candle, Ellsworth loomed over her knife in hand, his gaze narrow and mischievous. She felt his repeated blows, the way the blade broke through her flesh. Things she had never before remembered. She didn't know how bad it had truly been. The fear she had felt.

Tears sprang in her eyes, terror filling her again. She hoped Pierce's men had captured Ellsworth and that he wasn't still out there. In the midst of all that, what might have happened to Miss Rosewood? There was still so much that could go wrong.

Locke's near-death had almost broken her. That familiar pain she'd endured with William had returned, fresh and raw again. She couldn't bear it. Even now, she felt its effects as sharp as the day she had discovered her brother's body. Like shards of glass, dread still lingered in the pit of her stomach.

She released the sheets and touched her cheek. What was sure to be an ugly bruise ached with pain. She wanted to forget everything about the day before, worrying instead about the day ahead.

She sat up. Drapes of the richest velvet disguised day or night, she wasn't sure. Across a rug-covered floor, a marble fireplace radiated gentle heat. With a chandelier and cavernous, ribbed ceiling, not even the antiquity of Blackthorne Manor could compare.

Locke was nowhere to be seen, but at least they were in this place together. Whatever would befall him would befall her too. Despite all that had happened and could still happen, she found solace in that reminder.

She supposed she had woken up in worse condition. She clutched her arms as if to make sure she was indeed wholly intact. She still wore her dress, smelling again the salt of the sea. She had been too tired to remove it. At the very least it was dry by now. In a place like this, however, it would not do.

Pulling the bell, not one but several servants arrived. Like a parade, they carried goods befitting her royal surroundings: kettle after kettle of steaming water, bars of soap, whole sprigs of lavender, and a large, copper tub. Two women stayed behind, presumably to help her wash.

But where was Locke? When would he come up to see her? When would he explain what was to happen?

Despite her persistence, the servants ignored her questions. They worked in silence, splashing water into the tub and burning incense in each corner of the room.

She breathed in the thick, heady soup of smoke. It was a strange, crisp aroma. She recognized cleansing lavender and soothing chamomile, but there was something else she couldn't place. She breathed it in deeper, trying to figure it out.

Each time, her panicky urge to ask questions lessened. The conflicts of the last few days drained away. Somehow, it was easy to forget. Rather than fight, she simply let the servants do as they would.

They stripped off her clothes and directed her into the bath.

With each exhale, she fell deeper into relaxation. It was like being seduced. She had no choice but to surrender. *Why not enjoy it?*

Her troubles were distant now. They couldn't touch her, not here. Here, she had no need to think. Here, her mind had been emptied.

Hands reworked her braids, buckets poured over her head, her skin scrubbed with soap.

Between tangles of smoke, she took in the ornamental gold that edged the ceiling. Just about every piece of furniture was draped with velvets, furs, and piles of pillows. She wanted to rub her cheek over each of them. But moving from the tub seemed impossible—a task she would rather not do.

When the smoke finally cleared, she found herself blinking as if waking from a long, undisturbed sleep.

Reluctantly and with pruned hands, she lifted herself from the water's clutches. In a methodical routine she remembered faintly, servants gathered round her. They laced up her corset and bodice with easy precision and pinned up her braids.

She was still too dazed to speak or ask questions, but with each breath of fresh air, she could feel herself returning to normalcy.

The silence, save for the gentle cracking of the fire, continued.

She was almost glad for it. Regardless of what had produced it—be it the calmed warmth of the bath or the sharply scented incense—she'd needed that hour of relaxation. Her frayed nerves that had once felt beyond repair were finally recuperating.

In fact, she'd never felt better. Standing there, she felt every bit of the woman she had once been. Looking up into the mirror, she almost didn't recognize herself. She was struck by the finery draped over her. Never had she seen quite this shade of purple both dark and luxurious, nor the kind of corded lace that capped her shoulders. Chantilly, perhaps? She couldn't be sure.

Between her fingers, she traced the delicately sewn floral

design. Surprisingly light, row after row of lace draped down the entirety of the skirt. Hours of work Mae didn't want to imagine. Wearing it, she didn't even mind the bruise that marred her face.

"Be bringing you down to Mr. Locke shortly…"

The servant, a freckled woman younger than herself, grinned at Mae in the mirror. She had noticed her friendly demeanor early on and had been grateful for it. If anyone was to give her relief from worry, it was she.

"Wonderful." Mae was sure the dress could induce the same stares she'd achieved the night of the ball. The simple yet elegant design suited her perfectly. Not an inch of fabric needed to be taken in.

"How did they know my size so exactly?"

"Oh, yes, that." The maid yanked the bodice strings tighter before tying. "You need not worry yerself with thoughts of the like. You'd sooner go mad. They just be knowing things 'round here."

Mae wondered what secrets, if any, the woman might be privy to. Did she even know what this place was? Despite a sudden urge to ask, Mae held her tongue. She focused again on her dress, twisting back and forth at the waist, allowing the material to swirl around her.

"The dress suits you very well." The servant stepped back to take in the sight. From her extended gaze, Mae knew she was being sincere. Though it gave her no added confidence.

When the maid led her down a flight of stairs, her nervousness was building. She had no idea what to expect or what she might need to be prepared for. Would there be fighting or mere surrender?

In a parlor well-lit by a series of windows, Locke had been pacing. At her arrival, he paused and for longer than what was polite, took her in. So much needed to be said, so many concerns that itched to leave her tongue. But with Pierce hovering, they could do no more than exchange meaningful glances.

Compared to his previous state, Locke seemed to have shifted into the skin of a different man altogether. In a pale-blue waistcoat, he had strayed from his usual darker shades into Pierce's more eccentric fashion taste. The color more than suited him—it brightened his features.

"You are well rested, I hope?" Pierce asked.

"I'm fine," she answered absently. She preferred to study Locke a moment longer but couldn't think of anything to say.

"I'm glad to hear." Glancing back and forth between his two guests, Pierce seemed to notice everything. No longer in his black cloak, he was dressed like any other gentleman of wealth in cool, silver buttons and patterned, red silk. He was no longer a dangerous enemy, but an eager host.

"Are you a recent acquaintance of Mr. Locke?" Pierce asked Mae without so much as tilting his head in Locke's direction.

Locke sniffed. Pierce was teasing her. He knew they had become so much more than acquaintances. What he was really implying was that she worked quickly.

Mae felt herself flush. The time between them had been short, but it hardly seemed like an acquaintance of only a couple of weeks. Acquaintances spent dinner and afternoons together, not the whole of their days and nights. She didn't want to be just an acquaintance, either. These past few days seemed to account for something deeper.

She settled on saying, "Somewhat."

Pierce led her to the settee, where further interrogation would no doubt begin. Smoothing out her skirts, she made herself smile. She would be pleasant at least for a little while.

"Tell me the story of how you met," said Pierce, still standing beside Locke.

Dear lord… Mae flushed again. This man was making it seem as though she and Locke were engaged to be married. She was almost angry when a worse realization dawned. Beneath all his words and forcefulness seemed an undercurrent of menace, an ulterior motive to get at something else.

"In a storm," Locke answered for her.

"A storm, you say? My, must be quite the tale."

"But surely not so interesting as yours," Mae put in before another question could come. Taking in the room's details, it was clear the man had an obsession.

Like her room, relics of no doubt priceless value decorated on every table, shelf, and bit of floor space, giving the room an ancient yet wild allure. Almost like a treasure room. Perhaps that was what the place was.

"You have quite the assortment of antiquities," Mae remarked. She would gladly accept the challenge of naming the culture and time period of each piece. She recognized the Greek vases first with their distinct warrior caricatures drawn in black. On the opposite wall hung a floral tapestry that seemed to speak of Italy or Madrid. The stone statues set into the walls were more difficult to place. If anything, the place seemed part Spanish monastery with its rich, wooden furniture and, given the room's gold-trimmed ceiling and classical paintings, part Louis XVI of Versailles.

"This place is centuries old." He gestured grandiosely. "The ruins they were built upon date back even further."

Mae swallowed at the historical significance. The place was a bloody museum. Though no one had ever paid any mind to style or consistency, the room was no less extravagant. If not pleasing, it was at least the most intriguing room she had ever seen.

"Perhaps after tea, you'd like a tour?" Pierce asked.

"A tour? A tour of what?" Locke flinched, allowing Mae to slip from his gaze. He glowered at Pierce. "Surely, you mean the outer gardens."

"God, no. What do you take me for? I mean to show her this very building. Every significant room."

Mae expected Locke to say, "Splendid," or something of that variety. Instead, he knitted his brows. "Do you really think that would be appropriate? For an outsider, I mean…"

"'An outsider'?" Pierce gasped. "Nonsense."

Mae questioned the word too. Most likely, he meant anyone

outside this secret society. Nevertheless, it had been a word she'd resented all her life.

Locke argued further, but Mae ignored this. She eyed the tea service ready for her to indulge in. The sight was repulsive. How could she so much as take a sip when Miss Rosewood was in their grasp somewhere? At least she presumed as much. The way Pierce's men had gone after the pair left few other outcomes.

"Forgive me." She sharpened her voice to a razor's edge. "I am rather concerned about my pupil Miss Rosewood."

"My apologies for not informing you sooner," Pierce replied. "She is quite safe, I assure you. As soon as we get a handle on things, we shall release her."

"'Release her'?" Mae shot up from her seat. "Do you mean to say she is locked away?" How her own situation was much different, though, she couldn't say.

Pierce opened his mouth then exchanged a look with Locke. "No need to fret. I can attest to her comfort myself."

"I must see her. She is my responsibility." Mae gathered her skirts. "Now, please."

"My dear." Pierce sought to calm her with a cooing yet sardonic voice. "There are other matters we must attend to first. Ellsworth—"

"Keep him, for all I care, but release Miss Rosewood at once."

"Mae." Locke placed a hand on hers, searing her skin. "She's on Ellsworth's side now. She made that clear on the coast."

Mae snapped her hand away. "I just need to speak with her. Miss Rosewood may be naïve, but she's not—"

"Pierce will release her. *In time.* I've struck a deal. Pierce has agreed to let you go as well. He will handle Ellsworth too."

"What? Why? In exchange for what?" Nothing, especially here, could come for free. "For the sapphire?"

"I've already relinquished the stone." Locke pulled at his cuffs, unable to meet her gaze.

"Then what? What will you exchange?"

"I've agreed to join them." Locke set his jaw.

"You what?" Her voice came out high and urgent. Had this all been for nothing? He couldn't do that, not after all they had been through, not with how much she—*bloody hell*. She caught herself.

Clutching at her neck, she sank back into the settee. When had this happened? Had it been in the theater? That day at the coast? As early as their first meeting in the forest? Whenever it had been, she'd felt the full force of it when she'd seen him bleeding on that rock. At that moment, she'd been willing to kill for him. No one could separate them. The thought she couldn't endure then, she couldn't endure now.

"It is a small price," Locke reaffirmed. "I am to travel the world, just as I've always done. I am to look after their ships."

"But—"

Before Mae could form her plea, Pierce cleared his throat. "Of course, you two need not be parted. If you are interested, we'd gladly accept you too, miss."

Locke cast her a hard, pointed look. This place must have been just as sinister as she thought. Or perhaps he wanted to stay, to be parted from her for good, to return to his true lover: the sea. Her breath caught in her throat.

"No." She swallowed a heavy lump of hurt. "Keep your deal."

"As you wish." Pierce bowed his head in concession. "Now you must be ravenous." He leaned over the tray. "How do you take your tea?"

Tea? Mae wanted to snort. How long was he going to keep up these pleasantries? Everyone in the room knew they were little more than prisoners. The thought made her want to scream. "*Really*, sir."

Pierce jerked upright—as anyone might have, given her extreme rudeness. But she would not be fooled by his kindness. He had no right to imprison them like this and Mae would not let him forget it.

"Have I done something?" Pierce asked stupidly.

Out of the corner of Mae's eye, Locke had stepped closer.

"I don't trust you," she said.

"Of course not. Such things don't happen instantaneously. You must try, though. Truly, I mean to be your friend. I want to protect you from this Ellsworth chap. Give you some justice."

"'Justice'? I can only assume you mean death."

"Yes, but…" Pierce held up a finger in pause. "We have a rule here. I must know the facts. I must know everything."

"You're saying that if I tell you Ellsworth's crimes, you'll… What? Have him killed? Murdered?"

"I will take the matter to the council first thing. If that is what will indeed keep you safe, I am sure they will agree."

"Council?" she questioned. "What Council?"

Pierce folded his arms behind his back.

"*Our* Council. The ruling body of everyone who belongs to the Silver Order. And"—he grinned—"even a few outside of it, though they may not know it."

Locke was suddenly on the settee beside her. "Tell me." *Forget him*, his eyes told her. And for a moment, they were in the theater again. Just them and all that empty space.

Mae took a moment to settle the chaos of her thoughts. She had never told anyone before, but already, the memories were clawing to the surface.

If only she had let William talk. If only she had believed… Things would have been so damned different.

"Start from the beginning." Pierce took up a cup of tea and sat down.

"I suppose that would be William's return from sea. Or maybe a month prior, when I'd lost all hope." She looked up from her hands at Locke. "I'd given him up for dead, you see." Who could have blamed her? For almost four years, not a single letter. After the first year, people had already begun to talk.

"Probably a shipwreck, pirates or the French, they said. I had prepared for the worst. Sooner or later, I'd have to oversee the family business. Even though no one prepared me for it, I'd have to make choices and give directives. We had a manager for the business, yes, but in his hands, things had taken a turn for the worse." She smiled at the next part. "It was the arrival of the letter that changed everything. A miracle. All of the servants declared it so. We had been at risk of losing everything—or at least what I thought was everything."

Because while she had inherited the family fortune and ship-building business, the family name would be lost the moment she married. A disgrace to all the generations of Blackthornes who had come before her.

She could still feel the relief in her brother's embrace all those years ago. She felt no trace of that joy now. Not even close. Since that day, her life had begun a downward spiral. She had lost her family's fortune regardless of her brother's return. And in the end, he'd still met with death.

"Our manager insisted I take out loans. It was foolish, all that I did to save the business. But what did I know of such things? I wasn't educated in those ways. I was taught to sing, draw, dance—nothing of business. It was of little surprise that the loss of our trade, our home, our legacy…fell to my lot."

Locke's mouth opened, ready to protest. "It was your manag-er—"

"I know that now. I should have sacked him. But I didn't."

"You merely trusted the wrong person," Locke said. Pierce nodded in kind.

Mae shrugged. How could she have known the manager would only sink them into further ruin? As far as she'd known, the business had prospered for years under that manager.

"In the end, there was only one thing I could do: marry well. *Ellsworth*"—she choked on the name—"had made his wishes known. He sought my hand long before William's disappearance. My father had hated the man, of course. He was our competition, our rival. So it wasn't until after his death that I began seeing Ellsworth at dinner parties and balls—rather, every social gathering I attended."

Mae shivered at the memory of his touch, the unwanted advances she'd often evaded. He was rooms away, somewhere far off in this place, but she had a sudden urge to flinch and push him back, to get away.

"Against my brother's wishes, I eventually accepted his proposal. I grew weary of it every day, but what choice did I have? We were about to lose not only the business, but our home. William was in no condition to work. He had changed. He drank heavily, stayed up till dawn, slept far into the afternoon…"

Mae trailed off, noticing Locke's troubled, almost-fearful gaze. She couldn't take it.

"I managed," Mae added, hoping the look would dissipate. There were so many things she could never say. That she much rather hoped to forget. When she began again, she tried to sound unaffected.

"He had gone mad—or at least that was what I thought. Not long after he'd returned and learned of Father's sudden death, he began rifling through the house, turning up shelves and whole pieces of furniture." Mae knew now that he had been searching for that alternative will.

"The cottage—that was where he discovered it. He tried so hard to tell me. If only I had known then. If only I had let him speak."

In the presence of the two men's watchful eyes, she tensed. When had the room become so stifling?

"Ellsworth and I—chaperoned by my lady's maid, of course, as if I'd ever want to be alone with that man—were watching the fire after dinner when William rushed in. He was frantic, not himself. He grabbed at me, twisted my wrist to take the promise ring from Ellsworth off my finger. 'You don't have to do it!' he shouted. 'I thought I'd never find it, but I found it, Mae. I found it!' I thought he had gone mad, so I called out for Ellsworth to help. Told him he was drunk."

In her head, she could still hear the struggle, the rustle of clothing, William's screams. "The worst of it is he *was* drunk. Too drunk to get out what he needed to say before it was too late."

Locke placed a hand over her shoulder, but she wanted him to do so much more. The past had returned to her so vivid, so fresh. The panic, the sorrow, the anger… All the feelings mingled together in a whirlwind that had left her reeling.

"Ellsworth took William into the next room to calm down. He must have found the letter on him then. I'm certain of it. Rather than leave us to our wealth, Ellsworth hoped to claim it himself. He had murdered for it. He murdered William."

Her poor William.

Not even time could lessen the pain. It could only be replaced with anger.

Since his death, she alone had known the truth. Something, whether instinct or logic, had convinced her that Ellsworth had been behind William's death. He'd known the house well enough by then, so he could have easily made his way inside without her knowledge. The possibility had been reason enough to decline Ellsworth's proposal and seek work. Days ago, the villain had even admitted to his actions. She'd been right to trust her instinct.

"When did you find his body?" Locke asked.

"That very morning when it happened."

Something had woken her early. Dawn had just spilled over the lawn. She had been admiring it when she had heard the thud that would forever echo in her memory. On the paved drive, his leg had been twisted around in the most unnatural manner. His head a pile of flesh and hair. Splashes of blood strewn everywhere, even across the white marble steps of the entrance.

Mae squeezed her eyes shut, but that did nothing to erase the memory from her mind. She heard her own scream, even felt the texture of the curtain as she'd gripped it.

Some people, she once read, forgot traumatic moments of their past, whole days altogether, but not her. As hard as Mae tried to forget, the memory lingered in fine detail. Even horrific memories of the cellar had managed to come back.

"Why did you not apply to the police?" Locke asked in soothing but curious tones.

"There was an inquiry. A short one," Mae said. "None of the servants had seen Ellsworth enter the house after that evening, so there was no witness, no proof." Just a conviction in her heart that had almost driven her mad.

Locke turned to Pierce, both their eyes sorrowful, their lips speechless.

LOCKE STEPPED INTO the hall. After Mae's story, he and Pierce had agreed to give her some time alone in her private chamber.

"She'll need the rest of the afternoon," Locke said. But Pierce wasn't listening. His thoughts were somewhere else. He held out the key, staring at its detailed, ethereal design.

"This fortune," Pierce said. "Where is it now?"

Locke shot toward him, his mood shifting from concern to blazing fury in less than a second. "Ellsworth murdered a man for the mere promise of gold, came near to doing the same to Mae, and you have a mind to—"

"Apologies." Pierce placed a hand on his shoulder, extending the other with the key on his palm. "Here, take it. Give it back to her."

Locke coolly pocketed the key. Everything was in order, it seemed: the fortune was back in Mae's hands, the sapphire back in Pierce's, but he still regretted the path that had led him here, the fact that he had partnered with Ellsworth. There seemed no end to his evils, no end to all he had wanted to gain.

Locke tightened his fists, only too willing to hand Ellsworth death himself. Alas, he didn't find himself reaching for his blade as quickly as he'd expected. He simply wanted him gone. He wanted Mae safe.

"Just trying to be practical," Pierce said.

"The man means to kill her."

"Locke, please. Rest easy. The man is as good as gone. And

the lady will be grateful for justice, won't she?" He tapped a finger to his chin. "I was thinking—"

"Damn your thinking!" Locke wanted to swing at him, straight into the jaw. "Is everything a series of favors and debts to you?"

"I am always thinking how the Silver Order might prosper and advance. As I should."

"Just have the deed done. Get one of your guards to do it. I care not."

"You wouldn't face him in a duel," he teased. "At dawn?"

"No."

He only wished there was something more to be done. Perhaps Pierce had a way to turn back time, to erase her tragedies. In all of it, she had been helpless yet so strong in the face of danger and despair. But short of turning back time, there was nothing much to do.

"Join me for tea?"

"I think I'll stay."

"Stand guard, will you?" Pierce teased for what best be the last time. He cleared his throat. "We'll talk details soon, you hear."

"Yessir." Locke came near to rolling his eyes.

Alone, he tried not to think once more of what Ellsworth had tried to accomplish in the cellar all those days ago. The feeling sank into his stomach like a brick. He had underestimated the man.

☾

OUTSIDE, MAE COULD hear the constant thudding of what could only be Locke's footfalls. She opened the door and leaned against the frame.

His steps ceased. "How do you feel?"

Frankly, Mae didn't know. She thought she would have felt

relieved knowing Ellsworth would soon get his due, but somehow, she didn't feel anything. She felt numb.

"Fine," she lied.

She grabbed Locke's hand and pulled him deeper into the room. A voice begged her to keep her distance. What she felt would only cause her pain. But she had had enough of being alone in that room. Hell, of being alone in general. And now she wanted only him, to feel the same comfort and protection he had provided these last few days. A feeling she wished she could hold on to forever.

Locke closed in and eyed her still-tender bruise. He grazed it with his finger, bringing back the shock of the blow. She had wished Ellsworth suffering then. Why didn't she now?

"He hurt you." Locke began the expected reassurances.

"Please." She held up a weary hand. She didn't care about any of that.

There was something else much more important that preoccupied her thoughts. What she'd merely thought had been lust was something much more. Nothing could eclipse it. So clear and unwavering, these intense feelings had been there all along, yet somehow, she had been so unaware. Until now—when it was too late. A fact that seemed to gnaw at her soul.

"There must be something we can do… You can't stay. We can escape. Make our way to London and from there—"

"Fate won't have it that way."

She hated that he sounded so cold, so distant, a world apart from how he had been these last few days.

"Then we won't leave it to fate." She remained resolute. "I stay. I don't care about the danger. No matter the consequences, I stay with you until we can—"

She pressed forward, but his stiff arm held her back.

"But why?" Mae gulped. He seemed so adamant about his decision when she had hoped to quite easily change his mind. Had she read him wrong? Didn't he want her like he had in the theater? In his eyes, it had been so evident then. Now they weren't eyes at all, but stone.

"Why?" Her teeth clenched, lips shaking. He couldn't end things here, not like this. Life could be utterly terrifying with him, yes, but it contained a certain spark long absent from her life. He was what she had been missing, precisely what she had craved, and she hadn't even known it.

"It has already been decided."

"But the fighting, the violence…" She could not allow him to live that way again. It had pained him too much. A pain that might as well be her own. "Don't pretend you want that life."

"Pierce said—" He sighed. "He said this place was my future…that they could see such things."

"Pierce doesn't control your fate." Her voice rang with angry disbelief. But if sapphires that gave everlasting life could exist, why not impossible visions?

"You're right. He doesn't. Truth is, I can see myself doing this. *For you.*"

So he cared for her, no matter how worthless that was now. Somewhere his future self had already made his choice and his past self was helpless to change it. A conundrum if there ever was one. It was so insane, she refused to try to make sense of it. She stuck only to a simple truth: a future between them did not exist.

"There's no changing it," Locke confirmed.

"Then it's a lie. It can't be true. Not when I know my own will," she bit out. "And my will is to have you in my future. I don't care about anything else or what anyone says."

"I told you I would keep you out of harm's way and I will," he said, the sight of him suddenly strange among the elaborately carved ceiling, lacquered walls, and velvet curtains. "Everything that has happened to you falls to me. After the cellar, the coast… At least give me this."

Mae opened her mouth to defend his efforts but stopped herself. Was that all that had made him do this? Just his guilt? Maybe she'd been a fool to believe in a future with him. He was too wild, the type who belonged to no one place and no one person.

She had sensed it from the beginning. Perhaps the Silver Order and another set of adventures was his future. Maybe a future with her just didn't make sense. She worried her teeth into her bottom lip.

"See here." He dug into his pocket and pulled out the key. "You still have your inheritance. You can have the life you were always meant to."

The words were like a swift jab to the heart. But diverting her gaze, she took the key from him nonetheless.

"I owe you many thanks," she murmured, the words sounding silly and meager.

"No need." He took her hand quickly, as if she might run off, and squeezed it hard. His brows pinched together in a rare expression of pain.

She could almost fancy a glimmer of love in his eye. As she retraced their brief history, she was certain he loved her, didn't he? She knew she did. More than anything. However unlikely it once seemed, he had become all the words she had forgotten these last few years: everything good, happy, and beautiful. All the things she never wanted to forget again.

Mae took him in, every inch of his face, her eyes running down to his neck. She wanted to reach out, to finish what he had started in the theater…but that felt impossible now. Like he was already a thousand miles away.

"History has a way of repeating itself, doesn't it?" Like William, Locke was as good as gone. And like William, she had no hope of forgetting these tragic memories.

"Put it behind you. All of it. Losing your home, what happened in the cellar—it will poison you if you let it."

"I know."

"You can still have a life. Travel. Find a simple-minded husband. Be happy."

Almost laughing, Mae shook her head. Despite his persuasive words, his eyes wanted something else. In them, she could see the truth.

"Miss Blackthorne?" At the sound of a different voice, she started, her shaky fingers wiping away foolish tears. She hadn't even noticed Pierce's approach.

"Feeling better, I presume?" He made his way down the hall. "I hope you don't mind, but I took it upon myself to find someone for you."

With a shriek, Miss Rosewood stampeded toward her. She leaped into Mae's arms with a tight, suffocating embrace.

Despite some slight shivering, Miss Rosewood didn't seem any worse for the wear.

"You must forgive me," she croaked as she quivered. "I was just scared. So scared. Mr. Ellsworth promised he'd help me find you two. That's all I wanted." She glanced at Locke but only briefly before looking down at her hands. "I didn't know what to think. I thought you were having second thoughts. My mother said it is only natural. I hoped I could change your mind."

"Miss Rosewood—" Locke began softly.

"I didn't actually believe you two could be together until I saw it. That was when I knew the engagement was as good as over."

"I shouldn't have entered into it in the first place." Locke bowed his head. "I had other motivations. For that, I am sorry."

"Thank you." Miss Rosewood sniffled.

"I'm sorry to you too," Mae added. "I should have been more honest about everything."

Things would have been so different. Most likely, Ellsworth would have been locked away in prison. At the very least, Miss Rosewood wouldn't have been ruined.

"I never should have believed Mr. Ells—*Ellsworth*," Miss Rosewood spat, her eyes pooling with tears. "He's ruined me many times over."

"What do you mean?"

"He attacked me." Miss Rosewood swallowed. "But I fought him off. Just like you told me. Remember?"

Mae nodded, grasping at her skirts, desperate to hold back her horror. At the time, Mae had hoped it was advice Miss Rosewood would never need.

"He must not have thought I was worth the fight," Miss Rosewood finished.

"This is all my fault." Mae shook her head.

"It doesn't matter." Miss Rosewood pulled Mae in for a hug. How slim she felt in Mae's arms. She couldn't forget that Miss Rosewood was little more than a child, so easily persuaded.

"I want to return to things as they were." Miss Rosewood accepted Pierce's handkerchief and dabbed her tears. "I want us to go home."

Mae stepped back, looking at Locke and Pierce.

Miss Rosewood sucked in a breath. "You're coming, aren't you?"

"I can't."

"But mother will be forced to find another—"

"It's for the best." Mae cut her off before she could even say the word. The old post was her past now. "As soon as it is arranged, you will begin your journey home."

"We are happy to make arrangements for you as well, Miss Blackthorne," Pierce said. "But are you sure you must leave so soon?"

"Yes," Mae confirmed, though shakily.

"My parents are going to be so angry." Miss Rosewood covered her face. "My reputation will never recover."

Mae rubbed a hand over her shoulder. "Your mother is clever. Maybe she's come up with a lie that could explain your disappearance. Society may never know."

Miss Rosewood scoffed. "She's not so clever as you, Miss Blackthorne. I need you, *please*."

"I'm afraid I can't." Mae assumed her governess tone and took in Miss Rosewood's state of dress. Not only was her gown dingy with dirt, it was also ripped across the bodice. Mae tried not to think of her in Ellsworth's company. She pursed her lips, lest she give a horrified expression. "We should find you a new gown. One to travel in."

"We shall find her something very suitable, indeed." Pierce gestured them down the hall and they all—save Locke— retreated. While Miss Rosewood beamed at the prospect, Mae looked back at Locke growing smaller and smaller in the distance.

Chapter Eighteen

Tour of Secrets

Miss Rosewood pounded her fist against the vanity, rattling the scent bottles and a steaming tray of food a servant had just delivered. "How could you wish such a fate on anyone?"

"Please, Miss Rosewood. He has done terrible things to Mr. Locke and me."

"I know he is wicked, but—aren't most men so?"

"No, Miss Rosewood. They're not."

"Now who's being naive?" She crossed her arms. "It's not over for me yet. I've been thinking, if I am indeed ruined, Mr. Ellsworth might be my only hope for a husband."

"*What?*" Mae gaped.

"We must force him to finish what he started with me." She clasped her hands together. "After he hears of my dowry, I'm sure my father can convince him to do the right thing."

"You cannot marry him!" Mae squeezed her eyes shut.

"You'd rather see me ruined? You'd rather see me end up like some old maid? Like you?"

Miss Rosewood pushed back the table, sending a bottle rolling and exploding onto the floor. Lord knew how much it was worth or how old. But somehow, Miss Rosewood didn't seem to notice. She was so absorbed with her own anguish.

Despite the insult, Mae did her best to stay calm. If she didn't convince Miss Rosewood otherwise, Ellsworth, had he the chance, probably would marry her, if only to obtain access to Blackthorne Manor.

"That day at the cottage," Mae said. "Don't you remember? He wanted to hurt me, most likely kill me. You saw for yourself."

"But why? You won't tell me why."

Mae held her tongue. If she was going to reclaim her fortune, she could not risk anyone knowing about it—particularly the servants that might linger in the hall. "I can't say."

"Why not? You always tell me everything."

"I can't this time."

"Then why should I obey you? You're not my governess. Not anymore," she added with an angry sneer. The fact had likely seemed a second betrayal.

"I still have concern for your well-being."

"You never did," Miss Rosewood snapped. "Don't you remember what you did? How you…" She shook her head, her sullen expression deepening.

"I don't expect you to forgive me, but you have to trust me, Miss Rosewood. Please. Someday, I shall tell you all. Then you will understand. I promise."

"Why are you speaking to me like this? I'm not some child."

Mae walked over to the vanity, where bits of broken glass were strewn about. Without assistance, she proceeded to pick the bottle up piece by piece. The scent of perfume was strong enough to make her nostrils sting.

"One might never guess."

"You're just jealous," Miss Rosewood said. "Mother always said so. She told me you lost your fortune and as punishment, you were disgraced."

The sting was instant. Mae's hand tensed, squeezing the glass in her hand. Wincing, she threw the pieces away and moved for the door.

"You have airs like you're something more, but you're not,"

Miss Rosewood continued. "You're nothing. You're no better than an adulteress, a murderess!"

Mae paused. It would be all too easy to dwell on that day in the cellar again. To bring forth the awful images her imagination alone had conjured. But rather than let the painful truth claim and consume her, she continued down the corridor, her footfalls loud and sharp. One day, Miss Rosewood would understand. One day, she would forgive her just as Mae hoped to forgive herself.

Seeking calmness, Mae paced up and down the hallways, trying to think, searching for a plan that might help Locke escape. But her mind was too troubled to focus and in the vast array of hallways, she quickly lost her way. If only Locke were near. If only they might cross paths again.

Where might he be? Busy planning his next voyage, his next fantastic adventure?

Mae picked up her pace. There wasn't time to hope for chance encounters. Like Miss Rosewood, she would soon be off in her own carriage, and Locke just another part of the past she was supposed to forget.

Hearing voices, she peered into a doorway. Two servants stilled in their chatter. "Yes, miss?"

"Mr. Locke. Do you know where he might be?"

"Likely the library. Down the stairs and first door on the left."

When Mae reached the room, she was hesitant to enter. She hated that this might be their last moment alone.

As easily as she had fallen for him, she could stop loving him, right? But she knew nothing about matters of love. Her mother had spoken about it only once, her accent growing thick, same as it had when she'd told Mae stories of home. She had said love was something one must have faith in. *Doubt it once and you stand to ruin it forever. Doubt can fester,* she had said, *"till it grows into a monster strong enough to conquer anyone."*

The advice seemed telling now. Knowing her husband's profession, had Tala ever doubted him? If only Mae could apply that advice. If only it could change Locke's mind and help her keep him.

Stepping closer, she peered inside. The room was tall, like all the others. It must have held hundreds of books, with some accessible only by ladders. Tasteful landscape paintings broke up the monotony. But it was the smell she really appreciated. The musk of books and the sharp smell of varnish filled her with the familiarity of her own library. When it had *been* her own, that was.

Nestled in the crook of an armchair, Locke was deeply immersed in reading.

"Who's there?" He turned around and took to his feet. She hadn't made a single noise and still, he'd sensed her. "*Mae.* Is everything all right?"

She nodded, wondering what bewilderment her face had betrayed. "You couldn't sleep?"

"Not much, no." He rushed close. "Your hand. What's happened to it?"

"Oh." She lifted up her palm, now pooling with blood. In her eagerness to find him, she hadn't noticed. "I dropped a glass. It's nothing."

"Here." Locke whipped a handkerchief from his pocket and placed it over the wound. From his neck, he lifted free the serum.

"Please don't bother." Mae tried to resist. "Just leave it be."

"And risk infection?"

"It's such a minor wound. I won't have you wasting it. Not when you have so many voyages ahead." Mae pulled back, surprised when he held her grip.

"Be still. It will only take a drop."

"You're sure?"

"They likely have more. Either way, I've no use of it."

"But think of the danger you'll face." Mae felt a tingle as the serum hit her wound. Slowly, the skin sealed back together, leaving mere remnants of blood. Just like magic—only it *was*, indeed, magic. A baffling sort of magic that made her head spin every time she witnessed it.

In this new life, she could only imagine what other mystical things Locke might discover. Just like it had in his past, traveling would offer adventure, but it could never outweigh the violence.

"You won't get yourself killed, will you?" She remembered his promise at the stream.

He didn't reply. With a gentle hand, he worked to wipe away the rest of the blood.

"You could write me, you know. Couldn't we find some place to meet now and then? I'd travel anywhere."

"It couldn't last." Locke dropped her healed hand.

"Why not?" Maybe she was being naïve, but in her heart, what they had was strong enough. Wasn't it?

"They have rules here."

"Yes, rules and dictates—which you hate."

"Enough not to want them for you."

Mae shook her head, grasping for another argument.

"Want to know what I'm reading?"

Mae was silent.

"Some rather boring piece on botany by none other than Pierce." He smirked, motioning her to a tall stack of books. "I've finally learned his full name. Alexander Pierce. He's written of all these on different plant species and their properties. Can you believe it? A bit of an obsession, don't you think?"

"Stop it. I don't care a whit for books at the moment," she snapped. He wanted to distract her. But how could she oblige? Her upcoming departure occupied all her thoughts. So much needed to be said. The unspoken words hung heavily in the air, like a poisonous fog. She could not ignore how heavily it affected her, how it made any effort to breathe difficult.

"What do I do? Where do I go?" Once she claimed her fortune, she would have more money than she could want, but without him, her future seemed dismal.

"Any place you desire."

"I suppose I should buy a home someplace far away. Italy, maybe." She looked at the flower designs that decorated the rug.

"Is it as wonderful as I've read?"

"It is." Locke dropped his book onto the armchair with a *thud.* "What about your family estate? Will you not try to purchase it from the Rosewoods?"

The question was clearly a test. So she held him in suspense, staying silent as she paced up and down the shelves. Her fingers graced the spines. All the while, she could feel him following, watching her every step. "Very well, you were right. I don't have a future there, only a past."

"What happened in the cellar..." Locke's tone dropped. "What you did...you can't let it possess you, either. One day, I promise you, you'll learn to forgive yourself."

Mae swept around. He had gotten so close, she nearly bumped into him.

"I hope you're right," she said. Perhaps acceptance was the best she could hope for.

"And you? Have you forgiven yourself?" She was thinking about that woman who was being held captive, the one innocent who seemed to trouble him most of all.

"I've made amends and I'll keep making amends," he said, as though it were perfectly routine. As though it were nothing more than a promise to attend Sunday church. Perhaps those past mistakes were the least of his worries. Soon, there would be new regrets to trouble him.

When he reached out, it took her a moment to realize he was handing her something. A book.

"I found it here," he said. "One of my favorites. And since your journey is sure to be a long one..."

Her heart sank. He had settled on his decision. That was clear enough.

"You don't think they'd mind, do you?" Mae grasped it in her hand. Her eyes were fixed on the cover, but she saw nothing. She didn't even read the title.

"Please. Seems Pierce will do almost anything to get in your good graces. Sometimes, I wonder..."

"Wonder what?"

Locke looked around before dropping his voice to an even softer whisper. "We have to make sure you don't learn too much."

"Is that why you thought the tour inappropriate?"

"I wasn't just being rude, if that's what you're implying." Locke plopped himself onto the settee. He stared into the barren grate of the fireplace. "We should ring for a fire, hmm?"

"Then what is it?" Mae took the armchair beside him. "Why was it inappropriate?"

For a long moment, Locke didn't answer.

"Locke, tell me. I beg you."

"Fine. Before the day is out, I think Pierce is going to do everything in his power to convince you to join his organization. Perhaps their numbers are declining and since you already know…"

Why couldn't he just agree? They'd have each other. Nothing else would matter.

"Don't worry." Locke reached for her hand again, wiping away a smear of blood he had missed. His finger traced the place where the wound had been, no longer visible. "You trust me, don't you?"

"Yes," she whispered, though her heart screamed it louder.

He shot her a ghost of a smile. "Good."

"It's just…you could get hurt. Perhaps… Why not agree? Would it be so terrible?"

"Are you determined to torment me?"

"It doesn't have to be like this." She studied his features with careful precision, fearful of the day she would no longer know them. Years from now, would he forget her entirely? Somehow, she knew he would not. She had seen it. The feeling in his eyes hadn't been fleeting.

"I know men like Pierce." Locke's coldness returned. "He's got everything: power, money, connections. But that doesn't satisfy him. All that's left to attain is what he can't have, what's not right to have."

"Could his group really be so terrible?"

"To get this sort of power and money requires the darkest deeds," he said. "Look at how they brought us here, forced against our will… You mustn't let him persuade you."

Mae swallowed. She knew that. But at the same time, she was willing to give herself to any future if it meant being with him.

A thought froze her in place. There could, after all, be far worse fates in the world. Loneliness among others.

"What happens if I learn too much?" Mae had to ask. "What will he do then? And what if that is a fate far worse than joining?"

"You mustn't think like that. For now, we stand our ground."

"I'd much rather us leave. Together."

"As would I."

"Then how can you stay?" She could not help herself. "How can you know Pierce's telling the truth? What if—"

A sudden knocking silenced her.

Pierce stepped in, looking regal in his finely tailored waist-coat.

"Forgive the intrusion."

How much had he heard? Mae knew Locke wondered too because in that moment, he stepped closer, his stance firm. She imagined him like this at sea holding strong against the massive waves. Never giving up.

"Can I interest the two of you in that tour?" Pierce smiled warmly.

Mae glanced at Locke. It didn't seem they had much choice.

Within the maze of the building, they passed a grand ballroom, multiple libraries, and whole galleries of paintings and sculptures. There seemed nothing secretive or sinister about it. If it was anything, the tour was long and mostly boring. Mae could only stand the hundreds of ancient relics for so long before they lost their intrigue. For her, that had happened rooms ago.

Pierce pulled ahead. "I've one last surprise."

Mae tried not to show her relief, though Locke heaved out a well-deserved "Good riddance." Judging by his glare, Pierce was unaccustomed to such insolence.

He stopped in a cold hall lit by a wall sconce and held out his hand. After glancing at Locke, Mae decided to humor him, not expecting him so come so close.

"No one outside our members has come this far. But you, my dear, are a worthy first."

Mae gulped, though it wasn't the words that made her heart flutter—it was the tone and hidden meaning behind each syllable. He spoke and heeded her every reaction, as if she were something more than a disgraced governess, as if the world weighed on her good opinion.

She had to know. "Surely, you don't esteem me so highly?"

"But I do," he said. "And for good reason."

So much meaning seemed to swim in his eyes, Mae wasn't sure how to respond.

"Are you certain about this?" Without falter, Locke was at her side again. He had made a point to keep close. He didn't seem to care that Pierce had noticed.

Mae wasn't half so concerned. Rather, her curiosity was growing with each second. She was eager to see the areas privileged only to a few.

Locke prodded her. "Mae."

"One last room," she said.

Down a set of stairs, they seemed to spiral into oblivion. At the bottom, the hall was thick with moisture but full of light. A series of medieval-style torches intensely illuminated an arched hall that seemed to stretch for miles.

As they continued down, something wicked and unworldly crackled in the air. The place had an invisible yet powerful aura all its own. But from what? What type of mysteries lingered in these bricks?

Pierce opened a door Mae hadn't noticed. No sound indicated hinges or the twist of a doorknob. But with a breath of warmer air, the opening beckoned.

At first, there was only blackness, then with a fast-building intensity, the darkness was no more. Before her, a tangle of vines ran along stone walls, bursts of red scattered amongst them. Her eyes strained against the glare, but once her vision had adjusted, individual petals coalesced into beautiful, blooming roses. Overhead hung dozens of tilted mirrors, their purpose obvious yet impossible. Were they really reflecting light from so high above? The years it must have taken to construct! The amount of funds necessary… It all seemed quite impossible. *But why?* Mae wondered. *Why have it so hidden away?*

"This place…" Mae struggled to find the words. She simply had to know more.

"Take this." Pierce plucked a rose from the wall and handed it to her.

Naturally, she buried her nose in it and breathed in deeply. It didn't smell like a typical rose, full of crisp sweetness. It smelled of so much more. She breathed in the cool soil, the freshness of a summer breeze, the heat of the sun beating on her face. Sensations she didn't think had scent, yet that was the only way to make sense of it. What she held in her hand was no typical rose.

"It's beautiful." She exhaled, her body going weightless. Her head was swimming and she felt capable of bursting into a thousand pieces. Steadying herself, she tried to gauge Locke's reaction. But he had none. He looked about the makeshift greenhouse, his lips tightly closed to a thin line.

"What's it for?" Mae asked. "What is the purpose of all this?"

"It's one of our best abilities as of yet—"

Locke stepped between them. "This tour is over."

He took her hand and led her away.

"I haven't even shown her the crystals!" Pierce shouted after them.

In the hall, Mae yanked her arm back, defiant. "I can handle myself."

He drew in a deep breath and released it. "You shouldn't have asked for an explanation. Don't you get it? Everything here, especially knowledge, comes at a price."

"She is already one of us." Pierce's voice followed. "What else is left for her? She has nothing to go back to. You made sure of that."

"I made sure everything was set to rights. She has her inheritance now."

"So she has money." Pierce had found that mocking tone again. "Do you think that's all she's meant for in this world? A life of luxury? She has another purpose, truth be told, and that is here. With us."

"We agreed." Locke stood inches from Pierce now, as if ready to land a blow. Mae took a breath to calm her heart, but there seemed no hope of slowing it.

"I am no one of consequence, I assure you," she said. "You don't want me."

"Have you forgotten your own name?" Pierce asked her.

"There is no pride in it."

"Ah, but when you join us—"

"Sir." Mae threw away the rose. "I'm afraid I must refuse."

There was something nefarious about the group she could no longer deny. Something Locke had seen all along. He was right. She had just been curious was all. But she could never accept their invitation in order to stay with Locke.

"You have such strength in your heart and quickness in your mind." He threw his arms out wide. "The murder of your brother—"

"Please stop." Mae felt herself pale at the words. She could endure the memories no longer.

"Never fear the truth."

"Truth or not, what difference is there? Everyone thinks his death was a suicide. That will never change."

"With us, you can build your family's legacy anew. That sapphire, the serum—they are but a taste of the discoveries we've made—a whole world that is just beginning to open up before you."

"You've shown me nothing but a pretty garden."

"It is far more than that, Miss Blackthorne. Of course, if you wish I show you—"

"Our agreement still stands," Locke barked.

"Ah, Locke wisely knows the cost of such a secret."

"This is all for naught. She won't—"

"Let her decide!"

"Why me?" Mae sounded meek amidst their shouting.

"In the years ahead, I can see—"

"No." Mae stopped his lies. "You're desperate." Locke had been right again. "You need me to increase your numbers. But no one has time to be part of this foolishness anymore, do they?"

"You know not what you speak." Pierce's low voice was injured.

At first, it seemed he might give up the fight when all at once, he raced toward her. But instead of reaching her, he slammed into the square of Locke's shoulders. "You don't know what we are offering you. Few will ever know the privilege!"

"Enough." Locke shoved him backward into the glossy, brick wall. In the tight tunnel, his words echoed over and over.

But Pierce would not give up, looking past Locke to Mae only. "You are loyal to Locke, I understand." He straightened his cravat. "But why? Did he not tell you of his plans? They weren't going to let you off unharmed. Far from it."

"*Pierce.*"

He didn't listen. "Ellsworth would never agree to give you a third of the fortune—not without the promise of your death first. We are speaking of murder now, Miss Blackthorne. Your very own."

Though she had been well-aware, hearing it spoken aloud hurt all the same. She knew what her father had done. The anger and sense of revenge that had filled Locke before he'd met her. What if he had been unable to stop Ellsworth? He'd been outnumbered, after all.

"I lied to Ellsworth." Locke's face reddened, his hand still on Pierce's chest. "I never intended… I never would have let it come to that."

"If it had been William instead of me…would you have even hesitated?"

Locke didn't answer.

"You shouldn't trust me. How could you?" Pierce continued, more sure of himself. "But perhaps, if I may be so bold, you cannot trust Locke, either."

Mae braced herself. The tension seemed to burst all around her, fogging her head with pain. Though she wanted to deny his claim, breathing, much less speaking, seemed impossible.

She wasn't surprised when Locke took Pierce by his white collar. Violence had seemed imminent from the start. Now that Locke had Pierce by the neck, he held strong.

"Release me." Pierce struggled to free himself, though his voice was oddly calm. "For both our sakes."

When Locke refused, Pierce shouted a command. In response, thunderous steps rattled the lanterns. Guards from both directions surrounded them in moments, pistols drawn.

"How about now?" Pierce asked, a smile creeping over his face.

The cocking of their weapons echoed for a few seconds.

Locke grunted, then with one more shove, relaxed his grip. He eyed his opponents. One guard, a young man with a closely-trimmed beard, strode toward him. His aim shook, unsteady.

"Sir?"

Pierce gave a flick of the wrist and with a soft sigh of relief, the guard and the rest of the men stepped back, sheathing their weapons.

Mae could endure no more. She would not wait for the fighting to commence yet again. "You have my answer."

She didn't wait for a response. She just needed to get away. Following the path from which they'd come, she took the steps and went down the hall until she had reached something familiar. Against the hard, wooden banister, she caught her breath. As hard as she tried to, she struggled to wipe away the images of a murderous Locke. In one image, he was choking Pierce. In another, he was stabbing William.

That speech was part of Pierce's plans to discredit Locke, she told herself. Pierce was after her, just like Locke had said. But she could not let him succeed.

At the sound of footsteps, she twisted around, feeling the coolness of the stone wall behind her. It was Locke.

"We must speak." His eyes pleaded. "In private."

CHAPTER NINETEEN

Nathaniel

LOCKE LED MAE down the hall in silence. He didn't know how to begin. He had expected her to say something, anything. But the silence continued, making him feel worse.

A thousand thoughts seemed to rush into his head at once. And in Mae's presence, he had no hope for focus.

They stepped up a staircase. Farther down the hall, he held open a door into darkness.

"Your room?" she asked.

Locke struck a match and lit the lamp. He was grateful one of the maids had taken the time to tidy up his quarters. His bedsheets, usually left in complete disarray, were in perfect order.

Still, inviting Mae to his room was hardly proper. He expected her to object at any moment. Rather, she looked around, evidently not knowing where to sit or stand.

"This is very untoward, I know." He shut the door. "But we must be alone."

Mae nodded, waiting for him to continue. He swallowed a burst of fear. No one else could put him on edge like this.

"Striking that deal with Ellsworth has become my lowest deed," he began. "I won't tell you I hadn't a choice. I did. Even if..." He paused, searching. "It should not matter what your father did. That is nothing to me now and what I said earlier is true. I was never going to allow Ellsworth to harm you. The fact that he did… It ate away at me."

"I'm no idiot." Mae sat down on his bed. "I knew it all along."

She had almost forgotten it entirely. Whatever thoughts he'd had then didn't matter. The new deal he had made had proven all she needed to know. Damn the rest.

Locke felt his jaw go slack. "Then why help us?"

"I thought I'd find a way to outsmart you two. I almost did, didn't I?"

"You should despise me."

"What he did to you was awful," she said. "My father, I mean."

"Yes, but I knew it could never justify—I don't know why I didn't see it coming. I allowed Ellsworth to come too close…"

She lowered her gaze. For her, there must have been no escaping the subtle anxiety his name produced. He hated that he was still out there breathing, even if it wasn't for long. His name served as a reminder for him too. He saw her in the cellar again, atop a heap of dirt and dust, bleeding, barely able to breathe. He had cheated death on many occasions but never had he been more grateful for the serum. The black magic had saved them both.

"Despite what you may think"—he sat beside her, some distance away—"I wasn't thinking of the sapphire that day in the cellar, not even revenge. When I look at you, I don't see Alastair. You remind me of a much greater man… Your grandfather."

A long pause came near to driving him mad. By the time she spoke, she was surprisingly calm. "Precisely how old are you?"

Locke tried to make sense of her expression. There was no disbelief, contempt or panic, only curiosity.

He rubbed the tensing muscles of his neck. He could not let himself feel relief yet. "I'm only three years younger than your father."

Mae did the math. "Fifty-eight," she murmured.

"Old enough to know Nathaniel for almost half my life." He hadn't expected speaking of her grandfather would pain him so much. But it did. The man had been like a father to him. His greatest ally.

"Your grandfather, he was the fiercest yet most considerate man I had ever known. At sea, he held himself to the highest code. Learned from the greatest teachers. A natural-born leader if I ever knew one. Together, we plundered more wealth than your family had ever seen."

Wealth that for years he'd believed had been meant to be his. And yet, he cared nothing for it now.

"And just how did you come to meet him?" Mild surprise flickered across Mae's features. "Tell me everything."

Her eyes demanded it. There was no backing out of the story now.

"I was alone," he said. "My father and mother both dead."

It didn't matter how many years had passed, Locke still remembered the exact moment he had discovered their bodies. They had been curled up in bed together, their skin as pale as milk and covered in sores. He swallowed, ashamed at all the bitter crying he had done. But there had been no one around to notice at the time. No one around to care.

"Smallpox had taken the whole village. So at thirteen, I set out on my own." To this day, he still wondered why he had been the only one to survive. Of all the better men, why him?

"My father taught me how to trap and hunt. After some wandering, I took up residence in the woods."

Was it his imagination or had Mae leaned in closer?

"Your grandfather and I were neighbors and for a while, we were nothing more," he went on. "Then one day, while I was foraging, I heard hooves. Fearing discovery, I climbed up a tree, but in my haste, I slipped…"

"My grandfather rescued you?"

"Nathaniel was hunting at the time. From the fall, I had broken a couple of bones. But taking me to your estate, he helped me heal. For days, he even kept me company.

"I think he knew my parents were dead. He never asked where I'd come from. He simply told me the forest was no place for a boy. I had never lived in anything more than a hovel. When I saw the great Blackthorne estate—"

"You lived there?"

"Yes. You can imagine my appreciation. Never had I seen halls so vast, walls so adorned, furniture with carvings so intricate. It was like living in a dream.

"And yet despite my modest upbringing, your grandfather treated me no different than his own son—your father—like I was one of his own. While I healed, he told me stories. He talked most of the sea: the strange creatures, the daring battles, the relentless storms. He said if adventure was what I was after, it was a good living in this world."

He smiled to himself. The memories almost forgotten had been the warmest he had ever known.

"'Are pirates not criminals?' I asked him. "'Why not join His Majesty's Navy or board a merchant ship?' 'Because captains are cruel and unjust and your wages may never come,' he replied. 'But as a pirate, I could experience great adventure.'"

He was grateful Mae could hear the tale now. He wanted her to know the kindness of her grandfather. He had been so many things to Locke: a father, a mentor, a friend.

"I don't know why he took me in. Perhaps he sensed something in me. Something like bravery, I'd like to think. He even taught me to read. I managed to learn quickly and caught up to your father. He was a great lover of books too."

"You knew him well. Perhaps better than I."

"We grew up together. 'Alastair, come meet your new brother,' your grandfather told him. 'He'll be joining us at sea.'"

"How old were you then?"

"Just fourteen, if you can imagine. Your father and I, we learned everything together—strategy, how to wield a sword, pistol, dagger—everything... He was a bit perturbed by my eagerness, I think. He was always trying to outshine me, even if I was three years younger and no blood relation. In my eyes, I could never compete."

Mae shook her head. "A simple ship builder. Until recently, I thought he was nothing more."

"People can be many things. I, too, wanted to be so much more than the shopkeeper my father had been. I decided I wasn't a child anymore. I would build my own manor. I would live independently and make a life of my own."

Secretly, he had aspired to build a home as great as the Blackthornes'. A dream that seemed silly and materialistic now.

"I almost succeeded," he said. "At sea, sailors quickly surrendered under your family's flag. We smuggled freshly minted coins en route, stole whatever we could from merchant ships, and traded the loot for gold or jewels."

But it hadn't all been gain, he didn't dare admit. He recalled the battles that had turned bloody. The terrible men who had deserved to die. The good men who hadn't.

"It was far more money than I could ever dream of, but soon, it wasn't about the spoils. It was about the adventure—though I suppose that was what piqued my interest in the first place."

"When did you find the sapphire?"

"I was twenty-five and I remained twenty-five until Alastair snatched the sapphire from me seven years ago."

"So even though you are far older, you've only aged thirty-two years...."

"It meant I could keep on smuggling and that's what I did. We kept on smuggling. Somehow, the gold was never enough. I was missing something and not a kingdom's worth of gold could fill that hole."

He cleared his throat as if that might rid him of the ever-present ache. "In the end, our good fortune didn't last. Laws were passed. The seas were better patrolled and officials stopped overlooking our crimes. I could sense the end."

"How long before anyone noticed you weren't aging?"

"It was your father and likely the servants too who first noted it when I returned to demand my share of our profits. Though I showed up at his doorstep, Alastair refused to me step inside. I wanted to tell him all. After thirty years at sea, I was supposed to be in my fifties, like your father. Instead, I looked as if I were still in my twenties. I had to tell him something. But he didn't even let me explain. He was convinced it had to do with the devil and demanded I leave.

"I was set to leave never to return again when he came to my manor in the woods." Locke tensed at the memory, his words rising. "He poisoned me. Right in my own home. With the very wine I had offered, he left me for dead. He watched me as I choked, smiled even as he swiped my sapphire. 'I always fancied this rock.' He laughed. 'Since the day you took it, I've wanted it."

"That's awful." Mae grasped at her throat. "I never thought him… I just never… All of this when I was just a child," Mae murmured. "All of this at a time when my father and I played guessing games, when he told me fairy tales on the lawn… I had no idea."

Seeking reprieve from the dreary subject, Locke regarded her in the haze of the weak lamplight. Her eyes shone the very same as they had that fateful day in the Northern Woods. Since then, she had changed him, just as Nathaniel had done.

She had softened him. And despite all his years, every experience and sensation with her felt like his first.

"You're nothing like your father. He was greedy," Locke said. "More so than I. Superstitious too. He had envied the sapphire for years—particularly all of the luck it seemed to bring me. What irony."

"He never did discover its power, did he?" Mae sounded disappointed, almost.

"Apparently not. Sometimes, I think he took it out of spite. He knew how much I liked the thing."

"But the poison—you survived somehow," she said with glossy eyes. The story had clearly made her emotional. Because of what she had heard about his father or himself, perhaps. Maybe both.

"Yes. Thanks to the serum, I could claim revenge. I thought I could surprise your father, hold his life for ransom, just as we did at sea. I wasn't expecting the Silver Order to find me. He demanded the sapphire, wherever it was, be returned. But there was no chance your father would return it. The sapphire, I suspected, had been stored up with our spoils, out of reach. I had no choice but to run. For seven years, that's what I did. I lived from city to city, smuggling and thieving as the opportunity arose. It was the only way I knew how to survive."

"When you returned, my father was dead."

"Nothing was as I expected. The business had faltered. Your father… How…" His voice quavered. "How did he—"

"Pneumonia," Mae said. "It happened so suddenly that winter. First a cough then an inability to stand and finally…"

"I see."

Mae disguised her pain well, but Locke could imagine the desolation of that winter and all the years that had followed, not to mention the last couple of weeks. He wished now that he had been kinder. If only he could manage to come up with better words of remorse. For her sake, at least.

"One day, that could be my fate too," Locke said, her gaze captured by his every word. Taking her hand, he placed it over his chest. She flinched at the pulsing of his heart like that of a frightened beast. "I have a heart, the same blood as you. A blade would stop its beating no different than yours. Without the sapphire, I'm aging again. My time here is limited too."

These last few days, every second, every word had become precious to him. The last decade seemed a century, but the last couple of weeks, an instant. A flame now extinguished.

"You can't stay." Mae stood up and paced away, her voice sharp and demanding. "I can't let you."

"Please abandon this fight."

"I've seen my future too, you know. I am always wondering

what has become of you."

"It doesn't matter. Those guards. They would be on us in an instant." He went after her, even if it was only a few steps in that room.

"They're afraid of you. I saw it in that man's eyes when we arrived. We could use that somehow." Her face brightened. "We'll escape. Right when Miss Rosewood leaves."

"I've already lived that life, Mae. I won't have it for you." He would sooner endure a thousand more years of it than allow that.

"Why? Because you pity me?" She pulled back. "Because you feel sorry for what has happened?"

"Yes." He closed his eyes.

"But—don't you feel anything for me?"

"Of course I do. Since the start." Finally, he'd said it. As much as he had dared to. Two insignificant words that meant so much. Pointless as it was.

"Truly?" Mae's mouth parted, her fingers twisting around each other. "But still you mean to stay?"

She bit down on her lower lip, her chin trembling.

"It's the rightest, most noble thing to do."

Soon, she would forget about him. She just needed time.

"Hang the noble…and honor and decorum and pride," she said in harsh reply.

Could he have heard her correctly? He tried to read her eyes, but a deep sadness in them had not wavered.

Then something in her gaze shifted. A look that made him itch with lust. He feared what he might do when she took another step forward. But it was not his actions alone he needed to control.

Stilling him, she came close.

"I don't care for any of it." She needed only whisper now. "Not in the least." She gripped his arms tighter. "Not since I met you."

He thought he knew what she wanted. But watching her, he hesitated. He had to see. To be sure she wanted this.

He sucked in a raspy breath. Though neither of them seemed sure, temptation persisted. Her scent too strong, her lips too close. He could not bear it.

Leaving his mind and all hope for reason behind, he pulled her in. There was only the taste of her, all sweetness and warmth.

She pushed back and, before he could think why, she pulled her dress down from her shoulders then tugged at her draw-strings. Her gown disappeared, replaced by her skin. Like gold, she gleamed in the gloom. In the next instant, he saw all of her, the dress now a puddle on the floor.

His jaw went slack, his body tightening at the sight.

For a moment, he feared interruption from Pierce, a serv-ant—anyone. But lifting her up into his arms, he would let nothing stop them now. Not even if the room around them burst into flames. He wanted to drink her in many times over and each time with less restraint.

The rules didn't exist. For one more instant at least, she was his.

🌙

LYING IN LOCKE'S bed, Mae inhaled. His scent was all around her. Wonderful sensations still pricked over her skin, filling her with warmth.

She did not want to leave, but her stomach rumbled for the dinner she had missed. She considered going to the kitchens herself but discarded the idea. What if a servant saw her leaving his room? What if—

Catching her off-guard, footfalls clicked in the hall.

A bad feeling settled over her. In the glow of the dying fire, she could only make out shadows.

"Locke?" Mae sat up. A figure was in her room now. But it wasn't Locke. The slim silhouette was that of a woman.

Miss Rosewood.

"What are you doing here?" Mae gasped. She was, after all, completely naked. In the weak light from the hall, Miss Rosewood seemed to know it too.

"I might ask you the same. If it were not so obvious."

"Miss Rosewood, please. You should not be in here." Mae wrapped a sheet around herself and leaped out of bed, grateful Locke was gone.

"Is that shame I detect?"

The comment should have awakened her inner rage. Instead, her voice softened. "You wouldn't understand."

Even if she had caught the attention of the servants too, she didn't care. That evening had been worth every risk.

"Why is that?"

Unable to see much in the darkness, Mae searched restlessly for her clothing piled across the floor. Reaching out, she felt the sheer fabric of one of her underskirts.

"Just turn around," Mae barked.

Miss Rosewood scowled but obeyed nonetheless.

Mae dragged on her clothing, but hang it, she was still missing her corset.

"I thought you were better than this." Miss Rosewood picked it from beneath the bed and threw it at her. "You're—you're not even married. Now that you've done this, he'll never ask for your hand. But—oh… This isn't even the first time, is it?"

"Why have you come?" She worked to finish lacing her corset, thankful the one they had lent her laced up in the front, not back. Otherwise, she would have needed Miss Rosewood's help and that was the last thing she wanted. It was more likely they'd never speak again.

Though sloppily, Mae stepped into her dress and pulled it up over her shoulders too.

"Here." Miss Rosewood gathered Mae's shoes. "You'll need these."

Mae took them. Already, she felt sorry. Considering all Miss Rosewood had been through, perhaps her anger was justifiable.

She deserved some leeway. "Miss Rosewood, I—"

"I know he chose you instead. I even released him from our engagement, but do you have to rub it in my face?"

"I didn't plan for this."

"What would you have me believe? That he forced himself on you?"

Mae bent down to the floor again. Where was her key? She was never to let it out of sight and here it was: missing. She really had been careless.

Frantic, she patted the floor around her until, beneath the bed, she felt it. She took in a breath of relief and tucked it away into the top of her corset.

She had no delusions. Despite what had just happened between them, Locke was still sure to stay here among the Order. But at least her future was safe, financially. In all other aspects, she hadn't much else.

"Is it not enough that you ruined me?" Miss Rosewood continued her flouncing.

"I didn't think you'd chase after us."

"I loved him. Of course I followed, I thought… I was so sure I could change his mind. I was so sure I could save him from a trollop like you."

The phrase, so malicious, angered her this time. What she had with Locke went deeper than those last few hours. What existed between them had been real—even if it could not last.

She was glad Locke wasn't here to hear this, but at the same time, his absence said everything. She had a feeling he meant never to return. Perhaps it was better that way, to end things like that.

"You're right." Despite being decent, Mae felt naked again. "He's already left me."

But this only seemed to infuriate Miss Rosewood further. Her face contorted with it. "Then why did you do it? He wanted to marry me first. But you stole him away. It was you. You sought to ruin me."

Where were these words earlier? Miss Rosewood had only wanted to make it seem like she had forgiven her. Maybe she was just trying to appease Pierce so he wouldn't lock her away again. Truth was, she really hadn't forgiven Mae at all.

"How long have you been planning this?" Miss Rosewood demanded.

That was the last straw. "I planned nothing of the sort." She grabbed Miss Rosewood's shoulders, seeing no other way to drive home the truth. "I didn't mean to do it. I didn't mean to betray you."

Miss Rosewood had to believe her. These last two years, she'd thought they'd liked each other. But Miss Rosewood wrenched away, not with a look of distress but with a smirk. *"Mr. Ellsworth."*

"He is only trying…" The words drifted away. Mae knew instantly what was to become of her. The name had been a signal. Inside the room, she could make out the outline of another intruder.

She didn't need candlelight to know it was him. When he entered the weak flicker of the firelight, the sight of him, disheveled and greasy with sweat, stunned her to silence. His eyes seemed set on two things: violence and suffering.

Mae fumbled backward, gripping the bedsheets, desperate to create distance, but it was no use. She was trapped.

Before she could scream, a hand clenched tightly across her face. And it wasn't just his hand. She felt the coarse fabric of a rag and a harsh chemical sting.

In the few moments before unconsciousness settled over her, she knew she was dead. For the best, she supposed.

She hadn't much of a future without Locke either way.

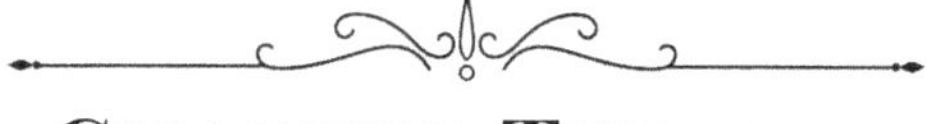

CHAPTER TWENTY

A New Ally

LOCKE WAITED OUTSIDE Pierce's office, his heart still roaring in his chest. All that had happened with Mae had given him hope. Now he had to squash it. He could not continue to linger in that dream.

He needed to at least *pretend* he could forget her. It didn't matter that she had heard his truths and, despite all his misgivings, she still wanted him, still trusted him enough to…

Lying with her was the closest he had gotten to living, truly living. He had never known the spoils that an honest life could bring, not until he had been with her. He was almost dizzy from the bliss. And he still had to give it up?

He stopped his pacing abruptly. Of course, those moments with her had changed nothing. He had to turn his back on her. Though he meant it for her own good, it certainly did not feel that way.

In the library, he had debated long enough. If he must do this, he would do it before his resolve weakened. Whatever the details Pierce needed to provide, he would gather and accept them.

His only fear was that this new life would continue for too long. The finest pleasures would never be enough to thwart his isolation. He'd soon become a machine. He fought back the anguish, feeling his throat, chest, and whole body harden to steel. Already, he wanted to return to his room, to escape within her arms.

He played their last few moments over again in his mind. He had watched her drift off to sleep, looking so peaceful, more so than any day since he'd met her. Somewhere in the night, he had fallen asleep himself, but when he'd woken early that morning, he'd known he couldn't stay. Taking in her beautiful face one last time, he'd been determined to remember every detail, storing it away for future use.

That should not have been their last time together. He clenched his fist, feeling himself giving in, not knowing if could stand a second longer of this fate.

At a flicker of movement, he looked up and stilled his grinding teeth. A guard, one with a short beard whom he recognized from earlier, appeared at the threshold. Pierce had been speaking to him for quite some time and Locke had grown tired of waiting. But as the guard brushed past, all that was forgotten. Something in the guard's sympathetic gaze cautioned him. Something was wrong.

Locke stepped into the doorway, taking note of the large office, preparing himself for anything, perhaps even a brawl.

At first, there seemed no hope of weapons. Carpeted in gold and green with shelves stacked full with books, the room held an air of pretentiousness rather than authority. But within the varied array of antiquities, his luck held true. Behind a glass display lay stone hieroglyphics and a pouch of excavation tools. If need be, the pick would serve him well enough.

"What is it?" Locke demanded, seeing Pierce's troubled expression. His heart thudded against his chest, fresh panic surging into his veins.

"Where did you last see Miss Blackthorne?" Pierce asked, quite calm.

"In my—why? Tell me what has happened." Locke was already inching toward the door, nervous for her safety. But he had to stay. He had to find out what was going on.

"Ellsworth escaped. It appears Miss Rosewood assisted in it. She, too, is gone. Seems you were right about her loyalties."

Locke nodded. Since he'd met Miss Rosewood, he'd known how naive and gullible she was, not to mention desperate for a husband. He wasn't surprised at all she had come to believe Ellsworth's manipulations.

Locke tried to speak, only his jaw went rigid. He swallowed. "When—When did this happen?"

"Sometime in the night, my men believe. He cannot have been gone for—"

Not bothering to hear the words, Locke cursed and raced out the door. Even that bit of explanation had stalled him too long. If Mae was not in his room, he would never forgive himself.

He ran faster, picking up his pace with every step. Climbing the marble steps, they never seemed to end. His lungs burned with exertion. He feared he might never reach her. He feared she was already dead.

Once in the hall, he closed the distance to his room in a matter of moments. He burst open the door and stepped inside. His heart seemed to freeze.

The bed, with sheets crumpled over to one side, was empty. But the smell of her was still in the air. She had been taken sometime within the last hour.

Like an idiot, he had been standing idle waiting for Pierce. How had he allowed this to happen? He paced along the edges of the room, looking for any clues. But it was pointless. Ellsworth had taken her and Locke knew exactly what he wanted.

Well, two things. Locke took up the pillow still dented from her face and squeezed it. Ellsworth could get the gold for all he cared, but he would never claim her life.

Shaking from head to toe, he remembered Ellsworth's nonchalant plans. To him, her death would be just one of many dark deeds in his ledger. Locke twisted the pillow and dropped it. Steps echoed in the hall.

Pierce had men crawling all over the place and Ellsworth had managed to escape? Just like that? Pierce had a hand in this. Damn him to hell.

Eager for a fight, Locke picked up the gas lamp and threw it to the floor. He found the largest shard and held it at the ready.

As the steps got nearer, the image of Ellsworth and his men overtaking Mae in the woods flashed across his eyes. The memory near paralyzed him. But with a creak of the floorboard, he was ready for blood again, ready to drown in it, if need be.

Silhouetted in the light of the hallway, a figure entered.

"Locke." Pierce stepped into a stream of light cast by the moon. All the color drained from his face. Locke stilled but didn't drop his weapon. He tilted it so that with the flick of the wrist, it might go diving into the man's neck.

He didn't care how many had to die for him to escape. He wouldn't fail this time. Pierce seemed to know this also.

"Once I strike the aorta, you'll be dead before your guards can scream for help. And I'm an excellent shot."

Pierce froze. "I don't doubt it."

"Now give me the truth."

"Fine," he breathed out. "I might have pulled my guards off their watch."

"Why?" Locke glared.

"I realized something. Without Miss Blackthorne, you're useless to me."

"You promised to let her go."

"Yes, but the life and vivacity that I saw in you was all but gone once you'd made your choice. And Miss Blackthorne… I thought maybe I could at least do with her alone, but then I came to realize without you, she'd be just as dead inside as you."

Locke couldn't help but smile at that.

"You can't imagine all the resources I've wasted bringing you here. It was high time my men focused on other more fruitful activities."

"It didn't matter what happened to us, eh?" Locke crossed his arms. He didn't believe the bastard for a moment. It was more likely that the man had gone so far as to order Ellsworth's release. Pierce couldn't just let Locke and Mae just walk away. Not now. They knew too much. Ellsworth, who already wanted them dead, would be the perfect man to do the dirty work.

Locke wouldn't have been surprised if Pierce had offered Ellsworth some kind of deal. He wondered what. He doubted any overture needed to be much.

He had probably requested Ellsworth to stab them both in his sleep. Pierce didn't know Ellsworth wanted Mae alive. At least for a long enough to find the vault. But Locke, he was supposed to be dead by now. Rather, he wanted a few words first, and maybe a few fists.

"I have another theory." Locke lifted his weapon an inch higher. Another guard would, of course, be waiting around the corner, but he didn't let that fear show.

Pierce swallowed, the sheen of sweat along his brow visible even in the darkness. "I could help you…"

"That's a start."

"I could return your weapons."

"Just like you returned Ellsworth's weapons?" Locke raised his brow.

"Plus some," Pierce put in.

"Then lead the way." Locke jiggled the shard.

With a nod, Pierce turned around back to the hall, albeit slowly.

Locke followed along, his weapon still poised.

Locke didn't know where this man was taking him and for all he knew, it could very well be a trap. But rather than continue to the stairs, Pierce stopped at a painting and pulled on its gold frame, revealing a dark, narrow passageway. He took a candle from a wall sconce and eyed Locke.

"You remind me a great deal of myself you know. Ruthless. Resourceful." Pierce laughed, no longer seeming to mind that a weapon was still trained on him. "Who would have thought I'd ever be comparing myself to a pirate?"

"As it is, I don't think you'd last a day amongst my crew."

Pierce laughed again, the boom of it echoing in the tight corridor. "Yes, well, I do like my comforts."

Locke continued to follow, the thud of their steps cutting the silence. He tried to see ahead, but the candlelight didn't stretch far. Beyond four or five feet was utter blackness.

"It was a mistake trying to kill you," he said plainly. "I see now that you might still be useful… as an ally."

"If I survive."

"A man like you? I have no doubt. How's this? I enlist two of my own men to your service. I'd be happy to provide the favor."

No doubt with an expectation of payment sometime in the future, just for letting him live. "As in two of your guards?"

"They'd be proud to follow you," Pierce insisted, keeping his steps quick. "But in exchange, I'd like for us to be allies."

Locke smiled—the man was quick on his feet. Luckily, negotiation came as natural as breathing to Locke as well.

"In other words, never attack your ships again."

"More importantly, I'd like you to keep a few things secret."

"Agreed. But keep your men." Their loyalty would be too hard to judge.

Pierce paused in his steps. "Are you so sure you won't need them?"

"Quite."

"The healing serum, then."

"You can take it." Locke reached toward his neck.

"No." Pierce stopped him. "It's the least I can do." The apology, if it was one, meant nothing to Locke. Pierce had let Ellsworth take Mae and there was no knowing how she might be suffering now.

Locke touched the serum. He was glad to have it—even if the thought of using it on Mae unnerved him.

A few more steps and Pierce stopped at a large iron door. He unlocked it with a silver key and swung it open.

Pierce's light flickered across the room. Lined up against the walls were weapons of every breed. From throwing knives to two large cannons in the back. It was a pirate's dream.

On the long, wooden table, his weapons were laid out in a row. Locke sheathed his blades first then stashed his pistols beneath his clothing.

"You'll need this too." From a wardrobe, Pierce produced a black cloak similar to those Locke had seen on the guards. "It will make us true allies."

Locke pulled his arms through the loose sleeves. It felt light but warm.

"Nothing can penetrate it. Neither a bullet nor a blade."

Locke raised his brows. He knew only heavy metals that could do as much.

Seemingly sensing his doubts, Pierce swiped a blade from his waist. "Are you brave enough to test it?"

When Locke nodded, Pierce thrust the blade into Locke's arm. Like metal, the cloak's material held firm. The fabric showed no sign of damage. "'Tis a special kind of silk. One of my more favored discoveries."

"Impressive." Locke touched the insignia patched on the sleeve: A simple rose with a dagger run through the center. The whole image was embroidered in silver thread. "I should be careful who sees me in the, eh?"

"Quite the contrary." Pierce sheathed his fine, silver-hilted blade. "Rest assured. Should any friends of mine see you in this, they will come to your aid. One never knows."

Did this mean they were friends now? The idea repulsed him. The moment Ellsworth was dead, he'd throw away this cloak. He vowed to never speak Pierce's name again. Locke squared his shoulders, ready to fly. "Now where's my horse?"

Pierce nodded and led him once more through the passages.

In the stables, even Gambit seemed to share a sense of urgency. Mounting him, Locke gave Pierce one last nod of goodbye, but hardly gratitude.

The man puzzled him. Even though Locke had come to the Silver Order as a prisoner, Pierce wanted only to be allies, maybe even partners. Now, Pierce must have known that to be impossible.

Locke twisted Gambit toward the fading light of day. Just before racing off, he pulled back. "I was right, wasn't I?" He shouted over his shoulder. "Your prediction was a lie." Mae had been right to fight it.

But by the time Locke had swung around, Pierce had disappeared back inside.

Locke shook his head. Pierce had fooled him. Of course his so-called future had been a lie. Maybe Pierce had hoped his acquiescence would lead to Mae's. But she had already known her future. She might have even pictured it. He knew he had.

In the end, Ellsworth's plans weren't going to succeed.

Locke focused on the swaying wheat fields ahead, wondering what the man had really seen. Was his future and Mae's still undetermined? He didn't want to know.

As Pierce had promised, the iron gate was wide open.

CHAPTER TWENTY-ONE
The Jump

AN ABRUPT HALT shook Mae awake. Before she could steady herself, rough hands threw her from a horse.

Sharp rocks cut into her knees. In the settling dust, a wave of confusion seized her to stillness. Her surroundings were like a nightmare. The trees were no longer black, but alight with the gold of a bonfire. She expected witches, even elves. Instead, stood a gathering of men and their tents.

Ellsworth's gang seemed almost refined in comparison. They donned what could barely be considered clothing, more like rags dinged with dirt, their hair matted and stringy. They laughed and argued, no doubt deep in their cups.

She was thankful for the darkness now. It was all that kept her shielded from view.

Mae pressed a finger to her temple. Her head still ached from whatever Ellsworth had used to drug her. How long had he been planning this? How, exactly, had he escaped Pierce's grips?

She felt the inside of her bodice. Ellsworth had taken the key too.

"Some distance, yes, but you'll find the journey worth your while, I assure you. The horses—magnificent, aren't they? They are yours." The voice was unmistakable. Mae looked over her shoulder. Ellsworth's lips strained into a smile. Though he had wiped his face clear of the sweat and dirt of before, his usual mustache had grown out to a frizzy, untamed line. His eyes squinted with exhaustion.

The very sight of him brought on the urge to run. But as she prepared her aching limbs, another set of hooves closed in.

It was Miss Rosewood. Her hair was wild from the wind, her posture straight, just as Mae had once advised her. *Run*, she thought. But remembering the night prior, a dreadful realization dawned.

Miss Rosewood had had a hand in this. She was angry with Mae. More than that, she was determined to have a husband. No matter how despicable.

Though in her mind, Mae wanted to deny it. The girl—she didn't care how naïve—could not have endangered them both like this.

"Miss Rosewood." Mae's voice croaked, her voice unrecognizable.

Her former pupil leaped down from her horse and headed toward her. For now at least, Ellsworth remained distracted by his transaction. If they were going to get away, they couldn't wait a moment longer.

"We have to run," Mae whispered.

Miss Rosewood pressed her finger to her lips, her eyes watering. "We're going home," she whispered.

"'Home'?" Mae questioned. If they were returning to Blackthorne Manor, they'd only be returning her to prison.

"You're going to help us find the vault, then everything will go back to normal. Better than normal, really. I'll be married. Frances said we'll be rich."

Mae cringed at the implied intimacy. "But the vault isn't..." Then Mae realized the truth with a tinge of relief. Ellsworth hadn't put two and two together when he'd caught them together along the coast. He'd thought they had just been running and doing God-knew-what. What would he do when he discovered the truth, that the vault wasn't anywhere near the manor? Mae didn't want to think about it.

"Miss Rosewood, please," Mae continued to plead. "You can't do this. You can't help him." Mae ground out between her teeth. "He'll kill me. He'll kill us both."

Miss Rosewood shushed her just like Mae had once done if she'd interrupted a lesson. "He promised he wouldn't hurt you. Don't you understand? This is the only way I'll be able to repair my reputation. I won't be shunned from society, Miss Black-thorne. I won't be made a pariah."

Mae buried her face in her hands. This was hopeless.

"Frances will make as good a husband as any," Miss Rose-wood said, like she was trying to convince herself more than Mae. "He will follow through with what he started. He has to."

"Miss Rosewood, please." Mae made one last plea, sinking her nails into the moist ground. Ellsworth was manipulating the young woman. How could she not see? Once more, Mae was at the man's mercy, but Locke couldn't rescue her this time. He was a prisoner of the Silver Order. What happened to her could no longer be his concern, she imagined Pierce saying.

Mae's only hope was appealing to Miss Rosewood. "Listen to me—"

"Oh, stop your pleading." Miss Rosewood looked down at Mae. "This will all be for the best. You'll see."

Just then, Ellsworth began to laugh, so loud and coarse, it was impossible to ignore. "No, you can't have these women." He waved the unkempt man away. "Put away your gold. They are mine."

Mae shivered at the implication. They were little more than captives now. It didn't take much to see that. Why didn't Miss Rosewood see the same? Mae tried to tell herself that her pupil didn't know any better, that she had failed her in the classroom in some way.

"Come." Ellsworth dragged Mae to a rickety wagon cart. "We have a fortune to raid."

He threw her in but didn't move away. He stayed close to speak to the driver.

A hum of disappointment coursed through her. There was no hope for escape. Not yet.

Miss Rosewood entered next and sat directly opposite, her face turned away, but her body oddly close. In the weak glow that penetrated, she looked quite changed. Her face was pale and devoid of its usual brightness.

"Soon, we'll see you off to London." Miss Rosewood shifted on the hard, cushion-less seat. "There, you can find work…and think of what you've done."

"This is immoral. Have you forgotten everything I've ever told you, Miss Rosewood?"

"Like what?" She eyed Mae suspiciously.

"The engagement I broke off—I never told you his name."

They stared at each other for a moment.

"It was Ellsworth," Mae revealed. "Ellsworth is nothing more than my brother's murderer."

"No man is going to be perfect." Miss Rosewood shook her head in denial, but a crack was spreading along her steel façade. "Especially if one is ruined."

"William told him about our fortune." Mae's voice grew louder. "One I knew nothing about."

"The fortune Ellsworth keeps speaking of? The one you're supposed to lead us to?"

"Oh, there's no doubt of that," Mae said. "And there's no doubting he killed William for it."

"Mother says his death was a suicide." Miss Rosewood's face turned a shade paler.

"It was not."

"But—But if it is true…no, you would have told me sooner."

"I'm sorry I didn't."

"He said your father owed him money." Miss Rosewood averted her attention to her hands. The crack in her mask had widened. Her fear was obvious now.

"Ellsworth lies. Don't you see it in his manner? In his face?" Mae reached out to touch her cold hands. "That vicious gleam in his eye? Haven't you noticed any of it?"

"What difference does it make?" Miss Rosewood's face went still, her voice dropping down to a meek whisper. "I have no choice."

"But you do. Would a life like mine really be so bad? It has to be better than a life with Ellsworth. I considered it when I lost everything and thought better of it. Much better of it.

"Surely, you have regrets." Miss Rosewood's voice croaked. She seemed so much older since they'd arrived at Pierce's manor. Older in appearance yet still so naïve.

Mae wanted to say as much but with the opening of a door, Ellsworth's wheezy voice filled the wagon. "Ladies," he said with mocking reverence. "We are off."

As he shuffled into his seat, Mae winced at his proximity. The urge for justice, she feared gone, had returned. She wanted to be free of him once and for all, to get the knife back in her hands like at the coast, and kill. But she had no blade, no weapon at her disposal.

Was it too late to do or change anything? Was she already doomed?

LOCKE TIGHTENED HIS grip on the reins and looked down at the camp of thieves. Ellsworth had gotten much farther than he had expected. Although Locke had been on the man's trail for hours, he was only now catching up.

In his haste, it seemed Ellsworth had had no choice but to resort to these scum of scum. Locke was painfully familiar with what these men would do for a guinea or two. He had crossed paths with them far more often than he had ever wanted. Thieves like them existed all across the globe. They eluded capture merely by their ability to leave town on a whim. They were more animals than men. Animals that he would never have anything to do with again.

They had undoubtedly killed a number of innocent men. But aiding in the kidnapping of an innocent woman… Damn it, they had gone too far.

He watched Ellsworth give orders to the driver of the wagon. All the while, the men argued and drank on without a care. Rage surged through his veins. They didn't know whom they were dealing with.

He kicked Gambit forward. Which way to turn? Was Ellsworth aware of the fortune's true location near Mae's summer home? Or did he think the vault, though not in the cellar, was still hidden somewhere within the estate?

He could bribe the men to learn Ellsworth's destination, but by the time the stealthy men negotiated a price, it might be too late. And going any closer to overhear Ellsworth's orders would mean discovery. He would not ruin his chances of surprising the man—at least not yet.

Only under penalty of pain would the men give away Ellsworth's destination quickly enough. As the wagon trudged away, Locke considered slashing the throat of every drunk man he set his sights on. He could practically feel the blood spilling over his hands and the justice that would soothe his soul.

He had killed many at sea in the name of his men. And if he stuck to another one of his old habits, he would kill all of them save for one. That man already weak with fear would undoubtedly give into his demands and questions at once.

It would take only a matter of minutes to complete the task. But somehow, he couldn't act. His desire to kill wasn't as it once was. He had softened.

He even felt glad for it.

He was no longer the same ruthless pirate unafraid to die because he'd had nothing for which to live. Now that Mae depended on him, jumping into a fight with twenty or so men seemed senseless. He would not risk himself, not when he was her only hope—not when he could so clearly see their future together.

There were other options before him. He could keep close to the carriage. Though it meant risking discovery, only then would killing be justified.

He found his knife at his waist, imagining the feel of it pressed against Ellsworth's throat. Yes, it would be a very justifiable murder, indeed. One of which he was sure even Mae would approve.

He only hoped he would be the one to suffer the deed. He imagined Mae with his blade in her hand again, so eager to kill. Above all, that was what he needed to stop.

With a bitter swallow of breath, Locke disappeared once more into the safety of the trees.

DURING THEIR LONG, restless journey, a thick stew of fog had settled over the road, dulling the afternoon sun.

She doubted a brighter day could improve her mood, anyway. No matter how hard she tried, her mind always returned to Locke.

She wanted that goodbye now, to savor that final kiss, to beg him to write. If she somehow managed to survive this, how would she find him? She didn't even know the town in which the Silver Order had been. Even if she had, the manor had been hidden away too well, their fences too high to breach. That, in addition to his voyages, which would be entirely unknown to her. But what did it matter? As hard as she tried, she could not picture a future beyond this.

With the slowing of the horse, the driver announced their arrival. They were pulling up to a train depot.

Ellsworth looked at them, daring them to make so much as a

single movement. "Don't waste your time." He lifted his coat to reveal a knife at his waist.

The driver held open the door.

But rather than let Miss Rosewood or Mae go first, Ellsworth pushed ahead. When Mae dismounted, he clasped her arm.

Outside, a mix of black smoke and fog darkened their surroundings. She had never taken the train, had only heard stories since the station had opened some months back. The talk was hardly enticing. The heavy smoke choked and even went so far as to blacken clothes.

To make matters worse, the platform was crowded with curious gentry and those clearly on summer holiday. As they worked through the smog, people jerked, shoved, and pressed against them.

"Stay close," Ellsworth breathed. As if she had a choice. He held his grip so tight, she couldn't stray an inch. Miss Rosewood, his more willing captive, he allowed to linger behind.

Mae could scream out, but she didn't doubt that Ellsworth would rather harm her right in this public thoroughfare than let her get away. Revenge, at this point, was more important. She could see it in his dark, gleaming eyes. Even if someone came to her aid, he'd probably hurt Miss Rosewood just to cause Mae pain.

Mae imagined how it might have looked from the outside. Her body folded into him, his hand coiled around her waist. Bloody hell, people probably thought they were lovers.

They blended in well-enough that as they walked toward the wooden platform, not a face turned in her direction. The bustle of society streamed around them and no one was the wiser.

"Eager to return?" Ellsworth put his lips to her ear.

Miss Rosewood huffed. She likely hardly expected a faithful lover in him, but watching it play out in front of her was a different thing entirely. Before Miss Rosewood turned away, Mae glanced tears in her eyes. Her shoulders were trembling too. Miss Rosewood would never speak up, Mae realized. She was in far too deep.

Mae tried to see it from Miss Rosewood's perspective. If she didn't marry Ellsworth, she'd be cast out of society. Her own family, so set on an advantageous husband for Miss Lenore, might abandon her too. She'd be alone in so many more ways than one.

"You have the key." Mae twisted against his hot breath. In her desperation and with his body so close, her eyes teared up. "You can find the vault on your own."

There was a pause of silence before Ellsworth laughed deep and low in his throat. "And give you up? Your father's most prized and favorite jewel?"

"He's dead. So is William. Is that not enough?"

When Ellsworth didn't answer, her panic grew more intense. She had no chance on a moving train. If she were to escape, she had to do so now—make a run for it on the busy platform, beg for help from one of the oblivious bystanders. But somehow, every opportunity seemed to pass her by. As it turned out, she was just a scared as Miss Rosewood. Her limbs kept freezing up, rooting her in place. What would happen to her? What would happen to Miss Rosewood? She hadn't long. In minutes, a beam of light grew larger down the tracks, followed by a series of whistles and a train attendant shouting in the distance. Although Mae resisted, Ellsworth and a long line of passengers pushed her forward. Even if she screamed, it would be covered by the train whistle now.

As Mae mounted the foot rail, they stilled again. The passengers ahead ducked beneath a low ceiling. Beyond that, she saw little else in the smog. Against the clamor of carriages and chatter, hearing was near impossible too.

The train whistled a third time, intensifying the chaos. Then in large, fat drops it started to rain. The crowd pushed harder. Mae gripped the handrail for support, but in the pandemonium, Ellsworth lost his hold. A gathering line of people pushed him farther away.

She was free.

She had only to alight from the steps and squeeze her way past a few shoulders.

The whistles blew again, this time with added strength. The train jerked forward. The screeching and grinding metal was so loud, it hurt.

Nearly losing her balance, she squeezed the railing tighter. The ground faded in and out of the fog. She had the chance to pick up whatever remained of her life.

Her chest heaved with each breath. The seconds kept slipping. The train was moving faster. And yet her mind continued to waver.

Could she really leave Miss Rosewood like this? Even if this young woman had led her into danger, could she really forget about her entirely?

No. If she had a single hair of morality in her body, she couldn't abandon her to a man like Ellsworth. The young woman had committed a betrayal, yes, but so had she. If she left her now, how could she ever hope for forgiveness?

She wasn't just some senseless social climber like Mrs. Wilson. She would never abandon a friend at the threat of scandal, much less violence. And she couldn't keep running and hiding from danger. She had done enough of that her whole life.

"Have you lost your senses?" A train attendant yanked her back and shut the door. Ellsworth stood behind him, his eyes shooting knives of anger.

For a moment, Mae resisted. Her body twisted, but the attendant held firm. Her only chance to escape and she had gladly let it slip.

☾

LOCKE SWEPT OUT of view behind a brick pillar, his mind still reeling at Mae's unwillingness to jump. She'd had her chance.

Why hadn't she taken it?

When Ellsworth had pressed forward through the train with Mae in tow, it had been all he could stand to watch. Did she doubt him, doubt he'd come after her? Perhaps she had reason to. He had made his deal with Pierce, hadn't he?

He didn't care. It didn't diminish his resolve, not even for a second. She hesitated for Miss Rosewood's sake. Perhaps Mae thought she could save her. She was too kind. As hard as Mae probably wanted to convince her otherwise, there was no overcoming her pupil's ignorance. He didn't care how good Ellsworth's manipulations were. She had seen enough of his deeds to see that he had no redeeming quality.

More than anything, it was desperation that drove Miss Rosewood, especially now that she was ruined. Perhaps he could understand that. Wasn't it desperation to find that sapphire that had forced him into the awful deal with Ellsworth?

Locke squeezed his fist. It took everything he had not to rush across the station, jump aboard the train, and rip Mae from Ellsworth's grip.

But that had been impossible. The train was traveling too fast. He had arrived too late.

He looked up at the clock tower. Even if he rode full-speed the entire way to the estate, he could never arrive before them. He cursed, squeezing his fist so tightly, he felt his nails break skin. He simply could not accept that sight of her had been his last.

If only he could feel her skin. He felt her absence most in his hands, her body so painfully not there.

Banging his head against the brick, he wondered how the devil he could reach her in time. Perhaps if the train was delayed…

Then again, maybe fate would be a cruel bitch, after all. Or had he simply committed too many crimes to ever hope for such a thing as love?

He was too selfish a man—nay, greedy pirate—for that. He thought he would die at the hands of the tempest sea. For so long, that life had ensnared him. Only now did escape seem possible. Only now did he feel he had the chance.

Not wanting to waste any more time, Locke tore himself away from the station and headed back toward Gambit. With renewed haste, he snapped the reins and kicked in his heels.

"SIT." ELLSWORTH SHOVED Mae and Miss Rosewood into the hard, wooden seats. Much like they had been in the carriage, Miss Rosewood sat next to Mae.

Hunching down in the seat across, Ellsworth took a surreptitious drink from his flask. A routine he continued until his eyes glazed.

Mae turned to the window, trying to distract herself with the grim, smoke-laden landscape that was now her world. So close by her side, Miss Rosewood seemed an extension of it. Though her face was still with numbness, her eyes were nervous with a constant sheen of tears.

The sight troubled Mae, but at the same time, her determination was building. For Miss Rosewood, she had to be brave. She had to find a way to escape this. Even if she couldn't marry, the young woman could still have a decent life. If nothing else, she could have freedom, independence. Wasn't that enough? She tried to convince herself of the same thing. If they both got out of this, they could be happy.

All around were staring eyes, both men *and* women, in the same dank and narrow place. Surely, someone would help.

She only needed to get Miss Rosewood on her side first.

With each sip from his flask, Ellsworth's lies were unraveling. Now that he was well into his cups, even Miss Rosewood had to see the danger of his stare.

Miss Rosewood had never been strong-willed, though. Too often, she followed, letting herself be influenced. In such close proximity, Mae would not get out a single whispered word, either. Here, it was hopeless. They needed to be alone. They needed to get off this train.

Another century seemed to pass before the train finally began to slow. But that hint of relief was quickly replaced by dread.

Mae's time was running out. Not a single delay or obstacle seemed to stand in Ellsworth's way.

"Another step closer." Ellsworth grabbed Mae and with Miss Rosewood following, they stepped off onto the platform. As the black smoke cleared, her stomach twisted in painful recognition. There was no mistaking the familiar buildings of Bristol.

As hard as she tried to break away from her past, it had pulled her back.

"What will you do to the Rosewoods?" Mae drifted through the station, listless.

"Mr. Rosewood won't be home. He's off in Scotland, no doubt, conducting a search for his daughter."

Miss Rosewood stumbled in front of them. "But I'm not in Scotland."

"Well, obviously. He merely thinks you are to elope."

"To elope! With whom?"

"With me, of course!"

"After a single evening? They can't think…"

But Mae was sure they did and judging by her stare, so was Miss Rosewood.

"I left them a note before we left." Ellsworth seemed pleased.

"What about Mrs. Rosewood and her other daughter?" Mae asked.

"My men have clear instructions to tie up anyone who gets in their way. That includes the servants. By now, my men might already be searching for the vault."

Mae looked down to hide her expression. *And they'll find nothing*, she finished in her head. How long would they continue to search before Ellsworth turned on them?

"What, you—but…" Miss Rosewood clawed at his arms.

"You promised to tell them of my return. My father—"

"—would be in far more danger had he remained." He flicked her away.

Lagging behind him, Mae could only feel pity. Was Miss Rosewood really fool enough to think he had informed her family of his actual plans to find the vault in their own home? Since they owned the estate, they could easily claim it as their own. Ellsworth would not risk that. He would sooner kill them all.

A cold burst of fear crept down deep into Mae's core. She needed to get away. *Soon.*

With his free arm, Ellsworth held open the door of a hired hack. She half-expected him to shove her inside. Instead, he motioned her. If she didn't know better, she might have confused him with a gentleman. This time, outsiders probably assumed they were relations, saving their conversation for an appointment of afternoon tea. But on the inside, Mae was dying bit by bit. In Miss Rosewood's eyes she saw the same.

"If you keep this tame…" Ellsworth lifted Mae's hand as she entered the carriage. "Perhaps I shall like you better."

Mae kept her focus on the empty seat, trying not to listen or pay him heed. Despite herself, she could feel Ellsworth's eyes all over her, drinking her in, as though she were something to be won.

"I could make you happy, you know… If you grant me—how should I put this—" He tapped the tip of his chin with his index finger. "Other favors."

Mae wanted to scream at the idea, but like a good prisoner, she bit her tongue. It was clear Miss Rosewood, who had already been seated, had heard the exchange. With her back straight and hands together on her lap, Miss Rosewood had the perfect posture of a lady—all except for the working of her jaw and grinding of her teeth.

Those intense eyes fixed upon the window were finally beginning to see. Life as a spinster would be far better than a life like this. Any life would be.

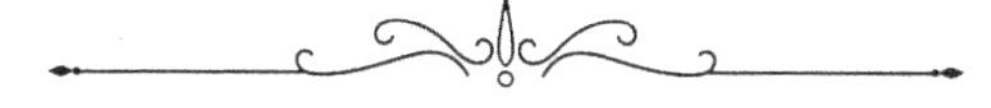

CHAPTER TWENTY-TWO

Old Tunnels

THE CARRIAGE SWAYED as the horses trampled their way around the next turn. Without pause, they pulled through the gate. It had been left open, as if in welcome. She prayed Mrs. Rosewood and Miss Lenore, defenseless as they were, had run off to the nearest estate as soon as they'd seen the men coming. The servants too. Whoever had taken their place would only mean them harm. Ellsworth's men cared for gold and little else. Most likely, they'd be willing to kill for it.

Mae peered out the window. The sun had set and darkness began its quick descent. In the distance, her home was little more than a shadow. Its darkened bricks and iron-spiked roofs rose higher as they gained speed again.

Mae struggled to make out any sign of life. Along the third floor of their quarters, the windows remained unlit.

The horses halted at the front entrance but received no welcome. That was a good sign, at least. Ellsworth alighted first. When Mae and Miss Rosewood followed, men poured out from the main doors, each of them wearing a scowl fouler than the last.

They were the same Cheapside-of-London-looking bunch as the two men before. Only there were a dozen of them, ready to do Ellsworth's bidding.

"Pretty, this one." A stranger with long, stringy dark hair, took hold of Mae. Completely surrounded, she saw no use in fighting. Still, she trembled in pain and disgust. Beneath the man's increasingly hard grasp, she was sure to bruise.

"Another!" A man with dirt on his face grabbed at Miss Rosewood. Unlike Mae, she struggled, throwing her arms out. "What do you think you are—Frances!" she cried. Mae winced at the plea. She had tried to warn Miss Rosewood. Why hadn't she listened?

"No need, Hans," Ellsworth said without real concern.

The brute threw Miss Rosewood forward. With a blood-curdling crack, she fell on her knees atop the hard brick of the drive.

"It's the other woman who's important." Ellsworth took hold of a lantern from one of his men and shined it in Mae's direction, but she could only see Miss Rosewood, struggling to smooth out her skirts and get to her feet.

Ellsworth did not so much as bat an eye. Stiff with focus, he turned to another man.

"Have you found it?"

"No, sir. But we dun just as you instructed. Got the master key, right 'ere." He fumbled in his pockets and handed it over. "We've access to every part of the house."

Ellsworth shoved the key into his own pocket.

"Mrs. Rosewood, her daughter? The servants? Where did you lock them away?"

"Ah, that, sir?" The man hesitated, shoving his hands into his fraying pockets. "I think they saw us comin'. They, uh, managed to flee."

At this, Mae heaved a breath of relief. Ellsworth, however, was not so pleased. "Escaped? *Escaped*, you say?" His face went still.

"Sorry, sir. We tried."

"Was not one of my instructions to bind them?"

"Sir, we—"

Ellsworth cursed then delivered a hard blow as quick as a snap of the fingers.

The man, gasping for air, cowered away.

Miss Rosewood covered her eyes.

"They wouldn't dare hide out in Locke's haunted estate, would they? They'd go to the next familiar neighbor. Has to be at least ten miles." Ellsworth heaved a breath, looking as if he wanted to hit someone else. He lowered his head in thought. "A pity it isn't winter. We'll have to work quickly now. Once we find the fortune, a bribe to one of the constables should do the trick."

Ellsworth strode into the manor and like clockwork, the men followed.

Glass crunched beneath Mae's feet. She hadn't known what to expect, but it certainly wasn't this. In the orange glow of Ellsworth's lantern, she took in the complete destruction of the foyer. Large, iron windows gaped open to the elements and paintings, torn and splintered, lay scattered across the floor. A consequence not of their search, but of careless men. The sight brought tears to her eyes. What purpose did this serve in their search? What had they expected to find?

She didn't want to think of the other rooms, the other valuables. She had to remember that they belonged to the Rosewoods nonetheless.

"Bring her here," Ellsworth said.

Nodding with servitude, Mae's captor dragged her forward.

"Now…" Ellsworth lowered the light. "Since the vault in the cellar was a trap…we're going to have to be a bit more careful, aren't we?"

With his free hand, he yanked Mae close. "You shall open all the vaults henceforth. What say you to that?"

Mae's head and heart seemed to throb in unison. She wanted to move back, if just an inch, but his grip was unrelenting.

"Don't resist me," he wheezed. "The true location of the vault. Tell me now."

"The old summer cottage." Mae dropped her head down.

Ellsworth eyes shot back and forth. "Lies!" he burst out. "That hovel is more than a day's ride—you are only trying to buy yourself more time."

"What do think Locke and I were doing there?"

"Given your state of undress at the time, lots of things."

Mae swallowed hard, her face reddening.

She just wanted this to be over. At this point, Miss Rosewood would be *lucky* if Ellsworth married her. After this, Mae doubted either of them would live. Truth or lie, death was inevitable either way. There was no doubting that. Her only hope was escape, which—Ellsworth was right—would indeed require time. If she failed to plan something, there would be no serum, no Locke to save her.

"The attic," she lied. Her only strategy was the place that would take longest to reach. Somewhere during that time, there'd be an opportunity to escape. There had to be.

Ellsworth beamed a wide, wicked smile. "Search the place thoroughly," he ordered his men. "Another one of you keep watch."

The man still hunched over from Ellsworth's blow nodded. The rest of them raced up the stairs.

"As for you, my darlings…" Ellsworth pushed Mae toward the hall. Behind her, Miss Rosewood's steps kept close.

Mae wanted to yell at her to run but struggled to find the words. She remembered Ellsworth's grip on her throat and heard again Miss Rosewood's bone-cracking fall to the floor.

Ellsworth peered inside a doorway. Looking satisfied, he forced Mae inside and motioned Miss Rosewood to follow.

"But not me, of course." Her lips and chin trembled. "I am to be your wife…you promised."

He laughed. "It is far more likely that I shall forget about you entirely."

With that, he shut the door, throwing the windowless library into complete darkness. On the other side, the key grinded in the lock.

The room fell into silence.

"Miss Blackthorne?" Miss Rosewood called out, her voice pained.

Mae didn't answer. She searched for the matches in the fireplace and busied herself with the lighting of the wall sconces. Ellsworth's men must not have gotten to this room yet. It had been left untouched.

Miss Rosewood swept around. In the new light, her face was expectant, ready for scolding. She looked no different than the days she had forgotten to do her readings.

Why hadn't Miss Rosewood believed her? Why did she let herself be fooled into thinking she had no choice? Was being an old spinster as Mae was destined to become really so bad? Being locked away in a cage was far worse.

More than anger, Mae pitied her former pupil. Miss Rosewood had been one of many foolish young women too eager to marry, but few had ever made mistakes as monumental as this.

Now Mae knew their fate all too well. Ellsworth's plan was simple enough. He wanted her fortune and to cover up his tracks and avenge his ruined business, her life. Miss Rosewood would of course suffer the same. Mae covered her eyes, too tired for tears.

"You lied." Miss Rosewood stalked forward, her steps loud in the quiet library. "The vault really is at the cottage, isn't it?"

Mae imagined those awful men rummaging through her family's long-forgotten, worthless things. Eventually, they would realize her lie. And sooner or later, they would be back.

"What does it matter now?" Mae asked.

Ellsworth didn't believe her. And it wouldn't save them— only a miracle could. Despite their helplessness, she clung to that remnant of hope. *"Failure is a state of mind,"* her father had once said, and she refused to submit.

"We have to do something…" Mae said.

This library had been one of her father's favorite rooms. Over there in that very armchair was where her mother had told her stories. Over there atop the low table was where her father and

William had liked to play chess.

The room was one of the oldest and also one of the most frequently used. So surely, it had been built with an escape. Almost every room in the house was connected to one. The only trouble was finding the trapdoor. William had shown it to her once, she was sure, but he'd shown her so many, she couldn't remember the precise access point. She'd have to search.

Mae ran her fingers along the shelves, knocking and listening for any sound that might indicate a pathway.

"Miss Rosewood, kindly help me."

Miss Rosewood dropped into the armchair and huffed. Mae expected tears at any moment, but there was simply no time for that. Nor time for kind words.

"It's not hopeless…" Mae tried to shake Miss Rosewood from her trance. "We can—"

Miss Rosewood cut her off. "Why didn't you jump off the train? I saw. You had your chance. Why—" She whispered softly now. "Why didn't you jump?"

A good question. Locke might very well have asked Mae the same.

Like a flame, he burst to the forefront of her mind. The sight of him in the cellar as he came toward her. His hair dripping at the ends near the stream. At first, the images warmed her, but with the recollection of recent events, her body, her face, and even her hands went cold.

"Tell me."

Mae sighed, at last giving in. The sooner she explained, the sooner Miss Rosewood might help. At least she hoped.

"I couldn't just…" Mae braced her back against the barren fireplace. "I couldn't just leave you with Ellsworth. My conscience would never clear me of it."

"Even after all I've done?"

"You were right earlier. You, against your own choosing, had been thrust into this mess…because of me." Mae bit her lip as the unexpected guilt dug deeper, hollowing out her insides.

"He was so kind to me at first. So full of compliments. I really thought he wanted to help me find you and Locke. I don't know why, but I believed him," Miss Rosewood mumbled in shame. "I should have known better. Only Lenore warrants that kind of attention."

"There are other things more worthy of your time."

"Like what? Drawing? Now that I am ruined, what else will I do with my time?"

Mae thought of Locke again and the miles that separated them. How much she so desperately wished she could hear his voice. No, Miss Rosewood hadn't been to blame for their separation. Pierce had been to blame for that. He had left Locke no choice.

"What about this fortune?" Miss Rosewood asked. "Didn't you know?"

"Not until after your engagement. No sooner. I swear it. Locke and Ellsworth were in league initially. They tried to make a deal with me to show them the vault, but Locke turned against Ellsworth to protect me and—"

"And that's how you fell in love?"

Mae nodded, tears springing to her eyes at the memory of all Locke had done to try and shield her from the Ellsworth.

"But never, not once, did you warn me of Mr. Locke's lack of feelings for me," Miss Rosewood continued.

"And how could I have done that? How could I possibly tell you to go against the wishes of your parents?" Mae demanded. "It may be my duty of look out for you, but I can't always speak my mind."

Miss Rosewood knitted her brow. "Still, you and Mr. Locke—"

"I didn't plan it. It just happened. I don't know how." Her mind returned to a whirlwind of sensations. The hot flush of her cheeks beneath his gaze, the way his touch set her skin to tingle. All the things she might never feel again. "In that, I was wrong. I chose wrongly." Everything she had done had been so wrong.

"Don't be sorry." Miss Rosewood shook her head. "Not for that."

Mae recalled the encounter in her father's office and the wild, uncontrollable feelings that had resulted. How could she allow such feelings knowing he'd been meant for Miss Rosewood? It had been depraved.

Starting at her tremulous hands, Mae was beginning to break down. She could stay strong and brave no longer. But why feel ashamed? Hadn't she every right to let the tears run? In the face of all Ellsworth's wrongs, tears were a small sort of justice.

"Your post wasn't so bad, was it?"

"No, not always. We got along well enough."

"Yes, and after this—if we make it out of this—we can be friends, can't we?"

Mae nodded. "We shall always be."

Miss Rosewood smiled weakly. "No matter how life seeks to separate us."

Or death, Mae didn't dare add.

"I wish…" Miss Rosewood covered her face. "Because of me, Ellsworth will get what he wants. He'll win. Oh, Miss Blackthorne." She sniffled. "Why didn't you jump?"

"He won't win." Mae swept away with the flash of an idea. She stared inside the fireplace. Something was pulling her inside. Was it her memory finally serving her or her brother taking her hand once more from the world beyond? She could almost fancy his icy grasp, tugging her fingers to the top corner of one of the bricks. She felt the tiny engraving: a pair of rearing horses, the Blackthorne sign of escape.

Just like that, her fears ceased. Why hadn't she realized it earlier? The escape wasn't behind one of the shelves, but behind the fireplace, like in so many other rooms. Her determination blossomed, giving rise to wild ideas.

"What's wrong?" Miss Rosewood jumped up.

"Ellsworth won't survive this."

"I don't understand."

Mae walked away in thought. Leaving wasn't enough. She couldn't simply leave and allow Ellsworth to take over her home like this. Her family's possessions would not be left to his devices. Not when there was something she could do.

"What are you doing?" Miss Rosewood followed Mae's movements. "What do you mean to do?"

Mae didn't answer. She took in the endless shelves of books, the thick, velvety tapestries and tufted, leather furniture, probably for the last time. There was only one option. One way that could send Ellsworth and his men running from the estate in regret. It would come at a high price, but trapped in her own library, it was easy not to care.

And there was no more time to waste.

With newfound determination, Mae strode toward a bookcase packed with various encyclopedias she had never read. But even if she had, even if those books meant the world to her, none of them mattered now.

At this moment, beating Ellsworth meant everything. Conceding to him meant losing it all.

She started with one book and tossed it to the floor, then began ripping the other books out of place in rapid succession. In great sheets, they fell to the floor.

"What in heaven's name…" Miss Rosewood gasped.

"We need to burn these if we're to start a proper fire." Mae moved on to the next bookcase and continued to push the books to the floor in loud, scattered thumps. "Grab me that tapestry."

"Are you mad?" Miss Rosewood went to her, her voice shrill. "We won't be able to escape. We'll perish for certain.

Mae stopped her work and raced back to the fireplace. Stepping on the ashes, she went inside. She felt for the engraving and pushed the brick inward. The back of the fireplace creaked aside, a rush of cold throwing back her hair.

"You don't know the estate like I do. No one does. This tunnel will take us to the western courtyard. From there, we can run to the closest estate. We'll be safe."

Miss Rosewood's mouth worked to find the words, but she was rendered speechless.

"Now help me." Mae pulled at the tapestries with all her might, tearing them down from their places on the wall—the places where they had hung for generations.

Material things don't matter and with time, everything changes, she told herself. Even stubborn men like men like who went decades without aging because of a sapphire. Her centuries-old home couldn't stand forever, either. Sooner or later, it all had to come down. But that didn't mean she had to fall with it.

"There." Mae pointed to one of the wall sconces. "That candle."

Nodding, Miss Rosewood obeyed, as eager as ever.

☾

LOCKE PRESSED HIS blade harder against the man's throat. The coarse brick of the manor grinded into his elbow.

"Two women. Where?" Locke demanded.

A dirt-lined face stared him square in the eye, unafraid. It was the one antidote to his fear tactics: an opponent deep in his cups.

The man had actually been doing a perimeter check—bottle of stolen scotch in hand. So when Locke had caught him by the arm, he hadn't put up much of a fight. The man had thrown a few awkward punches then gotten himself crushed against the wall.

With a frown, the man sighed at the bottle, now spilling its contents across the lawn.

It was truly pathetic.

Locke twisted the blade an inch. At last, *that* got his attention.

"Real fine pig sticker you got." The man snickered with his east-of-London accent. *How typical,* Locke thought. *Ellsworth's favorite kind of scum.*

"The women," Locke barked again.

"What women?" There was a tone of idiotic excitement in his

voice. "Where?"

Locke groaned with frustration and slammed a fist into the man's gut.

He coughed and strained for breath but didn't speak. Locke sighed. He hadn't thought it would be so difficult with a drunk. Was he going to have to break skin? He did not want to, but if there was no other choice, he would not hesitate.

"I won't ask again…" Locke roared, summoning true rage in his voice—a voice he had used on cocky, drunk bastards like this at sea.

"Aye. Those 'uns," the man spit out, close enough so that Locke could smell the scotch gone rotten on his breath. Ellsworth was out of his mind to hire men such as this.

The dandy knew nothing when it came to assembling a crew. It filled Locke with hope. These men would give him no trouble at all. If it came to it, he might have to take on as many as six at a time. Minus this one.

"Tell me." Locke slid his blade down his cheek, quickening the man's breath. "Or I'll run you through."

Finally shaking, the man peered to the left. Locke followed his gaze. Smoke billowed from the opposite end of the manor. A fire? How had he not noticed?

Panic pounded through him, building with every second. The need to act made his whole body quake.

"There, I'd wager." The man tilted his head, his eyes widening at the discovery. "Though dead, I presume."

Unable to stop himself, Locke struck the man's jaw with the hilt of the blade. "You best hope otherwise."

Sadly, the blow didn't improve Locke's mood. And worse, the man had barely seemed to notice it.

Too drunk to feel any pain, contempt flashed across the man's glazed stare. "You bleedin' bastard."

Locke looked down at the victim, pondering his options.

He could kill the man quite easily, but if he was going to find Mae, his hands would be free from blood. So with the blade's hilt,

Locke brought it down hard across the man's head.

The man dropped to the ground. With one last groan of frustration, Locke ran off toward the growing smoke, not liking the silence in the air. He hoped for screaming. It would at least mean she was alive.

☾

MAE HUNCHED OVER and coughed into her fist. The smoke from the library had already begun to seep into the escape tunnel. In the faint candlelight, streams of smoke reached out like gnarled fingers. The floating poison stung deep inside her nostrils and drew out unstoppable tears.

Miss Rosewood's condition was even worse. Each of her breaths were huskier and shallower than the first.

"How much farther?" she rasped. The tunnel should have led directly to the courtyard, but it kept going with sharp turns that seemed to weave in the shape of a "Z."

So far, it wasn't connected to any other rooms. Mae dreaded the idea that they might have been in one of the original tunnels, built over a century ago.

Even so, they had to keep moving. Bringing on real panic, the air grew warmer, drier. The fire that started with a pile of books had caught quickly. Behind them, wood snapped and crackled.

She had hoped the intense wind of the night and dryness of the day would be to her advantage. But now there was no turning back, no matter what they faced in the courtyard.

Mae held out her candle. In the building smoke, she could barely see. Then, at last, she saw something.

"Here it is," she breathed, the discovery quelling her panic.

She slid a hand along the cracked and splintered wood of the door, colliding with something strange. A flat board…nails…. As her fingers followed the length of it, she felt the coarseness of brick too. Frantic, she searched for the doorknob. She found it quickly enough, but twisting and pulling on it with all her might, it barely budged.

"What's taking you so long?" Miss Rosewood coughed again.

Mae almost let the despair consume her. But what good would that do? She took a deep breath and held back a sudden urge to scream. She endeavored instead to be brave.

"It's blocked. We have to go back." Mae tugged Miss Rosewood before she could protest. "Here. Cover your mouth with this." She tore off a piece of her skirt and handed it to her.

Through it, Miss Rosewood rasped for air, sucking in what she could.

Besides running faster, there was little else to be done. With every step, the smoke seemed to thicken.

"We have to get out!" Mae shouted.

Seeing through the smoke was all but impossible now. She prayed the fire hadn't spread out of control. They couldn't be trapped. Fire, she had heard, made for a terrible, slow, and agonizing death.

She stilled. Echoing inside the tunnel, shouting ebbed in and out of range. Mae blew out the candle and dropped it. Ellsworth's men had discovered the blaze, the knowledge filling her with a mixture of hope and fear. They would be putting it out. Now was their only chance of escape.

Mae moved faster, not allowing herself to slow even as instinct told her to run from the smoke. She could see the exit now: an orange haze that stabbed her eyes.

Fire tumbled toward the ceiling and all around them. The smoke had become so dense, it seemed a solid entity. Flames darted wildly along the entire east wall.

The men, meanwhile, were doing little good with flower vases. And despite the smoke, Mae and Miss Rosewood were spotted at once.

"Stop them!" the figure of a man shouted.

Mae leaped into a sprint, her heart beating in her skull, perspiration dripping down her face. Miss Rosewood squeezed her hand harder. The raging fire would be enough to elude the men. It had to be.

But reaching the stark coolness of the hall, Mae knew the men weren't far behind. If either of them were to escape, they needed to separate.

"Run to the stables." Mae embraced Miss Rosewood. "Mount the first horse you can and head south."

"But…you… What will you do?" Miss Rosewood struggled to catch her breath.

"I'll catch up, I promise."

Even Miss Rosewood seemed to recognize the lie, but with a shove from Mae, she fell into a stride. By the time the two men had found their way out of the room, Miss Rosewood was gone. Safe.

Mae had never felt more alone. When a tight grip enveloped her, she swung her arms out, thrust back her elbows, and pounded her fists. But no matter how hard she struggled, it proved futile. The arms did not loosen an inch. The poisonous smoke had rendered her weak.

"Where'd the other girl go?" her captor barked into her ear.

"Doesn't matter," his partner replied. "The house is doomed. Well done, lass. Well done."

CHAPTER TWENTY-THREE

Poison

MAE AWOKE ATOP the jagged bricks of the courtyard. She didn't know when she had fallen unconscious, only that her lungs still burned and her mouth tasted like ash.

A thud and the splintering of wood forced her to sit up.

The fire, beautiful in its orange, raging brilliance, danced along the night sky. She gripped the dead vegetation beneath her.

This hadn't been a dream. Nothing could be more real. The blaze roared, too loud to ignore. And every now and again came the sudden crash of what she imagined to be a banister, chandelier, or support beam. There was no coming back from the fire now.

There was no more searching for her family vault in this place.

Her body, stiff with cold, savored the fire's radiating warmth, but as she tried to move closer, something pulled her arm. She looked down. A chain glistened around her wrist. Like an animal, she had been chained to a stone statue of a woman, one of the many that decorated the formal gardens. Was she just imagining it or was the figure's stony face lined with green tears? Mae felt just as stiff and immobile, just as trapped.

Toward the house was a flurry of activity. Ellsworth's men

moved in and out of doors, raiding her home like savages. They lugged entire cabinets, trunks, and even her father's carved desk onto the lawn. From every part of the house, the fire raged on, the bricks of the manor sparkling brightly.

"Awake, I see." An unfamiliar man appeared, his white shirt wet with sweat. "Go get Ellsworth."

A man lugging a trunk some distance away dropped it where it lay and took to the house. Some minutes past, Ellsworth was upon her, a beaming smile on his horrible face.

Mae struggled against the restraints, the chains clanging in protest.

"A bit of bad luck, all this," Ellsworth said.

When he turned back toward the manor, the fire seemed to take on a new intensity. New tendrils of flame had broken through several windows, forcing her back. The dry heat burned her eyes.

"Need I remind you that neither gold nor diamonds burn?" Ellsworth spat. "Nor vaults. We'll be searching through the ruins soon enough."

How could she think she could stop such a monster? She hadn't even fazed him. Not for a second.

Mae shivered in the mix of cool wind and fiery heat. How long before he realized there was no other vault at the manor? What would he do then? Did it matter? At least Miss Rosewood had her freedom. At least someone did.

"How about we find us a better view?" He brandished a bottle of wine, no doubt stolen.

When he unlocked the chain, she considered trying to hit him. Useless, yes, but it might at least inflict pain. Then another thought occurred to her, a near-smile touching her lips. "Might I suggest my father's favorite bench?" She tried not to look hopeful.

"Yes, why not?"

Mae surrendered to his grip as he dragged her to the marble bench. The same one she had searched with Locke. A moment that seemed centuries ago.

"Very nice," Ellsworth remarked. Given the slight rise of a hill, it indeed offered the perfect view.

Mae didn't bother taking it in. She sat down quickly, the renewed thought of revenge tasting bitter at the back of her throat. All she needed was a moment of distraction, a moment that Ellsworth might look away.

"There's no need for this." Mae thought to give him one last chance at decency.

"Come now," Ellsworth said. "I'm enjoying this."

"Our families are rivals no longer."

At that, Ellsworth's happy expression broke.

"You're entirely clueless." He yanked her in close, their noses almost touching. "You think I'm vindictive, but this isn't revenge. It's *redemption*."

"And William?" Mae croaked. "Was he just another means to that end?"

"Your brother was already dead. And you knew it."

Mae felt her face crumple at the memories of William's drinking, the mornings she had found him unconscious on the stairs, often in his own vomit. She could not bear the idea of servants finding him like that. So often, she had cleaned him up herself. She had spent months doing that.

"He was sick. I wanted to make him better. I—"

"I did you a favor. It was no trouble, really. I found it on him that night, you know—the night you had me drag him away. I thought, hmm… Maybe he had discovered something. The very fortune those legends speak of. Well, he had."

Mae jerked hard against his grip, but he held her still, pulling her even closer.

"I waited till you went off to bed. Then I took a candlestick to his head. Don't worry, he was already half-gone from liquor. Smell made him a bloody pain to drag to the roof." He released her an inch. "I didn't just do it for the money, you should know. Everyone wanted you once."

Mae was surprised at the rush of memories that came. Yes,

there had been other men, but she had disparaged them all. She had been a different person back then, too picky, perhaps, but they had never been quite to her liking.

"Don't forget the ones your father scared away with his reputation," Ellsworth put in. His face twisted. "I was supposed to be the one who won. The one who rescued you… That was how people would see it."

Mae felt her stomach turn. What if she hadn't known? What if she had married her brother's murderer?

The idea was so despicable, she screamed out. She could bear it no longer. She beat her fists against him with all the strength she had left. But he simply moved back, letting her fall to her knees. She couldn't hurt him if she tried. Her throat still ached, like someone had taken a razor to it, and she was so utterly exhausted. On the weed-laden ground, she rolled on her back. Tears spilled down the sides of her face.

"He was too much of a drunk to know what to do with the fortune," Ellsworth continued. "And you! Without a man, you would have thrown it all away too. When, my darling, when will you see that money belongs to those who will make proper use of it?"

"And you think *you're* the one to do it?" Mae demanded. "You, who bankrupted your own business?"

She didn't know why she bothered. The rivalry between their families had gone on too long, had poisoned Ellsworth to the point of insanity. And there was never any sense in reasoning with a madman. There was nothing human about him in the least. He was a machine, bent on this so-called redemption regardless of what she said or did.

Ellsworth braced his foot against the bench. Using a corkscrew, he opened the bottle. "Chianti 1820. This year any good?"

Mae's teeth ground into her lip, not caring when she began to draw blood. That year, she had been a mere child playing in that very courtyard, back when it had been green and full of life.

How could she have known that one day, she would be beneath this great tree drinking that very bottle of wine, watching her home go up in flames? And despite her lifelong love of the place, the fire had been her doing?

She imagined what the scandal sheets would say. She could see the headlines and how little everything, her story, her tragedy, would mean to readers. It would be just another scandal to add to the list.

But it wasn't over yet. She could still change the ending. She remembered her younger self sitting on that very bench, listening to another one of her father's stories about the Northern Woods. A place of great danger, he had often told her and anyone else who might listen. It was he who had stirred up tales about the place. Now, she knew why. All those years, the forest had belonged to his enemy.

"How could a place so beautiful be bad?" she had asked him.

"Looks can be deceiving," he'd said, repeating the old adage as he'd picked at a branch that had drooped down in front of them. She'd reached for the seedpod in his hand, but he'd swept it back. *"Remember what your mother told you about this tree?"*

She had nodded. *"Their seeds look harmless, but they're really…"* *Poison.*

Mae snapped out of the memory, looking up at the tree above. Years later, it looked exactly as she had remembered. Its placement had been no accident. The tree had a purpose. Once more, Mae felt that familiar weight of duty. Her family wanted revenge. Her ancestors, every one of them, seemed to whisper in her ear.

How much she craved for Ellsworth to release that bottle he held tightly in his hand. She could think of nothing to distract him. If she asked for a drink, would he keep his eyes on her? Would he become suspicious when she tried to turn away? Perhaps this was useless. Even if she could distract him, how long might the poison take to work? He might die, yes, but so might she in the meantime. Just as she had failed at her grand plans of starting the fire but keeping it contained, she might fail at this too.

"Beautiful sight, isn't it?" Ellsworth sucked in the air and let it out in a rush.

Mae never wanted to see his dark, disturbing eyes ever again. Watching him drink wine straight from the bottle tormented her. He had not a care in the world. As if gazing upon stars, he watched the flames lick at the sky.

What might her father say? What might he have done? What would he have told her to do?

"What is it?" He roared as one of his men waved for attention.

"The fire is making re-entry impossible sir."

"I won't hear of it." Ellsworth pulled himself away.

As Mae had hoped, he left the bottle vulnerable on the bench. But for a long moment, she couldn't move. Ever since Ellsworth had admitted what he'd done to William, she had wanted revenge. Perhaps even before then. Now that the opportunity was before her, she doubted herself.

Like that night in the cellar, she had few options, all of which had devastating outcomes. The events of the past, the death she had handed out—rightfully or not—seemed to form a pattern. She feared she was incapable of reversing its steady progression, of returning to the person she had been before all this. What her family had been before her brother had left for sea.

Had her family been unable to stop its progression too? Had they hoped to get out of piracy years ago, the moment hard times had been behind them? Years before the greed and violence had corrupted them?

She tried to slow her breaths, remembering Locke's consolatory words that night in the tunnel. But had that man she'd murdered really been so bad? Perhaps he'd just been unlucky in life with no other life to which to turn. A boy who might have lived a better life had he had a better upbringing?

She could not erase that doubt from her mind.

This was different, though. Ellsworth…

He was making his way back.

There was no time to hesitate now. She wanted to survive—she knew that much. Still feeling weak, Mae lifted herself up. With no further thought, she took up a seedpod from the bench, broke it apart, and spilled its contents into the bottle.

Ellsworth was steps away, still standing tall with hands on his hips and hardly surprised that she hadn't decided to run. To her delight, he took another gulp of the poisoned wine straight away. With that, she had sealed his fate.

"Delicious." He swallowed and extended the bottle toward her. "See for yourself."

Mae shrank back, her heart halfway to her throat.

"Fine." He took another gulp.

For some minutes, they sat in silence, listening to the steady crackling of the fire and the occasional whisper of the wind. Her heart leaped every time he sipped from the bottle. Would it take the hours she had feared? Had the seeds lost their potency? Perhaps if she had taken a pod straight from the branches…

"This heat won't do," Ellsworth suddenly said, sweat glistening on his forehead. She noted that his breathing had quickened too. A consequence of the fire or poison? She could not tell.

☾

LOCKE PRESSED HIS back flush against the wall. He needed to keep to the shadows and move quickly.

All the while, his eyes stung from the smoke and sweat trickled down his forehead. A voice needled him—he was too late. She was already dead. How could he have done this to her? How could he allow her to be taken in the first place?

He sidled along a bay of windows blown out from the heat. Outside, Ellsworth's men and their piles of loot surrounded the west wing. None of them, no matter how intrepid, dared to enter the building now. The fire had grown too large. It had reached every wing.

None of this fazed him, though. As he listened for screams and even sniffed for burning flesh, he was ready to go deeper into the flames. He had no qualms about that. The only trouble was the rooms, winding halls, and the hours it might take to find her. And the house could collapse at any moment. Beneath it, they would both perish. But if that was how it had to be, so be it.

He stepped farther down and paused at the opening of another hall. The fire roared at the opposite end, his face burning from the heat. Amidst the shouts of arguing men and the snapping of fire, he could discern nothing. Fatigue had long begun to set in. He feared it would weaken his senses. As hard as he strained to listen, he might miss something. Perhaps the tiniest whisper that would lead him to her.

He moved toward another series of doors. He didn't care how intensely hot the fire grew, he told himself. If she died, there was nothing he could do, no way he could ever make amends.

He listened again. The house had become a furnace, the tip of his ear searing with pain. In a matter of minutes, the entire wing would be engulfed. He wouldn't be able to endure the heat. As hard as he might try, he wouldn't be able to get any closer.

Then, somehow, he heard it. The slightest whisper of a scream reviving him from his previous stupor. The raging fire with its great gusts of heat and crackling laughter confused its direction. Though it seemed distant, the scream was all the hope he needed.

He moved back toward the brilliant flames. Though it had yet to sound again, he ignored this. There would be no second chance. He didn't have time to consider the consequences. From the moment he had left Pierce, he had been more than willing to risk everything. Most importantly, he had been willing to die.

EVENING PASSED INTO deep night, Mae and Ellsworth's journey

marked only by the line of trees growing taller in the distance. Across the open field, the fire cast an orange haze. The leaves of nearby trees had begun to smolder too. Soon, whole branches would be consumed by flames and she with them.

"This way." Ellsworth dragged Mae forward, his ironclad grip reminding her of those pain-filled moments in the cellar.

"Tell me where you are taking me."

He pointed to an old work shed, some several yards away. "There, we'll have some privacy."

With that, her future seemed to crystalize, becoming clearer and all the more chilling. She could not have deserved this.

Panic squeezed her heart. The poison, what seemed her only hope, had not worked. She struggled to remain calm. Tears ran hot down her cheeks and her breaths would not slow. She needed to save her strength, to gather the courage already worn quite thin.

"Easy now. It's just until the fire goes down, then we search."

That could be all night, Mae feared. Perhaps more.

She thought to run, but walking at their pace had already proved laborious. She could barely focus her steps across the cold, bleak ground. The grass had faded away, her surroundings little more than a watery blur. Her steps just a pounding in her head.

Only after she nearly tripped did her senses return. Focusing her eyes, she realized they had crossed a trodden path. The scent of freshly turned soil filled her nose. She looked behind her. The trail was more distinct.

Did she dare consider it? No, it had to be. She was certain. The broken soil was from horse hooves, traveling full speed toward the estate.

Mae pulled back, hopeful that some traveler had seen the rising flames. She ignored Ellsworth's tugging. Like a sudden mirage, she saw Locke again—riding through the woods, lantern in hand, their paths edging closer.

But as Ellsworth forced her forward again, this lone traveler, whoever he was, seemed impossible. The marks were much older, perhaps even from Thomas.

The same fate that had once been on her side had betrayed her ever since the coast.

"I told you," Mae spit, the truth perhaps her only chance. "The vault isn't in the manor!"

It seemed she had no choice. She could not endure a whole night alone with Ellsworth. The thought made her stomach roil. However much was in her family vault, it wasn't worth her life.

Ellsworth turned to her abruptly, stopping them among the patch of thorns. "What did you say?"

"The vault is where you and Miss Rosewood first met us," she said breathlessly. "At my family's summer cottage… I wasn't lying."

"And why should I trust you?"

Mae struggled for argument. Before long, he was dragging her again. She did not know how much farther she could go. She felt dizzy. Dread weighed down on her too. Like a heavy stone atop her chest.

"Tell me the truth and you'll get your share. You can even have mine." He grinned. "When we marry."

"*Marry?*"

"Yes, of course. I wanted to kill you at first, I'll admit. But perhaps marriage is our true destiny. Suits me better, I think."

He really had gone mad. How could he think to force her? Did he have some terrible means to make her agree?

Horrified, Mae thrust her elbow into his stomach and gave a tug that only made her captor laugh.

Mae screamed out, not caring who heard, not caring if it captured the attention of the other men. Screams—though hoarse and ragged—were her only hope.

As if in reply, a deafening series of crackling caught her attention. The roof had finally given in, breaking into what sounded like a thousand pieces. A giant puff of smoke rose into the sky. When it dissipated, the fire burned brighter, illuminating the grass and trees ahead.

In the new burst of light, she saw something. Silhouetted against the firelight, it was just a blur, but as it approached, she saw more clearly. The rider! Not any rider, but a guard donning the black cloak of the Silver Order. She recognized it in the intense new light. Only then was it visible. In the darkness, it was no more than a glimmer.

She screamed out, calling again for help. Ellsworth quickly smothered her, his massive hand squeezing so tightly, she could barely breathe.

Ellsworth changed direction toward the woods. There, he could easily hide with her. Pulling ahead, he moved even faster. After her previous screams, Mae barely had the strength to resist. Perhaps this was why the woods had always frightened her. Perhaps it was because it was the place in which she had been destined to die.

She wondered where the guard had gone, why she didn't hear the approaching hooves. In her final moments of desperation, had she imagined him? She couldn't believe that. No matter how unlikely it seemed, she still strained to listen. She struggled against the man too, her moans muffled in his palm. Her tears dripped down onto the grass.

Stupidly, perhaps, she thought she heard something—the slightest wisp of air—when amidst the steady roar of fire came a hard *thud* right next to her ear. Ellsworth yelped, releasing Mae and slamming to the ground.

A blade jutted out from his chest. Locke's blade, its hilt embossed with black onyx.

In awe, Mae bent down and yanked it free from Ellsworth's flesh. Nausea washed over her. The knife dripped with blood and more of the red liquid gushed from Ellsworth's wound. He was dying, wailing and groaning in pain.

More men began taking notice. Against the haze of the fire, their black shapes turned in her direction. Someone had said something. Then, one by one, they dropped their loot and came running.

She nearly ran off right then. But, remembering the key, she could not leave it. Cringing and shaking, she found it in Ellsworth's front pocket. That, along with her father's watch. She took both and put them down her bodice. She looked down at him. Not quite dead, he was still struggling for air, maybe even for words. As much as she wanted, she didn't have time to sneer or utter her own words of vindication.

Still holding the knife, Mae shifted to run. But at last hearing the hooves, she swept around.

The attacker dropped down from his horse. For some rea-son—she didn't know why—her heart swelled with hope. There was something familiar about this figure, about his determined gait. Rather than demand his identity, she stood silent. Ellsworth was dead. Miss Rosewood was safe. That would have to be enough.

It's just another guard, she told herself. Locke had given the blade to one of the men. With that, he had washed his hands of her. She could not forget that he had wanted this. At Pierce's manor, he had asked her to leave. Despite all that existed between them, somehow, he had been able to bear parting from her.

For a moment, the memory made her angry. He had been a fool to let her leave. He had to have known something like this would happen. That she might as well be dead without him.

The stranger stepped closer, his face silhouetted once more against the firelight. And yet she knew him at once. Since that first night of the storm, she had grown to know every angle of his face, no matter how obscure in the night. This time, there would be no pause, no awkward hesitation between them. The moment she was within reach, she was in his arms, pressed against him, the feel of him distinct.

"Locke?"

She let the knife slip from her grip, taking in the ash and soot that smeared his lips and cheeks. His impossible presence revigorated her exhausted spirit.

They hadn't a moment longer, though. Untangling from him,

she looked toward the approaching men, their shouts and shrieks gaining distance.

Locke threw his cloak over her shoulders and waved forth Gambit. There didn't seem enough time to breathe.

The other men were still some distance off. On foot, how long might they have? Minutes?

A crunch of grass caught Mae's attention. Forever, that innocuous crinkling would always signal danger. All too often, it had. And now was no exception.

Clenching his chest, Ellsworth staggered toward them. In his other quivering hand, he aimed a pistol.

Instantly, smoke blossomed in the air, blinding her. In the agonizing seconds it took to clear, everything changed.

Locke lay stiff on the ground, gasping in pain. Ellsworth was at Mae's shoulder.

"The key." He grabbed her again. "Hand it here."

"No, Mae, don't!" Locke's voice rang out.

Ellsworth came toward him, Mae blocking his path.

"You!" he grunted. He need only hit her, shove her, but still, she remained—even when he pulled out a knife. It was the only thing she could think to do after all Locke had done.

With no further warning, he pulled the knife high and drove it into Mae's shoulder, knocking her to the ground. Locke called out, seemingly certain she was dead, or at least dying. But clenching at her chest, her belly, her sides, she found no blood. Only a slight, dull pain in her shoulder. Somehow, she wasn't injured.

"Damn woman!" Ellsworth kicked her aside.

Only then did she find the knife, twisted on the ground. How it had happened didn't matter. Locke and Ellsworth were diving at each other's throats and wounds. Though both were stripped of weapons and injured, the fighting did not wane. Blood dripped and at times streamed onto the grass.

Her heart beat hotter in her chest, her hands twitching. She couldn't... She wanted to be free of this violence, but seeing

Locke in this struggle, she was desperate to do something. Anything.

Gambit, back from wherever he had run off to, crossed her path. She thought to shove him away. Then, glistening in the moonlight, she saw it, hanging off one of the saddlebags—the thing that would no doubt secure her place in hell.

And yet she did not hesitate.

She tossed the knife away and grabbed the pistol. On the ground, Ellsworth locked his hands around Locke's throat and squeezed tighter. Locke's eyes seemed to bulge, becoming distant and glazed. She could not let it go on. She had to take the shot quickly.

First, she had to focus, to breathe. Mae steadied the weapon. At this point, all she could do was pray.

She took a deep breath and pulled the trigger. The fierce explosion, though expected, still sent her backward.

In the dissipating haze, Ellsworth was no more than a crumpled body along the moor.

Mae dropped the weapon and went to Locke.

Not all was right. Beneath her grip, he tensed.

"You're hurt," she said.

"I'm fine." He sat up and pulled her toward Gambit without pause. "Come. Foolish men never accept defeat."

Seeing he was determined, Mae mounted, her cloak billowing in the wind as they raced away.

A line of trees closed in. The shadow of branches darkened the night, the black pillars flickering fast as they plowed inside.

Meanwhile, Locke heaved for breath. The air, though fresh, cool, and full of the sharp scent of earth, wasn't enough for him.

Still, they didn't stop. They weren't safe just yet. Mae was afraid they might never be.

"Here." Locke finally brought Gambit to a halt. He could ride no longer. He was shaking.

Mae looked about the woods, her eyes adjusting to the darkness. Shouting still lingered in the silence. Between the trees, lanterns flickered. Ellsworth's men had pressed on. How long would they search for her? Till morning? Detection would be far easier during the day.

Before Mae could help, Locke fell from Gambit into a shallow ravine. A soft shattering of glass met her ears. She dismounted and rushed toward him, desperate for the sound not to have been what she thought it had been.

With some effort, she turned Locke over. He had landed on a large, smooth rock, shattering the bottle of serum into bits.

She cursed, taking what she could of the moisture—dirt and all—onto her fingertips. She hated herself for not thinking of it sooner.

She had to work fast. Picking off as much glass as she could, she slipped her fingers onto his mouth and pressed them against his tongue. She repeated this until she felt something warm.

Blood was seeping from Locke's side through her dress and to her knees. Why hadn't the serum stopped the bleeding? Was it too late? Even the serum had its limits. Wherever that line was drawn between salvation and death, it was a fine one. Why had he insisted on healing her wound in Pierce's library? That tiny drop was significant now. It could have saved him.

Mae leaned back. The rise and fall of his chest was jagged and sporadic. She ripped away his shirt, working to find the wound. Her fingers came away bloodied, though none of the gore fazed her. She tore her skirts and soaked away as much as she could. At last, she found it—right along the claw of his tiger tattoo. The jagged hole wasn't disappearing like the one on her palm had. It was smooth around the edges; it had healed, though only by half. When blood rushed up again, she pressed down.

Locke groaned, his eyes fluttering awake.

"You're still bleeding. Help me, Locke. *Please*." He must have known what to do. All those days aboard a pirate ship—hadn't they ever had a doctor?

"Yarrow," he managed. "You'll find it in Gambit's bags."

Mac nodded. She had seen the plant—a natural astringent—in

books, but in this darkness, she was worried she might not find it.

"In the leather satchel." He gripped her slick, bloodied fingers. "All of it. Bring it to me."

Mae placed his hand over the bundle of skirts and went toward Gambit. She found it in not the first or the second, but the third bag, and brought it to him.

By then, Locke's body had gone still. His eyes were closed, his hand barely clutching the bloody cloth.

"Locke." She shook him then put her ear to his chest. She jolted at the beating. It was waning, weakening with every second.

Faint as the wind, he took in a breath.

"You found it?" He took her hand.

"Yes." She picked it out from the pouch. "Yes!"

"Chew it," he instructed, motioning to her mouth.

Mae obeyed, alternating between chewing and pressing it onto the ugly wound. The plant tasted horrible, sucking every last bit of moisture from her mouth, making her even more desperate for the water she'd long craved. But the more she chewed and applied, the less the wound seemed to bleed until finally, it stopped altogether.

She wiped the sweat from her brow, feeling a hot smear of blood take its place.

"I've had worse." Locke groaned and shifted slightly. She didn't realize until now that he hadn't made a sound all this time. She wondered if he was in shock. Or if he had just gone numb altogether. "Don't believe me?"

"Of course I do," Mae said shakily, suddenly unsure about the night ahead. She turned up to the sky in prayer. It was alive with streams of smoke and a haze of red.

Mae whipped off her cloak and stretched it over him. His eyelids flickered, fighting against the desire for sleep.

"Forgive me."

"For what?" Mae asked, incredulous.

"For making you do that earlier. Making you kill him."

"I had to… I needed to…"

When she had tried to poison Ellsworth, it hadn't been a simple act of survival, either. Ellsworth had no longer meant to kill her. What he'd wanted, though, had been far worse.

"Still, I wished I had spared you the act." He coughed. "Where do you think I'll end up?"

"What do you mean?" Mae searched his face. It was calm and serene without a hint of fear.

"Heaven or hell?"

"Heaven or hell? Why, heaven, to be sure."

Locke smiled, perhaps a bit deliriously. "You haven't a clue how much I've wanted you to believe that."

"Of course," Mae said over and over again. "Of course."

"Here." Locke gathered the cloak around him and shoved it toward her. "You should keep this on." Even in his condition, he still gave orders. For a moment, she almost laughed.

When his eyes shut, sadness swept over her again.

"Just rest." The words comforted her too as she slipped next to him. She tried not to think about the moist dirt, insects, or the men who still searched for them. It was only a matter of time until they realized their master was dead. With no treasure to be found, either, she prayed they'd disperse, passing over Blackthorne Manor like a bad storm.

She pulled the cloak around her too. The material, whatever it was, was warmer than wool.

She wouldn't let Locke give up. She couldn't let him think that he would die for her. She held on to him tighter, letting her warmth infiltrate the skin that seemed to grow colder with each second.

She stared at the forest, her breaths as quiet as she could manage. For a while, no one seemed about. Then, in her exhausted state, she began to see figures. Little movements in the brush. She was not afraid, though, not like she had been that night of the storm.

No longer foreboding, the forest had become a place of protection. Even in the darkness, it wasn't eerie, but quiet and serene. Here, she wanted to forget her wrongs, her guilt, her past decisions that had turned morally gray.

Visible in the moonlight, a mist had begun to form between the trees. The white haze hovered like ghosts—benevolent ones, she wanted to believe. Maybe even her ancestors. If they remained through morning, they could very well escape. If only Locke could last until then.

And if he didn't… Her name demanded she carry on unfazed by all that had happened, demanded that she too become wild and always drifting like the sea. But she couldn't. She squeezed her eyes shut. She refused.

In the mossy dirt, she drew him closer. She felt it then. The slightest shift in her bodice. The last piece of her family legacy. She dug it out. The forest, the smoke, everything disappeared. Once more, she was lost in the key's gold-and-silver intricacies.

Beside her, Locke had fallen asleep, his breathing deeper and steadier. She would not wake him, though. She let him rest. She decided she would wait until the smell of smoke faded and the morning light began to filter through the trees. Only then, when she saw Locke wake too, would she dare to hope.

DROPS OF RAIN pricked at Mae's skin. The haze of light beyond her eyelids indicated early morning. But she refused to wake. Without Locke, what had she left? Eternal sleep seemed a far better alternative.

When a distant crash vibrated the ground beneath her, she surged forward. Was her home at last succumbing to the flames? Was it now no more than a pile of soon-to-be forgotten memories? She looked about, expecting to see it, but she was in the Northern Woods, the cloak draped over her. Alone.

She threw the cloak aside and stood up into a warm, lingering fog. Besides the tinkling of rain, the trees around her stood still and silent.

She closed her eyes, trying to remember the night before, not caring how the rain drenched her. She remembered Locke's struggles for breath. Had he healed, after all?

She walked farther into the mist but hesitated before calling out his name. She had heard of fogs like this. They had frequented her father's stories and in them there had always been something hiding. But those stories were nothing more than fairy tales, right?

She stilled, going over the possibilities. Perhaps Locke had not left the Silver Order. Had he only returned to save her? She shook with sudden anger. She would follow him if she had to, demand that he—

Catching signs of movement, Mae looked out.

Hidden in the fog stood a figure, but a figure she recognized nonetheless. As he gained on her, she had not a doubt.

She didn't hesitate.

In his arms, she ran her fingers around the back of his neck, noting his warmth despite the rain. He didn't speak a word. He merely held her. In a sudden gust of cold, she shivered. Maybe this was a ghost. *His* ghost, wanting to say one last goodbye before evaporating into the mist.

But the feel of him was too solid and when he said her name in one long, lingering breath, all those ideas seemed silly. Without his healing serum or the sapphire, he was an ordinary man now— someone she could grasp on to.

Still, she looked around, expecting one of Ellsworth's men to snatch him away at any moment.

"They're gone," he said. "Someone would have seen the fire by now. Fire brigade will be soon on their way."

"Thank God." She tightened her grip, feeling him stiffen.

"The wound is not quite healed," he said. "Though soon it will be."

Mae could scarcely let herself believe, but in his beaming

eyes, she could see their future was finally sound. Better than sound, really.

"About the fortune… I…"

"Forget your fortune," he commanded, reaching into his pocket. In his hand, a ruby ring shimmered in the weak haze of the morning sun. "I took it that day at the coast…for you. But if we sell it, it should be enough for us. For a short while, at least."

Breathless, she took the ring and squinted up at him. Dirt and shiny sweat mangled his features. And yet, he had never looked so endearing.

She stepped back. "Even without this fortune…you still want me?

"How could you doubt it?" Locke pulled her back into him, face to face. "I care nothing for gold. Adventure requires none of it."

"And I?" she asked. Before he could answer, she pulled out the key. "Should I be opposed to such things?"

His eyes went wide. He took her face in his hands, his eyes smiling into hers.

"I can cheat fate, too," she told him, her heart pounding and aching with joy.

It was a feeling she had known so briefly, it almost felt new.

EPILOGUE

MAE HELD DOWN her fluttering, wide-brimmed hat and gripped the handrail of the steamer. The brilliant blues and purples cast out by the setting sun were at their peak. The colors were whipped up by the same wind that threatened to blow her to sea.

Despite the foreboding harshness against her cheek, she pushed away any lingering feelings of apprehension. She'd wanted this journey for too long to doubt it. This was who she was now: brave and with a new tenacity for not just any life, but an extraordinary and thrilling one.

At least that was what Locke—Ethan—had told her. Particularly in the weeks following the fire, when her nightmares had become more frequent. One day, they would lessen, Ethan had reassured her.

She could already feel herself growing stronger and more sure of herself. She needn't hold on to the past or worry any longer. Not with Ethan beside her.

Beside her, he was so unflinching, even against the wind. With his head tilted defiantly and his hair swept back, he seemed to savor the relentless gusts.

"You'll get your sea legs soon, Mrs. Locke." He side-eyed her.

"Has a ring to it," she smirked.

It had been three weeks of waiting before their quiet ceremony, but finally, their license was valid. Mae had feared an obstacle or two, but as it turned out, the cleric hadn't even asked for a baptismal certificate. On the paperwork, Ethan had simply written in a false birth year. It didn't sit well with her that their certificate contained a lie, however. Even if it was as insignificant as his age.

But to assuage her, Ethan promised to renew their vows in every new country they visited, where they didn't need to bother with formalities like paperwork. In that case, she expected to marry him many times over.

It would likely be years before they returned to England.

Thinking now of her afternoon rides and her horse, Thomas, a pang of sadness struck her heart. As they slipped farther from land into sea, she could feel herself changing.

Hell, she already was. The newly discovered fortune in their hands would have been enough to change anyone. Her father always said that money was the best way to determine one's character. She wondered how his fortune had changed him, if that was what had made him so consumed with greed and jealousy. Or if she had really ever known him at all. He certainly hadn't been the man she'd wanted him to be, but, while she'd been growing up, he had still been the father she'd needed. He and William had protected her from their way of life for years. For that, perhaps she should have been grateful.

Mae could only wonder how she and Ethan would fare now that they had their riches. They had already given some of it away: first, to the servants of Blackthorne Manor who had always served her family well. Mae had insisted they be given enough not just to feed them while they found new work, but to comfortably retire. Next, to repay debts Ethan sustained during his more desperate times and even to help some of the families of Locke's old crew. If only to soothe their blood guilt, they'd given funds to charities too, namely the orphanage Ethan had talked about, along with the farm that had taken Thomas and the other horses in.

"I've been meaning to tell you." Fed up with the wind, she

took her hat from her head and held it down at her waist. "I'll be sending off another request to Mr. Milner."

Mr. Milner, her new solicitor, handled what he believed to be the entirety of Mae's fortune. In actuality, it was a mere ten percent of her—and now Ethan's—wealth. The rest remained locked away in the family vault.

Ethan raised his eyebrows.

"While you were seeing to our travel arrangements earlier, I received a letter…from Miss Rosewood."

Ethan started. "Miss Rosewood, you say? She's doing well for herself, I hope."

Mae nodded, though they had both read of her daring and brave escape in all of London's newspapers. "She apologized for the falsehoods."

Ethan shrugged. Of course, neither of them blamed her. After catching up to the servants hiding out in the Nettle Estate, she'd had to tell the constable something. Once he'd told her about Ellsworth's body, she had surmised enough to know it had been best to lie and keep out the truth of Mae's fortune.

No one could have predicted the interest the papers would take.

At first, Mae had feared for Miss Rosewood's closely guarded reputation, but as it turned out, she had claimed to be kidnapped from the start, and her heroism in winning her freedom in the grips of robbers had made her quite the sensation in the eyes of London society. Mae had underestimated Miss Rosewood. All on her own, she had come up with a rather clever way to save her reputation.

"Miss Rosewood tells me she's already found a husband—a baron of something or other. She says they are quite the match."

"And you believe her?" Locke raised a brow. "It's only been a few months."

She preened. "Don't forget: you and I fell for one another in even less time."

"Our time together was different," Locke said firmly. "Much

different."

"True, but her message sounded happy, truly happy. I do wish we could make it to the wedding. We'll have to make up for our absence with a gift. A *grand* gift."

Mae didn't like to decline Miss Rosewood's invitation, but in addition to having a long list of sights to see, Mae needed to keep her identity and new wealth a secret. At least for a little while. Among the gossipers, new legends were already taking shape. From the letters she had traded with Grace, there was still quite a bit of talk about the fall of the Blackthorne family and a man who could supposedly live forever.

Still, Mae felt safe.

Besides themselves and those of the Silver Order, only Miss Rosewood knew the true location of the vault. And even if she could find the vault's location somewhere along the rocky coast near the summer cottage, Mae trusted her to keep it secret. She already had.

"What, exactly, do you have in mind?" Ethan asked.

"How about a carriage or two?"

"You can't wait until we reach our destination? You could find something there. Maybe an elephant she'd like for travel instead?"

"We could always try to find one in Shanghai. I hear they are abundant."

Ethan laughed. "You make it sound like we'll never settle down."

"Not for a long time." Mae folded herself into his arms, allowing his body to shield her face from the wind.

"You're missing the sunset," Ethan half-whispered into her hair.

Mae waved it away, pulling him back toward their room instead. These days, she found herself more impatient for their new moments alone. There was no telling how long they had. Without the sapphire and serum, their time now would always be fleeting.

As Ethan gripped her warm, smooth skin, Mae remembered how little she cared for the safety of those trinkets. Not tonight, not even that morning in the forest after she'd been certain Ethan would survive.

Although fear and doubt had filled her then, there had also been that moment when she'd found Ethan among the mist. The moment when he'd seen the key. The excitement, the urgency… All the joy she'd felt then, she'd owed to the pain, death, and danger of the days before.

Like a true Blackthorne, she had come to terms with that price. There was no use denying it. Life, she knew now, glittered more brilliantly and beautifully with death on their heels. Far more than any sapphire could.

About the Author

Ella Leon writes historical romance with a twist of magic and suspense.

During her 9–5 career, she has delved into many different styles of writing: journalism, public relations and marketing. Fiction, however, is where she finds the most freedom to transform the page. Like the Victorians she writes about, she loves all things gothic and supernatural. Unlike the Victorians, she is a feminist who enjoys exploring the precolonial past.

When she's not writing, you can find her spending time with her family or tending to her rose garden. She lives in the Chicago area.

Links:
Website: ellaleon.weebly.com
Facebook: facebook.com/ella.leon.author
Tiktok: tiktok.com/@ella_leon
Threads: threads.net/@e.k.toth
X: @Stoeverit

* 9 7 8 1 9 6 5 5 3 9 5 7 6 *